Would he be the first? . . .

Meredith had brought with her several long night-gowns, but the nights here were so fierce and humid that she had taken to sleeping in the nude. It was something she had never done before and, at first, she had felt shame at the wantonness of it. Stepping out of the last garment, she breathed a sigh of vast relief. She started to reach across the pallet to snuff out the lantern, and froze at the sound of the tent flap rustling.

Cooper Mayo was just stooping down to enter the tent.

"What are you doing in here?" she demanded, her voice sounding shrill and high.

Already inside, Cooper stood stock still at the sight of her nakedness. Desire blazed in his eyes.

"If you don't leave at once, I'll scream!"

"I doubt very much that you'll do that, boss lady. The men would laugh among themselves at the antics of the *gringos*. To their way of thinking, what we're about to do is the most natural thing in the world."

"We're not about to *do* anything!" she said furiously.

"Yes, we are. You've been an itch in my blood since I first clapped eyes on you, Meredith, and by God, it's time I did something about it. It's been in your mind as well, you can't deny it."

His mouth descended on hers. Then those big hands were on her body, touching her intimately. Despite the strength of his hands, his touch was surprisingly gentle, and his hands were knowing.

Meredith felt her body responding to his caresses. Filled with self-loathing, she fought him. She was a virgin by choice, not from prudery or coldness . . . but to lose her maidenhood in this steaming jungle, and to a man like Cooper!

She fought him, silently, well knowing that she would indeed be the object of derision if she aroused the camp. His strength was to much for her; and even as she struggled a part of h̲ submit. . . .

Love's Magic Moment

Patricia Matthews

PINNACLE BOOKS • LOS ANGELES

LOVE'S MAGIC MOMENT

Copyright © 1979 by Pyewacket Corporation

All rights reserved, including the right to reproduce this book or portions thereof in any form.

An original Pinnacle Books edition, published for the first time anywhere.

First printing, April 1979
Second printing, May 1979
Third printing, July 1979
Fourth printing, September 1979
Fifth printing, August 1980

ISBN: 0-523-41200-2

Cover illustration by Lou Marchetti

Printed in the United States of America

PINNACLE BOOKS, INC.
2029 Century Park East
Los Angeles, California 90067

This book is dedicated to my many dear friends at California State University, Los Angeles.

CEREMONIAL CITY OF TONATIUHICAN

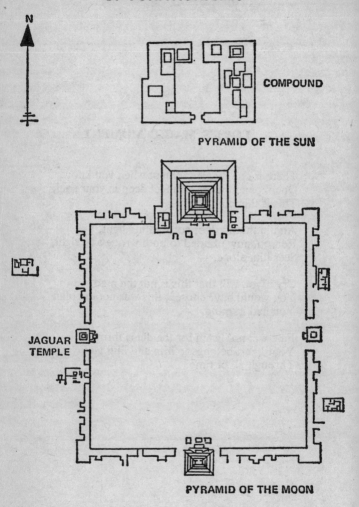

N

COMPOUND

PYRAMID OF THE SUN

JAGUAR TEMPLE

PYRAMID OF THE MOON

M.L.

LOVE'S MAGIC MOMENT

There is one magic moment when you know,
One moment when you feel deep in your soul,
This is the one.

And in that flash of coruscating light,
Reason, now blinded to both wrong and right,
Sees him alone.

Cry if you will that this is not the man
You would have chosen, this was not the plan
You had in mind.

Fate will not listen for the die is thrown,
Your heart belongs to him and him alone.
Through all of time.

LOVE'S MAGIC
MOMENT

Chapter One

The heat was oppressive and the humidity lent a heaviness to the air that caused it to press against the skin like a vast, damp blanket, entangling the limbs and sapping the body of energy.

Meredith Longley leaned back against the stiff, leather seat of her compartment and gazed indifferently out of the grimy window.

The sound of the train wheels formed a monotonous accompaniment to her thoughts— *clikata, clikata, clikata*—each *click* measuring off the miles from New England and home, and the progress deeper into Mexico to an enterprise with which Meredith wasn't certain she felt at ease.

Through the window, in the waning light, she could see that the junglelike landscape of eastern Mexico had changed, and that now the train was climbing, slowing as the tracks became steeper, more winding.

As the outside light faded, her window darkened, and soon Meredith could see her own reflection in the glass: a slender ghost of a girl with hair piled in a pale mass atop her head; a square, dimpled chin; and eyes that showed only as dark smudges. Did she really look that bad?

Turning up the wick of the coal-oil light in a bracket by her side, she reached into her handbag and took out a small mirror with which she examined her face.

Yes, the face was pale, and the brown eyes were ringed with dark shadows, shadows that had slowly come into being over the past weeks of her father's illness, shadows that were only now beginning to fade.

Meredith put the mirror away before she could see the quick tears that sprang to her eyes; she was angry at herself for the melancholy mood that seized her whenever she thought of Martin Longley. Would she ever stop missing him? Constantly, she found herself thinking of him as alive, turning to ask him an idle question, finding something of interest that she had to tell him, and then experiencing the shock of remembering that he was no longer there to communicate with.

He was supposed to have been with her now, on this archaeological expedition. They had been planning it for months—this excavation of a site that might in the end rival Heinrich Schliemann's discovery of Troy only three years before in 1871.

Even now, her imagination kindled at the thought of the ruined city hidden in the Mexican jungle, unseen for hundreds of years, until it had been discovered recently by a *mestizo* hunter; a city that her father had thought to be the fabled *Tonatiuhican,* House of the Sun; a city so old that it had already been a legend when the conquering Spaniards had landed; a great religious center of the Nahuas, which supposedly concealed a fabulous treasure called by the Spaniards, *El Tesoro del Sol,* the Treasure of the Sun.

It was to have been her father's most impressive excavation, the one which would have established his name forever.

As if Poppa needed that, she thought. His name was already well-known and respected in his field; his place at the University was secure, and students thronged to his classes. Meredith had been proud not only to be his daughter but his prize student as well. And now he was gone, and she was making the trip without him.

After her father's death, she had given no thought to continuing with their plans until her brother, Evan, had convinced her that the site should be investigated, as a memorial to their father. How could she possibly say no to that?

Martin Longley had been an exceptional man—there was no other word that adequately described him. Totally involved in his work for most of his life, he had not married until he was forty years old, when a beautiful student caught his eye and his interest, and persuaded him that he needed a partner in life as well as in the field.

It had been a singularly happy marriage between two people with a closely shared interest, and had been brightened by the birth of two children: Evan, born when Martin Longley was forty-two years old; and Meredith, born when her father was fifty.

It was a close family, and both children shared most aspects of life with their parents, but it was Meredith who inherited her parents' avid interest in the past. Protected darling of her father's autumn years, she was pampered and given undue attention, yet still was subject to the discipline of the working household.

When Meredith was twelve and Evan twenty, Marie Longley died of pneumonia, leaving a void in the family that Meredith felt it was her responsibility to fill. She became her father's close companion and partner, going with him on expeditions and trying to keep his cluttered affairs in order. Since Evan had only scorn for what he called "this obsession with dead people and where they lived and died," it was only natural that Meredith gradually began to take her mother's place as her father's right-hand helper and assistant.

And a month before, at seventy-two, her father had died with a suddenness that she found hard to comprehend. It was then that Evan had decided they should carry on their father's wishes, and excavate the city in the jungle. So here they were, on a rattling, incredibly dirty train, racketing through the jungle and mountains on their way to Mexico City, where they were to meet Dr. Ricardo Villalobos, Professor of History at the University of Mexico.

Her father and Dr. Villalobos had been friends for some years, and Dr. Longley had greatly respected the younger man's ability. Since affairs in Mexico were unsettled because the Revolution was still active in some places, it was thought best to have a representative of the University with them on the expedition. Indeed, having Villalobos along had already helped in getting the papers and permissions necessary for their departure . . .

Meredith's reverie was shattered by a sharp rap on the compartment door, which was pushed open to admit the blond head of her brother, outlined in the flickering light of the passageway.

"Meredith! What on earth are you doing sitting here like this? I'm going to dinner with Harris in a few minutes. Want to join us?"

Meredith nodded. "Just let me freshen up a bit."

"Right!" Evan withdrew his head and shut the door.

Meredith was always puzzled by her feelings for her brother. The thing that concerned her was the fact that she was not certain that she liked him very much. They had never been close—perhaps because of the difference in their ages—but it wasn't only that. Evan always seemed so distant, so removed from things, that she found it difficult to communicate with him. He was always so intense, so busy, so . . . so sober. It had taken her several

5

years to realize that he had absolutely no sense of humor, which was a little strange since their parents had had a marvelous sense of the ridiculous. Meredith wasn't even sure what Evan did for a living. She had the dim impression that he had something to do with investments.

But now, she reminded herself, she was going to have to work with him, as she had with her father, although it could never be the same. She had respected her father's experience and ability, but she really knew nothing about Evan's knowledge of archaeology. Since he had never shown more than a layman's interest in it, his knowledge was undoubtedly limited.

Finishing her brief toilet, Meredith went out into the narrow passageway and started toward the dining car. Although the railroad, recently completed from Vera Cruz to Mexico City, was being hailed as the finest in all of Mexico, the cars on this particular train were ancient and in poor condition.

Evan's compartment was the next to last one in the car. Approaching it, Meredith wondered if she should knock on his door in passing. She halted abruptly, hand raised to knock, and a figure collided with her from behind. She lost her balance and started to fall. Strong arms went around her, and she found herself being held closely against the linen of a man's coat.

"Sorry, ma'am," said a deep voice somewhere near her left ear. "I didn't mean to knock you down."

Flustered, Meredith pulled back. She was conscious of the smell of tobacco and bay rum, and as she raised her eyes, she saw a broad-cheeked, suntanned face almost intimidating in its strength.

The man's arms opened reluctantly to release her, and then a swerve of the train threw her against his chest again. He laughed easily, a deep rumble of sound, and Meredith found herself piqued by his easy assurance and self-confidence.

His eyes were the brightest blue she had ever seen. He was wearing a white linen suit, with a black string tie, a white planter's hat, and Western boots.

Rescuing the remnants of her dignity, Meredith again pulled away, lifting a hand to her hair. The man took two steps back, his coat swinging open, and Meredith saw a pearl-handled revolver strapped around his waist. She stifled a gasp. She knew that men often went armed in this revolution-plagued country; even so, the sight of the revolver startled her. She saw that he was appraising her boldly.

"Well now," he said admiringly, "if you aren't the prettiest lady that has fallen into my arms in quite some time." He spoke with a Texas accent.

Meredith felt her lips tighten. He really was insufferable. "As I recall, it was *you* who ran into *me*, sir, and if you will kindly move along, I'm sure that I shall be able to navigate the passageway with no difficulty, once you are out of the way." She knew that her tone sounded waspish, but his evident conceit had nettled her and

7

temporarily put her off-balance, a feeling which she did not enjoy.

He raised one heavy, dark eyebrow and smiled sardonically, "You are right, ma'am, of course. I do apologize for being so clumsy."

Meredith shot him an angry look from under lowered lashes. Was he laughing at her? The audacity of the man!

Before she could frame a retort, the door of the compartment next to Evan's swung open and a woman in a pale yellow dress emerged.

Dark eyes widened at the sight of the man in the white suit. "Coop! I was wondering where you were!"

"I was just coming to fetch you, Rena." That eyebrow arched at Meredith again, and his grin was mocking. "But I ran into a slight delay. Oh . . . forgive my bad manners, ma'am. This lovely lady is Rena Voltan, and I am Cooper Mayo."

"I'm Meredith Longley," Meredith said tightly, a part of her mind wondering why she bothered to give her name to this insufferable oaf. Her gaze clung to Rena Voltan. She had olive skin, shining blue-black hair, and a striking figure. Meredith knew that alongside this woman's seductive beauty, as blatant as a shout, she must look as nondescript and colorless as smoke.

Putting a long arm around the woman's shoulders, Cooper Mayo said, "Rena is a witch, you know."

"And I have cast a fatal spell on you, Coop."

8

"A man couldn't be under a better spell, my dear."

Witch should probably be spelled with a *b*, Meredith thought, then blushed at her crudeness. Still, she couldn't remember when anyone, man or woman, had aroused in her such animosity at first sight, as did Rena Voltan.

She said coldly, "If you will allow me, I am expected in the dining car."

"Certainly, Miss Longley." Cooper Mayo doffed his wide-brimmed hat, those bright blue eyes wicked and knowing. "It is *Miss*, I trust?"

Without answering, Meredith gathered her skirt, turned, and hurried with all the dignity she could muster toward the dining car. She could feel the heat of her face. He would probably be watching her, she knew; they would both be watching and laughing with shared amusement.

The dining car was about two-thirds filled and Meredith, eyes slowly adjusting to the brighter light, looked for her brother and Harris Browder. They were nowhere in sight.

She approached the steward, who by now knew the names of all their party. "Have you seen my brother?"

The steward shook his head. "No, Señorita. He has not been in yet. Would you like me to seat you?"

Her feeling of crankiness grew. Why wasn't Evan here?

"Oh, very well," she said crossly, then smiled at the steward to let him know that her displeasure wasn't directed at him.

The steward escorted Meredith to their table and handed her a large menu. She already knew it by heart and was not really tempted by the items offered. Still, she looked at it idly, just to have something to do. She always felt ill at ease, eating alone. What were you supposed to do with your eyes? It wasn't polite to stare at others, so there seemed nothing to do but to look at one's food or at the table. Where *was* Evan?

At that moment the dining car door opened and the tall man named Cooper Mayo came into the car, the dark woman on his arm. Meredith lowered her eyes quickly, but not before she had seen him smile in her direction. Lord, he was huge! No decent person should be that tall and obtrusive.

Fixedly, she stared at the fly specks on the dirty, white cardboard menu.

"Well, what shall we have tonight, Meredith? The leathery chicken, or the charred steak?"

Meredith, startled, looked up at the sound of Harris Browder's unctuous voice. Browder was short but powerfully built, middle-aged, and had an obnoxious personality. Meredith had never understood the friendship between Evan and Browder.

She said, "Where's Evan?"

Browder shrugged. "I don't know. He came knocking on my door a half-hour or more ago. He should have been here before me."

"Well, he's not, as you can plainly see."

Browder sat down. "Something must have

come up. I wouldn't worry about it." He picked up the menu. "What are you going to have?"

"I'm not hungry . . ." A movement to her right caught Meredith's eye, and she turned slightly. Cooper Mayo and Rena Voltan were being seated opposite her across the aisle. Cooper nodded, and smiled easily. He had the most perfect teeth Meredith had ever seen. They seemed, somehow, an affront.

Meredith turned back to Browder, and the thought of being alone with him didn't appeal to her. She said, "I think I'll go and see what's delaying Evan. You go ahead and order."

She left the dining car quickly, carefully avoiding the gaze of Cooper Mayo. The passageway of her car was deserted except for the porter, Juan, sitting on a stool at the far end. Meredith rapped on Evan's door; there was no answer. She tried the door handle and found it locked.

She called, "Juan? Would you come here, please?"

Juan got up and slouched toward her. "Yes, Señorita Longley?" he said, his Indian-brown face impassive.

"Have you seen my brother?"

"Not since he went into the compartment and closed the door." Juan's English was quite good.

"You sure he hasn't come out?"

Juan shook his head. "No, Señorita, he has not. I have been watching. The only people in the passageway since Señor Longley went into

11

his compartment have been you, Señor Mayo, and the Señorita Voltan."

Meredith gnawed her lip in indecision. Then she said firmly, "Would you open the door, please?"

He looked alarmed. "He may not wish to be disturbed, your brother."

"But if he is in there, he would answer my knock," she said impatiently. "He may be ill. I will accept the responsibility, Juan. Open it!"

With a fatalistic shrug, Juan took a ring of keys from his belt and unlocked the door. Opening it with a flourish, he stepped back.

Meredith moved forward, calling, "Evan?"

She stopped short just inside the compartment. It was empty; there was no doubt of that. The curtain over the grimy window was raised. Her mind groping with the problem, Meredith crossed to the window. There was room enough for someone to get out that way, if a person wished, for some strange reason, to jump from a moving train, but the window was firmly latched and the layer of dust on the sill was undisturbed.

Meredith was stunned by the incredible fact that Evan had somehow vanished without a trace from a locked compartment!

She backed out of the compartment, hand clapped over her mouth to stifle a cry of distress.

A glance showed her that Juan had returned to his stool at the far end of the car. In the dim light he looked as brooding and inscrutable as an Aztec stone idol. Meredith opened her mouth to summon him, then changed her mind. He would probably dismiss her fears for Evan as *gringa* imaginings.

Quickly, she returned to the dining car, and Harris Browder. As she sat down, he looked up, then craned his neck past her.

"Where's Evan?"

Leaning across the table, she said in a tense whisper, "He's vanished, just disappeared!"

Browder gaped at her. "Vanished? What are you talking about, Meredith?" His voice rose. "He couldn't have just disappeared!"

"But he has," Meredith insisted. "The door to his compartment was locked. When he didn't answer my knock, I called the car porter. Juan said that Evan had not left his compartment since going inside. I insisted that Juan unlock the door, and Evan simply wasn't there!"

Browder made a face of disgust. "Paugh! You can't trust these damned Mexicans. He probably dozed off, and Evan left the compartment without being seen. This peon doesn't want to admit that he was napping on the job, afraid he'll get fired."

"I just have this feeling that something is wrong." Meredith shivered, goose pimples popping out on her arms.

"Women's intuition?" he said with a condescending sneer.

"You can call it what you will," she said heatedly, "but I think we should do something."

"What would you suggest?" he said with heavy sarcasm. "Search the train?"

"Yes! I think we should."

13

"Meredith, this is a big crowded train. Besides, Evan is able to take care of himself."

Meredith realized that their voices were rising, and she saw with dismay that people were staring at them.

As her gaze swept across the table opposite them, Cooper Mayo leaned forward. It was obvious that he had overheard. The dark woman across the table from him was smiling with secretive amusement.

Cooper said, "I couldn't help overhearing, ma'am. Has something happened to your brother?"

"Do you know Evan?"

"I know him, yes," he said cryptically.

In her concern for Evan, Meredith's dislike of the big man had temporarily abated. "Have you seen him?"

"Not within the past hour." He shrugged. "But shortly before our encounter in the passageway I saw him enter his compartment and lock the door."

"I was just there. The door was still locked, and the porter swore that Evan hadn't left the compartment. Yet, when he opened it, Evan was gone!"

"Vanished into thin air, as the saying goes?" His eyebrow arched.

"Yes!" She stiffened. "Are you laughing at me, sir?"

"Not at all, little lady. I am taking you most seriously. Seriously enough, that I think something should be done about it. I . . ." He tossed his napkin onto the table and stood up, his bulk

14

towering over her. "Suppose I roust out the conductor, or whoever is in charge of this miserable train, and have him institute a search? Car by car?"

Meredith said eagerly, "I would appreciate that very much, Mr. Mayo . . ."

"See here, fellow," Browder blustered. "I don't see that you have any business butting in here!"

"Don't you now?" Cooper's blue eyes turned to ice. "And just who might you be, to have any say in this?"

"I'm Evan's associate."

Hurriedly, Meredith introduced the two men. Neither offered to shake hands. Cooper ignored Browder and looked down into Meredith's eyes. "Up to you, ma'am. It's your brother missing. Do you want the train searched?"

Meredith nodded. "I do! Yes, I do!"

Browder said, "Meredith, do you think this is wise? We don't even know this fellow . . ."

Meredith whirled on him. "Harris, stay out of this! Something has to be done, and *you* seem reluctant to act!"

"Did you ever think that Evan might be engaged in something and doesn't want to be found?" he said sullenly. "You know the temper he has. Suppose," he leered, "he's with a woman?"

"Maybe I don't know my brother as well as you seem to think you do, but I have a strong feeling about this. Something has happened to

15

him. Now, if you refuse to act, stop balking me."

Harris retired into sullen silence, turning to stare out the window.

Meredith looked up at Cooper Mayo. "I would appreciate your seeing what you can do. I had thought of talking to the conductor, but I know from experience that a woman is taken lightly down here."

Cooper dipped his head. He said warmly, "It will be my pleasure, ma'am." He started up the aisle.

Rena Voltan reached out a hand to touch his sleeve. "Are you going to just leave me alone and helpless, Coop?" she said with a pout. "While you chase around on a fool's errand?"

"My dear Rena, you have not been helpless since the day you left your mother's womb." His laughter was low. "I'm sure, if you wished, a snap of your finger would have some handsome fellow in attendance before I get out of this car."

The woman withdrew her hand, sitting back. Dark eyes blazing, she snapped, "Be careful how you talk to me, Cooper Mayo!"

"Why?" The broad shoulders moved in a careless shrug. "You'll cast another spell, perhaps? An evil one this time, Rena?"

"I just might!"

"Well now, that could be right interesting," he drawled. "Reckon I'll have to take my chances, won't I?"

He went down the aisle, his stride sure, adjusting gracefully to the sway of the speeding

16

train. He walks as though he own the earth, Meredith thought; yet it somehow seemed to enhance his charm.

The Voltan woman aimed a baleful glare at Meredith. She looked cruel, somehow evil. Meredith met her gaze steadily enough, yet she felt cold inside.

Then a waiter stopped by the table, blocking Rena Voltan from Meredith's view. "Señor, Señorita? You wish to order dinner now?"

"I think I've just lost my appetite," Harris Browder muttered sourly. "Tell Evan, when he shows up, that I'll be in my compartment." He got to his feet and left the dining car.

Meredith ordered a meal she didn't really want, her thoughts puzzling over Browder's behavior. She did not like the man; aside from his obnoxious personality, she had heard that he was a womanizer, and that his romantic pursuits were on the bizarre side. She had heard rumors to the effect that he had been involved in a number of scandalous escapades, involving women complaining to the authorities that he had physically abused them. He had barely escaped going to prison several times.

She had discussed this with Evan when she learned that Browder was accompanying them on the expedition.

Evan had laughed. "I'm not concerned about Harris's love life, dear sister. What he does in private is none of my affair."

"From the things I've heard, it's not all that private," she had retorted.

"Yes, I know he's not as discreet as he should

17

be. We've had a talk about that, and he's promised to behave himself."

"But I don't understand why you even associate with him!"

"Because he's got a talent for making money. Every time I'm involved in some deal with him, I end up making money."

"Are you sure these deals are legal?" She had recognized the question as unwise before the words were out.

Evan had glared at her, his temper flaring. "Are you accusing me of doing something criminal, Meredith? Because if you are, I warn you that you're on dangerous ground."

"No, of course not, Evan. I'm sure you're doing nothing knowingly illegal. But how do you know that Harris Browder isn't?"

Unappeased, Evan had said, "Harris isn't a crook, if that's what you're hinting at, and I don't wish to hear any more on the subject!"

That unsatisfactory conversation had done nothing to reassure Meredith about Harris Browder, but since he was Evan's friend, she concluded that she didn't have to like him. She was vague about why he was even along. A few times she had tried to draw Browder out, and discovered that he knew even less about archaeology than did Evan.

Now the man's behavior was even more baffling. Did he know what had happened to Evan, and wished her not to know? *Was* Evan with a woman?

Meredith realized with a jolt that she knew absolutely nothing about her brother's love life,

or even if he had one. He never talked about
women, and she had never seen him in the company of the same woman twice. She had wondered, fleetingly, if he ever intended to get
married. Yet he was still young; it was not
thought unusual for a man in the last half of
the nineteenth century to remain single beyond
thirty. A man was supposed to become reasonably well-fixed financially before taking a wife;
at least that was the approved procedure.

With a start Meredith noticed Cooper Mayo
returning from the front end of the train.
Trailing him was a plump, middle-aged man in
a conductor's uniform. They came toward her
slowly, the conductor making check marks on a
sheet of paper in his hand.

Glancing across the aisle, Meredith saw that
Rena Voltan was gone. As he drew abreast of
Meredith's table, Cooper winked, then leaned
over to say in a low voice, "I've got the conductor moving on it. He has the passenger list, and
is now checking the names off one by one.
We've checked every nook and cranny, starting
in the first car, and will go all the way back to
the end car. So far, no luck, Miss Longley. I'll
get back to you in here if there is any news. Or
if there isn't any." With that white-toothed
smile, he went after the conductor.

Sighing, Meredith pushed her plate away,
food scarcely touched, and gazed out the window at the darkened landscape. The train was
laboring up toward the plateau now. Tomorrow, they would be in Mexico City. If Evan was

19

not found by then, what would she tell Ricardo Villalobos?

More importantly, what would happen to the expedition now?

It was over an hour before Cooper returned to the dining car. All the diners had finished and left, and Meredith was alone. The lights had been dimmed and the waiters were waiting patiently at the front end of the car for her to leave.

She looked up as Cooper slipped into the chair opposite her. He placed a flask on the table.

"Brandy," he drawled. "I thought you could use a drink. I know I sure as hell could."

He turned, beckoning one of the waiters over. "A pair of clean glasses?" Before the waiter could voice a protest, Cooper passed him a silver dollar.

With a quick smile the waiter said, "*Si*, Señor Mayo. At once!"

Meredith was waiting impatiently for Cooper to face around. "Well? Did you find my brother, Mr. Mayo?"

Cooper shook his head solemnly. "I'm afraid not, ma'am, not hide nor hair. The conductor did a thorough job, I was right on his as. . . his tail every second. Everybody but your brother is accounted for, and we looked in every place large enough to hide a cat. Your brother is not on this train. If I hadn't seen him with my own eyes earlier today, I would begin to think he'd never been on board at all." He squinted at her. "We looked in that compartment of his, of course, and I see the mystery. How he could get out with the door locked, Juan's eyes on him every minute, is beyond me."

"I just don't understand it." Meredith sat back, discouraged. Then she glanced out at the dark night. "What did you mean, 'get out'? That implies that Evan vanished on his own! Granting that he would want to, how? This train has not made a stop since I saw Evan last."

"One alternative is," he raised and lowered his hands, "that he was thrown off, bodily. You'll pardon my bluntness, ma'am."

She looked at him in shock. "Are you trying to say someone deliberately threw him off this train? *Killed* him?"

He shrugged. "Under the circumstances, it's a possibility that must be considered."

"But who would have a reason to do that?"

"Does your brother have any enemies?"

"Certainly not!" She hesitated, then said slowly, "But I must confess that I really don't know Evan all that well."

"Most men have an enemy or two."

"Do you, Mr. Mayo?"

He grinned lazily. "I have enemies by the score, ma'am. A man in my profession attracts them, it seems."

"And just *what* is your profession?"

"That question is a little hard to answer," he drawled. "I usually call myself a soldier of fortune."

She was frowning, intrigued enough to want to pursue the line of questioning further, when the waiter arrived with clean glasses. Cooper poured brandy generously into each glass and shoved one across the table. "Here, you could probably use this."

"I don't often drink strong liquor."

"Well, I do. Often." He was smiling slightly. "With what you've been through, I should think a jot of brandy would be welcome about now."

Meredith eyed the glass dubiously, but she picked it up.

Cooper extracted a long, thin, brown cigar from a leather case. "With your permission, Miss Longley?"

"You have my permission, sir."

As Cooper held a match to the cigar, rotating it until the tip was burning evenly, Meredith distractedly drank from the glass. She drank too much and almost choked, but by the time she had her breath back, the brandy had a soothing effect on her tension.

Cooper studied her through eyes slitted against a thin haze of smoke. A smile curved his sensual mouth. "Feel better?"

Meredith nodded reluctant assent.

Cooper said abruptly, "What will your brother's disappearance do to your expedition?"

She stared. "How did you know about that?"

"I heard, somewhere," he said indifferently. "Why? It's no state secret, is it?"

"No, but . . ." She sighed. "To tell you the truth, I haven't thought that far ahead. I don't really know. It was actually Evan's idea, in the first place. I'd like to go ahead . . . after all, archaeology is my field, and I'd like to carry through as a sort of memorial to Poppa, but without Evan, I don't know. He was in charge of all the arrangements. I may have to abandon it."

He gave her a veiled look. "Abandon the search for *El Hombre de Oro*? It strikes me that's a prize worth any effort."

"I'm interested in artifacts, not treasure . . ." She broke off, a cold chill going over her. "How do you know about *El Hombre de Oro*? That is a secret!"

"Must not be such a great secret, if I know about it, wouldn't you say?" His look was ingenuous. "Actually about all I know is that in English it means Golden Man or Man of Gold, and that it's a half-sized human male figure, made of solid gold, with gems for eyes. Must be worth a lot of money."

"It's nothing but a rumor," she said tightly. "There are no facts to support its existence."

"When something that valuable is involved, a rumor is all that's needed to start a stampede."

Anger and contempt made her voice sting. "I gather that you're joining that stampede?"

"I don't know for sure." He was smiling. "But I must admit that it sounds mighty tempting."

"There's no way anyone can benefit from finding the Golden Man, if indeed it does exist. The Mexican government will have first claim."

"Oh, I wouldn't be too sure about that, Miss

23

Longley." His shrug was eloquent. "There are ways."

"That *is* what you're after! You called yourself a soldier of fortune a bit ago. Fortune hunter would be more apt." A chilling thought wormed into her mind. She said rashly, "Maybe *you* had something to do with Evan's disappearance!"

Those blue eyes frosted over. "I concede that I may be a fortune hunter, ma'am, but I am not a killer. I would advise you to curb your tongue."

"I will tell you this, Mr. Mayo . . ." She shot to her feet. "If I so much as see you lurking about the site of the excavation, I shall immediately notify the Mexican authorities!"

Cooper's smile was cynical. "Then I'll have to be careful that you don't see me, ma'am."

Chapter Two

Smoke drifting lazily up from his cigar, Cooper watched Meredith Longley walk out of the dining car, her back ramrod stiff. Outwardly he showed a calm, wryly amused countenance, but he was disturbed. He had been out of bounds with her, he knew, and certainly premature in mentioning the gold statue.

But from the moment he'd heard of the possible existence of *El Hombre de Oro*—from Rena Voltan—the old familiar excitement had him in thrall, the thrill of the hunt, the search for forbidden treasure.

Much of the time the hunt itself, the chasing down of rumors, was all that came of it, but the possibility of finding the prize, the pot of gold at the end of the rainbow, was as exciting as anything else in life to him.

Only twice had Cooper's treasure hunts been really profitable. Once, he had found a sunken Spanish galleon off Key West in Florida, and a rotting chest that burst open to spill riches into his hands, enough to keep him in luxury for a full year in New York. The other time had been the discovery of a lost gold mine in Arizona. That time he had been in the employ of another man, and Cooper's share had been piddling considering the riches the lost mine had coughed up. That, he was determined, would never happen again.

Cooper was honest enough to admit to himself that, the excitement of the hunt aside, greed had a lot to do with it. Damnit, he *needed* money! His finances were in poor shape. In between hunts for lost treasure, he took any job offering excitement and good pay. Some of the jobs he'd hired out for just skirted illegality. He supposed he was fortunate that he had never been in trouble with the law; since most of his employment took place in South and Central America, and Mexico, Cooper was not always too scrupulous about hewing to the letter of the law in those countries.

That was one reason he regretted speaking so rashly to Meredith Longley. The last time he had been in Mexico, he had hired out as a fighting man; unfortunately the side employing him had lost and he was out of favor in certain quarters. He would do well to keep a low profile. If she did actually alert the authorities that he was in their country, he could very well end up in jail.

Cooper really had not intended to return to Mexico this soon, but from the moment Rena had confided in him, the lure of treasure was too strong to resist, and here he was!

From Rena he had gotten the approximate location of the proposed excavation; it was a district familiar to him. It had been his hope to talk his way into a job with the expedition, perhaps as a hired gun; the region was infested with defeated revolutionaries and bandits, and *gringos* were not looked upon kindly. For this reason, Cooper had approached Evan Longley about a job, and had received a curt brush-off. Now, with Evan's mysterious disappearance, Cooper would have to play it by ear.

He certainly hadn't made a favorable first impression on Meredith Longley!

With a wry chuckle he drained the brandy from his glass, pocketed the flask, and stood up. There were still ways; there was *always* a way. In his checkered career, Cooper had learned to improvise. No matter how well-planned an expedition of this sort might be, things always went awry. He would just have to wait his chance, and hope he would be there to make his invaluable services available.

He gave the hovering waiter a salute and left the dining car. In his own car he paused a moment before Rena Voltan's compartment, wondering if he should try to soothe her ruffled feathers. Also, he was curious. Since learning from Meredith that the possible existence of *El Hombre de Oro* was supposed to be a secret, Cooper had to wonder how Rena had learned of it.

Rena was something of a mystery woman. Cooper had met her in Galveston, striking up an acquaintance that had ripened almost at once into a steamy affair.

He smiled to himself as he mentally compared Rena and Meredith Longley. Rena conveyed an aura of sexuality almost visible, while Meredith was rather prim—what Cooper thought of as "New England proper." Yet there was an unexploited beauty about her and a feeling of great sensuality held tightly under wraps. Her hair was pale gold in color, and he thought it would look like champagne pouring, if she would wear it loose and flowing. Also, he glimpsed a splendid figure under all those layers of clothing; if she could only be persuaded to dress a little more daringly. Not *quite* as daring as Rena, he thought.

Was she a virgin? He was almost sure she was . . .

Cooper smiled wryly. He had seen Meredith only at a distance on the ship from Galveston, not even knowing who she was until this evening, and he had talked to her a total of about twenty minutes, and already he was wondering how to get her into bed. He had better watch it!

Cooper liked women and he recognized, without undue vanity, that he was attractive to them. He'd had enough ready conquests to be aware of that. Yet there had been times in the past when he had let the pursuit of a woman interfere with his performance of a job, or a treasure hunt. Twice, he had lost good jobs because of a woman; and once, he had dallied too long with a woman and allowed a competitor to get a head start on him. This had been down in

Central America, and the prize had been a rich treasure in another hidden city in the jungle. His competitor had come out of the jungle with enough booty to make him a wealthy man for life.

The parallel between that time and this one was much too close for comfort.

He decided not to knock on Rena's door, and went on down the passageway to his own compartment. He was momentarily surprised to discover the door unlocked, and his first reaction was one of wariness.

Then he smiled to himself, knowing what he would find inside. Pushing the door open, he was assailed by her perfume, a scent as heavy as musk. The compartment was dark, but there was enough light to show him that the bunk was made and Rena was lying in a naked sprawl across the narrow bed.

Her golden complexion and the lush contours of her body reminded Cooper of a Rubens nude, and he immediately felt a familiar heaviness in his loins.

"Well, are you coming in or not, Coop?" she asked languidly. "I don't know as I care for just anybody wandering along the passageway and seeing me like this." Her laughter was throaty. "After all, I have my reputation to consider."

"So far, I've seen you worry little about your reputation, Rena," he said dryly. But he closed the door, isolating them in the warm darkness of the compartment. "I had the impression you were angry with me, my dear."

"I was. You were rude, rushing off like that. Cooper Mayo, the white knight," there was a sneer in her voice, "rushing to the rescue of a damsel in distress."

"A man must do what he must," he said amusedly.

"It's not very flattering, to be deserted while you chase off on an errand for another female."

Cooper frowned in the darkness, his temper stirring. "No woman has strings on me, Rena. Don't ever forget that!"

"Oh, I'm well aware of your touted independence, Cooper Mayo. Except that's not the whole truth, now is it? You think I don't know that you're cozying up to the Longley woman in the hope of getting some inside information about the treasure? Better yet, hoping to get your hands on it first!"

"Speaking of that . . . Meredith Longley told me that the existence, or non-existence, of *El Hombre de Oro* is supposed to be a dark secret. So, how did you find out?"

"Oh, it exists, lover. Be sure of that. As to how *I* found out . . . I have ways. An enterprising woman always does."

"Or a witch," he said, laughing.

"Or a witch. Coop . . ." She stirred, the silken sound of her flesh moving on the sheets exciting him. "Are you going to join me here, or talk all night? I've been waiting here forever, it seems."

"Well, since you asked so nicely . . ." He was already getting out of his clothes.

She said breathily, "Ah, that's my Coop."

Shortly, he was nude. He stepped to the bunk and Rena's hand reached out, stroking his muscular thigh. Her hand moved to his loins and expertly fondled his maleness.

"You are much man, Coop, more man than any I have ever known. They have a word down here. *Macho*. It means much man, all male." Her voice was husky and thick. "That's you, Cooper Mayo!"

Cooper stood quietly under her caressing hands. No other woman in his experience had ever been so frank and open about sexuality. Even those he had known with passionate natures rarely admitted it, until they were so caught up in need, or ecstasy, they could no longer exert control over themselves.

He was not sure that he *liked* Rena a great deal. She was too aggressive by far, there was a cruel, almost sadistic streak to her nature, and Cooper had a strong suspicion that she would stop at nothing to gain what she wanted. However, he had never been overly concerned about the morals of a woman, and Rena's ability and eagerness to provide pleasure was what interested him at the moment.

She murmured, "Now, Coop?"

"Now," he said, and got onto the narrow bunk with her. The confinement of their bed of pleasure had been no hindrance during the train trip thus far; nor was it now. Rena accommodated herself to his large body, taking him inside her with a gasp of delight.

It was Cooper's way to approach a romantic interlude in a more leisurely manner; he liked to dally with a woman, caressing and teasing, until she was in a torment of need. He always found it more satisfying for himself, as well as for his partner. There was none of that with Rena. She was greedy in love as in everything . . .

What the hell, he thought, this is no time to be dissecting the character of Rena Voltan.

He gave himself up to pleasure, all thought driven from his mind. He drove himself vigorously into her eager body. Under him, Rena writhed and tossed, moaning with delight. Her nails raked his back. Cooper knew, from earlier encounters, that his back would be covered with tiny slashes, like those left by an angry cat.

Rena attained a peak of ecstasy, but she never slackened, exhorting him on to greater effort. Finally Cooper groaned aloud with pleasure, and Rena rose and clung to him, her body spasming under his.

After the storm had subsided, she made pushing motions against his chest, and Cooper sat up on the edge of the bunk. No languor and tenderness of after-love for Rena. When the act of love was over for her, it was over—until the next time.

Cooper found and lit a cigar, the match flare brightening the interior of the compartment for a moment. In the light her hair was a dark tumble and her face had the sleepy, contented look Cooper had seen on the countenances of jungle cats after feeding.

"Give me one." She extended her hand. "I left my little cigars in my compartment."

Cooper found another cigar and gave it to her. She was the first woman he had ever known who smoked, and not only in the privacy of her own quarters. She brazenly smoked her little, twisted, Cuban cigars in public, delighted, he was sure, in the shock waves she caused.

He struck another match for her. Cigar clenched between her perfect teeth, she drew on it and exhaled smoke.

He placed a hand on her thigh. "Something I want to ask you, Rena . . . do *you* know what happened to Evan Longley? Nobody else seems to know."

He could feel her thigh muscles tense under his hand. But her voice was unruffled as she replied, "Coop, you are being rather nosy this evening. I've been bombarded by questions since you came in here."

"I'm curious by nature, especially when a prize such as the one we're seeking is involved. And you haven't answered my question."

"Of course I know nothing about the disappearance of this Longley person! Why should I know anything? The man's nothing to me."

"Not exactly true," he said mildly. "He's the one leading this expedition. For all I know, he may be the source of your information about this *Tesoro del Sol.*"

"Fishing, Coop?" she said with a taunting laugh. "Why don't you look at it this way: if something's happened to this Longley person, that's one less to share, or to get in our way, when we find the treasure."

"That's a pretty cold-blooded way to look at it."

"Just practical, I'd say." He felt her body move in a small shrug. "Don't tell me it hasn't crossed your mind. With him gone, his sister will still go ahead with the excavation."

"Don't be too sure about that. She seemed doubtful when I talked to her a bit ago in the dining car."

"Then if she doesn't, we'll go ahead on our own. Listen to me, Cooper Mayo . . ." Her voice became intense. "There could be a fortune involved here, and damn anyone, or anything, who gets in the way of me finding it!"

"You told me that the Longleys have the only map showing the location of *Tonatiuhican*. You also told me that your plan was to follow them to the site. If Meredith Longley doesn't go ahead, how do we proceed on our own without the map?"

Rena said calmly, "Then we steal the map."

He drew back from her. "That's going a little far, Rena!"

"Is it?" she laughed. "Ethics, from Cooper Mayo? You're willing to steal the gold from them, but not a map? How do you explain that, Coop?"

"We were discussing taking the idol from her brother," he said stiffly, "not a helpless woman, damnit!"

"Helpless? Don't let male gallantry cloud your good sense. In fact . . ." Her voice dropped to a mere whisper. "I've been thinking.

34

When we get our hands on the map, it might not be a bad idea to eliminate her entirely. She might have committed enough of the map to memory to find the lost city."

Harris Browder was troubled and angry. Unable to sleep, he had left his compartment and walked through the darkened train to the observation platform behind the last car. He stood alone now on the platform, in the warm darkness, the landscape a blur as the train sped along.

Despite his scoffing at Meredith's fears, Browder had felt the first twinges of alarm when she informed him that Evan had disappeared. Then, Browder had sought out the conductor after the search of the train had been completed, and learned that Evan had indeed vanished.

That was when Browder began to grow angry. Was Evan trying to ditch him? After he, Browder, had scrounged up the money necessary to finance this expedition, with Evan's promise of equal shares in whatever riches the treasure brought, had Evan used some ruse to disappear and find the ancient city on his own?

"If the bastard has, I'll strangle him. So help me, I will!" Browder said aloud, his hands clenching into fists. He pounded them on the railing.

It didn't concern him that Evan might be the victim of foul play, or some sort of an accident. If that had happened, the end result would be the same; he would be out of pocket all that expense money, and with no way to recoup.

Evan's sister, the ice maiden, would faint dead away at the least hint of skullduggery. Browder knew she didn't care much for him, and the feeling was mutual, except for one difference—he would dearly love to get her into bed, and find out just how hard it would be to melt that icy exterior. He'd seen enough of her to realize that she was a juicy morsel under all those clothes.

But she would never stand still for selling the gold for personal profit, or any other valuable artifacts they might find. Browder had heard her expound on the subject. Anything they found at the excavation was for the benefit of humanity, for exhibition in museums, to throw light on the ancient history of mankind.

Browder didn't care a fig for mankind or its enlightenment. He was interested solely in the benefit of Number One, and by God, if Evan Longley was up to some shenanigans to do him out of his share, he would regret it!

For most of his forty years, Harris Browder had been engaged in one illegal activity or another, and had been shrewd or lucky enough to escape punishment for his deeds. A couple of times he had carried off big coups, but nothing on the scale of this one. If Evan's estimate of the worth of the treasure was accurate, a half share should come to at least a hundred thousand dollars!

That, in Browder's book, was a big payoff, one worth killing for, if it came to that. He had killed men before, and for less; he would do it this time, if need be!

First, he had to watch himself around Meredith, and not antagonize her again. With Evan gone, she had the map and other vital information. Browder had pressured Evan for a copy of the map, but Evan had kept putting him off, promising to do so once the expedition was underway.

So now he had to play it cagey with Meredith . . .

A thought struck him. If he could somehow manage to get his hands on the map, he would no longer need Meredith or Evan. He could proceed on his own, and to hell with the Longleys!

In fact, then he could afford to hand Miss High-and-Mighty Longley her comeuppance, and in the doing give her a taste of what a real man was like!

Meredith had also had trouble sleeping. After leaving Cooper Mayo in anger she had returned to her compartment, but there was too much on her mind to allow her to sleep. After an hour of tossing and turning on the narrow bunk, she got up and put on her clothes again, anxious to escape the compartment, which had become as smothering as a prison.

She started through the cars, back toward the rear, intent on getting a breath of fresh air from the observation platform. Entering the parlor car, she found it deserted; there wasn't even a porter on duty, and only one lamp burned dimly. The parlor car was usually strictly male territory, where the men could smoke their cigars, drink whiskey, play cards, or simply swap dirty stories. The presence of women, if not forbidden, was certainly frowned upon.

The events of the night suddenly crowded in on Meredith. What if Cooper Mayo was right and Evan's unexplained disappearance had been foul play? If so, would she be the next victim? It smacked of melodrama, yet she knew now that the thought had been nudging her mind since Cooper had hinted at violence.

If such was the case, however unlikely, she would be an easy target, alone on the observation platform. Reaching a sudden decision, Meredith sought out a chair in one corner of the parlor car and sat down.

Something else Cooper had said was on her mind now. She had to reach a decision about whether or not to go ahead with the excavation. Most of the details of arranging things had been in Evan's hands, true, yet she had been on expeditions with her father, and had enough experience to know what to do. Also, Dr. Villalobos could handle much of the rest. If *he* wished to go ahead now that Evan was missing. Of course, the archaeologist was a friend of her father, not Evan. In fact, to the best of her knowledge, Evan had never met the doctor.

The map showing the location of the ancient city had come through Dr. Villalobos. It had come to her father some months before his death, along with a letter from Dr. Villalobos claiming that he was not in a position to finance an expedition on such a long shot. The Mexican government, to date, had not shown a great deal of interest in looking for the lost cities in Mexico that many archaeologists, Dr. Longley among them, believed existed; and Mexico, having recently emerged from a bloody and costly revolution, had other concerns, so Dr. Villalobos wrote that he could not go to the government for financing.

Martin Longley had arranged financing through a grant from the college where he taught, but that had been withdrawn on his death. Evan had managed to raise the money; just how, Meredith did not know, and she hadn't questioned him about it. Yet the money was available, and many of the expenses of the expedition had already been paid. If she canceled the excavation now, the monies already spent would have been for naught.

Yes, she would go ahead with it. Unconsciously, she nodded her head vigorously.

The rear door to the parlor car opened and a man entered. Meredith shrank back in her chair, hoping that in the dim light her presence would go unnoticed.

As the man came down the center of the car, she saw that it was Harris Browder. She had no wish to speak to him, but a small sound of recognition escaped her before she could stifle it.

Browder stopped in mid-stride, squinting in her direction. "Meredith! You're still up?"

He came over, taking the chair across from her. "Have trouble sleeping, too, did you?"

"Yes," she said coolly. "I'm worried about Evan."

"Me, too." He nodded at her look. "I know what I said before. I want to apologize for that. I was wrong. I thought it was just one of Evan's little games, but I talked to the conductor awhile ago, and he told me that Evan is definitely not on this train . . ."

Meredith studied him intently. He seemed sincere enough, yet she was sure she detected a sly look in his eyes. The impression could be wrong, however, springing from the fact that she didn't like the man.

Browder was going on, "But I'm sure Evan will turn up eventually." He broke off to stare at her. "I hope you won't think I'm being nosy, Meredith, but I do need to know . . . are you going ahead with the expedition?"

"Yes." Then she said more strongly, "Yes, I'm going ahead with it. I think it is what Poppa would want."

"Good!" Browder nodded vigorously, obviously greatly relieved. "I would hate to see the project collapse at this late date. I have an investment to protect. And I'm sure Evan will be pleased, when he pops up again."

She leaned forward to inquire what he meant by having an investment to protect, but Browder was already getting to his feet.

He said, "I think I can sleep now. You'd better turn in, too, Meredith. You must be worn out." He smiled. "Good night."

She leaned back, keeping her silence, as he went on out. At least she understood better Evan's association with this man; evidently he had helped raise money for the financing of the expedition. But why? Why in heaven's name would Harris Browder put money into an archaeological expedition? It was a puzzling question, one to which she could think of no ready answer. She determined to follow it up at the first opportunity.

Lost in thought, Meredith dozed for a few minutes, and dreamed of a golden city buried beneath wild jungle growth, and a squat golden statue with eyes that blazed with ruby fire. In the dream she approached the statue closer and closer, and then it began to fall from its high pedestal, toppling toward her. She turned to flee, too late, feeling its gross weight crushing her . . .

She awoke with a muted cry, glancing around sheepishly to see if she had been observed. The smoking car was still empty.

She got up and hurried along the train to her sleeping car, anxious now to browse over the map and other information Dr. Villalobos had sent to her father.

In her compartment, the door bolted, she got down the leather portfolio in which all the papers were kept. Evan had wanted to carry it with him, but Meredith had insisted she keep it in her possession so that she could make a thorough study of the material.

She opened it and reached inside, then removed her hand with a gasp of dismay. It was empty!

Peering inside, she could see nothing. Disbelieving, she turned it upside down and shook it; nothing fell out.

Meredith sank back against the cushions, her mind racing. She distinctly remembered checking inside the portfolio on boarding the train in Vera Cruz; the papers had all been intact then. Now they were gone!

Could Evan have taken them? To her knowledge he had not once been inside her compartment.

There was only one other explanation. Tonight, during her absence, someone had entered the compartment and stolen the contents of the portfolio!

Chapter Three

Amidst the noise and confusion of the huge train station, Meredith looked for Dr. Ricardo Villalobos.

It seemed a hopeless task to single out one person from the ever-moving throng. Hawkers, selling their wares, cried out to everyone who would listen: "Señor, Señora, a lovely *reboza*, made of pure wool! A silver pendant, Señorita, in the shape of a dove! It will bring you luck! Combs for your hair, pure tortoise shell!"

Here in the station could be found all of the different types and divisions of Mexican society. Wealthy Spaniards in their narrow dark clothes, white shirts and wide-brimmed hats walked disdainfully next to Indians in their baggy white pajamas and colorful serapes, and *mestizos* in everything from native costume to European dress.

And then there were the visitors—those who came to look, and those who came to stay—the

Americans, the Chinese, the Africans, the Europeans.

As she stood on the steps of the train, looking down on the crowded platform, Meredith swayed. She hadn't been eating or sleeping well, and the outrageous noise and rank smell of the crowded train station made her dizzy.

As she closed her eyes, trying to get a grip on her faculties, she felt a firm hand on her elbow. "Señorita Longley?"

She jumped with surprise and quickly opened her eyes. Looking up at her solicitously from the bottom step was Ricardo Villalobos.

Meredith found herself flushing. Dr. Villalobos was a darkly handsome, fine-featured man, with thick black hair and intelligent black eyes. He looked every inch the Spanish Don, an appearance which was not entirely misleading even though he was a professor of history. His family had been one of the first to settle in Mexico, for an ancestor had accompanied Hernando Cortez on his journey of conquest.

"Dr. Villalobos," Meredith said. "I was looking for you, but the crowd is so . . ."

"Yes, isn't it?" He smiled. "Come, let me help you down. You look pale. Was the trip uncomfortable?"

She nodded. "Yes, and more. I have a great deal to tell you."

Taking Meredith's weight on his arms, he helped her down from the train. She felt her face grown warm at the touch of his hands.

Meredith had met the doctor some years earlier, when she had visited Mexico City with her father. She had been only sixteen, and shy to the point of pain. He had been very gallant with her, with a seriousness that she felt disguised a degree of amusement, but nevertheless she had developed a tremendous crush on him, the memory of which now caused her discomfiture.

"I am so sorry about your father," she heard Ricardo saying as her feet touched the platform. "I wanted to attend the funeral, but circumstances were such that I simply could not get away. Your father was a good friend to me, and I received much instruction and enjoyment from our correspondence. I shall miss him. I think I can understand how great is your own loss and feeling of sorrow."

His compassion brought back memories of her father, and Meredith's eyes unexpectedly filled with tears. Unable to speak, she had to turn away.

Ricardo took her hand. "I am sorry, Meredith, if I have awakened painful memories. We shall speak no more of it just now." His voice became brisk. "I must express my pleasure that you have decided to continue with the expedition."

Her emotions under control again, Meredith said, "My brother encouraged me. Truthfully, I might well have dropped the project if not for him."

"Speaking of your brother . . ." His gaze raked the crowd. "Where is he? I have not met him, and have been looking forward to doing so."

Meredith took a deep breath. "What I am going to tell you will seem very strange. I . . ."

Ricardo looked at her with concern. "What is it, Meredith? Is something wrong?"

"Yes, I'm afraid there is. You see, Evan has simply vanished."

"Vanished? Where? When?"

"From the train, but it will take time to tell you, and I should see to my luggage first."

"Do not concern yourself about that." He took her arm. "I have a man here. He will collect your luggage. Is there no one with you then?"

"There is someone else, my brother's associate, a Mr. Harris Browder. He is looking after the unloading of the equipment."

"Then I must also offer him the hospitality of my hacienda. Come, I will put you in my carriage, and then return to find him."

As they left the huge station, Meredith found herself hanging back, until her companion noticed that something was amiss.

Ricardo looked at her questioningly. "You pull back, Señorita Meredith. Is something wrong?"

Meredith, her throat suddenly dry, swallowed. "No, not really. It's just that Harris already has a place to stay, and . . ." She broke off, not wishing to tell him that she would prefer that Harris Browder be quartered somewhere else.

"Of course, I understand," Ricardo said, but he looked slightly puzzled. Meredith looked

46

away, before he could see something that she didn't wish him to see.

With a firm hand on her elbow, Ricardo urged her along. Looking around the vast station, Meredith saw Cooper Mayo, his great height making him stand out above the crowd. He was staring at her speculatively.

Automatically, Meredith started to smile at him, but froze when she saw Rena Voltan by his side, supervising an entourage of porters as they wrestled with a mound of luggage. She was smoking a small cigar.

Meredith turned her face away, and let herself be guided on outside the station, to Ricardo's carriage. Although she had to admit to herself that the big man aroused her curiosity, she sensed a danger in him that frightened her. Rena Voltan, on the other hand, frightened her in a different way. Meredith felt that the woman was like some fierce, wild animal, beautiful to look at, but dangerous to turn your back on. At any rate, the pair of them had nothing to do with her.

It was a fine, clear day, and Meredith enjoyed the ride to the Villalobos hacienda. She found Mexico City very beautiful—the ornate churches, the brilliant flowers everywhere, the colorful dress of the people. It was a warm and lovely city, marred only by the sight of the many ragged beggars, lifting their wasted faces and thin arms to the passing throng. On Meredith's first visit to Mexico, she had wanted to give to them all, and did until her purse was empty; but there were still hundreds waiting, importuning, pulling at her skirts with stick-thin fingers. Now she knew better than to give publicly, except in unusual cases.

Ricardo gave her little time to look at the city, pressing her for the details of Evan's disappearance. She quickly told him what she knew.

His dark face somber and mystified, he said, "Have you contacted the authorities yet?"

"No," she said with a helpless shrug. "I thought that perhaps you could do something. I hate to say this, but I'm not sure just how concerned the authorities will be over the disappearance of a *gringo*."

He nodded. "You are probably right. I will confer with the police later today, and see if I can . . . How do you *gringos* put it? Light a fire under them?" His smile took the sting from his words. "The Villalobos name may not mean as much as it once did, but I do have *some* influence. But about your continuing with the excavation . . . how will you be able to do that, now that the map is stolen? As I wrote Martin, the copy I sent to him is, to my knowledge, the only one in existence."

"That's no problem. I committed it to memory." She smiled. "You probably don't know this about me, but I have what is known as total recall, a retentive memory."

"There are a great many things I don't know about you, a lack I hope to correct while you are in my country." He returned her smile, then became serious. "But the map is only one of your problems. There is still a great deal to do. Supplies must be purchased, laborers hired, and I think it would be wise to take along a few guards, men who know how to handle weapons. Mexico is still in a great ferment, as you well know. Men who were revolutionaries have now become *bandidos*."

"I thought that you could help with those matters," Meredith said carefully, and then, as a sudden fear touched her, "You *are* still accompanying me, are you not?"

"I planned to do so, and have been looking forward to it." Ricardo was frowning. "But I may not be able to get away at once. The way matters stand now, you may have to proceed without me, and I will catch up to you later. I shall be able to help you with employing a crew for the expedition, but you will need a strong man in charge, a man with some fighting experience, since he will, in effect, be in charge of a small army. It had been my assumption that your brother would fill that need. But now that he is not with you . . ."

"I know," she said soberly. Unaccountably, into her mind came the image of Cooper Mayo. She disliked the man, true, for his arrogance and self-assurance, yet wasn't that the sort of person she needed to command the expedition? Evan was capable enough for that chore, at least he had assured her that he was, but she would not use Harris Browder for that job. Not only did she doubt his competence, but she despised him.

Ricardo was speaking, "Over the years I

have assembled a fairly good crew that I use on my own digs. They have gained valuable experience at excavating, and are to be trusted." His smile was wry. "With the possibility that treasure will be uncovered at the site, you must have people you can trust."

She looked at him with interest. "Then you believe that the treasure, *El Tesoro del Sol*, does exist?"

"So the *mestizo* hunter told me." He shrugged. "He was delirious from jungle fever, but in his delirium he kept babbling about *El Hombre de Oro*, the golden man, and of cups and plates of solid gold."

"But if there is a treasure, why didn't the hunter keep quiet, and return for the treasure himself?"

"He was dying, and he knew it. He knew of my interest in ruins, and since he knew he would not live to benefit, he came to me with his knowledge. And the map, which he told me he drew while he was still lucid."

"Are *you* interested in the treasure?" She looked directly into his eyes.

He looked momentarily taken aback, then he threw back his head and laughed. "I do admire your American honesty, Meredith, your directness!"

She flushed, but said doggedly, "I'm sorry if I offend you, but you still haven't answered me. Is your interest in this excavation due to the possible treasure?"

"No, Meredith, I assure you that is not the case." He sighed. "While it is true that the cycle of revolutions has sorely depleted the Villalobos family fortune, I am not yet destitute. Besides, I did not say that *I* believed in the existence of a treasure, only that the hunter did. And you are not being logical. If my interest was in enriching myself, would I have informed Martin? Would not it be more likely that I would have found some way to proceed on my own?"

"That's true," she admitted with a nod. Yet there was still a worm of doubt in her mind. She gave a mental shrug. "Forgive me, Dr. Villalobos. Since last night, I seem to have become suspicious of everyone. By the way, do you know a woman named Rena Voltan?"

His gaze sharpened. "I have heard of her, yes. Why do you ask?"

"She was on the train, with a man who somehow knew about *El Tesoro del Sol.*"

Ricardo tugged thoughtfully at his lower lip. "I have not met the lady personally, but she has a rather . . . well, unsavory reputation in my country."

"In what way?"

"It is said . . . well, it is believed by some that the woman is a *bruja*, a witch."

"A witch!" She laughed uncertainly. "You can't be serious!"

"Oh, but I am. You may not believe in witches, Meredith, nor may I, but many in my country do. I have heard dark tales of the witchcraft rites she has conducted. It has even been said that she has had people killed to suit her pleasure. Yet, strangely enough," he smiled slightly, "she is accepted in most sophisticated circles. As a curiosity, perhaps."

"Is she Mexican?"

"Quien sabe?" He shrugged. "Who knows? Some say she is Spanish, some say she is Indian, and some say she is a mixture of both. I have even heard that she traces her ancestry back to the Incas."

"Does she have a profession? Aside from witchcraft, that is?"

"Again, nobody seems to know. The only solid fact is that she appears to have ample funds. She spends money lavishly."

Meredith suppressed a shudder. She remembered Cooper Mayo remarking that Rena was a witch. At the time Meredith had thought he was joking; now she wasn't so sure. She said, "The man with her was named Cooper Mayo. Is that name familiar?"

"I don't . . ." He broke off, snapping his fingers. "I have heard that name, as well. A man of many parts. A gun for hire, an adventurer. He was employed for his knowledge of weaponry during the late revolution. By the losing side, unfortunately for him. He had to flee, and is now persona non grata in some quarters, I understand. Those who have fought by his side, or against him, have a name for Cooper Mayo. The Wildman from Texas!"

"Well, whatever he is, he appears to be quite friendly with the Voltan woman."

The carriage swerved sharply, turning off the main road toward Guadalajara. They were on the outskirts of Mexico City now, and the

road they were on, lined with tall trees like
stately sentinels, led to the Villalobos hacienda,
which could be glimpsed up ahead, the whitewashed courtyard walls like snow in the noon
sun.

Meredith knew a little of the history of the
Villalobos family. The name had once meant
wealth and power in Mexico, and the hacienda
was quite old. The land for miles around had at
one time belonged to the family, but time and
revolution had eroded the family fortune, and
now only the hacienda remained in Ricardo's
possession.

Ricardo was the last of the Villalobos clan.
When Meredith and her father had first met
him, Ricardo's parents were still living and
their hopes had been high for their only child.
It had been their expectations that Ricardo
would somehow manage to recoup the Villalobos fortune, and add renewed luster to the
name. But instead he had chosen a different
life, finding his interest in the past, not the
present. It had been, and still was, his conten-
tion that the past should be preserved and made
known to the world. From what Martin Longley had told Meredith, she gathered that Ricardo had no interest in rebuilding the Villalobos family fortune.

As more of the hacienda walls came into
view, Meredith saw a profusion of flowers;
bougainvillea as bright as flames climbed up
the wall.

The carriage drew to a halt before iron gates,
and the driver got down to open them. Then

they drove into the courtyard, a beautiful inner garden alive with color. It was true that Ricardo might live in what he called "genteel poverty," yet he still maintained the hacienda in good condition, and kept a small but very efficient staff to serve his needs, and those of his guests.

The house itself was typically Spanish, with thick adobe walls and a tile roof. The main house and its wings formed an enclosed square with a fountain in the center, and many rooms opened onto the inner courtyard.

Ricardo stepped down out of the carriage and held out his hand to Meredith. "Welcome to my hacienda, Meredith. The staff has been informed of your arrival, and they will strive to make your stay pleasant and as comfortable as possible."

Meredith said graciously, "I'm looking forward to it."

Giving her his arm, Ricardo led her to the heavy front door. It opened before they reached it. A thin, young girl with bare feet, and a large, middle-aged woman stood smiling at them.

"This is my housekeeper, Dolores, and her daughter, Luz."

The big woman smiled broadly. In Spanish she said, "We have been looking forward to your visit, Señorita Meredith. My condolences on the sad death of your father."

"Thank you, Dolores," Meredith murmured.

"I give them into your hands, Dolores," Ricardo said, then turned to Meredith. "I'm taking the carriage back into the city, where I will consult with our chief of police about your missing brother. Perhaps I shall have some good news for you on my return. I shall see you at dinner." He nodded again to Dolores. "I would like dinner served at eight, Dolores. See to it that the señorita has water for a bath."

Dolores led the way down a cool hallway to the south wing of the house. The bedroom was cool, a breeze coming in from the courtyard. The furniture was massive, and dark in color, but there were vases of flowers placed on every available piece of furniture.

"I would very much like a bath," Meredith said.

"*Si*, Señorita," Dolores said. She bustled from the room, long skirts rustling.

Before a tub of water was brought in, Ricardo's man arrived with Meredith's luggage. Removing her shoes and loosening her bodice, Meredith found a tablet and pen and ink on a desk-table against the wall. She sat down and began to sketch the stolen map from memory. She would have drawn it the night before on the train, but she had been too distraught to concentrate properly.

From time to time, she closed her eyes and let the details of the last map shape themselves on her mind-screen, a trick she had developed after realizing that she had total recall of anything she read. She was about half-done when Dolores and Luz came in with a wooden tub of steaming water. They left the room, Dolores returning a few moments later with a bar of soap and an armload of fresh towels.

"Do you require any assistance, Señorita?"

"No, thank you, Dolores," Meredith said, getting up. "I can manage on my own."

When the housekeeper had gone, closing the door after her, Meredith undressed. She sighed with relief when she was finally free of all the confining garments, particularly the tightly laced corset, which had left deep marks upon the flesh of her torso.

Finally she stood before the full-length mirror, not out of vanity, but to see if she had lost any more weight. She had lost a considerable amount since her father's death, and her appetite still wasn't the best. Certainly she would not gain any weight on this trek into the jungle, as the heat, the hard labor, and the poor food would further inhibit her appetite.

She looked at herself critically. She had a good body: firm, high breasts, fully developed yet not too large; a trim waist broadening into the harp-shape of her hips; and slim, strong legs. Her flesh had a rosy tint in the dim light of the bedroom, giving her skin a healthy look, but she was far too thin. She would have to try to make herself eat. She would need the strength for the trip ahead.

No man had ever seen her unclothed body, and at the thought, Meredith's skin took on an even rosier tint. Without thinking, she moved her hands feather-light down over her breasts and across her slightly concave stomach. No prude, and certainly not cold toward men, Meredith had often wondered how a man's hands would feel on her body. Her skin tingled at the light touch of her own fingertips.

A man like Cooper Mayo? A big man, with great strength. Would his touch be gentle, and loving?

With an exclamation of annoyance, Meredith turned away from the mirror, and tested the water in the tub. It had cooled slightly and felt just right.

Stepping in, she lowered herself into the oblong wooden tub with a sigh. It was the first real bath she had had since leaving Boston, and it was sheer luxury!

She hadn't realized how weary she was until the warm water began to relax her. With an effort she roused, took the bar of soap and a washcloth, and began to wash. By the time she was finished, the water had become cool. She stepped out of the tub, dried herself with the big, fluffy towel, touched her body here and there with lilac water, and slipped into a loose robe.

Opening the hall door, she called to Dolores to come for the tub. The big woman came sweeping down the hall with the barefooted girl in tow. "Would you like something to eat, Señorita Meredith?"

Meredith shook her head and yawned. "No, thank you. I can wait until dinner. I feel like I could sleep forever. Would you wake me in time to dress?"

"*Si*, Señorita."

"*Gracias*, Dolores."

When they were gone, Meredith stretched out on the big bed, and was asleep in moments. She slept deeply, dreamlessly, until Dolores rapped on the door, calling out, "Dinner will be served in an hour, Señorita."

Meredith saw by the big grandfather clock that it was after seven. Pulling the drapes from across the doors to the patio, she saw that the shadows were lengthy. The days this time of the year were long. She smiled to herself. She knew that it was the custom here to dine late, sometimes as late as nine or ten in the evening. The early dinner hour was a gesture of consideration for her, Meredith well knew.

Feeling rested and refreshed, Meredith returned to the map. After fifteen minutes of concentrated work, she leaned back, studying the finished product. She was satisfied that it was an accurate facsimile of the original. She would have to make another copy for Dr. Villalobos before she departed for the site of the excavation.

Another knock on the door aroused her from her study of the map. It was Dolores. "Should I assist you in unpacking, Señorita?"

"Yes, Dolores, please."

Together, they unpacked the trunk containing Meredith's clothes, and she chose her best frock, a light green, multilayered silk dress to wear to dinner.

Dolores beamed her approval of Meredith's selection. "I will press out the wrinkles for you."

As Dolores hurried away with the dress,

Meredith began putting on her numerous undergarments. Dressing was a lengthy process, and she was just getting into her corset when Dolores returned with the pressed dress. After helping Meredith lace up the corset, and assisting her into the dress, Dolores stepped back, her broad face lighting up with approval. "You are beautiful, Señorita! Señor Villalobos will be enchanted!"

Meredith felt a flush burn her face, although she knew that Dolores was merely being polite.

After she had donned a pair of dainty slippers, she followed Dolores down the hall and into the dining room. Ricardo was already seated at the long table, sipping at a glass of Madeira.

The room was brilliantly illuminated, with candles striking shards of light from the silver. Snowy linen graced the table, and the heavy, dark furniture had been polished to a high gloss.

Ricardo, slim and elegant in evening dress, rose and came toward her, his dark eyes glowing with admiration.

"My dear Meredith, you are a vision of loveliness!" he murmured. Taking her hand, he brought it to his lips, bowing slightly.

The touch of his lips to her hand sent a shiver up Meredith's arm and she disengaged herself from his grip as soon as she could without being obvious about it.

"You look very handsome yourself, Señor."

"It's kind of you to say so, Meredith, but when are you going to call me Ricardo? I am, after all, not that many years older than you, more *your* contemporary than your father's, yet you make me feel like an elderly relative!"

Meredith flushed. "Very well, I shall call you Ricardo, if that is what you wish."

He smiled and offered his arm. "It is most certainly what I wish!"

He escorted her to the table, to a place set to his immediate right. When Meredith was seated, he poured Madeira from the crystal decanter, then resumed his own seat at the head of the table. She looked around the lovely room. The pair of them seemed lost—two at a table designed to seat at least twelve people.

She was pleased and yet uncomfortable at being alone with Ricardo. She felt unnerved, unprotected, thinking of his first name, as if his full name and title was a sort of charm that would protect her from . . .

She must *say* something, start the conversation going again. She took a sip of the wine, then leaned forward. "What did you find out about Evan?"

Ricardo's face turned thoughtful. Before he could speak, Dolores's daughter, Luz, came in with a tureen of soup, and filled their bowls.

When she had left the room, Ricardo said soberly, "I am afraid that I have little news of your brother's fate. I did have a long conversation with our chief of police. He is a good man, more dedicated and efficient than most, but he is quite harried at the present time. However, he did promise to investigate Evan's disappearance. You will be staying here for at least a week, I trust. Hopefully, by that time he will have news for us." He hesitated, his face clouded.

Meredith, about to taste the soup, lowered the spoon back into the bowl. "What is it, Ricardo? There is something you are reluctant to tell me, I can sense it."

"Yes, there is something else he told me." He sighed. "It seems that your brother was in Mexico City, less than a month ago."

Meredith felt a sense of shock. "But how can that be? Why on earth would Evan have been here? And he would have told me!"

"Apparently he did not," Ricardo said grimly. "I am afraid there is no doubt. The police records show that he was here for at least four days."

Meredith's thoughts were racing. "It's true that he was away for a time, following Poppa's funeral. But his business demands that he travel a great deal. I was so distraught about Poppa's death that I didn't question him."

"But that isn't all, Meredith." Ricardo seemed even more reluctant to proceed.

"What is it, Ricardo? Tell me!"

"During his stay here, your brother was seen in the company of Rena Voltan."

Chapter Four

"A party!" Meredith frowned. "I don't know. There is so much yet to do. I . . ."

Smiling, Ricardo said, "Come, Meredith, a party is just what you need. You have been working hard for a week now. You need to relax."

"We have much to do, you know that, and little time to do it in."

"My dear Meredith." He took her hand. "The party is partly in your honor. The Mendeses are dear friends of mine. In fact, Luis Mendes is one of the few in my country with any interest in our past. He is a wealthy man, and without his contributions to the University, I doubt very much if there would even *be* any classes in archaeology. He is excited that a North American archaeologist should be interested in excavating here."

"Does he know we are seeking *Tonatiuhican?*"

"No, no." He shook his head impatiently.

"All he knows, all he wants to know, is that you are conducting an archaeological expedition here. I really do think it would be to your advantage to attend, Meredith. We have so far failed to find a man suitable to act as trail boss and guard, and Luis has a wide acquaintance. He just might be able to find someone suitable."

She sighed. That much was certainly true. She said, "Nothing about Evan yet?"

"I'm afraid not. I had a brief conversation with the chief just today. They have uncovered nothing."

"Not even a . . ." Her breath caught.

Ricardo shook his head. "Not even a body."

She felt a surge of hope. "That should be a good sign then, don't you think? If Evan had been killed, either falling from the train accidentally or thrown off, wouldn't his body have been found by this time?"

"One would think so," he said gravely, "but don't get your hopes too high. Unfortunately, his body could have been discovered and robbed, then disposed of. Even if just for his clothes . . ." As she winced, Ricardo patted her hand. "Forgive me, Meredith, for being so brutal, but it is a possibility you should prepare yourself for."

All of a sudden, she was weary of frustration, and of worrying about Evan. She said, "I think you may be right. A gala evening might cheer me up. Heaven knows, I could use some cheering."

"Excellent, Meredith! It *will* be a gala evening, that I promise you. When Luis Mendes gives a party, it is the event of the social season!"

The Mendes estate was situated on Chapultepec Hill, with Chapultepec Castle dominating the heights above. As Ricardo's carriage slowed on the approach to the hill, Meredith looked up at the magnificent castle, where the Emperor Maximilian had lived in splendor during his reign of Mexico.

Ricardo said musingly, "Luis Mendes was one of the few members of the Mexican nobility to align himself with Benito Juarez during the Revolution. He was scorned as a traitor by those of his own class, but his foresight proved correct. Since he did support Juarez, even giving him financial aid, his fortune was not confiscated after the Revolution. Many of his class in Mexico City still spurn him, claiming he became a traitor for that very reason, to save his own skin, as you *gringos* say.

"But I know that is not true. Luis believed in the Revolution, and still does, although he does not approve of much what has happened since." Ricardo's expression became melancholy. "Would that my own father had had Luis's foresight. I would not today be living in genteel poverty. But enough of this dreary past history." He turned a bright smile on Meredith. "You look especially beautiful tonight."

"Thank you, Señor." Meredith was warmed by his compliment. Against her better judgment, she had purchased a new gown for the occasion, a confection of dusty pink silk, with a ruffle of paler pink at the low neckline and a full skirt, tiered and gathered behind into a fashionable bustle, which was caught with pale pink bows and bands of ribbons. It was beautifully made—the Mexican seamstresses were extraordinary—and Meredith knew that she looked exceptionally well in it.

The carriage drew to a stop before huge gates set in a high wall. The gates stood open, and Meredith had a glimpse of the people inside. The wall was flush with the street here. Torches flickered inside, and she heard the sound of lively dance music. The street was lined solid with carriages of every description, the liveried drivers gathered in small groups, talking and smoking.

Ricardo stepped out and held a hand up for Meredith. Once on the ground, she accepted his arm, and they walked through the gateway along with other elegantly attired couples. Ricardo seemed well-acquainted, having a smile and a word for almost everyone.

They went directly into the house. Like most houses of the affluent in Mexico City, it was thick-walled and whitewashed, but unlike the Villalobos hacienda, this one was two-story. Every room in the house was brilliantly lit with candles.

Inside the foyer, they were met by a handsome couple. The man was tall, dark, with a thick shock of white hair, and he was splendidly attired. The woman by his side was about his age—close to sixty, Meredith judged—but she was still slim, with a coil of black hair untouched by gray. Her gown was long, elaborately embroidered. A mantilla graced her shoulders, and she languidly waved a fan in one slender hand, although the evening was cool.

"Ricardo, my friend!" the man exclaimed. The two men embraced, then Ricardo bowed over the woman's hand. He murmured, "Consuela, you grow lovelier every time I see you."

"And you, Ricardo, are an outrageous flatterer!"

Although they were speaking in Spanish, Meredith had enough command of the language to understand them. Ricardo took her hand and drew her forward.

"This beautiful young lady is my house guest, Meredith Longley. Our hosts, Meredith, Luis and Consuela Mendes."

Luis Mendes bowed over Meredith's hand. In impeccable English he said, "I am delighted, Señorita Longley, to welcome you to my house. I have heard much about you."

Consuela Mendes took both of Meredith's hands in hers and said graciously, "You are most welcome to the House of Mendes, Meredith."

Luis Mendes said, "We must find time later to have a quiet talk. I am much interested in your archaeological expedition in my country. If I may be of assistance in any way, I am at your disposal."

Other arriving guests were crowding in behind them. Luis Mendes gestured. "But for now, enjoy yourself."

As Meredith and Ricardo proceeded on into the house, the music began again; it was not lively music this time, but a waltz instead.

Ricardo said, "As your escort for the evening, I claim the first waltz, Meredith."

He led her down a wice hall toward the back of the house. Through open French doors, Meredith saw a spacious patio, bright with flowers, a sparkling fountain in the center. The splendor of the ballroom wrung a gasp from her.

Great chandeliers blazed overhead, and the floor was polished to mirror brightness. Beautifully attired women and gentlemen, heads high in the consciousness of their own sartorial elegance, whirled about the room. Meredith noticed that a number of Americans were present. The orchestra, consisting entirely of stringed instruments, was at the far end of the large room.

Ricardo held out his arms and Meredith moved into them. Ricardo was a marvelous dancer and she gave herself up to the stately waltz. She was glad she had agreed to come. For a while at least, she could forget her many problems and enjoy herself.

The waltz ended with a polite round of applause. Ricardo said, "I see champagne on the side table over there. Could I fetch you a glass, Meredith?"

Before she could reply, a deep, familiar voice said at her elbow, "Miss Longley? An unexpected pleasure, seeing you here."

With her pulse accelerating, Meredith turned. Cooper Mayo was dressed as she had seen him on the train, his rugged face wearing that lazy smile.

"Mr. Mayo," she said formally, "I, too, am surprised to see you here."

"Oh, Luis and I are old friends." He arched an eyebrow at Ricardo.

"Oh . . ." Flustered, Meredith performed introductions.

The two men, eyeing one another warily, shook hands.

"I met Mr. Mayo on the train," Meredith said. "He was kind enough to help in the search for Evan."

"Yes, I have heard of Mr. Mayo," Ricardo said dryly.

"Have you now?" Cooper raised an eyebrow. "Good or bad?"

"A little of both."

Cooper laughed heartily. "That's a better report card than I usually get." As the music started up again, he looked down into Meredith's face. "May I have this dance, ma'am?"

"Why, I . . ." She glanced at Ricardo to find him smiling sardonically.

He stepped back. "I have no claim on Meredith, Mr. Mayo. You certainly have my permission, sir."

Without another word, Cooper swept Meredith into his arms and waltzed her out onto the floor. While not as smooth as Ricardo, he danced well enough.

"Seems like a nice fellow, your friend."

"I am his house guest while in Mexico City." Realizing belatedly how the bald statement probably sounded, Meredith flushed, but she decided not to elaborate.

"Well now, how about that?" He laughed softly. "Properly chaperoned, I hope?"

"That, sir, does not concern you, but, yes, I am well-chaperoned. Ricardo has a staff of servants. And speaking of chaperones . . . where is yours tonight?"

"Huh? Oh!" He threw back his head and laughed. "You mean Rena. She's around somewhere. We came together, if that's what you're getting at. But let's get one thing straight, little lady . . . Rena is not my 'chaperone,' just a friend. No woman has any strings on me."

"I'm sure I couldn't care, one way or another," Meredith said tightly.

"No?" His blue eyes got that mocking light. "Why did you inquire about Rena then? Afraid that she might cast a spell on you?"

"I don't believe in witches."

"I didn't either, until I witnessed some of the things she can do. At least, *seem* to do." He was grave now. "In Galveston, I saw her do some spooky things."

Interested in spite of herself, Meredith said, "Such as?"

"Such as, I've seen her perform her mumbo-jumbo rituals, and men have done her bidding."

"That proves nothing, sir. Men are notoriously fallible where women, certain women, are concerned."

"I saw her perform a ritual against a gent who had insulted her. The next day, this particular gent turned up dead."

70

"I have seen very little of her, but she strikes me as a person who would not hesitate at murder." Then she remembered what Ricardo had told her—Evan being seen in the company of Rena Voltan here in Mexico City. "Did she know my brother?"

"I believe so, yes." His gaze was sharp. "Why do you ask?"

"Oh . . . it's just a rumor I heard." She looked away from his inquiring gaze.

"You're wondering if Rena is responsible for your brother's disappearance, right?"

Fortunately, the music stopped at that moment, saving Meredith a response. She started to move away, her gaze sweeping the ballroom in search of Ricardo.

Cooper caught her arm, holding her. "Oh, no, you don't escape me that easily!"

They had stopped at the side table with the champagne bowl. Cooper guided her over to it, never letting go his gentle but firm hold. "Dancing makes me thirsty."

She said dourly, "It strikes me that it doesn't take a great deal to make you thirsty."

Unoffended, he nodded. "Right. I'm from Texas, you know, and we Texans are well-known for our thirsts."

He accepted two brimming glasses of champagne from the serving woman and gave one to Meredith.

As Cooper took a sip of his, Meredith said, "I have heard that you're known down here as the Wildman from Texas. Is that true?"

71

He glanced at her over his glass. "Now where did you hear that?"

She gave a vague shrug. "Is it true?"

"True enough, I reckon." He grimaced. "I never cared much for the moniker. It brings to mind the picture of a man with uncombed hair and beard, and mad eyes. But names of that sort tend to attach to a fighting man." He took a drink of champagne. "Speaking of names . . . Meredith strikes me as unusual for a lady. It sounds more like a man's name. How did you happen to come by it?"

"Meredith was my mother's last name, her maiden name."

"I like the name, and I must say, looking at you now," his eyes were admiring, "you look every inch the lady. And a lovely one."

Flustered, she was at a loss for an answer. Fortunately, she was saved one by Ricardo's appearance.

"Luis would like a word with you, Meredith," he said. "The guests have all arrived, and he is momentarily free of his hosting duties. Come along." Offering her his arm, he nodded formally at Cooper. "If you will excuse us, Señor Mayo?"

"With reluctance." Cooper dipped his head. "Thanks for the dance, ma'am. May I now lay claim to a second before the evening is over?"

"We will see," Meredith said, and sailed off on Ricardo's arm.

Cooper watched her progress amusedly. Aside from the fact that she just might be the way through which he could end up with a fortune, he was attracted to her. She was a contradictory female—one moment sophisticated, in command of herself, and the next moment shy, even timid, uncertain of her femininity. She certainly seemed confident enough in her knowledge of archaeology. Although he understood that she had always worked in the shadow of her father, he was more and more sure that she was fully capable of directing this excavation. If *El Hombre de Oro* was not a myth, Meredith Longley was competent enough to find it.

And that was his chief interest in the woman, wasn't it? Her leading him to the treasure?

He snorted softly, drained his glass, and looked around for Rena. She would be anxious for a report. He had very little to report as yet, but he had made some progress; he had made a good start at getting back into Meredith's good graces.

Meredith accompanied Ricardo from the ballroom and down a long hall. He explained, "Luis is waiting for you in the library, Meredith."

She was a little nervous. "Do you know why he wants to talk to me?"

Ricardo shrugged. "About the excavation, I should think. As I told you, Luis has only a layman's knowledge of archaeology, but his interest is much more than a layman's. I haven't told you this, but Luis was instrumental in getting the necessary permits. He has much influence in high government circles. Alone, I doubt that

73

I could have managed it. So, for that at least, you owe him an audience."

He paused to rap on a heavy door. A voice from within called out, "Come in!"

Ricardo opened the door and ushered Meredith inside. The library was a large, dark room, with a huge, ornate desk, and three walls of books. The elegant Luis Mendes got up from behind the desk, a smile on his face, and came toward them.

"Señorita Longley, it is gracious of you to spare me a few moments of your time. May I offer you a glass of champagne?" He took a magnum from the ice bucket on the desk, and poured into a stemmed glass. Not wishing to seem impolite, Meredith took the proffered glass.

"Ricardo, my friend?"

"No, Luis, thank you. I will leave you two alone, for your talk."

Luis Mendes nodded. "I shan't keep her long. I am sure you do not wish to be deprived of the company of such a lovely lady for any length of time."

With a nod to Meredith, Ricardo left the library.

"Now, Señorita," Luis Mendes said briskly, "tell me about your expedition."

Meredith said slowly, "What can I tell you, Señor? I have been working hard this week on the final details, which ordinarily my brother would have handled . . ."

"Yes, I have heard about that unfortunate occurrence. You have my sympathy. Have you found everything you need? May I be of any assistance?"

Meredith fought back an impulse to laugh. His eagerness was that of a small boy on Christmas morning, incongruous in a man of his age. "Everything is going fairly well, I believe."

"Tell me," he said, pacing back and forth, "what exactly do you hope to find in this lost city?"

Meredith tensed, then said carefully, "Well, as you probably know, the city, *if* it is there, is very old. If we are able to uncover artifacts of that life and times, the excavation will be of incalculable value, throwing light on an era in Mexico's past that is still very much a mystery."

"Fascinating, absolutely fascinating!" Luis Mendes said breathlessly. "How I envy you, Miss Longley! The people of Mexico, in these troubled times, very much need to be made aware of their proud history and how far back it goes."

He stopped to smile apologetically. "You must forgive me, but this is a subject dear to my heart. How long and hard I have argued with my compatriots that it is necessary to instill a feeling of pride in the people. But people in high offices contend that, with the revolution so recently behind us, there are other matters more pressing. I claim that is precisely the reason why we should support archaeological explorations. I will be frank with you, Señorita," he was pacing again, "I would much rather one of our own people conduct these explorations, but we do not have the background for it. I have bent every effort to expand our archaeological program at the University, and met resistance every step of the way. To that extent, I would much prefer that Ricardo be in charge of this expedition. Not that I have any strong animosity toward North Americans, I hope you believe that." He flashed a smile at her. "But it is our country, after all, and it should be *our* people."

"I understand perfectly, Señor Mendes," Meredith said, "while at the same time I am grateful for this opportunity."

"That is an excellent attitude. I applaud you. Now . . ." he said, rubbing his hands together, "if I may beg your further indulgence, I would love to hear more details."

To her surprise, Meredith found herself telling him about how such an excavation was conducted—the extreme care with which each artifact must be uncovered; the use of a fine brush to remove all dirt and other foreign matter adhering to the precious finds; the painstaking attempt to reconstruct any objects broken before removal from their resting places; and many, many other details. Meredith warmed to her subject, and realized that she liked this man.

When she finally ran down, Luis Mendes rubbed his hands together again and sighed. "Fascinating, absolutely fascinating! You have chosen a marvelous profession for yourself. If I were only younger, I would study for it myself."

"It is absorbing, I agree." It was Meredith's turn to sigh. "But there are problems, aside from the minor details, details that my father used to handle, and that Evan was to take care of this time."

He was instantly alert, eager in his desire to help. "Perhaps there is some way, then, that I may be of assistance?"

Meredith remembered what Ricardo had told her. "There is one pressing problem," she said. "Everything is pretty much taken care of, but I need a man with experience to take charge of the crew, to act as a sort of trail boss."

"A man with archaeological experience, perhaps?"

"Not necessarily, but it would be wonderful if such a man could be found."

He mused for a moment. "You will be venturing into dangerous territory. I should think that a man with perhaps some military experience, a strong man able to command men, hold them firm against threats, would be of value."

"That would seem to pretty well sum up what I need," Meredith said. "Do you know such a man?"

"It so happens that I do." He smiled. "In fact, he is here tonight, a man by the name of Cooper Mayo."

"Cooper Mayo?" She stared in astonishment.

"You sound as if you know the man."

"I do, yes. I met him on the train from Vera Cruz." She decided against explaining further.

"But from what Ricardo has told me, I gathered that he fought on the wrong side in the Revolution, and is not welcome in Mexico."

Luis Mendes was nodding. "That is quite true, but I happen to like the man. Oh, not that I approve of many of the things he does. He is an adventurer, a rascal, delighting in flaunting authority. But he is a courageous man, extremely capable in crisis situations, a leader of men, and an expert with weapons. I had a few words with him earlier this evening, and he informed me that he is seeking employment.

"A word from me in the right places, and he will be free from harassment by our police, if he can manage to restrain the reckless side of his nature."

Meredith was silent in thought. She walked over to the window to stare out onto the patio. The leaping fountain reflected the light of the torches, and the couples strolling hand in hand. The scent of fragrant flowers drifted in through the open window.

Cooper Mayo did sound like the sort of man she sorely needed, in spite of her dislike for many of his traits. She had considered placing Harris Browder in charge of the crew, and had immediately discarded the thought.

Could she trust Cooper Mayo? Was trust that important? The important factor at the moment was to negotiate the difficult journey to the site. Once there, she would need someone in charge to insure that everything went smoothly, and to see that intruders were kept away. Cooper had made no secret of the fact that he was much interested in *El Hombre de Oro,* yet Meredith had strong doubts that it even existed. It had been her experience that legends about fabulous treasures always sprang up around any discovery of an ancient, lost city, and in the majority of instances the legends turned out to be pure fancy.

She suspected that would be the case this time; in fact, she rather hoped it was so. An expedition such as this was difficult enough, without the presence of treasure seekers. She personally knew of several digs that had been totally destroyed by treasure seekers. All it needed was a rumor that something valuable had been found, and they came—trampling the site; crushing artifacts beneath their boots; and destroying priceless pottery in the hope of finding a bit of gold. Months of hard work could be destroyed in a few hours. She did not want that to happen here.

And if, by some chance, there should be a treasure? Well, Ricardo would arrive at the site before the extensive digging was underway, and he would see to it that what was discovered did not fall into the wrong hands.

She faced around. "Do you recommend Mr. Mayo, then?"

Luis Mendes nodded. "For a man to fit your needs, yes."

"All right," she said in decision. "If he will accept the job, it is his."

"Shall I so inform him?"

She hesitated, then said slowly, "No, since I

will be his employer, I think it best that I do that."

"You are correct, of course." He smiled his approval, and came toward her. "I wish you good fortune in your venture, Señorita, and how I do yearn to be with you. Perhaps . . ." He brightened. "Since you will probably be there for a time, perhaps I could arrange to visit the excavation site when you are well along?"

"You would be most welcome, Señor Mendes," she said sincerely. "I shall look forward to it."

"Excellent. It is settled then. And now," he said, holding out his arm, "I shall escort you back to the ballroom, and claim a waltz, as is the privilege of the host."

"I would be honored, Señor."

The orchestra was tuning up for a new piece when Meredith reentered the ballroom on the arm of Luis Mendes. She took a swift look around, but did not see either Ricardo or Cooper Mayo.

She didn't see Rena Voltan, either, which pleased her inordinately. Maybe the woman wasn't present; it could be that Cooper had been teasing her. Meredith thought of asking her host if the woman had been invited, but decided against it.

Luis Mendes was a marvelous dancer, his age certainly no hindrance on the dance floor.

As he swept her gracefully across the floor, a stray thought crossed Meredith's mind. Had she agreed to employ Cooper Mayo simply to separate him from Rena Voltan, and have him all to herself? What an utterly ridiculous idea!

She lost herself in the stately waltz, enjoying it without thought of anything else. So absorbed did she become that she didn't realize the music had ended, until she heard that familiar rumble of Cooper's voice.

"You promised me a second dance, ma'am."

"I said I'd think about it." She turned to face his lazy grin, infuriating in its assurance.

"So? Now that you have thought about it?"

Luis Mendes smiled paternally at them. "I will leave you in Cooper's capable hands, Señorita Longley." He bowed formally. "May I express my great pleasure at your allowing an old man to waltz with you?"

He turned away into the crowd. As the music started up once more, Cooper took Meredith into his arms and danced her out onto the floor.

"Nice old gent, for a Mexican," Cooper said.

Head back, so she could look up into his face, Meredith said sternly, "Do you find it necessary to sound so patronizing?"

"Did I sound that way? Didn't mean to."

"Señor Mendes speaks highly of you, by the way."

"Is that right? A kind word is always appreciated, since not a great many come my way."

"So highly, in fact, that he recommended you for a job with our expedition."

Surprised now, Cooper missed a step. "A job with you? What job might that be?"

"I need a man to take charge of the excavating crew, a foreman, if you will. And to see to it that we are not plagued by vandals."

"I don't recall asking you for a job."

"Does that mean that you're turning it down?"

"No, no, not at all," he said quickly. "But I must be honest with you. I know almost nothing about archaeology."

"That's not the important thing. I'll admit that I would have preferred a man with knowledge in the field, but your other talents are more needed. What is necessary for you to know about excavating a ruin, I can teach you."

One eyebrow arched. "I must be honest about something else, ma'am. I was a poor student. Fact is, I was booted out of a number of schools." The blue eyes were bright with amusement now.

Annoyed, Meredith snapped, "For trying to seduce your teachers, no doubt!"

"Now how did you know that, ma'am?"

"Because you're the most conceited man where women are concerned I've ever met!"

"If a man doesn't think highly of himself, any lady of his acquaintance ain't likely to, either," he said with mock humility.

Meredith was growing uncomfortable at the turn the conversation had taken. The music ended just then, and she extricated herself from his arms with relief. "You still haven't answered me. Do you want the job or not? I'm not so desperate that I have to beg."

"Oh, I want it," he said promptly. "But I wanted to be completely honest with you."

Was there a satirical glint in his eyes? She said, "Just like that, you accept? Not even bothering to ask how much I'll be paying?"

"I'm sure you'll pay a salary adequate for the job. You see how I trust you? No need for sordid haggling over money."

"That's a strange remark from a man who labels himself a soldier of fortune. I should think that would be the first thing . . ." She broke off as she saw Rena Voltan bearing down on them. The woman looked extraordinarily beautiful in a scarlet Spanish dress, complete with fan and mantilla. She was smoking a small cigar.

Meredith said hurriedly, "I will be in touch with you tomorrow about the details. Right now, there is someone I must see. Goodbye for now, Mr. Mayo."

With that she was gone, hurrying away before she had to speak to Rena Voltan. She ignored Cooper calling after her, "But you don't even know where I'm staying . . ."

Cooper stood staring after Meredith bemusedly. Absently, he took a cigar from his pocket and bit off the end preparatory to lighting it. He was of two minds about the result of the conversation. He had come here tonight with the intent of seeking a job with the expedition. Now that it had been offered to him, he wasn't sure he was all that happy about getting it . . .

A low voice said behind him, "Well, Coop, how did it go?"

He turned, gazing down into Rena's face. He said, "It went fine, I'd say."

From behind the fan she said tensely, "But did you get the job?"

"Oh, I got the job, all right."

"Do you think she's at all suspicious?"

Considering that Meredith had approached him about the job, Cooper thought, I would hardly think she is suspicious. He lit the cigar before answering, "In my judgment, I would have to say that she's not in the least bit suspicious. She thinks I'm a man down on his luck, badly in need of a job."

Rena relaxed. "Good! Now we can start to work in earnest. And Coop . . . just so she *won't* become suspicious, I think it'd be better if we not be seen together for awhile."

"What? You mean I'm to be deprived of the pleasure of your company?" His tone was lightly mocking. "I'm deeply hurt."

"I'm sure," she said tartly. Then her features softened a trifle and she said throatily, "Just think, the next time we get together, we will have something to really celebrate. Just hold that thought!"

"I'll try, Rena. I'll surely try."

Chapter Five

Harris Browder was livid when Meredith finally informed him that she had employed Cooper Mayo, and placed him in charge of the crew. They were in an old building that had once been a stable; Meredith had rented the building for a month to use for storage of all the expedition equipment, and now they were getting everything ready for their scheduled departure in the morning.

"What the hell did you hire that showboater for?" Browder exploded. "You had no right!"

"I had every right," Meredith said, managing to keep her voice steady despite the tension she was under.

She was not used to being in charge, making decisions, and it had been difficult for her to face Browder with the fact of what she had done. Still, inexperienced as she was, she knew that if she did not stand firm, she would lose control of the expedition, and she was determined that this should not happen.

"Aside from the fact that I don't trust the bastard," Browder said, "it's a needless expense. I can handle the job."

Meredith hesitated, knowing that she was on dangerous ground. Despite her dislike of Browder, she did not want to openly antagonize him. She said, "I think we need his special talents."

Browder scowled. "Just what special talents are you referring to?"

"I understand that he's very good at handling guns."

Browder sneered openly. "And I understand he's very good at handling women!"

Meredith managed to keep her temper and reply calmly, "I have been told that the country we're going into swarms with bandits and revolutionaries who refuse to concede defeat. We will be a prime target for both. Mr. Mayo not only is familiar with the country, but he has fought in the Revolution."

"*Paid* to fight." Browder snorted. "How can you trust a man like that? He'll sell out to anybody offering more money."

"I don't believe that. But disregarding that for the moment," she looked at him steadily, "would *you* be able to direct a defense against a raid by bandits?"

"I don't know why not. They're only Mexicans. Don't let them bluff you, and they run like rabbits." His manner was confident, but Meredith could see through it to the bluster underneath.

She said quietly, "I don't happen to share that opinion. These Mexicans you are so contemptuous of fought a bloody revolution only a few years ago, and they had courage enough to defeat a powerful army. No, it's decided. Cooper Mayo will be in charge. If I'm wrong about him, the blame will be on my head, not yours."

He hesitated for a moment, then blurted, "But it's *my* money you're spending like water!"

"Your money!" She stared at him, recalling his earlier statement.

"Where do you think Evan got the money to finance this whole thing?"

"I don't know, he never told me. But I still don't see how it concerns you."

"Because it's *my* money, damnit!" he snarled. "He came to me, and I scrounged around for the bucks he said he needed."

Truly bewildered, Meredith said, "For heaven's sake, why? I recall your saying something about an investment, but why should you be interested in an archaeological dig? It's not a business proposition from which you can realize a profit."

His reply was sullen and evasive. "That's for me to worry about."

"But of course! You've been taken in by that nonsense about finding treasure! Did Evan convince you that we'd find great riches, and he'd share it with you? If he did, I'm sorry for you. But no matter. Listen to me, Harris. There is *no* treasure. It's all a myth. And even if there was, you'd profit nothing from it. Whatever we find there will be reported to the Mexican government, and will end up in museums."

"So you say."

"I do say, yes. I'm sorry if Evan led you to believe differently, but that's between you and him. My advice to you is to take the first train out, and return to the United States," she took a deep breath, "because you're not going along on this expedition."

He went pale with anger. "Do you think you can just kiss me off like that? I have an agreement with Evan! If you think I'm just going to walk away, without the money I've sunk into this thing, you're even dumber than most females!"

Meredith tightened her lips. "Harris, I've tried not to fight with you for Evan's sake, but now it's clear we can never work together. It may be your money Evan used to finance this trip, but all the permits are in the name of my brother and I. As for your money, I will see that it is paid back when I return to the States. If you won't leave Mexico, then I'd advise you to find Evan, and settle with him. Because as of this moment, you are no longer connected with this expedition."

"You icy bitch, you can't do this to me!" Trembling with fury, he took two steps and seized her arm in a cruel grip. "Nobody does that to Harris Browder! I'll break your goddamned arm for you!"

A voice drawled, "Anything I can do, Meredith?"

Browder snarled, "Butt out, Mayo! You're not wanted!"

"I think that's for Meredith to say," Cooper said easily. "Meredith?"

"I just told Mr. Browder that he's no longer a part of this expedition," she said. "But he refuses to leave."

"If the lady handed you your walking papers, Browder," Cooper said, "I'd suggest you hit the road. And take your hand off her!"

"I don't take orders from you!"

"Now that's where you're wrong, my friend."

Almost before Meredith realized what was happening, Cooper seized Browder by the arm, spun him around and away from her, and then stepped in quickly, his right fist smashing into Browder's cheek.

Browder careened backward, landing on his rump on the dirt floor. The crew of Mexicans Meredith had hired were gathering around now, silently watching the scene.

Rubbing his cheek, Browder glared up at Cooper standing over him. "You're going to be sorry for this day, you bastard. I'll get even with you, you can be sure of that!"

"I never worry much about the future, friend, and I'm sure as hell not going to lose any sleep over any threat from the likes of you," Cooper said contemptuously. "Now, get! If you don't get out of here, I'll throw you out." He made a move as if to bend down to seize Browder again.

Browder scuttled across the ground on his back, his terrified gaze never leaving Cooper's face. "I'm going, I'm going!" At a safe distance he got to his feet, shaking his fist. "I'll get even with both of you for this! If you think I'm leaving Mexico, you bitch, you're crazy!"

Cooper growled threateningly, moving forward. Browder ran, disappearing out the stable door. Cooper laughed shortly, brushed his hands together, then faced around. Seeing the circle of watching faces, he ordered the men back to work.

Meredith, still shaken by the encounter, ran her fingers into her hair. "He's a vicious, despicable man. Do you suppose he'll make good on his threat?"

Cooper took her hand and patted it reassuringly. "Don't fret, my dear. Of course I'll keep an eye out, but in my opinion he's about as dangerous as a rattler with its poison sacs removed. All he can do is hiss. Now, I've got to hustle these men along, if we're going to be ready to hit the trail in the morning."

Meredith watched as Cooper moved among the crew, firm in his orders, without being arrogant. He got along very well with the men. Speaking fluent Spanish, he was in command every moment, yet at the same time the men respected him—more, she suspected, than they would have most Americans. She was growing more confident every day that her decision to hire Cooper Mayo had been a good one.

There still was no word of Evan, and Meredith had almost resigned herself to the fact that he was probably dead. She felt guilty that she couldn't find it in herself to grieve for him.

90

But coming on top of the recent death of her father, it was too much . . .

"Well, I think everything is pretty well under control now."

Not noticing his approach, Meredith was startled by the sound of Cooper's voice. She said, "We'll be ready to leave on time?"

"I see no reason why not." He was studying her closely. "You looked rather sad just then, Meredith. What is it? Your brother?"

"Partly that, and the death of my father. I still keep thinking that any moment Poppa will come into the room, and everything will be the way it was."

"Once we're on our way, you'll be so busy you won't have time to think of such things. Now, I told the men to take off for home, to say their farewells to their families, and report before dawn in the morning. So, why don't we go somewhere and I'll buy you a drink, and a bite to eat?"

Meredith felt herself go tense inside. It was the first time he had asked her out socially. She forced herself to relax, and said with a touch of malice, "Won't Rena be jealous if she hears of it?"

"I'm my own man, Meredith, and do as I please," he said tersely. Then he smiled. "Besides, Rena is gone."

"Gone? Gone where?"

"No idea," he said with a shrug. "She doesn't bother to keep me informed of her comings and goings. She left her hotel a couple of days ago."

Although he seemed completely honest and

candid, Meredith had an uneasy feeling that he knew more than he was telling. She said lightly, "Then I will accept your invitation, sir. It will not do to let Cooper Mayo spend a lonely evening."

Meredith was astonished by her boldness, and then decided, with a recklessness unlike her, that it was time she came out of her shell a little.

They left Mexico City early the following day. The men had been busy since long before dawn in the old stable, loading the mules with sleeping tents, bedding, the necessary supplies, and the equipment they would need at the site of the dig.

In addition to Cooper and Meredith, the expedition consisted of an even dozen men. Five of them were students of Ricardo's from the University. They had had some experience on digs, under his supervision. The rest of the crew were local men, who would do the heavy labor and stand guard. The men were all wearing pistols and carrying rifles. Today, Cooper carried his Colt in plain sight, and there was a repeating rifle in a scabbard on his horse.

There were two people present to see them off. One, Ricardo Villalobos, Meredith had expected, but she was a little surprised to see that Luis Mendes was with him.

Meredith now stood talking to them, while Cooper got the mule train started on its way. Meredith was wearing a sturdy riding outfit— boots, corduroy breeches, and a tough, fringed jacket. Within a few days, they would be riding through rough country, and less hardy clothing would be torn from her in a matter of hours.

"How I wish I was accompanying you, Señora Longley," Luis Mendes said with a melancholy smile. "That is why I am here, this morning, to see you on your way. My best wishes go with you."

"Thank you, Señor Mendes," Meredith said, warmed by his words. "I shall look forward to your visit."

"I will do everything possible to arrange matters so I can make the trip," Luis Mendes said.

"When can I expect you, Ricardo?" Meredith asked.

"As soon as possible. I certainly want to be present when you uncover the first artifact."

"The moment I locate the city, I'll send word to you. I only hope the city is there, so there will be artifacts to uncover," Meredith said fervently. "I remember the first expedition on which I accompanied my father. The ruined city we were searching for either did not exist, or it is lost forever."

"That will not be the case this time. I feel it, in here." Ricardo placed a hand over his heart, then smiled at the theatrical gesture. He took Meredith's hand and bowed over it, touching it with his lips. "*Vaya con Dios*, Meredith."

"Thank you, Ricardo . . ."

At that moment Cooper called to her, and she turned to see him standing beside his horse, a big bay. The mule train was already wending its way along the road.

Flustered, heart beating fast with excitement, Meredith said, "Goodbye, Ricardo . . . Señor Mendes."

Meredith hurried to her waiting horse, a dappled gray. Cooper stepped up to offer her a hand into the saddle, but she waved him off and mounted easily. When she glanced around, she saw that Cooper had also mounted up, and was kneeing his horse over to her.

With that mocking glint in his eyes, he said, "Self-sufficient, aren't you, little lady? Won't even let a man give you a hand. The men of Texas are accustomed to being gallant to the ladies."

"You are not hired to be gallant to me, Cooper," she retorted. "Let's get that straight right now. On this expedition, I expect you to treat me just like you would another man."

"Well now," he drawled, his gaze sweeping over her, "I don't think that'll be easy, even in that outfit you're wearing, but I'll try. You're the boss."

Meredith felt her face grow hot, but looked him steadily in the eye, determined not to let him see that he had the power to discomfit her. She said coolly, "See that you don't forget that, Mr. Mayo."

Cooper smiled, and touched the bay in the flanks. The horse moved out at a fast clip, soon catching up to the mule train. Meredith noted that Cooper rode very well, his big figure seemingly a part of the horse. Face still burning, she looked quickly away. Glancing behind her, she waved to Ricardo and Luis Mendes, then urged her own horse into a trot.

The stable she had rented was located in the southwest section of the city, so they did not have to ride through the busy streets. They headed in a generally southwesterly direction, and were out of the city proper in a short while. Meredith knew that the going would be relatively easy while on the plateau, but that it would become rougher once they dropped down into the jungle valleys.

Although Cooper didn't push the caravan hard, Meredith was grateful when they finally struck camp for the night. It had been some time since she had been astride a horse, and she was sore and stiff before the day was over. They camped near a stream, and a bucket of warm water was brought to her tent, the first one erected, and she washed as best she could and stretched out on the folding canvas cot. She was tired enough to fall asleep at once.

It was dark when she awoke. She could hear muted voices outside the tent, and see shadows flickering on the canvas walls. Somewhere, a guitar strummed softly, and a male voice sang plaintively in Spanish of a lost love.

Meredith quickly dressed in fresh clothing and ducked under the tent flap. A few yards away Cooper leaned against a tree trunk in front of his own tent, a long cigar, trailing smoke, in his hand. In the light from the cooking fire, his face looked saturnine. He was drinking from a tin cup. At the sound of Meredith's footsteps, he looked up.

"Why didn't you wake me?" she demanded.

"Why?" he asked innocently. "I figured you needed the rest."

"There were things I could do. I told you not to coddle me!"

"I don't see it as a matter of coddling," he drawled. "The caravan was placed in my charge, and it is my responsibility to see that things go smoothly. When we get to this lost city of yours, I'll turn the reins over to you, and confine myself to guarding your operation against attack."

More subdued, Meredith said, "I want to feel that I'm doing my part."

"Meredith, when we start to move through the jungle, we're going to be in constant danger. A lawless band of marauders would consider these mules, the supplies, and especially the guns, a real plum. And if they see a woman along, especially a pretty white woman, they'll start to paw the ground, like a bull about to mount a heifer!"

She stiffened. "I don't appreciate your crude metaphor, Mr. Mayo!"

"Appreciate it or not, it's the truth. If I have to be blunt, or even crude, to make you keep in the background as much as possible, so be it." His grin was infuriating. "Now why don't you just unruffle your feathers and," he slid down to the ground, patting a place beside him, "sit down here. Supper won't be ready for some time. I have some prime whiskey here that I'll

96

be happy to share. I can't offer any ice, just cold spring water, but it makes a mighty tasty drink."

Reluctantly, she sat down beside him. "As I've mentioned, I don't drink strong liquor."

"My advice would be to change your habits, then. We're going into fever and malaria country. Strong drink helps as well as anything to ward off bugs."

He splashed whiskey into a tin cup, adding water, and gave it to her. "Drink up."

Obediently, Meredith took a sip, shuddering at the strong taste. They were silent for a little while, a companionable silence, and Meredith began to relax. Then Cooper spoiled it. "When do I get a gander at this map, so I'll know where the hell I'm leading this outfit?"

"You don't," she said curtly. "I'll give you directions when needed."

"That's what I like in my employer," he said in a dry voice, "complete trust."

"It's not a matter of trust. If something goes wrong, you won't know the location of *Tonatiuhican*; therefore, you shouldn't be in any danger. Besides, I have no intention of letting the map out of my possession again."

"Again?" He twisted his head around to stare at her. "What do you mean?"

"The original was stolen from my compartment on the train from Vera Cruz."

"Any idea who the culprit was?" he asked casually.

"No. Some suspicions, but no concrete knowledge."

97

"How did you recover it?"

"I didn't."

"I'm afraid I don't understand. The map was stolen, you didn't recover it . . . how the devil do you know how to get where we're going?"

"I made a new map, from memory," she said somewhat smugly.

His initial look of astonishment was replaced by one of admiration. "Now that, my dear, is what I call one hell of a memory! I'll have to watch what I say around you, or my words may come back to haunt me."

Obscurely pleased that she had gained an advantage over him, however slight, Meredith took another cautious sip of the whiskey.

Cooper was staring off into the distance, a thoughtful look on his face. "You know what this means, don't you? Not only are we going to have to be on the lookout for *bandidos*, but it appears to me that another bunch is heading for this lost city of yours. Else why would they steal your map?"

Meredith grew still. "I hadn't thought of it that way." She laughed suddenly.

"What's so blasted funny?"

"It just occurred to me . . . Mexico is full of cities dating from lost civilizations, and for years nobody cared. Now, somebody cares enough to steal a map."

"I hardly think that was the reason the map was stolen, just to find a lost city," he said grimly. "There's somebody out there who believes the treasure you say doesn't exist, does exist, and they're hot on the trail of it."

"Well, good luck to them," she said with a shrug. "If there is such a thing as *El Hombre de Oro*, let them find him. I'm interested in other things, and even if they do get to the city first and find the gold figure, they'll never get it out of the country."

"Lady, you don't seem to understand." He sighed. "This puts us in more danger. You may be telling the truth when you say you're not interested in finding the loot . . ."

"I am telling the truth!" she said hotly. "I'm an archaeologist, not a fortune hunter!"

". . . but that doesn't mean others will believe you," he continued doggedly. "And it could well be in someone's mind to not only get there first, but to stop you from getting there at all."

"I can't believe that someone would kill me just to keep me from finding a city that may not exist, and a treasure that is probably a myth." Despite her disclaimer, a small chill passed over her.

"You're an innocent, Meredith. Until you've seen gold fever seize people, you can't understand what I'm talking about. It brings out the worst in the best of men!"

"Even you, Cooper?" she said softly. "You admitted being a treasure hunter, to being interested in the gold."

He looked taken aback for a moment, then smiled without humor. "Even me. It's a fever that can addle a man's senses."

Subdued, she said, "Well, you're honest about

it, at least." Trying for a lighter touch, she added, "I guess I'll just have to watch you."

"That's not a bad idea," he said shortly. He fell silent, brooding off into the night again.

The silence stretched for so long that Meredith became uncomfortable. Finally she blurted, "How did you come to choose your profession? If you can call it that."

He gave a start, scowling at her as if he'd forgotten her presence. He gave a short laugh. "That's not an easy question to answer. I often think that I should have been born fifty years earlier, or maybe even back before that."

"That's a strange attitude."

"Not so strange. Back then, a man could do pretty much what he wished, so long as he was man enough to get away with it. Now the world's become too tame, hemmed in by social mores and laws. Look at my home state, Texas, for instance. In the middle part of this century, it was wild and free. Now, what's left? Pushing cattle." He made a contemptuous face. "Sure, you read stories about the wild, wild West. Believe me, it's not that wild. The buffalo are long gone, fur trapping is no longer profitable, and the old gunfighters are either dead or dying out. Despite all the tales about the romantic life of the cowboy, cowpunching is nothing but hard work, a deadly bore."

"So you hired your guns out to other countries?"

"In a manner of speaking, yes. It makes for an exciting life, as well as a lucrative one. Usually." He frowned over at her. "But not always for my gun. I have a few other talents, you know."

"But here in Mexico . . . why did you hire yourself out to the regime in power at the time? From what I understand, Maximilian wasn't Spanish, and was a despot as well."

"The answer is quite simple." He shrugged. "They offered more money. Juarez, at that time, could barely feed his army, much less pay the salary that I required. Politics concern me very little, ma'am."

"You don't much concern yourself with right or wrong, either," she said tartly.

"Now just what does that mean?"

"It means that the cause of the revolutionaries was right. They were battling oppression."

Instead of being offended, Cooper was amused. "One thing I've found in these banana republic revolutions, most other wars too, is that the side that wins is the one that's right."

"That's a despicable philosophy!"

He laughed. "Did you hire me for my philosophy, or to get your crew to this lost city safe and sound?"

Somewhat discomfited, Meredith retorted, "I've always thought that a person's philosophy determines what he is. Your philosophy, if it could be called that, reveals a flaw in your character."

"Could be. But then I've never claimed I didn't have a few flaws." He grinned lazily. "I've learned that a man without flaws is a dull clod, and the ladies seem to find a man with

101

flaws much better company than the perfect gent. Now ain't that the way you look at it, ma'am?"

Meredith said stiffly, "I'm sure that I've never looked at it one way or another. And I didn't hire you just for your company!"

"Strikes me that was implied as a part of our bargain. If we don't find each other good company, it's going to get pretty damned dull after awhile."

Meredith gasped. "Our bargain implies no such thing! *I* certainly had nothing like that in mind when I hired you!"

"Didn't you now?" he drawled. "Maybe you did, and just won't admit it to yourself. But you will, I'll bet my boots on that."

Meredith was seething. The insufferable conceit of the man!

She started to get to her feet, but Cooper caught her hand, not cruelly but firm enough to hold her still.

He said, "There's one sure way to find out how we're going to get along."

Before she fully realized his intention, he had pulled her against him. His breath smelled of whiskey, as his mouth drew closer and closer to hers.

"What are you doing?" she demanded.

"This."

His mouth was close now, almost touching hers. Belatedly, Meredith placed both hands flat against his chest and pushed with all her strength. Cooper merely laughed, and gripped her shoulders with his big hands. Struggle as she might, Meredith could not free herself. She knew it would be useless to cry out for help; it would be an occasion for laughter among the men, instead of alarm.

Finally realizing that further struggle was a waste of time, she stopped, willing herself to endure the humiliation with as much dignity as possible. Faintly to her ears came the guitar music, and her senses seemed sharper, more attuned to the scented tropic night.

Then Cooper's mouth was on hers. Against all her resolve, the touch of his lips set up a quivering deep inside her, and she felt herself go soft. She felt boneless, lightheaded. She had been kissed by other men, a few times, yet those kisses had been tentative, almost chaste. This man's kiss was rough, demanding. Her heart began to beat wildly, and she wanted desperately to return the caress.

A groan came from Cooper, and his arms tightened around her, drawing her down onto his broad chest. Meredith felt her breasts flatten against him, and the nipples tingled, sending currents of delightful sensation through her body. In another moment her will to resist would melt away. Dimly, Meredith realized this, and she began to struggle again, muttering, "No, no!"

Finally Cooper relaxed his grip and leaned back with a smug smile. "That was just a getting-acquainted kiss. It wasn't so terrible, now was it?"

Through the tears of anger burning her eyes, his face was little more than a blur. She brought her hand around with all her strength and slapped him across the cheek.

"You are a contemptible man, Cooper Mayo! I have never given you any indication that I would encourage such an advance!"

Her open hand had left a red imprint on his face, and Cooper reached up to touch it with the tips of his fingers, but that maddening smile remained in place. "Now you're not going to tell me that you've never been kissed?"

"I have been kissed, yes, but by gentlemen who asked my permission first!"

"Couldn't have been much of a man if he felt he had to ask permission."

"They *were* gentlemen, at least," she said, her fury still blazing.

"Well then, that explains it." He spread his hands. "No one has ever accused me of being a gentleman."

"That's obvious." More in control of herself now, Meredith stood up. In a cold voice she said, "I want to make one thing clear. This is never to happen again!"

He grinned up at her. "You mean, if I want to kiss you, I have to ask permission first? Unh-uh, that's not my way, little lady."

"Now you listen to me, Cooper Mayo! For the rest of our time together, you will keep your distance from me. If you try to touch me again, I will . . ."

His smile widened at her hesitation. "You will what?"

"I will discharge you."

"And take this caravan into the jungle on

your own? Come now, my dear Meredith. That is impossible and you know it. For one thing, these men will not take orders from a woman, and at the first sign of danger they would take off, leaving you alone."

She knew that what he said was true. In a voice that shook slightly, she said, "Then I will return to Mexico City and hire another man to take your place. After all, we're only a day's ride away as yet."

"And tell people what? That you returned because a man kissed you? You'd be a laughing-stock, and I think you have too much pride for that." His voice changed. "But don't worry yourself. I have my own pride. Flaws I may have, but forcing myself on a woman is not one of them." He smiled again. "I will just have to be patient and wait until you're willing."

"That, Cooper Mayo, will never happen!"

He stretched. "Don't be too sure of that."

"Oh! You *are* an impossible man!"

Anger flooded her again, and she turned on her heel, going toward her tent. A shout sounded from the cooking fire.

Cooper called after her, "Your dinner's ready, boss lady."

Although Meredith was hungry, she said, "I'll skip dinner, thank you."

Chapter Six

Meredith was quite cold to Cooper during the next few days, keeping her distance and speaking to him only when necessary. At first he took her coldness good-naturedly, even with indulgent amusement, but as the days passed she noticed that his temper grew shorter and he was quite curt with her. She also noticed that, in the evenings, he was drinking more and more, coming to dinner in a surly, almost drunken state.

She took an obscure satisfaction from this, and also experienced a great relief. Despite her anger at his being too forward, she found herself remembering his kiss, remembering the hard strength of his body against hers, and the leaping response within her at the touch of his lips. At night her dreams were feverish, chaotic. She would dream that she was being held in his arms, and he was making ardent love to her. She would awaken slowly, still caught up in the dream, her traitorous body still yearning for the reality of his caresses.

This angered her even further, and alarmed her. She was afraid that if he forced himself on her again she would not have the will to resist.

They were deep into the steamy valley now, the city far behind. Occasionally they came upon a small village, and were greeted by wide-eyed children and grave, curious adults. The villages had small plots of cleared ground for growing crops, but the verdant undergrowth approached threateningly on every side and Meredith realized that the villagers were engaged in a never-ending struggle to keep their villages from being swallowed up.

Fortunately they were still on a well-traveled road, since a few larger, more prosperous cities were along it, including the lovely towns of Cuernavaca and Taxco, but beyond Taxco, they would have to branch off the road, heading west, directly into the jungle toward the Sierra Madre range. Meredith looked forward to that with dread; they would have to make their own trail, hacking their way through the rank jungle undergrowth.

To get away from Cooper, Meredith took to riding at the front of the caravan, often so far ahead she was out of sight of the lead pack mule.

The first time she did this a scowling Cooper came thundering up to her. "You shouldn't be riding up here! Suppose we're attacked unexpectedly? You should be back in the center, where someone can keep an eye on you."

"I'm seldom out of sight of the column."

"But you're more vulnerable up here. I forbid you to ride this far ahead."

"*You* forbid! Don't forget that you're working for me, Mr. Mayo."

"I have enough to worry about without having to look out for you," he said in a grumbling voice. "Damn foolish female."

"You are in charge of the men, but not of me. I do not take orders from you."

"You are in my charge, woman!" Then he broke off, shrugging. "Be damned to you then. If anything happens, it's on your own head."

"That's right, it is." Realizing that she was behaving contrarily, perhaps even foolishly as he had charged, her anger was such that Meredith drummed her bootheels in the horse's flanks and rode on ahead.

Seething, Cooper sat on his horse, watching her ride out of sight on the trail ahead. He lit a cigar and blew an angry cloud of smoke at the insects circling his head like a halo.

Meredith Longley was the most exasperating woman it had ever been his misfortune to encounter. She could be warm and charming when she chose to be, but at a wrong word or action on his part, she could turn cold and scornful.

He laughed shortly, slapping at an insect burrowing into his neck. He was honest enough with himself to admit that the fact she seemed unmoved by his advances was probably what he found so frustrating; Cooper wasn't accus-

109

tomed to female rejection. There had been moments when he had glimpsed a vulnerable side to Meredith, which was what had prompted him to kiss her that first evening on the trail. That, he realized now, had been a mistake. He should have waited.

He sighed. It was going to be a long, hard trip, and would be even more difficult when they finally arrived at the site of the excavation. With Meredith the only woman within miles, it was going to be damned hard to keep his distance.

The hell of it was, he admitted to himself, he liked her—most of the time. She was direct, honest, and apparently she did not possess the deceit and deviousness he had found in many women. Before, it hadn't bothered him whether or not he liked the woman he was in pursuit of. A woman like Rena Voltan, for instance, he accepted for what she was, with his eyes wide open, and took her for the pure animal pleasure she willingly supplied.

Maybe that was another mistake; maybe he should try to be more forcible, overpower Meredith. This was something he was usually adverse to doing. If a woman didn't want him, damned if he would force himself on her!

Yet, he understood that some women preferred it that way. Could that be the way with Meredith? There were unmistakable signs that she was attracted to him—or so it seemed to him.

His thoughts turned to Rena Voltan; she was supposed to be out there somewhere, trailing them a safe distance back. That had been her plan, when last Cooper had seen her.

But now he wasn't so sure. After learning from Meredith that her map had been stolen on the train, he had to wonder if Rena hadn't managed to get her hands on the original. If such was the case, she could already be somewhere up ahead of the caravan, and could arrive at the site of the excavation before they did.

He tossed his cigar into the underbrush and drummed his horse on ahead. Meredith was long out of sight, but despite her waywardness, Cooper felt that it was his duty to keep his eye on her as much as possible. He had the feeling that his emotions toward her would have to be resolved, and soon.

Cooper's anger did not abate appreciably, but lingered on through the afternoon and into the evening, causing him to drink more than usual. Never before in his experience had any woman gotten under his skin as had Meredith. Why this one, instead of the others he had known?

Drinking, he brooded on the problem, back propped against a tree, watching her move back and forth between her tent and the cooking fire. She didn't approach him, or even glance in his direction. From all the indications she gave, he might not have existed. The night was steaming—sweat was rolling off Cooper, made worse by the alcohol in his blood—but Meredith seemed relatively unaffected by the heat. Before supper, she had put on fresh clothing. She wore a white blouse that molded her firm breasts, and a dark riding skirt. Her hair was up in a bun, and as she bent over, Cooper could see her slender, white neck.

He ached to kiss that neck, and longed to let down her hair and run his fingers through it.

He ate very little dinner, and returned to the tree to drink again. With dinner over, the fires were allowed to die and darkness closed in.

Cooper sat on. Inevitably his head swung toward Meredith's tent, lit by a faint lantern glow. Watching, his breath caught, as her shadow moved back and forth between the light and the sidewall. From the blurred moments, he knew that she was undressing. It was inadvertent on her part, he was sure. He could see nothing but shadows, yet the scene was perhaps more tantalizing than if he were inside the tent.

He took a drink, and closed his eyes. It didn't help. Erotic images flickered before his mind's eye, and his vaulting need made his blood run thick and hot. No matter how he tried to cast them out, the images continued.

With a muttered oath, he got to his feet, the whiskey bottle thumping to the ground. He pushed himself away from the tree and strode toward the tent.

Meredith had brought with her several long nightgowns, but the nights here were so fierce and humid that she had taken to sleeping in the nude. It was something she had never done before and, at first, she had felt shame at the wantonness of it. Yet it was so much more comfortable than trying to sleep in a nightgown that it was now becoming almost a habit, done without a second thought.

Stepping out of the last garment, she breathed a sigh of vast relief. She started to reach across the pallet to snuff out the lantern, and froze at the sound of the rustling tent flap.

Cooper Mayo was just stooping down to enter the tent.

"What are you doing in here?" she demanded, her voice sounding shrill and high.

Already inside, Cooper stood stock-still at the sight of her nakedness. Desire blazed in his eyes. The tent was far too low for him to stand upright, but he was nonetheless threatening, even in his crouched stance.

Meredith's stasis broke and she doved for the lantern, blowing it out with one breath. Then she rolled over, scrambling for something to cover her body. Her hand touched a rough blanket and she pulled it around her.

Out of the corner of one eye, she saw his shadowy figure advancing toward her. The sound of his heavy breathing was loud in the small tent.

"If you don't leave at once, I'll scream!"

"I doubt very much that you'll do that, boss lady." His voice was husky with passion and whiskey. "Even if you did, no one would come running. The men would laugh among themselves at the antics of the *gringos*. To their way of thinking, what we're about to do is the most natural thing in the world."

He came down on his knees beside her, one hand groping for the blanket.

"We're not about to *do* anything!" she said furiously.

"Yes, we are. You've been an itch in my blood since I first clapped eyes on you, Meredith, and by God, it's time I did something about it. It's been in your mind as well, you can't deny it."

He closed his hand on the blanket and jerked it away.

As he leaned toward her, Meredith could smell the whiskey on his breath. She turned her face aside. "You're stinking drunk!"

He chuckled. "A little drunk maybe, but not that drunk."

His mouth descended on hers. Then those big hands were on her body, touching her intimately. Despite the strength of his hands, despite his liquored state, his touch was surprisingly gentle and his hands were knowing.

Meredith felt her body responding to his caresses. Filled with self-loathing, she fought him. She was a virgin by choice, not from prudery or coldness, but because her parents had instilled in her the belief that a woman's virginity was her most precious possession, to be given as a prize to the one man in her life—the man she would marry and spend the rest of her life with.

But to lose her maidenhood in this steaming jungle, and to a man like Cooper . . .

She fought him, silently, well knowing that she would indeed be the object of derision if she aroused the camp. His strength was too much for her; but later she was to wonder if she had fought whole-heartedly, for even as she struggled a part of her yearned to submit.

He was sprawled across her now. Somehow in the struggle, his clothes had become loosened, and she felt the hard thrust of his maleness. Belatedly, she realized that her struggles had only succeeded in arousing him further. Meredith relaxed, going limp. She *had* fought; she had refused to willingly submit to his lust. What more could be expected of her?

This conclusion imbued her with a feeling of self-righteousness, and she whispered through clenched teeth, "I won't fight you anymore, Mr. Mayo, but I'll make you rue this day. I swear this to you!"

His short laugh sounded coarse. "You'll come to think differently, Meredith. You'll see."

"Never! I will despise you until my dying day!"

Her words barely penetrated Cooper's consciousness. At another time they might have given him pause, but he was too consumed by need to heed them now. Meredith felt his hands spreading her thighs, and felt the probing of his hard member at the secret place, which heretofore had been inviolate.

She squeezed her eyes shut, turned her head aside from his hot breath, and tensed herself against the expected pain. Yet he was gentle, and even in her ignorance of men, Meredith knew that this was not usual. There was a moment or two of discomfort, but when he thrust himself all the way inside her and began to move slowly, the discomfort lessened and she relaxed, determined to endure until his passion was spent.

But even then, instead of pounding at her as she had anticipated, Cooper did not hurry. He kissed her breasts and she could feel the nipples become swollen. Then he was seeking her mouth. She refused to turn her head. He placed his hand on her chin, his fingers digging into her cheek, and forced her face around and up.

His mouth was warm and incredibly soft. She would not open her lips to him, but now the movement of his body inside her was arousing unfamiliar sensations, not at all unpleasant. In spite of herself, she began to weaken. Her lips parted and his tongue invaded her mouth.

All at once, she found her hips moving in counterpoint to his, and she raised her head a trifle, her mouth responding. Cooper took away his lips for a quick breath and a rumble of laughter burst from him, triumphant laughter, almost gloating, and a part of Meredith's mind despaired of what she was doing.

But now her pleasure was growing, a feeling of unbelievable pleasure radiating out from the center of her being. She had the strange feeling that she was about to burst clear of her physical self, and soar free in ecstasy. A guttural moan escaped her lips.

At the same moment Cooper went rigid. "Ah-h, dear heart! Meredith, Meredith!"

He shuddered mightily, and shuddered again.

A measure of sanity returned to Meredith, as she sensed rather than felt that he was still while her lower body was yet moving against him. By a great force of will, she made herself go still, and full awareness flooded back, followed by a surge of revulsion. She pushed against his chest. "If you have finished what you came to do, I would appreciate you removing yourself."

Cooper moved, and she heard rustling sounds as he adjusted his clothing. She snatched up the blanket and pulled it over herself. She could see the outline of his body squatting nearby.

"I'm not going to say I'm sorry, Meredith, because I'm not. I suppose I was . . . well, impulsive," he said, a sheepish note in his voice.

"Impulsive! You call rape impulsive?"

"Oh, come now, my dear. Let's not get melodramatic. You do tempt a man something fierce."

"Tempt? Oh!" Her breath caught. "How can you say that? I have never given you the least encouragement. On the contrary . . ."

"Perhaps not intentionally. But you are a beautiful woman, and just being near you . . ." There was a hesitant note in his voice. "I had suspected you were a virgin, and my suspicions have been confirmed. It will be better the next time, I promise. The first time for a woman is . . ."

"The next time!" she exploded. She sat up, the blanket falling away from her breasts. Hastily, she pulled it up. "There will be no next time, do you understand that? We are too far along on our journey for me to send you packing. I suppose you took that into consideration," she said bitterly. "But if you come near me again, I will kill you, Cooper Mayo. Tomorrow, I am going to arm myself with a pistol and keep it beside me at night. If you so much as stick your head inside this tent again, I will blow it off!"

Chapter Seven

Rena Voltan and her small crew of armed toughs were not far behind the Longley caravan; they were, in fact, less than a half day's ride to the rear. Rena kept them at just enough distance so their presence would not be discovered. Since the Longley caravan left a clearly marked track, she was content to follow in its wake.

Contrary to Cooper's suspicions, Rena did not have the stolen map showing the directions to *Tonatiuhican*. Evan Longley had promised her a copy, but then he had done his disappearing act. When she had learned that he was gone, Rena had searched his and Meredith's train compartments thoroughly, but had found nothing.

Her rage at Evan was monumental. She had devoted considerable time and effort into seducing him, on his earlier trip to Mexico City, because he had hinted at the possibility of finding a great treasure.

In turn, he had confided to her his future plans, and had promised her a share of the riches if she would aid him in smuggling the treasure out of Mexico. She had agreed, thinking that once she had a copy of the map, it might be possible to beat the legitimate expedition to the treasure. Now, she was left holding the poverbial empty bag, and Evan, in all likelihood with the map, was heading toward the lost city.

Also, her pride was stung. She had rather enjoyed Evan. He was handsome to look at, a pleasing lover, and as amoral and unprincipled as herself. However, she was not used to being on the unsatisfactory end of an arrangement. She had set out to use him* and he had tricked her. He must not be allowed to get away with it.

After Evan's disappearance, mutual anger had brought Rena and Harris Browder together. When she had allowed Browder to join her group, Rena thought wryly that treasure hunting, like politics, made strange bedfellows—not that she and Browder were literal bedfellows as yet. Although Rena liked men of varied shapes, sizes and natures, Browder was not a type she cared for. He was crude, not at all handsome, and could, she suspected, be brutish in bed, although the last trait she did not necessarily consider a liability.

Thinking of sex turned her thoughts to Cooper Mayo. She could almost hear his drawling voice: "Not your type, my dear? I didn't think there was any such animal."

Of all the men Rena knew, and there were many, Cooper Mayo had the ability to arouse her more than any other. Wise about herself, Rena knew that it was probably because he refused to bend to her will. Most men soon became putty in her expert hands, but Coop remained his own man at all times. She was looking forward with great anticipation to the time they would spend together, once she had collected the treasure of the ancient city and escaped Mexico with it.

When Harris Browder had come to her in Mexico City the day before the Longley expedition was to depart, Rena had laughed at him. "What makes you think I have any interest in this 'lost city' of yours? And even if I did, why should I take you along, Browder? I hardly know you."

"Because I'm the one who came up with the money to finance Evan!"

Rena shrugged, blowing smoke. "That's your problem. And his."

Browder scowled threateningly, small eyes narrowing. "It'd be yours, too, if I went to the authorities with what I know. These greasers wouldn't take too kindly to the plans you two have for smuggling all that gold out of Mexico, without giving the Mexican government their share!"

"What gold?" she asked innocently. "I don't know what the hell you're talking about."

"Oh, yes, you do," he said meanly. "Evan told me all about the woman he met in Mexico City who knew ways to get the loot out of the country."

"Evan talks a lot, doesn't he? What else did he tell you?"

"That you were pretty damned good in bed," Browder said bluntly.

Rena kept her face a mask to conceal the sudden anger she felt, but in that moment she determined that Evan Longley would pay, and pay dearly, for that particular indiscretion.

"Are you threatening me, Browder?" she said softly.

Browder took an involuntarily step back, blinking. He said hurriedly, "No, no. But it's to our mutual advantage if we team up. Surely you can see that. I'm not asking for a fifty-fifty share, just my investment back and a small profit." He added bitterly, "And a chance to get my hands on that double-crosser, Evan Longley!"

"We have that common goal, certainly."

Since Rena instinctively didn't trust the man out of her sight, she made up her mind to let him accompany her. It would be easy enough to dispose of him somewhere down in the jungle, and there was always a chance that he might be useful. She said, "All right, you can come along with me."

"Thanks, Rena. You won't regret it."

"That remark of Evan's . . . I hope you don't have any ideas about sharing my bed?"

"Not at all," he assured her. Then his eyes got a sly, lecherous look. "Not without your permission. But that, too, could be to our mutual benefit."

So far Rena had not given her permission. But as the nights passed, she was becoming restless, alone in her tent. The five men she had hired to accompany her were all Mexicans—sullen, dangerous men, killers all. Even if she had the inclination, Rena wouldn't trust one of them in her bed. They might cut her throat while she slept, just for the hell of it. And so, of necessity, she slept alone, a circumstance not at all to her liking.

One particularly sultry evening, she decided to give Browder his chance to prove himself. During the trip, she had been wearing boots and trousers, but on this evening, before supper, she put on a colorful peasant skirt and a low-cut bodice, leaving her full breasts unfettered. Before going out, she dabbed perfume behind her ears and in the cleavage between her breasts. Cooper, on getting his first whiff of the scent, had laughingly labeled it. "Mantrap," he said. "Brewed in your witches' cauldron, no doubt." This wasn't far from the truth.

Carrying a bottle of potent tequila, Rena joined Browder where he sat near the small cooking fire. His eyes widened at the sight of her seductive costume, and he scrambled to his feet.

"Rena! You look . . . uh, different tonight."

"A woman must look feminine once in awhile," she said boldly. "In this damned jungle, you can forget what sex you are, if you're not careful."

"A man would have to be blind to mistake you for anything but what you are," he said with clumsy gallantry.

"Why, Harris, how nice!"

She laughed inwardly at the look of bafflement in his eyes. She had kept a distance between them until now, and clearly he was struggling to fathom the reason for the sudden change.

They sat down close together. Rena called to the cook for two cups, a slice of lemon, and salt—the necessary ingredients for the proper drinking of tequila. When the items were brought, she splashed generous portions of the liquor into cups, and they drank.

Rena took out a cigar and leaned toward Browder for a light. The blouse billowed out from her body, and she saw Browder's eyes fasten greedily on her bared breasts. She looked at his groin, pleased to see his immediate and unmistakable reaction.

Noting the direction of her glance, Browder started to shift about, then relaxed, making no further attempt to hide the bulge.

Rena looked up to meet his eyes, a secretive smile on her lips. Anticipation stirred in her. It was going to be a night to enjoy. No subtleties, no protestations of love, only raw animal lust. She knew that at a sign from her, he would gladly rip the clothes from her body and take her by the fire, in full view of the men. For a dangerous moment she was tempted to encourage him; it could be exciting, a new thrill. She decided against it. The crew members could easily become aroused enough to attempt a mass sexual attack. That prospect in itself did not frighten her, but if such a thing happened she might lose control of the crew, and that would never do.

Browder said, "We haven't been exactly chummy the past few days . . ."

"Understand one thing, Browder," she said coolly. "I am in charge here. Whatever we do, will be on *my* terms. I have had things on my mind, and have not been inclined toward chit-chat."

"Oh, I understand that, Rena," he said hastily. "But I was wondering how we're going about this deal. Just how do we grab the loot?"

"We wait. We follow the Longley caravan and watch at a distance. When they find this lost city, when they find the gold, then we make our move." She added bitterly, "If Evan had come through with a copy of the map, we could have gotten there first and been long gone before the Longley woman even arrived."

He peered at her. "I was wondering about that, too. You don't have a copy of the map then?"

"I most certainly do not." She blew smoke angrily. "I went through her things on the train. There was no sign of it."

"What happened to it, do you suppose?"

She shrugged. "I have no idea."

"Then how do you suppose Meredith is finding her way, if she doesn't have the map?"

125

"I don't know that, either. It's possible she does have the map, and I just didn't find it."

"What happens if they try to stop us? This Cooper Mayo is a hardcase, I understand."

"If they get in our way, we do what is necessary. Kill them, if need be. The men I've hired are hardcases, too, experienced gunmen."

"If we have to dispose of Meredith Longley, I'd like to get my hands on her first." His smile was a leering grimace. "Her, with that ice maiden, 'don't-touch-me' manner of hers. I'd like to put some good male fire into her, and see how she acts then."

Rena studied him speculatively. "Is that the way you like to take your women, Browder? Rape them?"

He laughed. "If there's no other way."

"If any man tried to take me without my consent, he would regret it."

Browder looked abashed. "I wasn't talking about you, Rena, but it strikes me . . ." He regained some of his boldness. "Maybe I'm wrong, but I kind of got the idea you liked your men rough."

"Rough is one thing. Rape is another."

She poured more tequila and they drank. The cook informed them that dinner was ready. Their fare was simple, standard Mexican food, highly spiced. When they were finished, Rena fired a small cigar, and sat cross-legged, careless of a length of leg exposed to Browder's lecherous gaze. Finally, she stirred and got up. She picked up the bottle of tequila.

"Would you like a nightcap, Browder? In my tent?"

Browder got to his feet with alacrity. "It would be my pleasure, Rena."

Rena went into her sleeping tent first, sitting on a blanket on the ground. She gave the tequila bottle to Browder.

He squatted on his haunches. "You don't want one?"

"I've had enough for one evening."

Enough light filtered through the tent wall for her to see him tilt the bottle back and gulp from it. The liquor ran down his chin. He wiped it away with the back of his hand.

Just like the crudest peasant, Rena thought with a shudder of anticipatory pleasure.

He raised up on his knees, fumbling with the buckle of his trousers. She scarcely had time to raise her skirt above the waist before he was on her, and inside her with one brutal lunge. Rena moaned softly.

The act was done in straining silence, as they coupled like two barnyard animals. Except for the connection of their sexual parts, they touched nowhere else. They clashed together like antagonists, each intent on his own victory of completion, with no concern for the other.

Browder was rough, cruel, in the seeking of his own pleasure. It was as Rena had suspected it would be, and it was the way she wanted it.

Bodies pounding together, they drove toward their final moment of sensation. And in that final moment, Browder finally put his hands on her. Big hands spanning her waist, he pulled her toward him, fingers digging into her flesh like iron clamps. He held her tightly while he groaned out his pleasure.

Finally, he let her go. Even in the throes of her own ecstasy, Rena knew that she would have black and blue marks in the morning. She lay still, face turned away, while he pulled up his trousers, and left the tent, stooped like a hunchback.

No further word was exchanged between them, yet Rena knew that he would steal into her tent every evening from this night forward. At least it would help relieve the boredom until they had attained their goal. Until she had attained *her* goal, she amended. When that was accomplished, she would see to the elimination of Harris Browder. Just like the Black Widow disposes of her mate when he is no longer useful, she thought with grim humor.

Well, many men had called her the Black Widow.

The first time had been when she was merely twelve years of age, in a remote mountain village in central Mexico. Her father had been a poor *mestizo*, who worked in the fields by day and drank away most of the night, to come home to their hovel and fall on her Indio mother, a repeated act that resulted in the birth of twelve children—half of whom died, in their early years, of disease and malnutrition. Rena, the eldest, had survived through sheer strength of will and an animal shrewdness the other children did not possess. Her name had not been Rena Voltan then, but Juanita Diaz.

The family had existed only one step away from starvation, but by dint of guile and the shrewd use of a ripening figure, Rena managed to find food in places other than her own hovel. Seemingly she had been born with full knowledge of the use of sexual wiles, and through agility and quick wits, she managed to avoid the clutches of the men she beguiled out of food until shortly past her twelfth birthday.

Pedro, a man of thirty, lived in a hut by himself without wife or children, a lifestyle unusual in the village. Since he had food to spare, and was not always sodden with drink as were most of the other men, he was a prime target for Rena. He was always good for a plate of beans, and a tortilla or two.

In addition, Pedro did not constantly eye her lustfully. In fact, Rena had begun to suspect that he was one of those men others whispered about contemptuously as being "womanly," and interested only in other men. For that reason she grew careless—a mistake she never made again.

Pedro was squat, strong as an ox, and usually spoke only in monosyllables. One afternoon when Rena was in his hut, head bent over a plate of beans, she suddenly felt his hand close around her arm in a cruel grip.

Startled, she glanced up to find Pedro's blazing eyes close, his breath hot on her cheek. She knew instantly what he was going to do and began to struggle—not from fear so much as from outrage.

She realized soon enough that struggling

would avail her nothing; Pedro was too strong, and she was too young and undernourished. Her struggles only inflamed his lust.

Soon, he had her on her back on the hard ground, her flimsy skirt pushed up above her waist. Roughly, he forced her thighs apart and rammed his swollen organ into her body.

The pain was sharp as a knife thrust. She cried out, beating her fists against him, but as he continued to push himself into her, a strange, hot pleasure began. Pedro, snorting like a bull, collapsed on top of her.

In a moment he lifted himself off her, and left the hut without a word. Rena lay still for a time, puzzling over her feelings. She was still outraged at being forced to submit against her will, but for the first time she had a dim understanding of the whispers she had heard about the nighttime activity of men and women.

When she appeared at the hut two days later, Pedro's dull, flat eyes showed a flicker of astonishment.

After they had eaten a plate of beans and rice, Pedro lunged across the earth toward her. Again, he took her by force, and again Rena fought him, more fiercely than before, but in the end he was the victor.

This time, the pain was less intense and the pleasure more prolonged for Rena, before Pedro gave his snort and collapsed atop her. In that moment, Rena fumbled for the kitchen knife she had concealed on her person, and drove it to the hilt into his back between the shoulder blades.

His body arched in a grotesque parody of the spasm of pleasure that had convulsed him only a moment before. Then he looked down into her eyes, and spoke more words than at any time since Rena had known him: "You . . . like Black Widow spider . . . make love . . . then kill."

Blood gushed from his mouth, and he rolled off onto the ground. Nimbly, Rena scrambled away to escape, soiling her dress. She had no need to check; she knew that Pedro was dead.

That very night, with her few belongings wrapped in a kerchief, Rena left the village of her birth. She knew that she would not be missed, and had little fear that her flight would be connected with Pedro's death. Even if it was, it didn't matter. And as for her going . . . well, girls often fled from the poverty and hardship of the mountain village, hoping to find domestic employment in the cities. The goal of most was Mexico City, and that was where Rena was headed.

By morning she was on the main road to Mexico City, barefooted and barelegged, her ragged dress deliberately arranged to reveal her ripening womanhood.

Most of the travelers on the road ignored her; aimless wanderers, male or female, along the roads in Mexico were not unusual. A few passing men made vulgar remarks, crude advances. A mere glance told Rena that they were as destitute as she. But finally, around noon, a middle-aged man came along, riding in a cart pulled by a tired burro. His name, he said, was

Ramon Arango, and he was on his way to Mexico City. She was welcome to ride along with him if she wished.

Rena assessed him quickly. He was more appealing physically than the men of her village, far better-dressed, and obviously had some schooling.

Making up her mind, she climbed into the cart with him. As they rode along, Ramon explained his business. He made regular pilgrimages to the more remote villages, purchasing native handicraft—shawls, lace, pottery, and the like—for a mere pittance, then selling the items for a large profit to the *Americanos* visiting the capital city. He hawked the items on the streets, or outside the great train station. The hawkers competing with him bought their wares in Mexico City itself, at a greater price, or made whatever they sold themselves.

"I have no wife," Ramon said with a sly, appraising glance at Rena. "Nor do I have a woman to share my bed. How old are you, girl?"

"I am sixteen," Rena lied quickly.

Satisfied, he nodded. "That is old enough."

When they camped that evening, Rena shared his blankets. Ramon was a good lover, but she found him disappointing in one respect. He was not rough in the way that Pedro had been, and did not provide her with the same thrill. So, in the week it took them to arrive at Mexico City, Rena undertook to instruct him, seeing nothing incongruous in a girl of twelve

132

instructing a man more than twice her age in the art of love.

By the time they reached Mexico City, Ramon was her willing slave. Along with further increasing her own knowledge of the sexual arts, Rena learned what a potent weapon she possessed. All she had to do to get Ramon to bend to her will was to refuse him her body. The first few times this happened, he raged and stormed, threatening to leave her or beat her. In the end he did neither, but always gave in to her demands.

He begged her to become his wife, but Rena had no intention of tying herself legally to any man. She had seen what marriage and the bearing of children had done to her mother, and other women.

She did stay with Ramon—for a few years. She began directing his business affairs as well. Knowing that her sexual attractiveness was not enough in itself to enable her to escape the trap fate had in store for most Mexican women, she set about becoming wealthy. Ramon was content to proceed as he had been doing. It wasn't a hard life and it gave him a fair living, but Rena was not satisfied with that. In a short time she had cajoled him into opening a small shop.

Since there were not enough Americans coming to Mexico City to make the sale of trinkets to them really profitable, Rena, always observant, decided that the sale of religious objects would be far more lucrative.

Rena had no religious beliefs herself, yet

133

faith ran deep in the Mexican people. What were the finest structures in Mexico? The churches. Every village and town had at least one imposing church; many had a large number. And even the poorest peasant always had coins to drop into the box just inside the church door. All homes were filled with objects of a religious nature—plaster saints, crosses, small religious paintings, and other items. Even the donkeys pulling carts in the streets had crosses hung around their necks.

Rena decided that there was money in this. Along the streets leading to every church were small shops selling religious items. The shopkeepers operated with a very small profit margin. Who would sell religious objects to the devout for a large profit?

Rena had no such scruples. For the store she wanted she chose a location on a street a block from Mexico City's finest cathedral, the largest church in the Americas, overlooking Liberation Plaza. Ramon, a devout man, balked at first when learning of Rena's intention, but he eventually gave in. He balked again, when he learned that it was her plan to buy the items they were to sell as cheaply as possible and mark the price up quite high, sometimes as much as fifty per cent.

"But Rena, this is unheard of!" he protested. "A person does not make huge profits by preying on the faith of others!"

"You may not want to, but you will." Rena, just turned fifteen, had ripened into a mature woman early. She postured boldly before him.

"If you wish ever for me to do to you what I did last night, you will do as I say."

As always, after being deprived of her favors for several nights, he capitulated.

It wasn't long before Rena thought of another way to further increase their income. With almost no education, she recognized the need for learning if she was ever to move in higher social circles. So, during the first two years they had the shop, she read incessantly. She knew how superstitious were the people of Mexico; in her mind she equated this with their religious fervor. But along with their religious beliefs, she knew the Mexican people secretly believed in the old gods and the old ways—in *brujas*, signs, portents and rituals.

Rena began to study the old arts, seeing them as a means to gain more power over the people. However, she was also fascinated with what she learned, and realized before very long that she had a gift for the ancient skills. Cautiously at first, she practiced the rituals and became expert at them. She was never really sure if she believed in what she practiced, yet she could not deny the results she often achieved.

Her interest, and growing expertise, opened a new avenue to more profits for the store. The same people who bought the religious objects also provided a lucrative market for the paraphernalia of magic. In a room in the back of the store, Rena had potions and spells for sale, and she also offered her own special services to those who had need of them. The people who required her services and specialty items were willing to pay almost any price.

Although Ramon suspected what she was doing in the back room, he kept silent. By now he was complaisant, well-fed, and content in their prosperity. Rena felt nothing for him now but contempt, and had long since taken other lovers. But, all the while her hoard of gold and silver was growing, as well as her fund of learning. Her reputation also grew, and many wealthy, powerful people came to her to purchase her skills.

Later, Rena realized that the turning point in her life came the day a man high up in government circles sought a secret audience with her. He had heard of Rena Voltan and her witches' powers. He had an enemy in high places, an aging but still powerful political leader. Could Rena bring about his enemy's death with her occult powers? If she could perform this service, she would be paid well, very well indeed.

Rene was shaken. It was the first time such a service had been asked of her. She almost refused, but the sum of money mentioned was great. She promised to see what she could do.

She had no way of knowing if any of the spells she cast were actually powerful enough to cause death, yet she did know that some human intervention was partially responsible for the successes she had so far enjoyed. She made a doll in the likeness of the intended victim, pierced the heart of the doll with a long pin, placed the doll in a box, and dispatched it to the enemy of the man who had employed her.

When he victim opened the box and saw the doll in his likeness, he gave a gasp, clutched his chest, and fell to the floor.

Rena was sure that the man's weak heart was what brought on his demise, not her witchcraft, but she received the credit for it, and a handsome fee.

Ramon also believed she was responsible for the man's death. He somehow learned of it, and this was finally too much for him to accept. "Rena, I have allowed you to amuse yourself with your spells and such, thinking it would do no harm. But this is going too far! You have been responsible for a man's death! I forbid you to continue with what you're doing. It is the devil's work!"

Rena was secretly amused by his attitude, but it gave her the excuse she'd long been seeking. "*You* forbid! Ramon, the time is long past when you can forbid me anything. If you don't like what I'm doing, leave!"

"The store is mine."

"So it is. Then I shall go, leaving you to sell the religious knickknacks to the fanatics."

Ramon, stricken, remained resolute, obviously convinced that she wouldn't leave. "Then go. I do not want a woman allied with the devil!"

Rena left, taking the considerable sum of money she had hidden away. She found quarters in a better part of the city and went into business for herself, limiting her clientele.

She was just eighteen years old.

For the next four years her reputation grew, and she prospered greatly. One reason for her prosperity was a refinement she had added. As insurance against her spells not working, she hired an assassin, a particularly villainous individual who killed as much for the pleasure of it as for the money she paid him. In this way, she never failed to bring about the death of anyone she was paid to dispose of.

She lived well, moving ever higher in the social life in Mexico City. She delighted in seeing fear leap into the eyes of those people meeting her for the first time, when they learned she was Rena Voltan. This fear gave her a thrill almost sexual.

Then it all came to an abrupt halt. Her hired killer got careless, and was killed himself while attempting to do away with a man. Somehow, the intended victim learned that Rena had been behind the attempt on his life. He was a powerful man, politically, and he got word to her that he would see her dead.

Rena deemed it prudent to leave Mexico for a time. Although she had been living extravagantly, she had managed to put aside a considerable sum of money. She traveled to Rome, London, Paris—all the fabled cities of the world—and finally came to the United States. There, she learned that the man who had threatened her life was himself dead, and she decided that it was safe to return to her homeland; her funds were running low.

Shortly after her return to Mexico City, she met Evan Longley and learned of the possibility of a great treasure in the lost city. If she could get her hands on that treasure, Rena thought, she would be rich beyond her dreams and could do as she pleased for the rest of her life.

Then, in a brief second visit to the United States, Rena met Cooper Mayo, while in Galveston waiting to board the ship to Vera Cruz. She was not in love with Cooper, for she doubted the existence of what men called love, but he could arouse her sexually as no man ever had. He amused her, and he was a strong man.

She wanted him. She wanted both Cooper Mayo *and* the treasure, and she intended to see that nothing stood in the way of her getting both.

Chapter Eight

The expedition had been on the move a little over two weeks, when disaster struck.

The going was difficult and slow, now that they were off the well-traveled path. Often, the men had to hack a way through the thick undergrowth with machetes. Occasionally they would come across an Indian trail going in the direction they wished to go, and when that happened, traveling was somewhat easier, but then the trail would change directions or fade away and they were forced to cut brush again.

The crude map Meredith had drawn from memory showed few landmarks—a hill, a stream, a strangely shaped tree. Without a compass they would soon have become hopelessly lost. They had difficulty, because of the heavy undergrowth, in finding the landmarks, but Cooper, seeming to have some kind of sixth sense, unfailingly found them. And each time he did so, he gave her an infuriatingly smug grin. He never called Meredith anything but "boss lady" now. That, and his condescending manner, enraged her, but she could only grit her teeth and bear it.

Meredith had lived up to her threat to Cooper, by carrying a pistol on her person at all times. And despite his angry glowers, she still rode at the head of the column, which was usually strung out on the narrow trail that had to be laboriously hacked through the undergrowth.

One afternoon, Meredith was riding a little farther ahead than usual, for they had come across a recently cut trail that the undergrowth had not completely reclaimed, giving the machete users a respite. With Cooper's warning in her mind, Meredith proceeded warily, hand close to the pistol in her waistband. Common sense told her that she should drop back toward the center of the caravan, but something willful in her refused to let Cooper know that she believed him right.

After riding at the head of the caravan for over an hour, Meredith glanced back and saw nothing but empty trail behind her. Quickly, she reined in, preparing to turn her horse about. But the trail was so narrow she realized that it would be difficult, and she decided to wait until the first of the pack mules came into sight.

In that instant a shot rang out behind her, followed by two more in quick succession. She heard shouts and they seemed more distant than she thought possible. Had she ridden that far ahead? And should she ride back toward the column, or remain where she was?

She tugged the heavy pistol out of her belt and stared at it helplessly. She had never fired a weapon in her life. Torn by indecision, she sat her horse for a moment, as the shouts and shots came much closer. Then a shot rang out very nearby and a bullet whistled over her head, rattling the leaves of the tree under which she sat.

Without warning her horse bolted, spooked by the shot. Losing her balance, Meredith had to drop the pistol and cling to the saddlehorn. At the animal's first startled leap, she had lost the reins.

Holding on as best she could, Meredith tried to soothe the horse with the sound of her voice, but to no avail; the animal plunged on. To her horror, Meredith saw the path close up before them, disappearing completely.

Without slowing the horse crashed into the thick undergrowth and lurched sideways, as a vine wrapped itself around Meredith's chest like an arm and swept her out of the saddle. She struck the ground hard. Pain twisted in her skull and she lost consciousness. . . .

Consciousness returned slowly, and painfully, as she tried to remember where she was.

Sitting up, she touched exploratory fingers to the growing lump on her skull. It was extremely painful, but the skin was unbroken, and there seemed to be no other physical damage, although her blouse was ripped away from one shoulder.

Gingerly, she got to her feet, looking around

her. The horse was nowhere to be seen and there was no sign of the trail. Everywhere she looked tall trees and thick vines pressed in upon her, like green walls. The heat was stifling, and perspiration ran down her forehead and into her eyes. She listened intently, but could hear nothing—no shouts or gunfire.

For the first time she gave serious thought to what had happened. The caravan must have been attacked, probably by revolutionaries. Had Cooper been able to rally the men to defend themselves?

Trying to decide in which direction the caravan lay, Meredith took a few steps and halted. What if Cooper and the others had been overwhelmed? She could be walking into great danger!

Yet, what other choice did she have? She could not survive very long by herself. And somehow, she doubted that Cooper could be defeated that easily, not unless attacked by overwhelming numbers; and by all accounts, the outlaw groups were small.

Determinedly, she struck out in what she believed to be the right direction, pushing and tearing her way through the undergrowth. In a short time her clothes were torn and filthy, and soaked with perspiration, and her hands skinned and bleeding. She kept on doggedly, but before long she had to face the truth—she was hopelessly lost. The sun was above her somewhere, but the jungle was so thick overhead she could not see it, only feel its intense heat.

It was evident now that she had been going in

the wrong direction; if not, she would have long since stumbled onto the trail. Too late, she realized that she had been foolish striking out on her own. Cooper would surely be looking for her now, and if she had remained where she was, he would have eventually discovered her. Now, it might be nightfall before he could locate the trail she'd left.

The thought of spending the night alone in this jungle filled her with dread. Exhausted and fighting back tears, she sank to the ground at the foot of a large tree. She was hungry and parched with thirst.

Cooper, where are you?

If he had loomed up before her in that moment, hat slanted at its usual cocky angle, wearing that insolent, taunting grin, she would have thrown herself into his arms without reservations, forgiving him for everything!

In matter of fact, was there really anything to forgive him for? Cooper was the ultimate male, maddeningly sure of his appeal to women, and undoubtedly he was positive in his own mind that she had wanted him to take her. There might even be a measure of truth in his charge that she had been leading him on, although she certainly had not been conscious of it.

Since that night, now over a week past, she had thought about it often, despite all resolves not to, going over and over what had happened. And she had to admit, in all honesty, that there had been a moment when she had responded to him.

Leaning back against the tree trunk, she dozed, and dreamed of riding into the lost city, with Cooper by her side. In the dream *Tonatiuhican* had not been swallowed up by the jungle, but appeared as it had been in the beginning, new and shining and golden—and empty, for there was not a soul visible. It was a city of the dead, or a city whose inhabitants, for some mysterious reason, had fled.

A rustling sound roused Meredith. She sat up, blinking, as a shadow fell across her. She was staring up into the grinning, brown face of a squat man, who wore a greasy sombrero and a serape. His feet were bare, and cartridge belts crisscrossed his broad chest, like an obscene cross.

With a strangled cry, Meredith tried to force her stiff muscles into action, but the man moved swiftly, grabbing Meredith by the arm. With a harsh laugh, he flung her against the ground, hard enough to drive the breath from her, then stood over her menacingly. Without once taking his eyes from her, he gave a shout: "Gabriel! *De prisa!*"

The first pistol shot had caught Cooper unawares. Lulled by the peaceful journey, he had ben dozing in the saddle.

But he came instantly alert before the echoes of the shot had died away, shouting orders and kneeing his horse along the caravan toward the front of the column. He had drilled the men well, and there was no panic. Quickly, they closed ranks and returned the fire, although

146

their attackers were hidden in the jungle. Aware of just how vulnerable they would be to a sneak attack from the screen of thick undergrowth, Cooper had given instructions that, if this happened, the men were to fire at will into the jungle on each side of the column, forming a wall of bullets that would keep their enemies from coming close enough to get a good shot at them.

The attack only lasted a few minutes, and there wasn't a single casualty—on either side, as far as Cooper could ascertain. After the relatively brief exchange of shots, the jungle fell eerily silent.

Cooper was puzzled. It had been a strange attack, carried out for no purpose that he could see. It did not seem logical that determined raiders would have been frightened off by a few random shots.

Suddenly, he thought of Meredith. Where was she? A quick look around told him that she was not present, and a fast head count revealed that no one else was missing. Cooper went down the line, questioning all the men. None knew of Meredith's whereabouts.

The man who had been in the lead with the first two pack mules told him, "I last saw her up ahead of me, Señor Mayo, on her gray horse."

"Damn the pigheaded female!" Cooper cursed loud and long, then instructed that camp should be made here, with guards posted, in the event that the attackers returned. Taking two men with him, he rode after Meredith.

About a mile ahead they came upon her horse. The animal stood with head hanging, and there was a cut on one leg.

Cooper sent one of the men back to the main body with Meredith's horse and instructions for the others to remain camped until he returned, then hurried ahead with the second man. As he rode, Cooper kept a sharp eye out for signs. After another few hundred yards, he saw where the fronds of a banana tree had been broken off and the ferns crushed.

Cooper and the Mexican slid from their horses, and leading the animals, followed the signs into the underbrush about twelve feet, where a large, trampled area told him that the frightened horse had thrashed about. Cooper concluded that it was probable Meredith had been thrown and may have lain unconscious for a time.

He swore aloud, but along with his anger came apprehension. His first thought was that she had been so far ahead of the column she might not have even known it was under attack. But if she had been thrown from her horse here, where was she?

Motioning to his companion to follow, he walked slowly, his eyes easily following Meredith's progress. In her blundering, she had left a trail that a half-blind man could follow.

It soon became apparent that she had lost her way, as the trail was leading in the opposite direction from the caravan.

"Damn stubborn woman," he muttered.

"Why didn't she have the sense to remain where she was?"

Then he paused suddenly, a cold feeling in his gut. Her tracks ended, but there were other tracks, both of bare and booted feet, and the hoofprints of horses, all of which led off into the jungle, angling in a westward direction.

Cooper stood, pondering. A suspicion began gnawing at him. Had the attack on the caravan been a ruse to spirit Meredith away? It didn't make much sense, but everything pointed to that conclusion.

To complicate matters, it would soon be dark, since darkness came swiftly in this climate, and it would be impossible to follow the trail at night. If Meredith's abductors kept going all night, they would have an insurmountable lead by morning and an excellent chance to cover their tracks.

There was nothing to do but push on and hope to catch up to them before dark. He looked at the man beside him, a small, sinewy Mexican, who was now showing the whites of his eyes like a frightened horse.

"We go back. Get the others," he jabbered in Spanish, as his eyes nervously searched the trees and undergrowth.

Cooper put a large hand firmly on the smaller man's shoulder. "No," he said. "We must go on. If you should go back alone," he added, "it would be very easy for our friends out there to pick you off." He snapped his fingers, and the other man winced.

"*Si*, we go," he said without much conviction.

Cooper mounted his horse with misgivings. He knew the man would be of little help, frightened as he was, but he was all Cooper had.

At least there was a trail to follow, though the bandits in these jungles rode small, wiry animals, tough little ponies capable of worming through even the smallest opening, and the trail they left was not easy to detect.

As they progressed, Cooper noticed that the signs showed a horse would occasionally break off from the main group, which was gradually diminishing in size. When they had come across Meredith, there had been approximately a dozen of them by Cooper's estimation, and now they must be down to about six.

Having little choice, he doggedly followed the trail of the main group. It could be that Meredith had been taken away by one of the riders branching off, but his instincts told him differently, and right now that was all he had to go on.

With the sudden advent of darkness, he had to give up the chase. They made a cold camp by the side of the trail, with tough jerky and water from their canteens for supper.

Cooper awoke at first light and started tracking again, the Mexican following disconsolately behind. Long before noon, the trail disappeared, as Cooper had feared would happen. The original band of twelve had been reduced to a pair of horses, and the tracks of those animals vanished abruptly on the bank of a stream. Cooper sent his companion in one direction, with instructions to scan the opposite bank for tracks emerging from the water. Cooper could see that the man wanted to refuse, but did not quite dare.

Cooper traveled along the stream in the other direction for over two miles. Finally, discouraged, he turned the bay back upstream. By the time he reached the spot where they had separated, the Mexican was waiting for him. He gave a doleful shake of his head.

"There is no sign, Señor Mayo. These *bandidos* have many ways of hiding their tracks."

"I had no luck, either," Cooper said with a sigh. "It looks like we've reached a dead end here. I can only hope that whoever stumbled across Miss Longley is bent on rescuing her, not otherwise."

In his heart Cooper knew that this was not true. Anyone familiar enough with the terrain here to be able to lose himself so easily would know the whereabouts of the archaeo¹ gical expedition. Had they wanted to return Meredith, they would have done so already.

His name was Gabriel Morales, and Meredith was frightened sick of him. He was a slender man of perhaps forty, with dark, Indian eyes and a somber, scowling countenance. A scar zigzagging across one cheek gave his features a sinister cast.

He could speak English, that much Meredith knew. After being summoned by the *mestizo* who had found Meredith, the man called Gabriel Morales had questioned her in a harsh voice, demanding her identity and the reason for her presence alone in the jungle. When Meredith spoke her name, his dark eyes had lighted momentarily, and she could have sworn that he recognized it. But nothing that had happened since bore that out.

After she had given her name, Gabriel had suddenly stopped speaking, scooped her up in arms that had astonishing strength for such a slender man, and carried her to his horse. He had placed her in the saddle and got up behind her, both arms around her, as he gripped the reins in front of her. His muscular forearms were rigid against the undersides of her breasts, and she was constantly aware of his touch.

Repeatedly she demaned to be let go and received no response. Wearying of that, she asked what they intended doing with her, and to that she received no answer, either. Gabriel Morales did not speak another word to her after hoisting her onto his horse.

As they rode along, he would motion from time to time, and one of the riders would branch off from the main group. Meredith had long since concluded that they were the most evil-looking bunch of men she had ever seen. They all wore tattered clothing, and looked unkempt and ill-fed. But their horses were well-cared-for, and every man was armed with side-arms and rifles, chests crossed with cartridge belts. Gabriel was alone in that he carried only one weapon—a pearl-handled pistol strapped to his waist, like Cooper's.

Cooper! Had he missed her? Was he searching for her? Or was he dead, and the members of the expedition scattered?

By the time darkness had fallen, the number of her captors was reduced to Gabriel and one other, the villainous-looking individual who had found her. Meredith surmised that they were expecting to be followed and Gabriel had sent the others off in different directions to confuse their pursuers.

At this thought, Meredith's flagging spirits soared. That had to mean that Cooper was behind them!

But as time passed, and there was no sign of pursuit, she grew more and more discouraged. Perhaps the fear of pursuit and capture was such an ingrained way of life with these outlaws that they divided into splinter groups as a matter of routine.

She had expected them to make camp when night came, but they kept riding. They had splashed into a shallow, swift-running stream before dark, and traveled down it for some miles, before Gabriel spoke in rapid Spanish to his henchman. With his knee Gabriel guided his horse out of the stream, then reined the animal in several yards back into the jungle. The second man remained behind. Gabriel lit a twisted, vile-smelling cigar, and smoked in silence. Listening, Meredith could hear brushing sounds behind her. In a flash of insight she knew what it was. He was covering their tracks!

Despairingly, she cried, "What do you want with me?"

This time, Gabriel answered her, in his perfect English. "Is that not a stupid question, Señorita? My *compadres* and I have been long in the jungle, and without the company of women."

Fear turned Meredith cold. "You intend to rape me?" she whispered. "All of you?"

His laughter was low. "Rape is a *gringo* word. Down here, when a man needs a woman, he takes her. We do not call it rape. But if such a fate horrifies you, perhaps we could ransom you. I understand some *bandidos* wax fat on the ransom money taken from *gringos*."

"I'm not worth anything to anybody!" Meredith cried.

"Not to anybody? Surely every person is worth something to someone, somewhere." There was a mocking note in his voice. "Perhaps, Señorita Longley, you do not know your own worth."

She tensed. "What does that mean?"

"You may take it to mean what you wish." His voice became harsh, almost contemptuous. "Do not concern yourself, Señorita. The men of Gabriel Morales will not ravish you." The *mestizo* rode up. "Is it done?"

"It is done, *jefe*." The other man grinned, showing gold teeth. "Not even the jaguar could follow our scent now."

Gabriel nodded, and said crisply, "Excellent! Now we ride to the hacienda."

They set out at a brisk pace, bearing away from the stream and in the direction of the mountain fastness. Meredith's spirits plummeted even further. Once in the unexplored

Sierra Madre mountains, they could remain hidden forever. Now, Cooper would never find her.

They pushed on through the night, climbing steadily. The going was better now, and Meredith noticed that they were following a dim trail.

Weary as she was, Meredith dozed from time to time, and would have fallen from the horse but for Gabriel's supporting arms around her.

Shortly after sunrise, as they were riding alongside a tumbling stream and rounding a huge boulder, they heard a sharp hail. Gabriel halted the horse and held up his hand. Looking up, Meredith saw a man atop the boulder, a rifle cradled in his arms. Gabriel called up to him, and the sentinel motioned them on.

As they rode around the boulder, Meredith saw that they were entering a narrow defile, sheer walls rising on both sides. If this was the only way in, the man on top of the boulder could stand off an army.

Shortly, the gorge opened out into a small, narrow valley. In the distance Meredith saw a cluster of adobe buildings with tile roofs. They rode in the direction of the buildings.

As they approached closer, Meredith realized that the distance had deceived her. What had looked like a prosperous hacienda was in actuality scarcely habitable, and in a state of disrepair. Portions of the outer courtyard wall had crumbled into decay; what had once been a flowering inner garden was choked with weeds; and the fountain stood bone-dry. In sections, the roof had caved in, leaving the rooms open to the sky.

As they rode into the courtyard, men rushed out to greet Gabriel. Meredith recognized several of them as members of the original party. They spoke to Gabriel in rapid Spanish, but Meredith caught enough to understand that they were pleased at how easily they had eluded the stupid *gringo*.

Gabriel dismounted, carrying Meredith to the ground with him. A plumb, scowling woman emerged from the house.

"Maria!" Gabriel exclaimed. "How nice to see your smiling face once more! I have been away too long."

The woman called Maria did not stop scowling, but it was clear that she was pleased by Gabriel's words.

"This, Maria, is Señorita Longley," he indicated Meredith with a gesture. "She is to be our guest for a time. Señorita, since we have ridden long and hard, without food, I imagine you are both hungry and tired. Maria will see to your needs."

He started to turn away. She said quickly, "Wait! Señor Morales, you say I am to be your guest for a time. For the moment, I will ignore the fact that I am a guest against my will. But for how long, and for what purpose?"

"Those are questions I have no intention of answering," he said with seemingly unconscious arrogance.

"I would advise you to try and accommodate

yourself to the circumstances. The surroundings are not palatial," he said with an ironic smile, "and the fare is simple. But it is the best I can offer you.

"One further word, Señorita Longley . . . I cannot spare men to stand guard over you, but I don't think I need to remind you where you are. You are many miles from civilization, with thick jungle every foot of those miles. Of course there are trails, but to those unfamiliar with them, they lead nowhere. Should you try to escape, it will be on your own head. Think about that very carefully before you try to flee. And now, if you will pardon me, I have matters to attend to."

Sweeping his sombrero from his head, he bowed, dark eyes expressionless, and strode away. The men followed after him. Meredith stood staring at his retreating form, baffled not so much by questions of why she was here, as by the man himself. Gabriel Morales was an enigma. It seemed obvious that he had some education and considerable intelligence, yet he showed a ruthlessness that frightened her.

Meredith shivered slightly, then junped as a heavy hand descended on her arm. She glanced around into Maria's scowling face.

"Come along," the woman said in Spanish. Not waiting for an answer, she pulled Meredith along into the hacienda.

Meredith's estimate of the dilapidated condition of the hacienda was unfortunately correct. Although the interior was clean, it was sparsely furnished, showing few signs of what must have once been impressive grandeur. Even the bedroom to which Maria escorted her had no furnishings—only a pallet on the floor, a bucket of water, a tin washbasin, and a rough towel.

In a surly voice Maria said, "There is water. I understand that American women wash all the time." She turned her head aside and made a spitting motion. "If you want food, come to the kitchen. I am no serving woman."

"I am grateful, Señora," Meredith said in a civil tone. She had started to speak in her halting Spanish, but something warned her that it would be wise not to let them know she spoke or understood their language.

Maria grunted and left the room.

Meredith washed as best she could. She looked with longing at the pallet, but she was famished and wished to see as much of this place as possible.

After tidying herself, she went out into the hall. She noted that while most of the rooms had no doors, hers was an exception. It had a heavy wooden door with a bolt on the outside. She wondered if she was to be locked up at night. Not that it made a great deal of difference, she reflected wryly, for Gabriel was right. No matter how desperately she might wish to escape, it would be foolhardy to try to flee this place on her own. And she had committed enough foolish acts during the past few days. If she had not been so stubborn and determined to show Cooper her independence, she might not be in this predicament now.

As Meredith started down the hall, a slender, brown girl, barefoot and in a ragged dress, rounded a corner, almost colliding with her. The girl couldn't be more than fourteen. Above prominent cheekbones, her brown eyes had the frightened look of a startled doe. Despite an undernourished appearance her figure showed signs of coming womanhood.

At the sight of Meredith, the girl stood frozen for a long moment, her only reaction a heightening of the fear in her eyes. Then her hand flew to her mouth and a mewling cry came from her. She whirled and ran back the way she had come, ducking around the corner.

"Wait!" Meredith called. "I won't hurt you!"

She hurried after the girl, but by the time she turned the corner, the girl had vanished.

Bemused, Meredith moved on down the hall. She could well understand why the girl might be frightened living among these brigands. But why be frightened of another woman? Then she concluded that, living here in the mountains far from civilization, it was quite possible that the child had never seen a white person.

Shrugging, Meredith dismissed the girl from her thoughts, and proceeded on toward the kitchen. She found it by following her nose. Maria was alone in the big, echoing kitchen. There was a table, covered with various foods in preparation and cooking utensils, and an open pit in the center of the floor over which was suspended a large pot.

Despite the fact that all the doors were open and the windows shutterless, it was stifling in the room. At the sight of Meredith, Maria frowned inhospitably, but she filled a plate with tortillas, rice and beans, and gave it to Meredith.

Meredith ate hungrily. Maria ignored her, going about her chores. After Meredith had eaten, she thanked Maria and wandered outside. It was shortly past noon and the hacienda seemed deserted. When she returned to the kitchen, she found that even Maria had disappeared. Then Meredith realized that it was siesta time. If she chose, she could walk away and just keep walking, without anyone stopping her.

The sun, away from the shade of the hacienda, had been fierce, and Meredith felt enervated from the heat and the heavily spiced food she had eaten. Well, when in Rome, she thought wryly, and went down the hall to her room. After removing her boots, she stretched out on the pallet and went to sleep.

Chapter Nine

Two days passed, during which Meredith was left pretty much alone, taking her meals from the surly Maria in the kitchen. The men gave her leering looks, but did not molest her. In all that time she did not see Gabriel Morales, and could only conclude that he must be away. She had almost given up hope of being rescued.

Occasionally at night she was disturbed by the sounds of drunken revelry, and once she was shocked awake by the sound of a woman's shrill scream. It wasn't Maria, she was sure of that, so it must be the girl she had glimpsed in the hallway. She thought of going to find out what was wrong, but realized at once how foolish that would be.

By the evening of the third day, Meredith was restless. She was bored here, with no one to talk to except Maria, who spoke to her only in grunts. Even Gabriel's disturbing presence would be better than this.

After supper she tried to sleep, but it was no use. Finally she got up and wandered out of the house. The courtyard was empty, and the hacienda behind her was dark and silent. Then she heard voices somewhere out in the night, and the soft strumming of a guitar. She remembered the nights with Cooper around the campfire, and longing swept over her. What she wouldn't give for everything to be as it once had been—on the trail to *Tonatiuhican*, with Cooper's comforting presence nearby. Was he, wherever he was tonight, thinking of her? Had she left an impression on him that night he took her by force? She had to admit that time had softened her reaction, and she had to wonder if she meant anything more to him than just a momentary gratification.

She laughed at herself. It was female vanity, she well realized, but she *wanted* him to remember her . . .

She stiffened suddenly. From somewhere she heard a muffled cry. She listened intently. Then she heard it again, and she could tell the direction from which it came. There was a crumbling, roofless outbuilding about fifty yards from the main house, a building she knew was used as a stable. Staring at it, she saw a faint glow of light coming from within.

The sound came again, recognizable now as a female cry, and she started toward the building at a run. When she reached the open doorway, she slowed to a halt and cautiously peeked around the door frame. What she saw appalled her. The girl she had seen briefly in the hacienda was on the stable floor, her flimsy dress shoved up around her waist. A man kneeled at

162

her head, pinning her shoulders down, and a second man was between her spread thighs, his trousers down around his ankles.

The girl screamed again, and with a sickening feeling Meredith realized that this was the sound she had heard before in the night. At the scream the man holding the girl laughed cruelly, and raised one hand to slap her.

In Spanish, he said to his companion, "Hurry it up. Our little wildcat is still full of life. If you take too long, you will be too weak to hold her when it's my turn."

Outrage drove Meredith out of concealment and into the light provided by one lantern on the ground. "Stop that!" she shouted. "You animals! Let that poor girl alone!"

The man between the girl's thighs paused in his activity, and turned a gaping face. The one holding the girl's shoulders laughed again. "The *gringa* lady. Maybe she is jealous, eh? Should we give her a chance to know what a real man is like? Eh, *compadre*?"

Before Meredith was fully aware of what was happening, both men sprang at her, the one still with his trousers lowered. Staring in disgust at his engorged organ, she did not react quickly enough, and they had her in a strong grip, one on each side of her.

In an instant they had her sprawled flat on the ground, one pinning her shoulders, while the second man had her legs spread and was trying to tear her trousers off. Meredith fought like a tigress, writhing and tossing. She took a deep breath and screamed with all her

163

lung power, although she sensed that it was futile. Who would come to her rescue here?

The one attacker had her belt unbuckled now and was pawing at the waistband of her trousers. His breath was hot on her face, smelling of garlic and tequila.

Then a harsh voice barked from the doorway. Both men froze. The voice snapped again, and Meredith recognized it as belonging to Gabriel Morales.

Reluctantly, the two men released her and stood up. Meredith, breathing hard, got quickly to her feet. Gabriel stood a few feet away. His face showed no emotion. He gestured curtly, and the two men turned away, disappearing into the shadows.

Gabriel said, "You are very unwise, Señorita, venturing out of the hacienda alone. If they had taken you, you would have only yourself to blame." He ran his thumb along the scar on his cheek.

"I came out here because I heard a scream . . ." She looked around, expecting the girl to be gone. But she was still there, on the ground, curled in a fetal position. Her eyes were blank and staring, showing no awareness of their presence. Her dress was still up around her waist. Meredith stooped and covered up the girl's loins.

Straightening up, she said angrily, "Those animals were attacking this poor child. I heard her calling for help!"

Gabriel gazed down at the girl dispassionately. "She is accustomed to such treatment.

Juana is Indian, and was starving until I took her in. My men are in need of female companionship. What other purpose in life does she have?"

Meredith gasped. "How callous can you be? Indian or not, she is a person, and as such is entitled to some consideration!"

"She is a nothing." His lip curled. "She is entitled to nothing. It is her lot in life to serve men."

"If she has come to accept such treatment, then why was she screaming? And fighting those animals of yours?"

His full lips curved in a smile, but his eyes did not change. "Some women receive pleasure from brutal treatment, is that not so?"

"No, that is not so! I certainly do not, nor do any women I know!"

"I will remember that," he said, his black eyes intent on her.

Meredith's face felt hot. "What do you mean by that?"

He said coolly, "You may take it to mean what you wish." He spoke in Spanish, "Juana, compose yourself, and go to the hacienda."

With a start of fright, the Indian girl crawled for a distance, then got to her feet and ran out of the stable.

"You are a contemptible man, Gabriel Morales," Meredith said. "If you treat your men in such a manner, I am surprised that they follow you."

"I treat my men as I please." His expression became set, and his eyes were hard as stone.

"What do you know of me, or my men? You are American, and know nothing of why I am as I am."

She recoiled from his icy anger. Then she said defiantly, "If those two are examples of your men, I have no wish to know anything of them. What are you going to do to punish them?"

His eyes narrowed. "Punish? Punish them for what?"

"For the indignity I suffered at their hands. For what they intended doing before you stopped them."

This time he threw back his head and laughed, a full-throated, roaring laugh. "The arrogance of American women! Why should you be treated any differently than Juana? Just because your skin is white and you have been pampered all your life by the men of your race? To men as woman-hungry as mine, you are a woman the same as any other. You can provide them with pleasure as well as Juana can, so I intend no punishment."

"Dear God! I've heard that many Latin men view all women as slaves for their pleasure, and now I believe it."

"We are outlaws, Señorita. What else could you expect?"

Curiosity drove her to ask, "And you, Gabriel? Is that how you look upon women?"

"Of course, Señorita. Did you expect more of me?"

"I don't know what I expected, but you do

seem a cut above the others. You obviously have some refinement, education . . ."

His face hardened again. "Losing a war, being hunted like a wild animal and forced to forage off the land, tends to strip away all refinement, all the aspects of civilization, from a man. I am concerned with only one thing . . . survival. And seeing to the deaths of as many of my enemies as I can before they manage to kill. me. But why should I explain myself to such as you?" He gestured. "Come, I will see you back to the hacienda, where you will be safe."

They walked in silence back to the hacienda. There was no sign of the two men, nor the girl Juana. Meredith was still furious at Gabriel, but as they entered the rear door of the hacienda, she got a glimpse of his face in the lantern light. It was dark and brooding, shadowed by melancholy, and the expression somehow softened the normally cruel cast of his features. Even the scar seemed less frightening.

On impulse, she asked, "Gabriel, I can understand how the life you're leading now could brutalize even the most sensitive of men. But how did you come to be involved in the Revolution? No matter how much you may deny it, I know you came from an aristocratic family."

He frowned at her. "Do you really wish to know?"

She flushed. "I wouldn't have asked, otherwise."

He studied her for a long moment, rubbing the scar. "All right, I will tell you. Will you share a bottle of wine with me?"

She hesitated, pondering the wisdom of drinking with him. Noticing his gaze on her, she said hastily, "Yes, of course."

He led her into the kitchen, where she sat on a bench at the table. Gabriel took a bottle from a dusty row on a shelf, and uncorked it, pouring wine into two tin cups.

With a twist of bitterness, he said, "It is raw, I know, but that is another refinement I gave up . . . fine wines."

Sitting down across the table from her, Gabriel took a strong pull of the wine. He began without preamble: "You're right, Señorita Longley, I have been educated, perhaps above my station. My father was an aristocrat, and my mother an Indian woman who worked in his home. I am what you would call a bastard. My father did not acknowledge me publicly, but he was a kind man, and educated me, and loved me, I believe, as much as he did his legal sons. As to why I joined the fight, well, I had little choice. I was very young when the Revolution began, but I grew old quickly. I saw my father killed, and four stepbrothers. I was forced to watch both my mother and one sister raped, then killed by revolutionaries. My father's land was confiscated.

"From that moment on I was no longer young. I was full of hate and bitterness. I swore to kill as many of my enemies as possible." His smile was bleak. "That is one promise I have kept. I have killed many. There was a time when I thought we would emerge victorious. But lack of support from the people, and bad leadership, led to our downfall."

"I can well understand your bitterness," Meredith said cautiously. "It must have been horrible for you, what happened to your family. But on the other hand, the people of Mexico, the lower classes, were long suppressed. From what little of your history I know, they were practically enslaved. In seventeen seventy-six, my own country went through the throes of a revolution, and probably for less reason."

He looked at her out of hard eyes. "But the people of Mexico exchanged one form of slavery for another. You have traveled in my country. Are the people better off than before?"

"I suppose what you say is true . . ."

"*Madre de Dios,* of course it is true!" He struck the table a blow with his fist. "This present government is corrupt; it is run by greedy, ruthless men, who wish only to further their own needs, with no concern for the masses. They would glady stand on a pyramid of the dead and the dying to attain the power and wealth they desire!" He gestured, slumping back wearily. "I know, history teaches that usually a revolution exchanges one despot for another. And what but words of justification could you expect to hear from an outcast, an outlaw, eh, Señorita?"

He drank wine, wiped his mouth with the back of his hand in a deliberately crude gesture, and looked across the table at her. "One word I will say in my own defense . . . I do not use the girl, Juana. I have not had a woman

169

in a long time, so long that I have forgotten what it is like."

His dark eyes, which she had thought of as cold, seemed on fire, and his gaze clung with a sudden hunger to her mouth, to the exposed curve of her throat, then moved on down to the swell of her breasts.

Meredith felt violated, outraged; at the same time there was a loosening inside her, a feeling of secret yearning that both frightened and angered her.

She said quickly, "That is commendable, I am sure, but that still does not excuse your allowing your men to abuse that poor girl!"

He slammed the cup down on the table. "They are men, and they have the needs of men!" He leaned forward, his winey breath fanning her cheeks. "Consider yourself fortunate, Señorita, that I have commanded them to leave you alone. It has not been easy, I assure you. They are surly and rebellious, demanding of me why I should protect a *gringa*."

"And whose fault is it, that I am here?" she demanded. "I didn't ask to be brought here. You have never told me the reason, nor how long I am to be held here."

"I am a *bandido*, what else could you expect from one of my ilk?" he said with a sneer. "You should be worth a great ransom."

"I've told you, there is no one who would pay ransom for me," she retorted. "Not one penny!"

"Enough!" he said. He drained the cup. Once again, he was his old, arrogant self, the few moments of near-vulnerability gone. "Enough of your prattle!"

Meredith stood up. She said coldly, "For a few moments I thought I glimpsed a sensitive person in you. It seems that I was in error. Good night, Señor Morales."

He sprawled on the bench, legs extended. Without looking at her, without speaking, he tipped the wine bottle up and drank from it, the thumb of his other hand caressing the scar.

Meredith swept from the kitchen, and down the hall to her room. Inside, she slammed the heavy door and leaned against it, breathing unevenly. She was filled with a vague unease; it had been foolish of her to anger him. Fervently she wished there was a bolt on the inside. There wasn't even a piece of furniture she could shove against the door.

Finally, she removed her boots and stretched out on the pallet. Sleep eluded her. The night was very warm, and her clothes restricted her. For some time she tossed and turned, ears straining for the slightest sound, but the hacienda remained quiet and still. Meredith felt strange, almost feverish. Her flesh burned where her clothing stuck to it. Half-asleep, she removed her clothes item by item, until she was naked.

After another interminable time, she sank into a light slumber, only to awaken with a muted cry as the door crashed open, banging back against the wall.

There was enough light to enable her to see a male figure in the doorway. Her first thought was that one of Gabriel's men had stolen into the hacienda; then the door closed with another crash, and Meredith started to scramble to her feet.

The figure was at the pallet in two strides, and a strong hand seized her shoulder, forcing her back down.

Gabriel Morales said, "You wished to know for what purpose I wanted you, Señorita Longley. Now you shall find out. You stated that no one would ransom you, so I must be repaid in some way."

Her skin burned where his hands gripped her. "You promised that nothing would happen to me!"

"I promised only that I would protect you from my men. But I am *jefe*, so I may satisfy my desires as I wish."

Meredith knew that no one would defy him, so it would be futile to scream for help, and he was too strong, too quick, for her to escape him. Even as she thought of this, a part of her mind derided her. How would she know if she didn't even try?

Belatedly, she tried to push him away, but Gabriel clamped his strong hands around her upper arms, and pinned her to the pallet. With one knee he forced her thighs apart, and she felt the rigid prod of his maleness against her inner thigh. Then he was inside her, taking her almost casually, contemptuously, and Meredith thought of animals coupling in heat.

Contrarily, the impersonality of it ignited a spark of arousal in her, and she had to fight against a desire to respond to him. She forced herself to lie inert under his pounding body. Fortunately, it was soon over, as he went rigid, his body finally still.

Then, as silently as he had taken her, Gabriel got to his feet.

Out of her shame and anger, Meredith cried out, "This doesn't make you any better than those two men in the stable, does it?"

Although it was too dark to see his features, she could sense him become still, and the anger emanating from him was almost a palpable force. He seemed about to speak, or strike out at her with his fist, but instead he turned on his heel and strode out of the room, slamming the door.

Meredith lay without moving for a long time. She felt used, brutalized, yet she could not forget that moment of wanting to respond, the dark thrill she had experienced. Hot shame flooded her. Was she a wanton? Had those few moments with Cooper Mayo unleashed a side of her nature she had never suspected?

She finally went to sleep struggling with the problem.

In the morning Gabriel Morales was not to be seen. He did not appear as the day dragged on, and Meredith finally concluded that he was gone again. Was it possible that he was also ashamed of his behavior of last night, and did not wish to face her? Somehow, she doubted that.

Late in the afternoon, as she was wandering

through the big hacienda, the girl, Juana, rounded a corner and faced her. As before, the girl froze.

"Please, Juana, I won't harm you," Meredith said in her halting Spanish. She advanced toward the girl carefully. "I would very much like to help you, if it is in any way possible."

Juana relaxed a trifle and did not flee, although it was obvious that she held herself in readiness to do so.

Meredith's heart went out to the girl. She still wore the tattered garment of last night, dirty and even more torn, and one bare arm showed the bruises where she had been held so cruelly. Meredith touched her fingers to the bruised spot.

She said, "Dear God, how those brutes abuse you! Can't you run away? At least *you* are familiar with the countryside."

"I have no place to go. I would starve. Here, I have food."

"But is it worth what you have to endure? Surely, you can do something!"

"I fight them," Juana said with simple yet touching dignity.

"But you can't fight them all off, I know that. It will continue to happen as long as you remain here."

"There is nothing I can do," the girl said with an expressive shrug, then started to turn away.

"Wait!" Meredith touched the girl on the arm. "There is one thing we can do . . . at night, why don't you come to my room, Juana?

Spend the night with me. That way, those louts can't get at you."

Juana's dark eyes began to glow, and a grateful smile broke. The smile transformed her face, and Meredith could see that she would be lovely one day.

Juana said eagerly, "You would do that for me, Señorita Longley?"

"Yes. After supper tonight, come to my room."

Juana took her hand and rained kisses on it. Embarrassed, Meredith finally pulled free, and the girl darted off, bare feet flashing as she ran.

Before Juana was out of sight, Meredith was already having second thoughts. She had no doubt that the men would hesitate to come into her room for Juana, since Gabriel had forbidden them to enter. But how would Gabriel react? He would likely be furious.

Meredith's head went back. She would face his wrath when it descended on her.

Another thought intruded into her mind. Was her gesture purely for Juana's welfare, or was she doing this in the hope that Gabriel would not barge in on her again, with Juana in the room? Meredith had to admit that she didn't trust herself. If Gabriel came to her again, her resistance might well be even less than it had been last night.

She drove such speculations from her mind. She could only hope that Gabriel would be absent for some time.

He didn't return that day, and had not returned when she finally retired for the evening, taking Juana into the room with her. The girl brought a straw mat into the room to sleep on, then insisted on helping Meredith take a bath. At first Meredith, unaccustomed to such attentions, tried to discourage her, but she finally submitted, amused at the thought that she might not only have saved Juana from nightly abuse, but gained a personal maid as well. The idea somehow pleased her.

Since she had no toilet articles with her, Meredith had not been able to brush her hair since the last night with the caravan. When she complained of this to Juana, the girl ran out of the room. She came back within a few minutes with a crude brush, and began brushing Meredith's hair. She was awkward at first, but she soon caught the hang of it. When she was finished, Meredith's hair was shining and she felt cleaner than she had in a long time.

By the time they were ready to retire, drunken shouts could be heard outside, and a voice yelled Juana's name outside the window. Shivering with fright, Juana huddled against Meredith, who held the girl closely and made comforting noises.

A short time later, heavy footsteps sounded in the hall and a fist hammered on the door.

"Juana!" a voice shouted in Spanish. "Come out here, you Indian bitch, and perform your duties!"

Juana burrowed against Meredith, shaking. Meredith held her tightly. She called out, "Go away! Juana is not serving as your camp whore any longer. If you try to come in here after her, I will tell your *jefe*!"

There was a silence on the other side of the door. Then a voice muttered drunken curses, and Meredith held her breath in suspense. After a moment the footsteps started up again, retreating down the hall, and Meredith breathed easier.

They lay side by side, with Juana on her straw pallet alongside Meredith, Meredith holding the girl's hand.

Meredith lay awake for a long time, listening tensely for footsteps outside the door, but finally all the sounds of revelry ceased and she went to sleep.

She was awakened by the noise of gunfire crackling outside. The faint, gray light of dawn spilled through the room's one window. Jumping up, she hurried to look out, but she could see nothing. The gunshots grew in volume, accompanied by shouts of alarm and the drumming of approaching hoofbeats.

Juana was sitting up, hugging herself, her eyes round with terror. Meredith fell to her knees beside the girl, holding her tightly.

Together, they waited in fear and trembling, their eyes fastened on the door.

Chapter Ten

As Meredith and Juana clung together in fear, the sounds of battle raged loudly but briefly. In what seemed to be only a few minutes, the sounds of firing ceased, and the courtyard became still.

After the cacophony of shots and screams, the sudden silence was threatening, and Meredith began to wonder if there was anyone left alive.

She made a move to disengage herself from Juana, so that she might go to investigate, but the girl cried out and clutched her arm. So Meredith subsided and sat quietly, smoothing Juana's hair and comforting her.

The moments passed slowly, with no sound save that of Juana's soft sobbing, and then Meredith heard male voices from somewhere inside the hacienda.

A moment later she heard the thud of footsteps coming down the hall toward the room. Despite her fear, she felt resigned to whatever might happen. Whatever it was, *whoever* it was, she would have to face it.

But in spite of her fatalism, she felt her body grow tense as she watched the doorknob turn slowly. Juana's head was bent, but Meredith gazed unblinkingly at the door as it slowly moved inward, then was thrust open with a crash.

In the gloom of the unlighted room, the only thing she could see clearly was a man's hand gripping a large revolver. She attempted to swallow, but her throat was closed and dry.

A familiar voice said, "Meredith!"

She glanced up, coming to her feet at the same time. A catch in her voice, she said, "Ricardo!"

Faint with relief, she ran into his arms. She buried her face against his chest, choking back tears.

Ricardo holstered his pistol and held her, murmuring words of reassurance. Finally, she stepped back. The first thing she noticed was that he was frowning in Juana's direction. Meredith turned and saw that Juana was looking at Ricardo with trepidation.

"This is Juana, Ricardo. Morales's men have been . . . she has been terribly mistreated." She held out her hand, and said soothingly, "It's all right, Juana. Ricardo is a friend. There is no reason to be afraid anymore."

But the girl was not reassured. Getting to her feet, she sidled around Ricardo, her eyes never leaving his face, and ran from the room.

Puzzled, Meredith said, "I don't know what's

wrong with her. She should realize that she's safe now."

Ricardo was smiling again. "These Indian girls have lived so long without seeing people other than those of their own village, that they are terrified of strangers." His face took on a look of concern. "Are *you* all right, Meredith?"

"I'm fine, now that you're here. But tell me," she said eagerly, "how did you find me?"

"Well, I started for the site a little earlier than I had anticipated. On the way, I was met by a man from your caravan, who had been sent back to Mexico City by Cooper Mayo to inform the authorities of your disappearance. This area," he indicated the small valley with a sweep of his hand, "has long been notorious as the stronghold of the *bandido*, Gabriel Morales. I had a strong feeling that you were in his hands, at least a feeling strong enough to gamble on, so I immediately recruited a band of fighting men, and headed here."

"But how did you get so close before being detected? I was brought in by Morales and his men through a narrow defile, guarded by a sentry, who could see anyone coming up the gorge."

"There is another way in, Meredith." His smile was wry. "As I told you, I did not fight in the Revolution, but I had friends on both sides and have long known of this place. If you are wondering why I did not pass my information on to the authorities, since Morales and his band are much sought after by the police, I knew Morales slightly in the old days and have

181

some sympathy for him. Not that I sanction his present actions." His face hardened. "And I certainly do not condone his taking you prisoner. I cannot fathom his motives for that."

"I'm mystified myself," she said. "He did mention something about a ransom, which is ridiculous on the face of it. Ricardo," she placed a hand on his arm, "were any of your men hurt?"

"Not a single wound. Nor were any of Morales's men injured, as far as I can ascertain. Apparently only a few were here, and those fled after a brief exchange of shots. That also puzzles me. And Morales doesn't seem to be here, either."

"He must have ridden away this morning, or last night." Her voice caught, and she looked away quickly.

"Meredith . . . did Morales harm you?"

Memory of the events of last night flooded her mind, throwing her into confusion. She didn't dare look at him, afraid she would give herself away.

"Did he?" He cupped his hand around her face, and forced her to meet his eyes. "Tell me! If he has harmed you, I will see that he pays for it, if it's the last thing I do!"

His dark face was set in harsh lines, and there was a strange look in his eyes. Meredith made herself smile, and said lightly, "What harm could come to me? Aside from holding me here against my will?"

He looked deep into her eyes and finally seemed satisfied that she was telling the truth.

182

He dropped his hand and said in a remote voice, "Gabriel Morales was once a gentleman, but many men in his situation revert to savagery."

In an attempt to change the subject, she said, "How soon can we leave this place?"

He seemed to have difficulty focusing on her. "Leave? Oh . . ." He smiled with an effort. "We can leave whenever you're ready."

"I'm ready now. I want to get back and continue the expedition . . . oh, Ricardo?"

"Yes, Meredith?"

"The girl, Juana. I want to take her with me."

He frowned. "Do you think that wise? This girl belongs here, with her own people."

"Her own people?" she said scornfully. "If you mean the men of Morales, they have made her life a hell on earth. I simply cannot leave her behind. She'll be dead before she's full grown."

"Meredith . . ." He sighed. "We have many unfortunate people in Mexico. You have seen the hundreds of beggars on the streets. Americans have a tendency to be too kind-hearted, and we always advise them not to give money to the beggars, as it only attracts scores more. This is somewhat the same thing . . ."

"I see no parallel at all. I will take Juana with me. She can work for me, become my companion. It will be helpful to me to have another woman along."

Conflicting thoughts spun through Meredith's mind as she talked. She had spoken on a sudden impulse, but now that the words were out, she knew it was what she wanted to do. But was it out of kindness to Juana, or as a gesture of defiance to Gabriel Morales, a means of showing him that Juana had other functions in life than to serve his band of animals? She said spiritedly, "Nothing you can say will dissuade me, Ricardo. I am going to do this."

He threw up his hands. "Then what can I say? We will take her along by all means. I only hope that you do not regret it later."

"I'm sure I won't." Another question came to mind, and she looked away before asking it. "The caravan . . . where is it? And Cooper . . . Mr. Mayo?"

"The caravan is camped in the same spot where you left it, so I understand."

"What is he doing? Waiting there for me to stroll back into camp? Why isn't he searching for me?"

"I don't know, Meredith. You will have to ask him that question yourself."

Cooper could not remember having spent a more frustrating week. After the trail had petered out and he could find no trace of Meredith, or her captors, he debated with himself as to what course he should take.

Finally he made the only decision that seemed feasible—he struck camp at the same spot where the caravan had been attacked, determined to remain there until their supplies were exhausted, or he received some word of Meredith.

He did not slacken his efforts to locate her.

Each day he rode out, searching for some sign, always hopeful that he might have missed something; and he questioned everyone he came across for some word of an American woman. He sent one man to Mexico City to notify the authorities, well realizing that he could probably expect little action from that quarter, and he dispatched several men to nearby villages to ask after her, hoping that the local people might be more willing to talk to men of their own race than a strange *gringo*.

To make matters even worse, he discovered that he missed the damned woman! When this fact dawned on him, he had to sit down and think about it.

Being in her employ and responsible for her welfare—a duty that he had failed miserably— was one thing, but missing her as a person was a whole different matter. She was cold, thorny, opinionated, stubborn as a mule, and from all indications, she despised him.

So why did he ache for her? Could he be in love with the woman? Cooper Mayo, in love? He scoffed at the very thought, yet he had to wonder. He had known many women, taking them as they came, but he had loved none of them. Of all the women he had known, Meredith Longley was an unlikely choice for him to fall in love with. He had heard that the ways of love were strange, but . . .

He dismissed the whole thing as ridiculous, putting it down to the remorse he was feeling over her disappearance. True, if she hadn't disobeyed him, if she had remained with the caravan, this would not have happened. Still, he should have forced her to stay within sight, roping her to her horse if necessary!

Ten days after Meredith's disappearance, he was sitting before his tent after supper, drinking and brooding, when he heard one of the sentries give a hail. Instantly alert, Cooper came to his feet in one smooth motion, the Colt drawn and ready. He saw the sentry herding someone toward him. Cooper thought that the figure seemed too small for a man; then as they drew nearer, he saw that it was Rena Voltan.

He holstered the Colt, and lit a cigar, while he waited for her. Despite the tropic heat, she looked cool and composed in a dark riding habit; and he wondered anew at the fiery passion that smouldered beneath that cool exterior. Uncomfortably, he realized that he was having a physical reaction, just at the thought of their past sexual encounters.

She stopped before him, her gaze dropping to his groin. She laughed throatily. "Missed me, have you, Coop?"

"Not particularly," he said in a growling voice. "Why are you here, Rena? I thought we agreed you wouldn't show yourself, at least until we reached the lost city."

"At the rate you're going, we'll never get there," she retorted. "That's the reason I'm here. You've been sitting here for days, and I want to know the reason."

He studied her intently. "You don't know?"

"Now why would I ask, if I did?"

"Meredith has disappeared. Ten days ago."

"How could that have happened?"

"You're sure you have no knowledge of it?"

Taking a small cigar from her pocket, she lit it, staring at him with narrowed eyes. "Just what are you trying to say, Coop? Do you think I'm responsible?"

"It had crossed my mind, yes. It's just the sort of stunt you might pull." He smiled cynically. "I've been thinking of going to look for you, if Meredith didn't show up soon."

"You can be sure that if I had her in my grasp, I wouldn't be here now. I would have wrung the location of this city out of her by now, and be headed there." Head tilted to one side, she blew smoke. "I don't suppose you got it out of her?"

"No, she said I'd be safer for not knowing, so I didn't push it, lest I rouse her suspicions."

"But I'll bet you roused something else, huh, Coop?"

He snapped, "Don't be vulgar, Rena!"

"Ho, ho! Touchy, are you?" Her grin was unpleasant. "Tried to get her into bed and failed, is that it? Must be the reason you're touchy. Besides, from what I've heard of Cooper Mayo, once he gets a woman into bed, he can worm anything he wants out of her."

He drank from the tin cup, refusing to look at her.

"So what do you intend doing? Are you going to camp here forever waiting for her to show up?" Her voice was threaded with anger.

"I've been looking for sign, asking questions.

Sooner or later, someone will leak word of her whereabouts."

"Damnit, Coop, she could have been seized by bandits, or dead by now. Then where are we?"

"You have a better idea?" he demanded. "Maybe you should try some of your 'witchcraft'!"

"I might just do that," she said calmly. "You're certainly not getting anywhere sitting here on your rear. You know, I scraped the bottom of the barrel financing this operation. If it doesn't pay off, I'm going to be broke."

"You may be anyway, even if the city is found. I'm beginning to think it's a waste of time. Meredith is convinced there is no loot at the excavation."

"The Longley girl is an idiot," Rena said. "She's one of those academic types, interested only in finding dead cities and artifacts left by dead people."

"Well, nobody could ever accuse you of that, Rena."

"You are damned right! And sarcasm doesn't become you, Coop," she said. "Especially since I know that you're as greedy as I am. Unless," she peered at him, "you've fallen for Longley."

"I've fallen for no one," he said, but he looked away involuntarily.

"Anyway, I'm convinced there is a treasure, enough to make us both rich."

"Your intuition tells you that?"

"That, and the fact that I've done some studying. The ancient tribes were known for making many objects out of pure gold, and there is no reason to think this city, if found, will not be full of gold and silver objects. All we have to do is find it. Then, together," she placed a hand on his arm, "we can go anywhere we wish, do anything we want."

There was a familiar, husky note in her voice, and Cooper knew what was coming. He was torn two ways. He wanted her; his mind was flooded with memories of their times together; but at the same time the thought of Meredith intruded into his mind, causing him to feel guilt.

Rena said softly, "It's what you still want, isn't it, lover?"

"Yes, of course," he said in a low voice.

She moved closer, rubbing against him. "It's been . . . what? Almost two weeks, darling. That's a long time."

Knowing Rena, he somehow doubted that she had been celibate during that time. She stood on tiptoe and kissed him, her lips hot and demanding. At times she was almost masculine, with hard, uncompromising edges, but in an instant she could become soft and desirable.

Cooper dismissed Meredith from his thoughts and returned Rena's kiss with rough ardor.

"Ah, that's my Coop," she murmured against his throat.

She insinuated a thigh between his, and he could feel the hard points of her breasts against his chest. He turned with her into the tent. Disregarding the frail folding cot, they made love on the hard ground, the first time without fully undressing.

Rena removed her undergarments, and raised her long skirt, at the same time managing to fumble with Cooper's trousers until his throbbing manhood was in her small hand. She tugged at him until he was over her, and then into her. She accepted his entry with a gasping cry.

It was wild and abandoned, and Cooper forgot everything else, lost in a cauldron of heat and passion.

It was an exercise in animal lust, and when he had finally shuddered out his release, he experienced a mood of depression and could barely restrain himself from ordering Rena from the tent.

He lay on his back, wondering at himself. The other times with this woman had been romps, times of release from sexual tension, and he had been able to walk away from the encounters without a trace of regret.

So, why was this time different?

Many reasons came to mind—he was frustrated and upset over Meredith's disappearance, and guilty about it; he was becoming disenchanted with Rena's schemes; he doubted the existence of the treasure; and Rena's attraction, while still powerful enough to appeal to his sexual appetite, was beginning to wear thin.

At that moment Rena stirred by his side, her experienced hands on him, and Cooper laughed silently at himself, as he felt his body begin to respond. As some wise man once said, the mind might be strong, but the flesh was weak.

"At least let's get more comfortable. This ground is hard," he said, reaching over to pull a blanket from the cot.

This time, they undressed, but their lovemaking was as urgent and frantic as the first time.

As they lay side by side, finally sated, Rena said softly, "I'll tell you again, Coop, at the risk of pumping up your male ego . . . you're the man for me."

He grinned. "Not just one among many?"

She made a sound of annoyance. "Now what does that mean? Do you always have to turn nasty? I have never claimed to be an angel. I have known many men, and probably will know many more. But I don't ask an oath of fidelity from you, so why should you ask it of me?"

"You're right." He added glumly, "Maybe we deserve each other."

"I prefer to think that we complement each other."

Sleepy now, Cooper was silent for a few moments, but something was still bothering him. "Rena?"

"Yes, Coop?"

"This map of Meredith's she claims was stolen . . . you know nothing about that, had nothing to do with it?"

"Why does everybody keep asking me that? Use your brain, for God's sake!" she said irritably. "If I had the damned map, why would I be frittering away time like this? I'd already be at the site."

"Yeah, I suppose you're right." He sighed. "Any idea who might have taken off with it?"

"Longley could be lying."

Cooper grunted. "Why would she do that?"

"I have no idea, but then how is she on the way to this lost city, if she doesn't have a copy of the map?"

"She says she drew one from memory."

"She must have a good memory. At least I hope so, or she's wasting her time, and ours. The only other person I can think of who might have taken the map would be her brother."

"Then that means he could already be there."

"That's what has been worrying the hell out of me."

Cooper was silent again, and in a few moments he heard her breathing become heavy. To his surprise, he felt her turn toward him, throwing one arm across his chest. She muttered something and snuggled close to him, as if for comfort and reassurance. It was something he would not have expected of Rena Voltan.

His first impulse was to throw her arm off and move away from her, but he stayed where he was and they went to sleep that way.

Cooper was rudely awakened by a scream of pure rage. He sat up, blinking in confusion. The first thing he noticed was that he had overslept—the sun was up. The second thing he noticed was that Rena was still beside him. She had also been awakened and was sitting up, her bare breasts bobbing.

And the third thing he noticed was Meredith Longley, half-bent over and just inside the tent flap. Eyes blazing, she was trembling with fury.

"Meredith!" He grinned with relief. "Hey, I'm glad you're back safe and sound."

"I can see that," she said furiously. "I can see that you've been worried sick. I can also see how you've been spending your time, instead of looking for me." She pointed an accusing finger at Rena.

It finally dawned on a befuddled Cooper that he was about to be hit by a storm.

"I *have* looked for you, Meredith," he said. "As God is my judge, I have."

Meredith said icily, "And she has been helping you look? Is that what you're going to tell me next?"

"No, of course not." Fully awake now, his own temper was stirring. "I hadn't seen Rena until last night."

"Why should I believe you? If last night was the first time, it didn't take you long to get her into bed, did it?"

"Now you listen to me, boss lady," he said harshly. "I work for you, yes, but my personal life is my own damned business!"

"Not when something like this takes place on my expedition! Then it's my business. If you want to use this slut," Meredith said scathingly, "take her out into the jungle, where she belongs!"

Rena was smiling, unruffled. "Why are you so upset, Longley? Coop is just an employee of yours, nothing more. Isn't that right?"

Meredith flushed, then bit down hard on her

lip. This time she spoke more quietly. "In that you are right, Miss Voltan, but it's the . . . impropriety of it. I won't have anyone working for me dallying with camp followers. That must be the reason you're here. Isn't it?"

Cooper said, "You're going too far, Meredith. There's no reason to be insulting."

"It's all right, Coop." Rena touched his arm. "Let her spill her venom. I must say I'm surprised at her emotional display," she said with elaborate innocence. "Harris Browder calls you the ice maiden. He should see you now."

"Browder!" Meredith exclaimed. "What do you know of him?"

"Why, Harris Browder is with me. You object to that? I understand you kicked him out."

Meredith stared. "But *why* is he with you?"

"Maybe he just likes my company." Rena's smile was feral. "You could ask him, if you like. My camp is only a few miles from here."

"I have no concern with Harris Browder," Meredith said. She gestured. "I want you out of here, Miss Voltan, dressed and out of here within ten minutes. If you're not gone by then, I will have you thrown out of my camp." Turning, she ducked under the tent flap.

Cooper reached for his trousers and pulled them on.

"Coop . . ." Rena tugged at his arm. "What is this going to mean to our plans?"

"How the hell do I know?" He vented his rage on her. "You shouldn't have come here, damnit! Now Meredith knows that you're around, and she has to wonder why."

194

"I noticed you seemed glad enough to see me last night."

She was right, Cooper knew, but he had no intention of admitting it to her. He threw on his shirt and pulled on his boots.

Rena leaned forward, ignoring the fact that she was naked and totally exposed. In a low, venomous voice, she said, "Don't cross me, Coop. Do and you'll be sorry!"

"It's hardly a question of me crossing you. I'll see if I can straighten this mess out. Now, you'd better get your clothes on and scoot out of here while you still can."

Without another look at her, he ducked under the tent flap and outside. Meredith was standing not far away, and he was dismayed to see Ricardo Villalobos with her.

He loped toward them. At the sound of his footsteps, Meredith glanced around and her face became a glacial mask.

"I suppose an apology is in order, boss lady," he said, with what he hoped was a disarming grin. "Although I don't think my morals are your concern, I *was* out of line . . ."

"Your apology is accepted, Mr. Mayo, but it really doesn't matter, since you will be leaving with your friend."

"Not from choice, I won't."

"The choice is already made. You are fired."

"Now look, Meredith . . ." He rubbed his chin. "I know you're upset and angry, but regardless of what you may think of me, you need me. So don't act foolishly out of spite."

Support came from an unexpected quarter,

as Ricardo Villalobos said, "He is correct, Meredith. You hired Señor Mayo for his special talents, and you may be needing those talents more than ever. The caravan has been attacked once, and may well be again. Without Señor Mayo, you would be most vulnerable. Do not forget that Gabriel Morales is still out there somewhere."

Out of pride and stubbornness, Meredith knew that she had gone too far to back down, and she was secretly glad that Ricardo had given her an opening she could use without losing face.

Cooper was speaking, "Would someone please tell me what has happened? Who the hell is Gabriel Morales, and what are *you* doing here, Señor Villalobos?"

"Ricardo came to my rescue," Meredith said somewhat smugly, "while you were idling away time here, dallying with your witch woman!"

Cooper started a hot retort, then switched his attention to Ricardo. "How on earth did you ever find her?"

He listened intently, as first Meredith, then Ricardo told him how she came to be rescued.

Dressed, Rena Voltan ducked out of Cooper's tent. A glance told her that Cooper and Longley were engrossed in conversation. They did not notice as she left quickly, heading back up the trail toward her own camp.

Hurrying along, her thoughts were troubled. She had the uneasy feeling that Cooper and Longley were emotionally involved, and Longley's violent reaction a short time ago only served to strengthen her conviction. If Longley was not at least partly in love with Cooper, she would not have been so angry.

But what concerned Rena was how it would affect Cooper. Would he become so enamored of Meredith Longley that he would back out of their agreement? Rena knew that Cooper loved money and the good life it would buy him, but she also knew that the emotion called love could do strange things to men. In the end, would he choose Longley's love over the gold?

In that moment she determined that Cooper Mayo would probably have to die. Even if she was wrong in her suspicions, the very fact that she was having doubts meant she could no longer fully trust him. And the fact that she had taken him into her full confidence, now sealed his fate. She would wait, wait until the treasure was uncovered—since he could still be instrumental in finding that—then she would contrive to eliminate him.

She told herself that this decision occasioned no regrets, no sorrow. True, he was the best lover she had ever known and a continued liaison with him would be pleasant. But she had no use for any man who would allow himself to become moonstruck over a woman. She would feel the same about it even if he had been in love with her. A man in love developed scruples, and could not be trusted.

The decision made, she strode briskly into the small clearing where her tents were set up.

Browder was pacing back and forth before

his tent. At the sight of her he scowled darkly, and hurried to meet her.

"Rena, where the devil were you all night? I've been worried about you, thinking that something had happened to you!"

"I don't have to account to you, Browder, for my comings and goings," she said in a cold voice. "And I should think you'd know me well enough by now to realize that I can take care of myself, no matter what the circumstances."

Somewhat taken aback, he recoiled. "I know you can handle yourself, but you don't understand."

"I don't understand what?"

"Not long after you wandered away last night, a messenger showed up here looking for you." Browder was growing visibly excited.

Rena said tersely, "A messenger? Who sent him?"

"Evan, Evan Longley!"

"Evan? Where is he?"

"He's at the site of the lost city. He's found it, Rena!"

"And the treasure, has he found that?"

Browder shook his head. "That, I don't know. The messenger didn't say, and I didn't want to give anything away by asking him. But here's the thing . . . Evan wants us to join him as soon as possible. The messenger is still here, ready to lead us there!"

Chapter Eleven

The Longley caravan was operative again, moving with painful slowness toward its goal. But Meredith knew, if the map she had drawn was correct, they should be getting close to the reported site.

She had finally let her good sense overrule her heart, and had said no more about firing Cooper. Actually, she was ashamed of herself for the flare-up in Cooper's tent. She had acted like a jealous harridan. Why should she concern herself with Cooper's behavior? He was nothing to her, just a valued employee, and as such his morals were certainly no business of hers.

Fortunately, Ricardo's presence with the caravan gave her a good excuse to avoid Cooper as much as possible. She was always careful to have Ricardo with her when it was necessary to talk to Cooper.

Meredith was glad that Ricardo had joined them for other reasons as well. He was a charming companion, and she could converse with him on many subjects, particularly archaeology. He was a cultured gentleman, not a rough-and-ready adventurer like Cooper Mayo!

Sometimes, she caught Ricardo looking at her in a rather strange way, his eyes thoughtful and sad. Each time she caught him at it, he glanced quickly away, and was then again his usual charming self.

Ricardo had not brought along a sleeping tent, and Cooper, on learning of this the first night after they resumed their journey, said, "You can use mine, Ricardo."

"Oh, no, my friend," Ricardo said quickly. "I ask no special consideration."

"It's not special, just practical. I'm accustomed to sleeping out, you're not. It's that simple. And I don't mean that sarcastically." He waved a smoking cigar, and slanted a sudden merry look at Meredith. "I'm sure the tent isn't haunted by Rena's presence, so you'll have nothing to fear on that score."

Ricardo laughed. "I would have no fear in any case. Her presence might be diverting."

"The woman has bewitched the pair of you, I do believe," Meredith said with asperity. Already regretting her words, she sought to change the subject. "But it is nice of you, Cooper, to offer Ricardo your tent."

"It's my pleasure." Cooper waved the cigar airily. "It's also a pleasure to have you talking to me again."

"I will be happy to talk to you, sir, so long as Rena Voltan is not the subject of the conversation."

"I'll try to oblige, boss lady, but I do think that your dislike of her is out of proportion."

"I'll be the judge of that, if you don't mind." She gestured. "Why is she tagging after us? Have you given any thought to that? Certainly you don't think it's only because of your many charms? Even *your* ego can't be that large."

Cooper shrugged. "I don't know why. I reckon I haven't given it much thought."

His glance had shifted away, and something in his voice struck a false note. Meredith pressed on, "There can be only one reason . . . she has heard about the supposed treasure!"

"I think you're overly alarmed."

"Am I? You said yourself that others might be after the gold. Gold fever, you said, does strange things to people."

Ricardo interjected, "I thought we had agreed, Meredith, that the likelihood of treasure being found was small."

"We did, but what we believe and what others believe are two different things." She turned her gaze on Cooper. "You made a point of that, as well."

Cooper had a glum look. "Perhaps you're right. Rena may have something like that in mind. But what do you suggest we do about it?"

"There isn't a great deal we can do, but keep a wary eye out." Her voice went up an octave. "And I would suggest that one thing *you* could do is keep away from her!"

Cooper's gaze locked with hers for a long moment, then he turned, strolling away.

Ricardo said gently, "Aren't you being a little hard on him?"

Meredith gave a start, tearing her glance away from Cooper's retreating back. She was shocked to realize that she was tense, hands clenched so hard that the nails were biting into her palms. She said, "If I am, he deserves it."

"Why? Because he is a man? Rena Voltan is an attractive woman, whatever else she may be, and Señor Mayo has been without a woman for some weeks."

Meredith chose a direct attack. "You mean, she's available and I'm not?"

Ricardo reared back, blinking. "That wasn't precisely my meaning, but yes, I suppose that is true."

"Would you avail yourself of her favors, if you had the chance?"

His look was unreadable for a moment. He smiled faintly. "I might. I am a man, too."

"I don't believe that. You are a gentleman."

His smile turned ironic. "You have much to learn about men, my dear Meredith."

She flared up. "Don't speak condescendingly to me! I'm not a child!"

"It seems to me that you are," he said soberly. "In many ways."

She got up without another word and made her way into her tent.

In the days that followed, there was a subtle change in Meredith's relationship with Ricardo Villalobos. It appeared to Meredith that their brief conversation, their most intimate to date, had broken some mental barrier in Ricardo's mind. Where before he had always kept a certain distance between them, even in private conversations, much of that reserve was now gone. He was still charming and fun to be with, of course, yet he was more apt to make personal remarks—a compliment on her appearance; unguarded endearments slipping out; offhand comments about the future that seemed to hint at some relationship extending beyond the termination of the dig.

Meredith had the feeling that something was pending, that an emotional crisis was approaching. It was an unsettling situation, one that made her uncomfortable at times, and yet it did not frighten her. It also tended to cause her to feign an intimacy with Ricardo in Cooper's presence; her behavior at times verged on the flirtatious. She felt shame afterward, but this did not prevent her from behaving in the same manner at the very next opportunity.

Infuriatingly, Cooper viewed her antics with thinly veiled amusement, and this goaded her into even more outrageous behavior.

They had been pushing hard for a week, and even Cooper was beginning to show the strain. Since now the men were forced to fight the jungle for every foot they traveled, they were all tired and short-tempered. The only person who seemed unaffected by the arduous journey was Juana. She was happy as a caged bird let free. However, she was always underfoot, trying to serve Meredith in every way possible, and Meredith had to restrain herself from snapping at the girl.

One evening, as they awaited supper, Cooper said, "How close do you figure we are to this city of yours, boss lady?"

Meredith thought for a moment. "If both my memory and calculations are correct, we should be quite close. Another week, I'd estimate."

"Then I have a suggestion. Everybody is worn out. I think we all deserve a day of rest. This is not a bad camping spot, with the stream over there. We need fresh meat. A couple of times lately I've seen wild boars nosing around. Why don't we rest tomorrow, and I'll take a couple of the men and spend the day hunting?"

The closer they drew to *Tonatiuhican*, the more eager Meredith became to reach it, yet she recognized the wisdom of Cooper's suggestion. They could all use a day of relaxation. She said, "Much as I hate to delay, I suppose you're right. Besides, I could use the time to wash a few things in the stream."

Since it was a day of leisure, Meredith slept late the next morning, and Cooper and his hunting party were already gone when she arose. She put on a Mexican skirt and blouse, bundled up her dirty clothes ready for washing, then went outside the tent.

Breakfast had been served hours ago. Ricardo was lounging beside the remains of the cooking fire with a cup of coffee. He got to his feet at her approach.

"Good morning, Ricardo," she said cheerfully. "Sorry I slept so late."

"Why not?" he said with an expressive shrug. "There is nothing left for your breakfast, only coffee. But I can . . ."

"I will make your breakfast, Señorita," said an eager voice at her elbow.

Meredith sighed in exasperation before turning. "It's not necessary, Juana," she said sharply. "I've told you there's no need for you to wait on me hand and foot!"

The girl's face fell, and she looked ready to weep. Checking her annoyance, Meredith reached out to touch the girl's hand. "I'm sorry, Juana, but I am a grown woman and can do a few things myself. I *like* to do for myself."

Juana's face lit up. "I will do the señorita's laundry!"

"No, I want to do that myself, as well. Why don't you . . ." Meredith passed a hand over her face. "Why don't you spend the day doing something for yourself?"

"There is no pleasure for Juana in that."

"Then it's time you were learning to take pleasure in yourself. I know what you can do . . . you seem to have a talent for finding fruit for us. Why don't you spend the day doing that? I know you enjoy it."

Juana's face bloomed with a broad smile. She bobbed her head and ran off, happy at being given an errand.

"Honestly, that girl will drive me crazy," Meredith said. "She's underfoot every minute. Every time I look around, there she is."

"You can't say I didn't warn you, Meredith," Ricardo said, and poured a cup of coffee for

205

her, while Meredith delved into the cooler for whatever she could find. She settled for half of a papaya. Spooning it out, she said, "Cooper has gone?"

"Oh, yes. He was off before dawn, I was told." He took a sip of coffee. "A very capable man, Señor Mayo." He looked at her keenly. "Do you not agree?"

She avoided his glance, shrugging. "He does what he's hired to do, I suppose."

"It strikes me you are underestimating him."

Her anger sparked, and she finally looked at him. "This is the second time you've defended Cooper. Why, Ricardo? What is he to you?"

"Why, nothing. Not really," he replied, taken aback. "I suppose I like to see any man assessed for what he is worth."

She jumped up. "I'd rather not discuss Cooper Mayo, if you don't mind. I have some washing to do."

He called after her, but she strode on to her tent, gathered up the bundle of clothes, and made her way into the trees to the swift-running stream.

The water was very cold, and the bar of soap she had brought was next to useless. In the end she had to wash the clothes as she had seen the Indian women do—beating them against rocks until she thought they were reasonably clean. Then she spread them across the rocks along the stream to dry.

She was soaked with perspiration from her labors, and drowsy. The water looked tempting, but it was too shallow to really bathe. In the end she loosened her blouse, took off her boots, and stretched out on her back in a hollow between two boulders, with just her feet trailing in the cool water. The sun was climbing toward noon, but the trees laced together overhead kept it from hitting her directly. She felt languid, her blood thick and barely flowing, and her breasts seemed swollen, even the nipples hard with an undefined sexual need.

She fell into a light sleep, only to awaken with a start as a shadow fell across her. Memory of the moment when she had been awakened by the *mestizo* in the jungle vivid in her mind, she sat up, her heart pounding. The sun had moved around far enough to send rays of light through a break in the trees overhead, and the male figure looming over her was a menacing shadow, the face hidden by a nimbus of sunlight.

"Cooper?" she said tentatively, "is that you?"

"No, Meredith. It's Ricardo." He squatted down, and she could finally see his face.

"Oh . . ." She laughed with relief. "You startled me, Ricardo. I guess I was sleeping."

"I know, I've been watching you. You looked so innocent, and so lovely." His voice was tight with emotion, and his face was grave.

Meredith suddenly remembered that her blouse was unfastened, and a quick glance told her that her skirt was well above the knees, her feet dangling in the water. Heat rising to her face, she made an involuntary move to straighten her clothes and then stopped, realizing that it would only make matters worse. Besides, she had nothing to fear from Ricardo.

"I think I fell in love with you the first time I ever saw you, Meredith," he said in a low, throbbing voice. "When you were just a girl with your father. Then, when you came back, a full-grown, beautiful woman, my love returned full force, but I did not think that I had a chance to win your love. We are, after all, worlds apart. Yet, these last few days with you, being close to you, you seemed to reciprocate my feelings and I began to hope."

Meredith was dismayed at his confession, and somewhere in her head was an echo of Cooper's mocking laughter. She had been hoist on her own petard! Yet, at the same time, she was deeply moved by Ricardo's declaration of love, and her heart went out to him. She was suddenly, and acutely, aware of his male presence, perhaps because always before he had kept a wall of reserve between them.

His hand came out and stroked her cheek. "Dear, dear Meredith, I do care for you, I do."

"I care for you, too, Ricardo, but in a different way. You are dear to me . . ."

Even to her own ears, her voice sounded blurred, and she seemed trapped in a sort of spell. Involuntarily, she returned his gesture, her hand going to his cheek. Ricardo seized her hand and carried it to his lips. His lips were warm and soft, and Meredith could feel her body quicken.

Later, she was never sure as to what happened in the next few seconds. Before she real-

208

ized it, Ricardo was stretched out full length alongside her, his hands on her. His touch was tentative at first, as if fearful she would repulse him. Meredith considered resisting him, sure that it only required a firm no to get him to stop, but the thought had little will behind it. Not only was she grateful for all the things he had done for her, but she was curious as well.

The times Cooper and Gabriel Morales had taken her had been rape, or very close to it. Would it be better if she was made love to by a man she liked very much, a man who did not take her by force? And was she an ice maiden, as Harris Browder claimed? Or was she capable of losing herself in love, in fire and passion?

His mouth was on hers now, and his hands were under her garments, touching her intimately. Passion flared, and she opened her mouth to his with a smothered gasp.

Sensing her ardent response, Ricardo was more forceful now. In a little while he leaned back slightly and quickly undressed her. Hazily, Meredith realized that men from the camp, or even Juana, could come upon them at any time, but by now her need was great and she did not care.

When she finally lay naked, Ricardo drew back. His gaze moved over her and he inhaled sharply. His voice muted with awe, he said, "You are beautiful, Meredith, a feast for the eyes." His fingers trailed along her inner thigh and Meredith moaned, writhing under his caressing touch.

Again, his mouth fastened on hers, the length of his body firm against her. She responded without reservation, returning caress for caress, and when she finally guided the hardness of him into her, she began moving in unison with him. There was no holding back this time, as there had been with Cooper and Gabriel; there was no need to hold back.

Her passion was just as fierce and demanding as his, and in a torment of rapture, Meredith gave herself without inhibition. As the end approached, Ricardo tightened his arms around her, corraling her wildness.

When they lay quiescent together, passions satisfied, Meredith was exultant. She was *not* cold. At last she knew that she was a complete woman.

Murmuring, she stroked Ricardo's moist hair, as his head came to rest on her breast. She could feel the strong, racing beat of his heart.

"I love you, Meredith," he whispered.

"I know, I know." It was on the tip of her tongue to say that she loved him in return, but something stayed her.

All at once, the myraid noises of the jungle crashed in on her, and from some distance away she heard a man's voice. It was as if, for a few minutes out of time, she had inhabited a web of silence spun by some magic spell, completely isolating her from the outside world.

But now the risk of discovery aroused apprehension. What if Cooper, Juana, or even one of the crew, should wander by and see them like this?

Trying to control her impatience, she pushed gently at Ricardo, and he reluctantly moved away.

Meredith reached for her clothes and slipped them on.

Cooper returned in triumph shortly before dusk, with two of the men bearing a boar lashed to a pole.

As Meredith and Ricardo came toward him, he said with a flourish, "Behold! The hunter returneth with his kill!"

His elation died within him as Meredith and Ricardo crowded around, voicing their delight. One look at the pair was enough to tell Cooper that something had happened while he was away from camp. There was a new intimacy about them, and a glow on Meredith's face that had not been there before. Also, Ricardo kept touching her from time to time.

Sometime during the day, Cooper knew, Ricardo had made love to her. The signs were unmistakable.

Cooper's first reaction was anger, and he had to restrain himself from confronting them with what he suspected. It would be a bad mistake, he realized after his initial anger had cooled. Besides, what was it to him if Meredith took Ricardo Villalobos for a lover? She had made it abundantly clear what she thought of Cooper Mayo, and that was enough to keep him at a distance. He had never in his life pressed his suit to a woman who wanted no part of him.

His thoughts were wry. Was it the blow to

his ego that had aroused his ire? He had never been spurned by a woman before, yet there was a first time for everything, he supposed. There was more to it than that, however. He had also never felt this deeply toward a woman, and it hurt. It hurt like hell!

There was a sadness in him, a feeling of loss, that he suspected would last for a long time.

He turned away abruptly from the happiness on Meredith's face, and began supervising the preparation of the boar for the evening meal.

There was always Rena to fall back on, he reflected, but she struck him as being a poor second best now. He hadn't heard from her since that morning Meredith had come upon them and ordered Rena out of the camp, but he knew that she was still behind them somewhere.

At least now, he could concentrate on the original scheme they had concocted to make off with whatever loot was found at the excavation. He could plan toward that goal now without the qualms of conscience that had plagued him for a long while.

Like the saying went, you couldn't change the spots on a leopard, and the spots on Cooper Mayo had been there too long. He should have known better than to even try. Cooper Mayo feeling pangs of conscience? Most people who knew him would collapse with laughter at that!

So, from this time forward he would devote his energies toward getting his hands on the loot, and Meredith Longley could go to the devil!

Chapter Twelve

Meredith soon noticed that Cooper's attitude toward her had changed. Where before he had been mocking and insolent, now he closed her out completely.

His indifference piqued her, and she was at a loss to explain it. There was no way that he could know Ricardo was now her lover, and even if he did, what could it matter to him? He had his witch-slut, didn't he?

After she had a little time to think it through, she came to wonder why she was so upset. She had wanted him to leave her alone. Now that he was doing so, she was unhappy about it.

With a determined effort, she tried to push thoughts of Cooper out of her mind, and turn her attention to Ricardo. Unfortunately, there was little opportunity for privacy, and very few chances for them to spend time together alone. In a way, this made the rare, stolen moments of love-making even more delicious.

Meredith was happy in her relationship with Ricardo, and in the flowering of her sexuality. Having never experienced love, she had no way of truly gauging her feeling for him. Perhaps there were no starbursts such as she read about in romantic novels, but he was a sensitive lover, a good companion, and was considerate of her needs. She felt a strong affection for him. Perhaps that *was* love. Why should she demand anything more?

Cooper Mayo was all male, handsome and charming, but if she had imagined in the beginning how thrilling it would be to have his love, she was now disillusioned on that score. The incident with Rena Voltan had driven all such thoughts out of her head. He was a hateful, deceitful man, concerned with only his own pleasure, with no respect for a woman's feelings.

As for Ricardo, he was euphoric, and in their private talks, he mentioned marriage and their future together.

"I think it's a little premature to talk of marriage," she told him. "Let's wait until the dig is finished. This is all new to me, you know, and I need some time to get to know you better, and myself as well."

"I thought we already knew each other quite well," he said in an offended tone.

"Don't feel hurt, Ricardo." She stroked his cheek. "Be patient with me."

"I am a patient man," he said, smiling now. "I shall wait."

However, he continued to talk as if their marriage was a fact. "When we are married, I will not ask you to give up your work. We have that in common, a love of the past. When things are better for me financially, I can resign my position, unless Luis is able to get a department of archaeology at the University, and we can work excavations together. It will be an exciting life, my love. You will see."

So enthusiastic was he, and so convinced that they would become husband and wife, that Meredith soon caught herself thinking of being married to him. Every time this happened, she scolded herself. There was a job to do first—the excavation of *Tonatiuhican*.

As the days blurred together, one after the other—so similar that Meredith often felt she was living the same day over and over again—she began to wonder if the city even existed. After so many days on the trail, civilization seemed far removed. Life seemed pared down to the basics of food, water, a few hours' sleep, and the need to make progress through a hostile jungle that fought them every step of the way.

One steamy midafternoon, after they had stopped for a meal and a siesta, Meredith sat studying the map, which she had spread out on her lap.

With a rather dusty forefinger, she traced their path with some anxiety. The last landmark shown on the map was a large outcropping of stone on the side of the mountain; they should have located it by now. They were traveling now through an area both mountainous and heavily forested, and the men were beginning to grumble at the continued need to chop their way through the jungle.

The map was rough, and the distances only approximate, but Meredith had calculated that they should be very close to this last signpost on the way to *Tonatiuhican*. Yet where was it? It should have been easily recognizable, because the stone looked much like the face of a jaguar in profile. Taking out her compass, Meredith looked at it carefully. They were going in the right direction, and they had come approximately the right distance. Where was the outcropping of stone?

Looking up, she saw Cooper dipping a cupful of water from one of the water kegs hanging across the back of a mule. He looked up, and his glance met hers.

With a wave of her hand, she motioned him over.

He drank the water, replaced the cover on the keg, and wiped his mouth on his hand, before sauntering over to her. He hunkered down in front of her, and pushed his hat to the back of his head, looking at her quizzically.

The jungle had taken its toll on him, too. He was no longer so immaculate, and his clothes showed signs of hard use. The planter's hat, for instance, was no longer white, but dirty, and sweat-stained around the band.

Yet, for all that, he still cut a dashing figure—the Colt on his hip, that maddening self-assurance still undaunted.

He was so close now that Meredith could see

the tiny hairs on his muscular forearms, and feel the force of his gaze. She began to think that she should not have been so impetuous in calling him over. However, she reminded herself, this was business. She was his employer, and as such, had every right to call upon his services.

Making her tone businesslike, and avoiding the use of his name, she pointed to the map. "The map shows that we should be coming across a landmark, a large, stone outcropping that looks like the face of a jaguar. As it's drawn, it looks like the outcropping is on the right face of the mountain. Have you noticed anything like that?"

He stared at her a long moment before answering, his expression thoughtful. "No," he said finally. "Of course, I haven't really been looking for such an outcropping, since you hadn't bothered to tell me that it even existed."

His voice was noncommittal and his gaze guarded, but still Meredith felt intimidated by his controlled anger. The reason she hadn't told him was because this was the last landmark, and she did not want him, or anyone else, to know this before they found *Tonatiuhican*.

This knowledge caused her to feel defensive. "I didn't tell you, because it wasn't time to tell you," she said coldly. "Now we are in the vicinity of the landmark, and now I'm telling you about it. I would appreciate it if you would do your best to locate it, instead of wasting time being sarcastic!"

He stared at her almost insolently, rocking

back on his heels. Then he smiled, and it was the old, familiar, mocking Cooper who said, "Why, of course, boss lady. I thought you knew that I always do my very best for you."

The look that accompanied this remark made her face grow hot, but before she could respond he had risen to his feet, tipped his hat to her, and was turning away.

A mixture of feelings swept over her, and she felt tears very close. She was tired, dirty, and worried. Nothing seemed to be going right, except her relationship with Ricardo. She turned her head, looking for him. She had not seen him during the time the caravan had been halted. Then she saw him, riding toward her from the head of the train. He dismounted near her, and walked over to her side, where he dropped to the ground wearily.

"I've been scouting up ahead, and I think I've found an easier way up that next slope. There is less undergrowth, and the mountainside is not so steep."

She gazed at him with approval. Even a coating of dust and sweat could not hide his good looks or his breeding. He remained a gentleman, even in these rough conditions.

She handed him the map, pointing to the last landmark. He was, she thought, the one person she could trust. "Ricardo, this is the last landmark, see? An outcropping of rock that looks like a jaguar's head, on the side of the mountain. By my calculations, we should be in sight of it, and yet so far I've seen nothing that might agree with the description as shown on the map. Did you see anything like this up ahead?"

Ricardo took the map eagerly and studied it. He shook his head in disappointment. "No. There is only the slope of the mountain, covered with trees and undergrowth. When we get farther up the mountain, I'll have one of the men climb a tree and take a look around."

He gave her a kiss on the cheek, gently, as if he knew her fatigue and depression. "I see that Cooper is mounting up, so we had better get on the trail if we want to make any distance before nightfall."

She allowed herself to be helped to her feet. Both home and *Tonatiuhican* seemed very far away and, right at this moment, she wished that she had never come here, had never agreed to the expedition. Her brother was gone, her innocence was gone, and so were all her illusions. She had found Ricardo, but was that enough to balance out the rest?

For two more days, the expedition toiled up the jungle-smothered mountain slope, while tempers frayed and water and food supplies grew dangerously low.

Each day Meredith looked in vain for the outcropping of rock that would mark the last signpost to the lost city, and each day she saw nothing but jungle.

Then, on the third day, they found it, or rather Cooper found it.

They had stopped to rest during the heat of the day, and since there was a stream nearby, all the water kegs and canteens were filled. Meredith and Juana were anxiously awaiting the completion of this task so that they might have a much-needed wash, when Meredith heard Cooper's voice calling her name.

She stood up and waved, and watched as he came toward her. Reaching her side, he leaned casually against a tree and began lighting a cigar.

"Well?" she said impatiently, anxious to get back to the stream.

He looked up. "You know that outcropping, the jaguar's head you've been looking for? Well, I think I've found it."

Excitement bubbled up in Meredith like a spring, and she could not keep the eagerness from her voice. "Where? *Where?*"

"Right over there, up the stream a ways." He pointed.

Meredith's feeling of excitement began to recede. "But how could it be there? It's supposed to be a large outcropping on the side of the mountain. This stream is in a ravine!"

He smiled slightly. "That's quite true. But in reading that map, you've been forgetting one thing."

She bristled. "And what is that?"

"You're forgetting that the map was drawn by an unlettered *mestizo*, with no training in map drawing or in art."

She frowned. "What do you mean?"

"Simply that he did not always draw things to scale. You remember that some of the other landmarks were either larger or smaller than they appeared to be on the map?"

Meredith said slowly, "Yes, that's true, but none of them were so far off that we couldn't find them."

He smiled again, this time the famous, self-satisfied, Mayo grin. "Well, we found this one, too, only this one is *way* off. Come with me?"

He held his hand toward her, and after a brief hesitation she took it, her anticipation such that for a moment she could hold no grudge. Almost pulling her along behind him, Cooper followed the stream uphill. Juana followed a few steps behind them.

He guided them to the very edge of the stream, to a place where they were almost standing in the clear water, and indicated a point farther upstream. "See? There!"

Meredith looked in the direction he was pointing, and saw nothing that she could identify as the landmark. Her anticipation once again faded and she said angrily, "I see nothing, Cooper. What are you talking about?"

"Look again," he said, moving close and taking her by the shoulder. "There, just beside the water."

She looked again, sighting down his pointing finger. There, at the side of the stream, water flowing around it, was a stone just about as tall as she was. The sun, shining full on the face of the stone, made it difficult to see the outline, but even so she could make out the unmistakable resemblance to the profile of a large cat.

She gasped. "But it's supposed to be huge, and on the side of the mountain!"

Cooper lowered his outstretched arm, but did not remove his other hand from her shoulder. "I've been trying to explain that to you. That's what you *thought* it was supposed to be. Although you haven't seen fit to show me the map, I'll warrant that if you look at it again you'll see that it's only a case of inexact rendering on the part of the *mestizo* artist."

She shook her head. "Well, it doesn't matter now, so long as we've found it."

She turned to him with a brilliant smile, all past animosities momentarily forgotten in the thrill of finding this last landmark. "Thank you, Cooper!"

He looked at her with obvious surprise, seemingly nonplussed. "Why, thank you, boss lady. Those are the first kind words you've spoken to me in some time."

His expression turned thoughtful, and for a moment Meredith again regretted her spontaneity. But then, it wasn't all that important. They were so close now that they must be almost upon the city itself. This little bit of foreknowledge could do him no good, nor her any harm.

"We must hurry," she told him. "It's important that we make good distance this afternoon."

"Sure, whatever you say," he said, still looking at her strangely, but she only smiled at him again, and hurried back down the incline, anxious to consult the map so that they might be on their way.

Upon studying the map again, Meredith saw what she had missed, or rather, what she had misread. The drawing of the stone was, of course, much out of proportion, but the main problem was the curving line she had taken to be the mountain slope. It was clear now, that this mark was supposed to represent the stream, and it was the stream bed that they must follow, up the mountain, to the spot where it originated. That spot marked the site of *Tonatiuhican*.

All afternoon they labored upward, following the stream bed. The men, even the horses, seemed to have caught Meredith's excitement. No one complained, and all seemed to have found a new energy.

Ricardo, riding behind Meredith, seemed to be the only one not caught up in the feeling of anticipation, but Meredith put this down to the fact that, as an amateur archaeologist, he had discovered other ancient cities in Mexico. As for herself, she felt explosive with tension— eager as a child on Christmas morning. Using her heels, she urged her horse forward up the widening ravine.

The sun was low, almost ready to drop behind the mountains, when the caravan reached the head of the stream.

The canyon had grown shallow, flattening out, as it reached a mesalike plateau, or shelf, several miles wide. Behind the plateau rose the rest of the mountain, looking awesome and a little frightening in the afternoon light.

There was complete silence from the men, as the horses stamped and milled around restlessly. They were all looking at her expectantly, and her heart was thundering in her rib cage. They were looking to her for an explanation, and she anxiously stared past them, searching for some sign that this was the right place.

It had to be! They had come so far!

The silence grew, as her gaze scanned the plateau. The shelf here was far less densely forested than the slopes below, although trees and other plants encroached from all sides. But there was nothing; nothing that could be . . .

"Meredith!" It was Ricardo, gently touching her shoulder, turning her, pointing to the far side of the plateau against the mountain.

He pointed again, and this time she really struggled to see.

There, barely discernible against the trees and the bulk of the mountain, was a shape, a dark mass rising taller than the tallest trees. Its form was that of a pyramid!

Meredith felt the tension drain from her, and she let out her breath in a long sigh. *"Tonatiuhican!"* she whispered.

The men heard her and repeated the name like a chant, growing louder with each syllable: *"Tonatiuhican! Tonatiuhican!"*

Chapter Thirteen

Guided by the Indian sent by Evan Longley, Rena and her crew made fair time to the lost city of *Tonatiuhican*, following the trail that Evan had left.

Rena drove her crew hard, from dawn until full dark, impelled by urgency now that her goal was in sight. She kept a close watch on Harris Browder. Now that he knew where Evan was, it would not be unlike Browder to slip away and try to get to Evan first.

On the last evening—the guide having told Rena that they should reach the city the next day—Browder asked worriedly, "Why do you suppose Evan got in touch with us now, after all this time?"

"I have no idea, Browder, but I suspect that it's because he's had no luck finding the treasure. If he had, knowing Evan, he would be long gone with it."

"How do you suppose he found this place on his own?"

225

"I asked the Indian that, and he told me that Evan came to him with a map and hired him as a guide. The Indian comes from a local village, and knows this area quite well."

"When I get my hands on Evan," Browder said darkly, "I'll break every bone in his double-crossing body, damned if I won't!"

"You'll do no such thing. We take it easy with him until we learn what he knows, if anything, *then* we'll deal with him."

Browder hit his knee with his fist. "He can't be allowed to get away with what he did!"

"He won't get away with it, Browder. But we'll do it my way, is that understood?"

Browder glowered at her, but he subsided, growling.

Rena had debated with herself if she should have Browder disposed of before they reached the site. Except in bed, he had been of no use to her so far. Yet, there was a slight possibility that he might come in handy in dealing with Evan. After all, they were both Americans and might confide in each other because of that, despite their differences.

So you live a little longer, Harris Browder, she thought silently, screening her face with a cloud of cigar smoke.

The next morning, when the Indian guide informed Rena that the lost city was just ahead at the top of the ravine up which they were climbing, she ordered him tied up. After that was accomplished, Rena told her men to draw their weapons and advance quietly. At the top

226

of the ravine, the jungle thinned out and the ground leveled off onto a large plateau.

In a low, tense voice, Rena said, "Careful now. Evan surely has a crew of armed men with him."

But as they moved cautiously across the plateau, an area relatively clear of trees, Rena saw that there was little need for caution. There was no one in sight, and nothing that might be the ruins of an ancient city. Then, as she lifted her gaze, Rena saw the pyramid rising above the trees.

She called to Browder, who was beginning to look angry. "There, behind the trees. That has to be it."

Browder's face cleared. "By God, it is! I was beginning to think we'd come all this way for nothing."

Rena motioned to her men and they moved forward. "Quietly," she told them. "I would like to surprise my dear friend, Mr. Longley."

When Rena's party emerged from the trees that surrounded the clearing at the base of the huge pyramid, Evan was in plain sight, blond hair covered with a sombrero, shirt open across his broad chest, directing several men who were digging a trench on the side of the pyramid base. Rena motioned to her own men to fan out, weapons ready, as she walked toward Evan.

At the sound of their footsteps, Evan whirled, his face breaking into a broad grin. "Rena! Sweetie, am I glad to see you!" He came toward them in great strides. "And Harris! I wasn't expecting you. But then," his grin widened, "I should have known you'd get together with Rena." He extended his hand.

Browder knocked it aside. "You double-crossing sonofabitch! You took off and left me holding the bag!"

"Aww, come on, Harris!" Evan's smile was ingratiating. "You're my old pal. I wouldn't double-cross you, you know that. I just thought it would be better if I came here to the dig, before my dear sister got here. If I could have found the loot first, I would have been in touch with both of you, you can be sure."

Rena knew that he was lying, but she kept her suspicions unvoiced for the moment, curious to see what other lies he had on tap.

Browder said, "How'd you get off that train?"

"Simple." Evan laughed. "I gave the porter a handful of pesos, told him to swear, under risk of death, that I hadn't come out of my compartment after going in. Then, when the train had to come almost to a stop where the roadbed was being repaired, I hopped off."

"Everyone thought you were dead," Browder growled. "Including me."

"That's what I wanted everybody to think," Evan crowed. "I had the only copy of the map, which I filched from Meredith. At best I thought that might discourage her, and she'd turn tail for home. At worst, I knew it'd take her some time to reconstruct it from memory and get a crew together. And it worked! I've been here two weeks now, and she hasn't shown up yet."

Rena said dispassionately, "You could have gotten word to me about your plan, or told me in advance."

"Nope. This way, no one knew, so there was no way anyone could suspect what had happened." He cocked his head. "You been desolated about my assumed demise, sweetie?"

Ignoring his jibe, Rena said, "I suppose then, since you've finally let us in on your whereabouts, that you've found the treasure?"

His face fell. "No, damnit, I haven't." He took a large bandanna from his pocket and wiped the sweat from his face. "There's a lot more to this than I figured. This place is huge. The big pyramid there," he gestured behind him, "is only one of four, and there are all kinds of great statues, and chunks of stone scattered all over this whole area. The whole city has almost been swallowed by the undergrowth.

"I started digging here, at the biggest pyramid, because I figured that since it's the largest it must be the most important, and if it's the most important, then there's a good chance that the treasure would be here. Right?

"So that's why I've got the men digging here. There're steps going down into the ground, and we've discovered a room down there, but it's choked with debris, an accumulation of centuries. Maybe we'll find something when it's all cleared out."

"I suppose you didn't think to hire somebody

with at least some knowledge of archaeology?"
Rena asked.

"No. I don't know anybody like that to hire,
and even if I did, I wouldn't risk it."

"It strikes me that you're fumbling around
like a blind man in the dark," she said with an
edge of contempt.

"That could be." He looked at her challeng-
ingly. "Do *you* know anything about archaeology?"

"A little. Since you came to me with your
story, I made it a point to study the subject. I
should think that you, coming from a family of
archaeologists, would have picked up *some*
knowledge over the years."

"I had other things on my mind," he said
with a sneer. "Who had time to learn about
dead people and dead cities?"

"There may not be any treasure, like that
damned sister of yours claims. And that means
that my money has all gone up in smoke!"
Browder started for him with a snarl.

"No, no!" Evan backed up, hands held out
before him. "It's here, I tell you!" He reached
into his shirt pocket, and then held out his
hand toward them. In the palm lay two gold
beads, each about the size of a man's thumb and
glowing with the mellow softness of pure gold.
"See?" Evan said, his voice shaking. "Look at
these! Pure gold. Feel them." He handed them
to Rena, who weighed them in her palm
thoughtfully.

She said, "You found these here?"

Evan nodded quickly. "While we were digging out the steps."

"Here, let me look at them." Browder stretched out his hand. Rena looked at him, making him wait, until his hand began to shake with eagerness, then dropped the golden pellets into his palm.

Evan dropped his hand onto Browder's shoulder. "I swear to you, Harris, you'll get your investment back, many times over!"

Rena knew that at least this time, Evan was speaking the truth. She also knew what she was going to do.

She said, "How many men with you, Evan?"

His glance was wary. "I hired five men, knowing there'd be digging to do."

"At least you had enough forethought for that," she said dryly. "Since your planning hasn't been the best, we'd better get organized. Your sister is not far behind, and she has quite a few people with her . . ."

He blinked. "Behind me? Hell, I was hoping she would give up this whole project when I took off like that."

"Well, she didn't, and she may show up at any time. So the first thing we do is post some lookouts to warn us of her approach. A thousand men could have barged in here, Evan, and you wouldn't have known until it was too late. Where is your camp?"

"Over there." He motioned to the west, on the other side of the pyramid. "We cleared a spot about two hundred yards back, near the edge of the plateau."

"I'm surprised you didn't set up camp right here at the base of the pyramid."

"Now, that's not fair, Rena," he said, with a hurt, little-boy expression. "As I told you, I was sure Meredith would turn right around and go home, so I wasn't expecting any visitors, aside from you."

"Well, it seems you're wrong, doesn't it?" she said curtly. "But never mind. Browder, see that our men set up camp at the place Evan selected. As soon as that's done, post guards all around this area."

Browder nodded, and left after casting a glowering glance at Evan. When he was out of hearing, Evan said slyly, "I'm surprised, sweetie, that you'd hook up with old Harris. How the hell did that come about?"

"You left us both in the lurch, so why is it any surprise that we'd team up?"

He sidled closer. "You know me better than that, Rena. I'd never leave you in the lurch." Placing a hand on her arm, he lowered his voice, "It's been a long time, sweetie. I've missed the hell out of you."

"Have you?" she said evenly.

"I swear." He ran his thumb up and down her arm. "Why don't we take a walk into the jungle, and sort of renew old acquaintances?"

"There isn't time for that now." Then she softened her harsh tone. "Tonight, after camp is set up, come to my tent, Evan."

"That's a promise?" he said, his eyes hot.

"That's a promise," she said in that same seductive voice. She became brisk. "Right now, I have things to do."

Evan turned back to supervising the digging, and Rena went around the vine-cloaked pyramid, to the area that Evan had cleared for a camp. At least, she thought, it's far enough back and screened by the jungle growth so it can't be spotted easily.

She found her crew busily setting up camp. She went from one crew member to another, whispering orders to each. Then she crossed over to where Harris Browder was putting up his tent. Hers was already erected.

Browder straightened up, wiping sweat from his eyes. "Evan had it in mind all along to leave us out in the cold, didn't he?" he said.

"It would seem so."

"Then let me kill him now," he said viciously. "He's no longer of any use to us!"

"In that, you're probably right. But I'll see to it in my own good time."

"But Rena, he can't be allowed to get away with it!"

"He won't get away with it. Nobody crosses me and gets away with it, Browder." She stared him down. "It would pay you to remember that."

"Just so *he* pays for it," he mumbled. His voice took on that annoying whine. "Rena, do you think Evan found those gold beads here?"

"You know as much about that as I do."

"But you don't have an investment to protect!"

"I have an investment in time, which I could

have turned to better use. But we've come this far, we have to see it through." She modulated her voice. "My intuition tells me that it's here. If we're patient, I think we'll both end up rich."

He brightened. "Your intuition, huh? And you're a witch, so you should know, right?"

"That's right, Browder. Now listen to me . . ." She placed a firm hand on his arm. "After supper tonight, I want you to retire to your tent, and stay there, no matter what happens, until I call for you."

"What do you mean?" He was frowning. He glared at her as enlightenment dawned. "I know what's up! You want to be alone with that bastard. Well, I won't have it!"

"Browder," she said in a voice soft with menace, "I'm getting sick of you dragging your feet when I tell you to do something. You'll do as I say, or you won't live to see the sun rise in the morning. These men are mine. They take orders from me, not you, and if I tell them to shoot you dead, they will be most happy to oblige, ridding the world of one more *gringo*. Is that clear enough for you?"

He went ashen, backing up a step. "All right, Rena, all right. You're the boss, I know that." His voice was sullen, and he wouldn't meet her eyes.

"See that you don't forget it."

That night, after supper, Browder made the excuse that he didn't feel well and retired to his tent, without looking at either Rena or Evan.

Satisfied, Rena lit a cigar and leaned back, giving her attention to Evan.

He was glum. "This whole project may be a waste of time, Rena. We dug out that whole underground room today, and came up with nothing. At least nothing worth anything, only a bunch of pottery, stuff like that. What my dear sister would refer to, reverently, as artifacts."

"Thousands of people used to live here, Evan. But time has hidden the places where they lived and worshipped. Maybe we'll just have to let your sister find the gold for us." Rena laughed. "We'll wait and let her do our work. She knows what she's doing, we don't. We have to be patient." She smiled inwardly, recalling that she'd said much the same thing to Browder. What a pair of blundering fools she had joined up with! She added in a soft voice, "I'm sure we can find some way to pass the time."

He cheered up, his look suddenly bold. "I sure as hell can think of one way. But what about him?" He jerked his head toward Browder's tent.

"What about him?" she asked carelessly.

"Is something going on between you and Harris?"

She retorted, "If something is, it's none of your affair."

"Oh, I know that," he said hastily. "I've never had any strings on you. But if we get together again, won't he be a problem?"

"I can handle Harris Browder." She ground out her cigar and stood up in one supple movement. "There's room enough in my tent for two. Unless you'd rather sleep alone in yours."

"Hell, no." He got to his feet with alacrity. "I've had enough nights here alone in that tent. Let's go, sweetie!"

He took her hand and they walked toward Rena's tent. Browder's tent was dark and quiet, but it was only a few yards from hers. Rena was confident that he was awake and listening to their footsteps. The thought of his jealous state at this moment both amused and excited her.

Evan's step faltered as they crossed by Browder's tent. Rena smothered her laughter, took his hand, and pulled him along. At the canvas flap she let go of his hand and ducked down inside the tent, already unbuttoning her blouse. She sank down onto the pile of blankets on the ground. Evan stumbled in the dark and fell to his knees, cursing.

"My, my, lover, you're eager," she whispered. "I must say I'm flattered."

"It's damned dark in here," he grumbled.

"I love the dark."

She found his hand and placed it on her bared breast, the nipple already stiff against his palm. Evan sucked in his breath and clumsily tried to embrace her. She eluded him with a laugh. "Get undressed first, Evan. You know that's the way I like it."

Muttering, he reared back and began tearing at his clothes. Smiling to herself, Rena finished removing her own clothes and stretched out. "I'm waiting."

"I'm hurrying, I'm hurrying!" he said, the sounds of ripping cloth an accompaniment.

In a moment he was beside her, his breath hot on her breasts, then her mouth. Her hands flicked over his body, finding him already aroused.

"It's been too long, I can't wait!" he cried.

"You don't have to, lover," she said in a low, guttural voice. "Now!"

Evan moved over her, and she fitted herself to him. They became one, already into the heated rhythm of intercourse.

Even as her passion began to build, a part of Rena's mind remained cool and detached. She reached under the corner of the blankets, and closed her hand around the hilt of the knife she had secreted there earlier. She brought it out, gripped firmly in her right hand, and waited.

As her ecstasy began, and as Evan shouted out his culmination, shuddering mightily, Rena struck, driving the knife between his shoulder blades with all her strength. Evan grunted sharply, his lower body still in motion.

The pleasure Rena experienced was so intense she came close to fainting. Her sanity returned as Evan slumped in her embrace, still in death.

With a supple twist she rolled him off and onto the ground. Even so, she felt the hot stickiness of his blood on one breast. Without bothering to wipe it off, she hurriedly slipped on her dress and boots, and left the tent.

At the entrance to Browder's tent, she called in a low voice, "Browder?"

"Rena?" he said instantly. "Is that you?"

"Yes. Get dressed and come to my tent at once. I need you."

Without waiting for an answer, she turned about and gave a shrill whistle, the prearranged signal to her men.

As she turned back, Browder arrived, breathless. "What's up, Rena?"

She knew that he had been lying in his tent fully dressed, and the fact tickled her. "Come inside." Motioning with her head, she ducked inside her tent. Browder crowded in after her, stumbling in the dark.

Rena thumbed a match and lit the whale oil lamp.

A gasp came from Browder. "Jesus Christ! What happened to Evan?"

"I should think that's obvious. He's dead."

"Dead? But how? . . ." He stared at her with wide eyes. "You killed him!"

"You wanted him dead, didn't you?" she asked amusedly.

"Yes, but I didn't expect you to do it."

"I've learned the hard way that it's best I handle things my own way."

She didn't realize that her pleasure was evident on her face, until he peered closely at her, then drew back, going pale. "You enjoyed it, didn't you?"

"Of course not!" she snapped. "But it was something that had to be done. Despite all your boasting, I didn't think you had the stomach for it, Browder. Now . . ." She became brisk. "We have to dispose of the body."

Recovering somewhat, he half-turned away. "I'll get a couple of the men and bury him."

"No, that's not what I had in mind . . ." She was interrupted by a pistol shot.

Browder froze. "What was that?"

"I gave orders that Evan's men were to be disarmed, and if any resisted, they were to be shot. I imagine that one of them must have balked. I want Evan's body taken to the pyramid and left in that underground room he uncovered. Then we'll move farther back into the jungle, set up a new camp, and wait for Longley to show up and find him." She smiled savagely. "Too bad I can't be around to see her face when she finds her dear brother dead."

"I don't see the reason for that, as much as I'd like to see her hurt. She'll only get the wind up."

"Don't be more stupid than usual, Browder. I *want* her to get the wind up. I want her to realize that her brother betrayed her, and that haste is necessary. With that prodding her, maybe she'll uncover the gold sooner." She gestured. "Come along, drag him out of here."

With evident reluctance, Browder grasped the body under the armpits and began dragging the dead man out of the tent. Rena, holding the lantern high, followed along.

Harris Browder was sweating heavily by the time he had dragged the body to the pyramid. Rena urged him on. Rounding the base of the large pyramid, they came upon several of the crew in a lantern-lit circle near the excavated steps. Rena saw that her crew held guns on Evan's men. Hands in the air, they wore frightened looks.

Coming up, Rena said crisply, "Are they all under control?"

One of her men grinned widely. "It is done, Señorita Voltan. They are now meek as sheep."

"I heard a shot."

The man nodded. "One of the sheep thought he was a ram. He is no longer with us."

Rena studied the cowed men, debating what course to take. Browder arrived dragging Evan's body, and pulled up alongside her, panting heavily. Rena noticed that Evan's men were eyeing his body with dawning comprehension and fear. It would probably be simpler to kill all of them, yet that could have repercussions later on. It was easier to cover up two killings than a half-dozen, and they looked cowed enough.

Making up her mind, she raised her voice. "Look upon your leader and think well on what has happened to him. I am going to release you to go home to your families, but you will keep quiet about what you have seen here. If you do not, you will share his fate! Is that understood?"

As she looked hard at each man in turn, she received only eager nods.

"Good! Let them go. And one of you," she gestured to her own crew, "help Browder deposit the treacherous *gringo*'s body in the underground room."

Chapter Fourteen

Meredith, urging her horse forward, started the expedition toward the pyramid in the distance.

No one mentioned resting, or suggested that they begin to make camp for the night. Now that the name had been spoken, the whole crew was afire with curiosity to investigate the ancient city.

There was little conversation as they followed the faint trace of a trail that led across the plateau. All of them seemed touched by the moment, awed and somewhat intimidated by the antiquity of the ruins they were slowly approaching.

As they crossed the level surface of the plateau, Meredith scanned it with an archaeologist's eye. There were many small hillocks, rough in shape and covered with vines and plants, that were probably ruined buildings, or perhaps giant statues, or *stelae*, that were typical of the ancient Mexican cultures.

At one point they came across the remains of a smaller pyramid, somewhat truncated as though some of the top stones had fallen.

Meredith called a brief halt, as she studied it. Covered with ferns and vines, it could easily be mistaken for a small, regularly formed hill.

Just past this smaller pyramid, Meredith noticed that the ground was very smooth and even, and in places showed patches of white, as if the entire area had once been covered with plaster. This section extended for a considerable distance, almost like a huge playing field for games.

When at last they reached the base of the largest pyramid, she gazed at its mossy slope in awe, feeling a thrill that she would not have been able to describe to anyone, except perhaps her father.

She placed her hand against the earth that now covered the stone, and had the feeling that she could draw a certain power from it. For a moment she closed her eyes, thinking of Poppa and what this would have meant to him.

The light was beginning to fail, and she turned to call to Cooper, intending to tell him to hurry in setting up the camp, when she heard a man shout.

Staring in the direction of the sound, she was startled to see a number of the men hurrying toward the right side of the pyramid. Curious and rather frightened, she followed them, almost running into Cooper's arms as she rounded the side of the huge edifice.

"What is it? What's wrong?"

Cooper didn't answer, but led her to the spot where the men were congregated. They made way for her, and in a moment she was looking down at a trench of newly turned earth and a flight of narrow stone steps leading downward.

Her hand flew to her mouth and she gave a low cry. "Oh, no! Someone has been here before us!" She turned to Cooper. "This is new. Freshly dug," she said in dismay.

He nodded, his face serious. "And I have the uneasy feeling that whoever dug it is still around."

At that moment, Ricardo pushed his way through the knot of men and to Meredith's side. He looked down at the trench and shook his head. "Carelessly done. I hope they have not damaged or destroyed anything."

Meredith turned to him and put her head on his chest. He stroked her hair with his hand. They stood that way for a moment, then Meredith raised her head. As she did so, she caught an unhappy expression on Cooper's face.

Cooper turned away abruptly and gestured to the men. "Spread out. Search the area. See what you can find."

He faced Meredith and Ricardo. "Maybe it's not so serious. Could be a local Indian who stumbled across it and decided to do a little looting. It happens all the time. If that's what happened, he may already be gone." His voice lacked conviction.

Meredith stepped back from Ricardo and stared grimly at the exposed steps. "There's still some light. Let's see what damage has been done."

"But it is late, Meredith, and it's been a long day," Ricardo said. "Don't you think it might be wiser to wait until morning?"

She frowned at him. "If I wait until morning, I won't sleep the entire night. You, of all people, should understand that, Ricardo."

He smiled, with that expressive shrug. "Of course. I feel the same. I was only trying to be practical. But who wants to be practical at a time like this? Here," he gestured to one of the remaining men, "fetch some lanterns, and hurry."

Meredith's nerves were wound tight. She was afire with excitement, as she always was during the first discovery on a dig.

It was true that in this instance her pleasure was considerably dampened by the fact that someone else had been here first, desecrating the site, but even so, it was like opening a door into the distant past. She experienced the usual thrill of anticipation, as Cooper started the way down the narrow steps, holding a lantern in one hand and his Colt in the other.

He called up to her, "Meredith, stay behind us until we find what's waiting for us down here."

"All right, all right!" she answered impatiently.

Amused by her eagerness, Cooper grinned, and went on down the steps with Ricardo behind him. Meredith was right on their heels.

The threshold was so low both men had to

bend down in order to proceed. Despite its being open, the underground room had a musty odor. Meredith was horrified at what she saw inside. Seething, she stood looking around, while the men went on ahead.

The digging had been hasty, clumsy. Dirt lay in uneven piles and shards of broken pottery were crushed underfoot like eggshells.

"Damn them!" Meredith exploded. "It's a crime, what they've done! All these priceless objects destroyed!" The wanton destruction brought tears of anger to her eyes.

Cooper, who had gone on ahead, called back, "There's something here in the corner." Lantern held high, he stooped to peer into the shadows. "Stay back while I investigate."

Ricardo said consolingly, "Don't be too upset, Meredith. This is only one room. I share your dismay at what happened here, but there will be other rooms you can . . ."

He broke off at a shout from Cooper.

Meredith started toward the shadowy corner. "What is it, Cooper?"

"Don't come over here, Meredith!" He moved quickly to bar her way.

"Why not?" she demanded. She tried to push past him. "What did you find?"

"Something you don't want to see," he said grimly.

"How do you know that? Do I have to remind you that I am in charge of this excavation?" Before he could stop her, she snatched the lantern from his grasp and dodged around him.

"Oh, Jesus!" He took a step after her, then

halted. Meredith, advancing a few steps, saw the figure of a man lying on his side in the dirt. She bent, holding the lantern closer, then cried out as she saw the knife protruding from the man's back and the dried blood. Now the light struck his face, and Meredith let out a gasp of recognition.

"Oh, dear God in Heaven, it's Evan!"

She fell to her knees, her hand involuntarily going to his face. She recoiled with horror at the icy touch of the dead flesh.

Cooper took her under the arms and gently moved her back. She turned and buried her face against his chest. "How long do you suppose he's been dead here like this? I pray not too long!"

"At a rough guess I would say he's been dead . . . oh, two days at the most."

"But why? Who would do such a thing?"

"Meredith . . ." He cleared his throat, and said gruffly, "You must face the truth. Your brother left the train so he could beat you here and get his hands on the treasure first."

Angered, she drew back. "What a filthy thing to say!" She lashed out with her open hand, striking him across the face.

Cooper didn't even blink, but stared back at her stoically.

"Don't, Meredith." Glaring at Cooper, Ricardo gathered her into his arms. "It is not necessary to be so cruel, Señor Mayo," he said.

"It's time the blinders were removed from her eyes," Cooper said stolidly. "And time she faced the truth about Evan Longley."

Meredith twisted her face around. "You don't *know* that it's the truth!"

"If you mean can I spell it out for you, chapter and verse, no. But be logical . . . why else would he disappear off the train, then show up here?"

She dashed tears out of her eyes. "Even if that's true, it doesn't explain his death. Who would want to kill him?"

"My guess would be a confederate. Obviously he wasn't alone here. No one man could do all this digging."

Privately, Cooper had a strong hunch that Rena Voltan was somehow involved in Evan Longley's death. The thought sent a chill down his spine, and he involuntarily aimed a glance toward the pale oblong of the door. If she *was* here, she still had to be around somewhere, and the thought made him very nervous.

"You have been obsessed by a treasure hunt. How do I know that you aren't responsible for this?" Meredith said wildly. "You could have come here while I was away!"

"You're not being at all logical," he said calmly. "In the first place, I had no idea where this place was located. You should know that better than anyone. But even more importantly, I've hardly been out of your sight since you rejoined the caravan, and your brother was killed recently."

"In that he is right, my dear," Ricardo said. "You have to be fair about this, upset as I know you must be."

In her heart Meredith knew that they were

both right, but she stubbornly refused to admit it. She sent a glance toward Evan's body and shuddered. "Do we have to just leave him there?"

"No, of course not," Cooper said. "I'll get help and move his body up above. We must . . ." He hesitated, then said slowly, "Forgive me for being blunt again, but he should be buried as quickly as possible, in this climate."

They buried Evan Longley by lantern light that very night, in a spot hacked out of the jungle within sight of the pyramid.

Although not religious, Meredith spoke a few words she recalled from her childhood studies of the Bible, as her brother was placed into the earth.

She turned her back to hide her tears as they shoveled dirt into the grave. She admitted that she felt as much guilt as grief. She had never cared for Evan, and had never been close to him. But even if what Cooper said about him was true, and she suspected that it was, he had been her brother and she owed him a measure of grief.

Ricardo stepped up to her, touching her arm gently, and said, "It's finished, my dear."

Meredith squared her shoulders resolutely, and turned with dry eyes to face the assembled crew. "We came here, all of us, to excavate the lost city. I intend for us to start work early in the morning, so we all should get a good night's rest."

The next few days passed in a flurry of activity, keeping Meredith too busy to dwell on thoughts of Evan's death. She had talked with Cooper and Ricardo about informing the police of Evan's murder, but in the end they had agreed that it would accomplish nothing and might delay their work. The camp had to be arranged in an efficient manner, and preliminary explorations had to be made. Also, the untrained members of the expedition had to be taught all the proper techniques.

Talking to the men through Ricardo and Cooper, she explained how important it was for them to be careful, even gentle in their digging; how they must not pick up any item which they uncovered; that it must first be sketched, and its depth and location noted. Meredith repeated over and over again how they must either call her or Ricardo, or failing that, Cooper, if and when they uncovered an artifact, no matter how small or seemingly unimportant they thought it to be.

Each novice was assigned an experienced partner from among the ranks of those men who had worked with Ricardo in the past, and Meredith had hopes that this method would insure a reasonably efficient dig.

About half of the men were put to work removing the soil and plants, which covered the surface of the pyramid, and the other men were set to carefully removing the shards and unbroken pieces of pottery from the room already excavated when they arrived.

Once this was done, Meredith and Ricardo

went over the underground room inch by inch. When the debris and the undamaged pottery had been removed, and the room cleaned, it proved to be of more value than Meredith had at first thought.

The floor and walls showed traces of the same plasterlike substance that she had seen in the main courtyard, and along the inner walls were a series of glyphs, still visible, although the colors had badly faded. Meredith excitedly began to copy these, while Ricardo carefully examined the walls. As the exotic forms began to take shape under Meredith's pen, she could hear Ricardo striking the walls, looking for a possible entrance to another room.

Almost hypnotized by the swirling complications of the strange figures she was copying, she did not hear Ricardo when he called her name. It was only when he touched her shoulder that she became conscious he was talking to her.

"Meredith, I think I've found something! Come over here." She had never seen him so stirred. His face, in the light of the lantern, seemed flushed and his eyes were very bright.

She followed as he led her to the inner right-hand corner of the room, and listened closely as he struck the wall with the handle of his pick. The stone gave forth a hollow sound that was different from that of the other walls.

"See here?" He held the lantern high, and the light fell full upon the corner. He pointed. "There, in the corner itself. See how wide the spaces are between the stones?"

She leaned forward and peered into the corner. What he said was true. The space between the stones, usually infinitesimal, was indeed a little wider, showing as a thin line down the length of the point where wall met wall.

Ricardo put his free hand around her and pulled her close. "You realize what this may mean?"

She nodded. Although not much was yet known about the Mexican pyramids, her father had believed that the ancient peoples here, unlike the Egyptians, did not build their pyramids primarily as tombs for royalty. Instead, Martin Longley believed, the pyramids had been built as temples to their gods. If this dead city was the fabled *Tonatiuhican*, this, the largest pyramid, would have been erected to *Tonatiuh*, the Sun God. And, if this was a door, it might lead to a great storehouse of artifacts.

"Oh, Ricardo!" She clung to him, weak yet afire with excitement. "We could discover something amazing. Something that will make my father's name live forever!"

"Yes," he said, turning to kiss her lips. "Oh, yes, my darling. And yours as well. Don't forget that."

"We'll start trying to break through the first thing in the morning," Meredith said.

The next morning several men were assigned to remove the stones in the corner of the room. However, moving the stones proved to be a difficult proposition, one that took some time. To make their task even more difficult, working space in the room was limited.

Meredith, her mind on a possible break-through, did not see much of Cooper. She knew that he had his men deployed to the best advantage, that he was helping wherever he could, and she appreciated that; but she was just as glad that he seemed to be avoiding her. She had enough on her mind as it was.

Juana was helping with the cooking now, and had proved to be quite adept with her hands. She learned quickly, and Meredith had taught her how to clean and assemble the broken pottery. The girl seemed content, and Meredith was pleased to think that she had made the right decision in bringing her along.

While the men were working to remove the stones, Meredith and Ricardo made an overall survey of the site. The area occupied by the inner city was far larger than Meredith had at first surmised. There was a huge courtyard, a great field, several city blocks in size. Rectangular in shape, it was bounded by the remains of at least four pyramids: the large pyramid against the mountain; a smaller one opposite it, at the other side of the courtyard; and two smaller yet, facing each other. Other mounds might be additional pyramids, or possibly buildings, and all were covered with earth and growing things.

In the area near the large pyramid, which Meredith had christened the Pyramid of the Sun, they found a number of stone *stelae*, fallen long ago and now covered with vines and ferns.

While part of the crew labored to find the passageway Ricardo believed lay behind the wall of the underground room, the rest of the men continued to work clearing the pyramid and cleaning the *stelae*, so that Meredith might study and draw them for the records.

For the moment all seemed well. The spirit of discovery had pervaded the camp and everyone worked from dawn to dusk without complaint. The novice workers were doing well, and there had been several good finds.

It was one of these finds that introduced the first note of discord.

Two days after work had begun on the wall of the underground room, one of the experienced workers, a young man named Raul, came running up excitedly to where Meredith was carefully copying the carvings on a broken block of stone.

"Señorita! Señorita!" he cried, then began to rattle off phrases in a Spanish so rapid that she could not make out a single word.

She raised a hand in protest. "Wait, wait! Slower . . . *Mas dispacio, por favor. Dispacio!*"

Raul took a deep breath, then began again, speaking almost as rapidly as before. This time Meredith did manage to catch a few words; enough to realize that he was talking about the room under the pyramid.

She got to her feet and he started away at a run. Quickly, she followed him. Had they broken through?

As she followed Raul down the stone steps, she could hear the sound of loud, excited voices.

Once in the room, she almost choked. The air was full of dust, which was settling all around her. She almost tripped over a block of stone, and then noticed that several more blocks littered the floor.

Dimly, through the cloud of dust, she could see Ricardo and several workers gathered in the corner. Ricardo was holding the lantern high, and beyond its yellow glow there stretched . . . blackness! They had broken through. There was a passageway, or at least another room.

She called Ricardo's name, and hurried toward him. He turned in her direction, and she stopped where she stood. His face looked so strange, so strained and wild. Then he saw her, and his expression changed to the one she knew so well— that of a kind and loving man.

"Meredith! What did I tell you? It's a passageway, and it stretches for a considerable distance at least."

She ran the last few steps to his side. "Oh, Ricardo! That's wonderful! Can you see anything?"

"Well, the passageway, of course, but there seems to be something in the middle, blocking the way."

He raised the lantern high and the light fell on a squat stone figure. Meredith's gasp was echoed by the men standing near her. The stone had been carved in the semblance of a rounded figure, with the head of a skull. The statue was not large, but it somehow managed to exude an aura of menace.

The man standing next to Meredith crossed himself, and whispered under under his breath, *"Madre de Dios. Ayudame!"*

Meredith stared at him. "What is it? What's the matter?"

"Mictecacihuatl," he whispered, and the others glanced at one another nervously.

Meredith looked up at Ricardo. "What is *Mictecacihuatl*?"

"Mictecacihuatl is the goddess of death." He turned to the men. "There's nothing to fear. She cannot harm you. Come, José, Raul, bring the dolly. We will take our goddess up into the sunlight where we can get a good look at her.

"Meredith, you had better get your notebook and make a note of just where the find was made. You can sketch her later, outdoors. If we're to explore that passageway, the goddess has to be removed from there."

Meredith went to fetch her pad, and by the time she got back the men were working with the heavy statue. It was clear that they did so reluctantly, and that they were afraid and ill at ease, but finally the goddess was hauled up the steps and out into the sunlight. Meredith got her first good look at the figure.

Carved from one stone, the body of the figure was actually only suggested. It was the face that dominated, a grinning skull with round, staring eyes. The figure wore a flat, round hat and long earplugs. An incongruity was the hair, or what seemed to be hair, that surrounded the skull in a style similar to that worn by pages in the royal courts in earlier times. The whole figure, save for the skull-face and hat, had been decorated with stylized carved designs.

Ricardo and the workers, after placing the statue near the base of the pyramid, returned to the room below. Meredith could tell that Ricardo was having difficulty with the men. Clearly, they had no desire to return to the room or the passageway, but Meredith was too engrossed in her study of the statue to give much of her attention to what was going on around her.

She did not even hear the rattle of stones above her. The first she knew of her danger was when she looked up to see a huge stone bounding down the side of the pyramid toward her with express-train speed. . . .

Chapter Fifteen

Meredith's senses were acute. She could hear the sound of the great stone as it struck the tiers of the pyramid above her; she could smell the odor of wood-smoke from the camp; she could hear the cries of alarm from the men nearby; but she could not move.

Immediately before her was the grinning face of death, and above her the actuality. She could only stare, as if hypnotized, as the heavy rock bore down on her, looming larger and larger.

And then, with a force that knocked the breath from her body, she was roughly thrust aside as something struck her shoulder a stunning blow. She sprawled on the ground, her face and nose in the dust. Choking and coughing, she raised her head.

Cooper was on the ground beside her, his clothes covered with dirt, and his face tight with anger. Meredith thought the anger was directed at her, and she knew she deserved it. Why hadn't she moved? She could have been killed!

She tried to swallow, but there was no saliva in her mouth.

Near her on the ground, she saw the stone. It was as large as a washtub, and carved in the likeness of a jaguar's head.

Finally, Cooper broke the silence. "Didn't you see it coming, for God's sake?"

She nodded. "I . . . I couldn't move. I'm sorry. It was stupid of me, but it happened so suddenly, and I was so caught up in my study of the goddess figure, that I just froze." She took a gulping breath. "Thank you, Cooper. You saved my life."

The harsh planes of his face softened, and he reached out to brush something from her cheek. In a voice almost inaudible, he said, "It was my pleasure, boss lady." Then, businesslike again, he helped her to her feet, and she vainly tried to dust herself off. They were surrounded by several of the workers, who talked quietly, in tones almost ominous, among themselves and pointed to the figure of *Mictecacihuatl*, and to the snarling jaguar head that had nearly killed Meredith.

She could feel their fear—could almost smell it—and she knew that it boded ill for the efficient working of the dig, but right now she was too shaken to try to placate them. As Cooper helped her to her tent, she kept pondering the strange coincidence of the fact that she had been studying the goddess of death when she had almost been killed.

Although Meredith made a point of appearing the next day, bright and energetic as ever, the atmosphere in the camp had changed radically, and definitely for the worse. Meredith asked both Cooper and Ricardo to talk to the men, offer them bonuses, anything to keep them content and working, but the damage had been done. In an aside, Cooper informed her that two men had slipped away during the night.

The remaining men went about their work, but slowly, with a good deal of grumbling and foot dragging.

Ricardo covered the statue of *Mictecacihuatl* with a tarp, and had it moved into Meredith's tent for study, but it was not a case of out of sight, out of mind. The men now gave Meredith's tent a wide berth, and eyed her askance, as if the power of death attributed to the statue had been transferred to her.

However, a cautious exploration of the passageway went ahead. Two of the young men who had worked with Ricardo before were willing to work with him in the rooms beneath the pyramid.

They found the passageway blocked at intervals; each time they progressed a few feet, a new barrier was discovered. They did come upon a second small room in which they found some well-preserved wall paintings, and a number of small jade figurines, which Meredith studied with great interest.

These figures mystified her. Quite Oriental in appearance, they had large, round, babylike heads, with crying mouths, and were carved with exceptional skill. She spent every spare minute with them, studying them until her eyes burned with fatigue and her head throbbed.

The discovery of the jade figurines was the last good thing to happen. It was as if Meredith's near-fatal accident was the trigger for a series of catastrophes. Equipment broke down. Artifacts were mysteriously damaged, or destroyed, or lost. A good portion of the crew came down with dysentery—it seemed as if trouble had been lurking in the wings, only waiting for an opportunity to overwhelm them.

Yet, they struggled on, and even made some progress.

Two of the crew, while righting a large *stele*, had the ground crumble away beneath them. Neither man was hurt, and they found they had fallen into a room of some size. Further investigation partially uncovered a building that Meredith thought might have been the living quarters for the priests who had attended the temples.

But even this discovery turned into disaster. One morning a black rooster was discovered at this spot, its throat cut and its blood splattered on the ancient stones. After that, none of the crew would go near it, and Meredith was forced to abandon investigation of that particular area.

That night she asked both Cooper and Ricardo to meet in her tent, for a conference.

Cooper arrived first, carrying a bottle of whiskey in his hand. Smiling ruefully, he set it on the table. "I figured we might need this."

For once Meredith didn't feel like making a flippant remark. She was too depressed. She smiled at him wearily. "For once, you may be right. That just might be a good idea."

Cooper's eyebrows climbed in astonishment, but he seemed happy to find her in a more agreeable mood than usual. "You look worn out."

She nodded. "I am. More than I can ever remember being. It's all this," she waved her hand, "all this trouble. All these things going wrong. It's like there's a . . ." She stopped.

Cooper dropped down into one of the folding canvas chairs. "Like there's a curse on us?"

She looked at him with some suspicion. "Well, yes. If I were superstitious, that's exactly what I'd say. It's what the men are saying, isn't it? That we're cursed?"

Cooper wrestled with the bottle, got it open, then poured a healthy drink into a water glass. "Yes, Meredith, it's what they're saying. And I believe it's what someone wants them to think."

Meredith leaned forward tensely. "Someone *wants* them to think? You think it's sabotage? But who would . . .? Of course! Rena Voltan!"

"It could be her," he said expressionlessly. "Or it could be that renagade bandit who abducted you. All I know is that there are too

261

many things going wrong, too many mysterious 'accidents,' and I don't like it."

"You do not like what, Cooper?"

Ricardo came in through the tent flap and dropped wearily onto the end of the cot.

"All these accidents," said Meredith. "We both think something peculiar is going on."

"Something like sabotage," Cooper added. "Did you know that two more men disappeared last night?"

Meredith said gloomily, "If this keeps up, soon there won't be any workers left."

"Then I guess we'll just have to turn to with shovels ourselves," Cooper said with a wry laugh. He held up the whiskey bottle. "A drink, Ricardo?"

Ricardo nodded. "Make it a strong one. I have more bad tidings. We just tore down one pile of stone blocking the passageway, only to find another a few feet farther on. It's maddening. If they, whoever they were, spent so much time sealing off the passageway, it must have been for a good reason. I keep thinking of what we may find if we ever get through these blockades, and it does not make for peace of mind."

Meredith smiled sympathetically. She knew how he felt; she felt the same impatience and frustration.

"Those jade figurines, for instance," Ricardo continued. "They are marvelous, from a really ancient culture, different than many things we have found near the surface. At least two cultures have lived on this site, Meredith, perhaps more.

"You cannot discount instinct when you are working an excavation, and my instinct tells me that there is something unusual under this pyramid, if we can only get to it before the entire crew deserts us, or our food supply is gone."

"That's why I asked you both to come here tonight," Meredith said. "What do you think we should do? What *can* we do?"

"We could send out a search party, try to find traces of our uninvited visitors," Cooper said slowly. "They must have a camp not too far away. But that would take time, and would also take men away from the work here."

Meredith said, "And we're shorthanded as it is."

Ricardo nodded. "Yes, and it would leave the camp relatively unguarded."

Meredith looked at him. His face was tired and drawn, but there was feverish excitement in his eyes. She had not really been alone with him since the discovery of the passageway, and although she knew that he was working himself to the point of exhaustion, she couldn't help but feel to some extent rejected. She knew this feeling was foolish. She was very familiar with the fascination a dig could hold for an archaeologist. Her father, when working on a site, had usually been unable to think or devote time to anything else, and Meredith often fell victim to the same malady; still, she longed for the comfort of Ricardo's arms, and his tenderness and attention.

Feeling guilty, she pulled her thoughts back to the matter at hand. There were more important things to worry about.

Looking around, she caught Cooper studying her face, and their eyes met. For an instant something stretched between them, something as real as a touch, and then his expression smoothed out.

Meredith spoke quickly, "Maybe it would be a good thing to talk to the men again, tell them what we think. It's clear that they're scared to death of anything that seems to be of the supernatural but sabotage they can understand. A talk might make things better."

"Unless they think that whoever is sabotaging us has a contact of sorts *with* the supernatural," Ricardo said slowly. "Meredith, what do you . . . ?"

At that moment, a shriek split the jungle stillness, and before they could react, Juana burst into the tent, disheveled and panting.

Clutching Meredith around the waist, she fell to her knees, crying loudly, "Aieeee! Aieeee! *Brujo*, Señorita Longley. *Brujo*!" The rest was a jumble of words that Meredith could not comprehend, and then she realized that the girl was speaking Nahuatl.

Cooper and Ricardo had already run from the tent, and finally Meredith managed to disengage the girl's clutching arms and follow them. Her attention was caught at once by the glow of a fire. Men were shouting and running toward the base of the large pyramid, one side of which seemed to be aflame. Moving to a better vantage point, Meredith witnessed a terrifying scene. High up on the side of the pyramid, at the third of the four tiers, stood a fearsome figure.

Fantastically tall, with a headdress of feathers and a mask for a face, the figure stood before a curtain of fire, which flickered with flashes of blue and green.

Now the figure slowly raised its arms, as if in a signal, and the men's voices quieted. For a moment Meredith could hear only the crackle of the flames, then a sonorous voice began chanting in Nahuatl. Meredith understood only a few of the words, yet it was clear that the voice was warning them, telling them that they must leave the site at once.

Before the voice died away, she saw Ricardo and Cooper charging up the side of the pyramid, but in the same instant they moved the fire went out and the darkness became total.

Pandemonium broke loose among the men, and for the next few moments Meredith had no idea of what was happening. Feeling utterly helpless, she retreated to her tent and to the frightened Juana, who cowered on her cot in the corner. She was trying to comfort the girl when Cooper and Ricardo returned. She looked at them expectantly.

Cooper shook his head with a rueful laugh. "Can you believe it, there was nothing there but the remains of the fire, nothing but ashes, not even coals. Whatever it was, it was a devilishly clever trick. We'll have a hell of a time with the men now. We'll never be able to convince them that that performance was not done by some supernatural creature."

"Dear God!" Meredith exclaimed. "What can happen next?"

They found out the following morning. When Cooper went to assign the work teams, he found that several more men had deserted during the night; this time part of the supplies and horses were gone as well.

Meredith was just getting dressed, when Cooper came to her tent with the bad news. It was like a slap in the face, but she had been hit so often lately that she was numb. She felt that whatever happened next, no matter how awful, she would not even feel it. She was wrong.

Cooper had barely finished telling her of the new defections, when a group of men dressed in police uniforms came into the camp clearing. They were armed with rifles, and their appearance was so sudden, and so unexpected, that Meredith's only reaction was shock.

The main body of the party stopped several yards short of her tent, but their leader, a slender, dark man with a full moustache, continued on toward her and Cooper.

Stopping in front of them, he made a full bow. "Señorita Longley?"

She nodded, too stunned to speak.

"I am Hernando Aragones, of the police of Acapulco. I am here to tell you that you must close down this excavation."

"In God's name, why?" she said despairingly. "For what possible reason?"

"We have been informed that an American was murdered here," he said stolidly. "My instructions are to close down the excavation until this murder can be investigated."

Chapter Sixteen

As Meredith and Ricardo plodded wearily toward Acapulco, Meredith was conscious only of an overwhelming feeling of depression. She said drearily, "Evan's murder may never be solved. We might as well forget about continuing with the excavation."

"Don't despair, my dear." Ricardo kneed his mount close, and reached over to pat her hand. "Perhaps it is not so bad as it seems."

"How can it be any worse?" she cried. "Perhaps I should just give up and go home. We've had nothing but trouble from the start; Evan's disappearance, then his tragic death; my abduction by Gabriel Morales. I was almost killed at the excavation, and now this!"

"Do not talk about giving up, or going home, Meredith." His voice grew urgent. "I will not hear of you going home."

"But what is there here for me, if I can't continue with the dig?"

"You will continue, Meredith," he said confidently. "Luis will help us. He has much influence, as I have told you. He will see that this affair is soon cleared up. We will be back digging within two weeks, at the very most."

After the excavation had been closed down, Ricardo had left immediately for the nearest telegraph office, taking Meredith and Juana with him. After an exchange of telegrams with Mexico City, they learned that Luis Mendes was in his winter home in Acapulco. Ricardo wired Mendes to expect them, and they set out for the port city.

Now Meredith said, "I hope you're right." She smiled slightly. "Oh, well, I suppose I could look upon these next few days as a holiday. God knows, I'm sick of life in the stink and heat of the jungle!"

"That's the spirit, my dear." A shadow crossed his face. "But I hope you didn't mean what you said literally. There is more than just the excavation to keep you here, isn't there?"

"I don't know what you mean."

"There is a hope in my heart that I might keep you here permanently, as my bride. We have talked of this. I have asked you, nay, begged you, a number of times. You always said you were too busy to think about it seriously." He looked into her eyes. "Well, for the next few days, you will not be too busy. Meredith, will you now consent to marry me? You know how much I love you."

"Darling, I know." Her breath caught. "But I . . ."

Encouraged by her seeming indecision, he

rushed on, "So you cannot say it is sudden. We could be married at Luis's hacienda in Acapulco. There will be plenty of time. Then we could return to the excavation as husband and wife. And there is a practical side to consider."

She said warily, "What do you mean?"

"As my wife, you will become a citizen of Mexico, and that could go a long way toward helping the authorities to open the excavation to you again. You will no longer be a hated American, but one of us."

"You really think that would help?"

"I do, my dear. Sincerely."

Conflicting thoughts tumbled through Meredith's mind. She was strongly attracted to Ricardo, and they had much in common, but did she love him? Was she prepared to commit herself to a permanent relationship?

And Cooper? What would his reaction be? She closed her eyes, and the image of his mocking smile filled her mind. But why should he care? He had his witch-woman. She experienced a feeling of vertigo and gripped the saddlehorn tightly.

"Meredith? Are you all right?"

She opened her eyes and smiled over at him. "Let me think about it a little. I'm so tired right now, I can't concentrate, but I will admit that the idea sounds appealing."

A radiant smile lit his face, and he said fervently, "You will never regret it, that I vow to you. I will make you the happiest woman on earth!"

Looking into his smiling face, Meredith was

moved by the fact that she could cause such happiness in another person. Unaccountably, she found herself thinking of her father, and his happiness when he was puttering about a new dig with Meredith by his side. And what did she have to go back to when she finally left Mexico? She had no family left, and she had never cared for the austere climate of New England, nor the dull academic life.

Poppa, she thought silently, what would you think? You knew this man, and called him friend. The words were almost a prayer.

"All right, Ricardo," she said abruptly. "I will marry you, if you're sure that's what you want."

The Mendes's winter hacienda in Acapulco was large, and almost as opulent as the house in Mexico City. Bougainvillea vines climbed the courtyard wall, the blossoms bright against the whitewashed adobe. Fountains sparkled in the courtyard, and flowering plants were profuse. A factor that made it even more attractive was its location—on a hill overlooking the glitter of Acapulco Bay.

It was late afternoon when they rode into the courtyard, and Luis Mendes came hurrying out to meet them, calling for a servant to care for their horses.

"Señorita Longley, it is a great pleasure to see you again!" Beaming, he helped her from her horse, then hurried around to embrace Ricardo. "My friend! I was delighted to receive your wire!" The face he turned to Meredith was grave. "And I am desolated about all the difficulties you have encountered, Señorita, most especially the untimely death of your brother."

"It has been a difficult time, Señor Mendes," Meredith said listlessly. "I do hope that you can be of some assistance."

"Be assured that I shall do everything within my power. I am eager to know the full story. What information I have is skimpy. But first, you must refresh yourselves. I shall expect you both in my study within an hour. Then we shall talk, and see if we cannot move against the obstacles you are confronted with."

Juana had dismounted from her mule, but hung back shyly. Meredith motioned her over, introduced her to Mendes with a few words of explanation.

Luis Mendes took Juana's hand and bowed over it, with as much respect as he would have shown a lady of the aristocracy. Juana turned a dark red, and looked around as though about to flee.

Hiding a smile, Meredith took the girl's hand. "Come along, Juana. I am dirty, tired, and stiff from the long ride. You have much to do to make a new woman of me."

Escorted by Luis Mendes, they went into the hacienda and down a long hall, where they were shown their respective rooms.

Mendes said, "I am sorry that my staff here is smaller, and I hope you will forgive me if my hospitality is not the best."

Meredith had to laugh at this man, the most

273

gracious host she had ever known, lamenting his poor hospitality. She sobered. "Señor Mendes, you do lift a person's spirits. I feel more cheerful than I have in some time."

At exactly six o'clock, Meredith and Ricardo were in Mendes's spacious study. Meredith, refreshed by a bath and clean clothing, was feeling much better.

Mendes served them glasses of dry sherry, seated them in comfortable chairs, and settled down behind his desk. "Now, I would be grateful if you could bring me up to date on the events leading up to this moment."

Taking turns, Meredith and Ricardo told him all that had happened. Only once did Mendes interrupt, when told of Gabriel Morales. He said harshly, "That donkey dung! A thousand pardons, Señorita, but this man has been a thorn in our side since the final days of the Revolution. It is past time he is made to pay for his crimes. And you may be sure, Señorita, that I will see to it that he is brought to jusice for the indignities you suffered at his hands. Pray continue."

At the end of their story, Mendes gazed out the window pensively, pulling at his lower lip in thought. Abruptly, he swung back to face them. "I have one piece of information that you are lacking. The reason that all this trouble descended upon you, the immediate reason, was a report to a policeman here in Acapulco. The peon who made the report told of an *Americano* being murdered at the excavation. The informer had been in the employ of your brother,

Señorita, and your brother . . . You will pardon me, but it would seem that your brother was bent on looting the site before you arrived."

"It's all right," Meredith said stiffly. "I found that hard to believe at first, but I have come to accept it as true. But there are two things I don't understand. First, if this man reported Evan's murder, surely he must have known who killed him. So why is it necessary to investigate? And second, why is it necessary to close down the excavation?"

"Yes, I can see your confusion." Luis Mendes made a steeple of his fingers, looking intently at her. "As to the first, this informer merely stated that Evan Longley had been killed. Unfortunately, the man has a reputation for being unreliable, and the policeman did not place much credence in his story. It was only when he checked with his superior that interest was aroused. His superior knew that your brother was the object of an extensive search. Even then, no action might have been taken, at least not immediately, but for the fact that *you* did not report your brother's death to our police. That aroused their suspicions."

"We thought of that," Meredith said, "but we concluded that it would not be of interest to them, since Evan was an American."

"Ah, I see." Mendes sighed heavily. "That shows prejudice on your part, does it not? Our police are as concerned with crime, especially murder, as their American counterparts."

"You're right, of course." Meredith felt herself flushing. "Perhaps it was a mistake."

"You are correct in that. It was a sad mistake." Mendes's gaze moved to Ricardo. "But I am surprised, my friend, that you did not see to it."

"I'm afraid I shared Meredith's view, to a certain extent," Ricardo said uncomfortably. "But the fact that we were excavating had more bearing on my decision. I feared that publicity and a police investigation would bring hordes of sightseers and vandals to the site, hampering our work."

"And perhaps the possibility of a great treasure to be found," Mendes said softly, "influenced your decision?"

"That does me an injustice, Luis!" Ricardo said hotly.

Mendes sighed again. "Perhaps, my friend, perhaps . . ."

Meredith broke in. "How did you know about the treasure?"

Mendes tented his fingers again. "This is my country, Señorita, and I have many sources of information."

"The treasure is a myth, nothing more!"

"Again, perhaps. But be that as it may, it approaches the answer to your second question. As you already know, it was difficult to obtain permission for a North American archaeologist to excavate the ancient city. I was able to get permission for you by exerting great pressure in high circles. But the moment word reached those same high circles of your brother's murder, and the possibility of gold and silver being discovered, it provided a ready excuse to close down the excavation."

Meredith slumped back, discouraged. "That means I might as well give up. They'll never allow us to resume digging."

"That is not necessarily so," he said, smiling. She perked up. "What do you mean?"

"It means that I will simply bring my influence to bear once again. But," he leaned forward, "I deem it wise to wait until this murder of your brother is solved."

"But that may never happen!"

"Do not be so pessimistic, Meredith . . . if I may be allowed the liberty of calling you that. Did you not say that you believed his associate, Harris Browder, to be in the area of the excavation?"

Meredith nodded. "The Voltan woman told me that, yes."

"And Señor Browder was disenchanted with your brother, was he not? So, he would seem a logical suspect."

"It's possible that Harris killed Evan, yes. But Rena Voltan is a logical suspect, as well."

"Ah, yes." Mendes looked out the window again. "Rena Voltan has an unsavory reputation in my country, and she is reportedly a witch." He smiled wryly. "The people of Mexico have a great awe of the supernatural. But she is also a woman, and we have a great reverence for ladies, and to suspect a lady of so foul a crime is unthinkable. But no matter." His shrug was eloquent. "Even if the crime is not solved, I suspect that the police interest in it will eventually subside. Meanwhile, you must be patient, and I must exact a promise from each of you." His face became stern. "Meredith, you must swear to me that, if anything of monetary value is found, you will at once report it to me, or to my government. Do you promise?"

"Of course I promise," she said in surprise. "I never intended doing anything else."

"And you, my friend?"

Ricardo flushed. "Do you need to ask this of me, Luis?"

"I do. If I am to intercede in Meredith's behalf, I have to be certain that any treasure found will find its way to where it rightfully belongs."

"You have my word," Ricardo said.

"Excellent!" Mendes leaned forward, smiling. "Now you need only show patience, Meredith. You shall be back at work on your excavation before too long."

After a moment Ricardo cleared his throat, and reached for Meredith's hand. "We have an announcement to make, Luis. Meredith and I are to be wed."

Mendes's lean face went blank with astonishment, and he stared at each in turn. A moment later he was beaming paternally. "That is excellent news! You will be married here, naturally. We shall have a grand wedding, one that will be the wonder of all of Mexico!"

When Rena Voltan learned that the Mexican government had ordered all work stopped on the excavation for an indefinite period, she was absolutely furious. It seemed that she was to be frustrated at every turn!

First, it had been Evan's defection; she had settled with him for that. Then his sister had mysteriously vanished for several days, delaying things and costing Rena money. The most frustrating things, prior to the present situation, had been learning that Evan had been unsuccessful at finding the treasure, and the postponement of her own search due to the arrival of Longley and her crew. She had tried everything in her power to kill Longley and frighten away her people, so she could be free to look on her own, supremely confident that she could find the loot. And now this!

Rena was not accustomed to being frustrated, by anything. Sitting before her tent, smoking her small cigar, she made up her mind that this would *not* be the first time. Now, what could she do? She knew very well how obstinate and slow government authorities could be. They might keep the excavation shut down for months, even years.

She stirred, as she saw Harris Browder hurrying up in the evening dusk. She had dispatched him to see if he could learn why the authorities were here, and the reason for the closing of the excavation.

"It looks like we're in bad trouble, Rena," he said, squatting down beside her.

"Did you find out what I sent you to find out?"

"Yes, and what I learned is the reason I say

we're in trouble! Somebody reported Evan's death to the police!"

Rena expelled an angry breath. "Who did that?"

Browder shook his head. "I don't know, but it has to be one of Evan's men we let go. The cat's out of the bag, however, so the who doesn't matter. The thing is, that's why they closed down the dig. It's to stay closed down until they figure out who killed him."

Rena struggled to contain a bark of laughter. Closed down because of Evan's death, and *she* had killed him! What irony! Still, she didn't regret the deed; it had been necessary. Her mind raced as she weighed this new development.

"Meredith has left the excavation, along with some Mex."

Rena's head came up. "How about Cooper Mayo?"

"He's still there, with what's left of the crew. The Mex I talked to said their orders were to remain there until they could start digging again. Rena . . ." His voice whined. "What do we do now?"

She motioned. "Quiet, I'm thinking."

"Maybe we should just give the whole deal up, swallow our losses, and get the hell out of here!"

"I don't give up that easily," she said absently.

"But it's different now! Damnit, there's a charge of murder hanging over us. What if they talk to others in Evan's crew? They can testify that you killed him! For murder, down

280

here, they execute you first and ask questions after!"

She frowned at him. "Don't forget one thing, Browder. Under the law you're as much responsible for Evan's death as I am."

"But *you* killed him! It wasn't my idea!"

Temper rising, she started to lash out at him, then subsided as the idea came to her.

What was the phrase? Sacrificial goat?

She smiled seductively and stroked his cheek. "Don't worry too much, Browder. I'll take care of everything."

"Everything?" he asked suspiciously.

"Everything. Meaning the loot isn't yet lost to us. Now, let's go to bed and get a good night's sleep."

Getting up, she let her fingers trail across his cheek, then took his hand and led him into the tent.

Like leading a goat on a tether, she thought, smiling to herself.

Chapter Seventeen

The wedding of Ricardo Villalobos and Meredith Longley was everything that Luis Mendes had promised it would be.

He and Doña Consuela had begun planning the fiesta and the marriage ceremony the very next day after Ricardo's announcement. Meredith was dazed by the speed with which the arrangements were made, yet there was still time for second thoughts. During sleepless moments in the stillness of predawn, she harbored grave doubts about the wisdom of what she was doing. She longed for the familiar surroundings of the dig. There, in spite of all the troubles she had been faced with, everything was simpler, uncomplicated by the emotions now tearing at her.

But by day, as the climactic moment neared, she was swept along by the accelerating pace, and had to admit that she enjoyed being the center of attention. Everything focused on her, as the soon-to-be-bride. Ricardo was banished to the background, and they seldom had a moment alone. They had not made love since the night before they arrived.

On the day of the wedding, Meredith was dazzled by the change in the walled patio behind the main house. During the past two days she had scarcely stirred from the hacienda, and in that brief time the courtyard had been transformed by the servants, under the stern and creative eye of Doña Consuela.

The eaves of the house were hung with many flowers, ivy vines climbed the staypoles, and palm fronds made shadowy bowers for matrons to gather under and exchange gossip.

Also hung along the eaves, mixed in with the flowers, were *piñatas*, those animal forms made of brightly colored paper that, when broken, spilled forth presents for the numerous children, who were always underfoot like noisy household pets.

A waxed square of canvas was stretched on a plot of ground for dancing, and there were five waiting musicians, wearing loose white clothing.

A cloud of pungent smoke hovered over the red tiles of the main house; a steer had been roasting in the courtyard all night. Long trestle tables, covered with snowy white linen, were set side by side, and servants busily served red wine, brandy, bowls of nuts, fruits, and melons to the guests.

Many of the women wore white Sonora dresses, with hoop skirts, and black lace mantillas or gaily embroidered silk shawls; and most of them had Spanish combs high in the backs of their elaborately constructed hairdos. Most of the men wore *vaquero* costumes—short, embroidered jackets studded with silver buttons, which glittered in the sun—tight riding trousers; and low-crowned, wide-brimmed vicuna hats. On many silver spurs jangled musically as they walked.

Meredith had had no say in the dress she wore—a gown of expensive, white lace that bared her shoulders and hugged her torso. It was an exquisite garment, made especially for her, and she thought that it was lovely, yet she felt that everyone present could see through the pretense and know that she was not a virgin, and thus not entitled to wear white. Of course, to have made such a comment to Doña Consuela would have caused a great uproar.

She was not allowed to show herself in the patio before the nuptials and watched the preparations from the second floor window overlooking the courtyard. She smiled as she caught a fleeting glimpse of Ricardo having a drink with Luis Mendes. He was dressed in dark, formal clothing, and the brief look she had of his face revealed that he was pale, and more grave of countenance than she had ever seen him.

Was he having his own doubts? Or was it just the usual nervousness of a groom?

Behind her the roomful of women chittered, and Meredith turned away from the window with a sigh. Despite the magnificence of the wedding, or perhaps because of it, she would gladly have settled for a simple ceremony. All day women had hovered around her. Only Juana took it all in stride. Meredith was amazed at the aplomb of the Indian girl; she had settled into her role of lady's maid to Meredith, and had assumed a proprietary, protective manner.

Meredith had all her undergarments on; the only items remaining to complete her preparations were the wedding dress and her shoes. It would soon be time—the ceremony was scheduled to begin in one hour, at four o'clock sharp.

Now Juana was making shooing motions and raising her voice. "The Señorita Meredith must rest until it is time. You leave her alone now!"

She began herding the women toward the door, like a flock of chickens. The women went, muttering in outrage. Meredith was amused at the once-shy Juana, and at the same time she was grateful. A few minutes of rest would be welcome. It had been a long, trying day, and it was far from over. She sank down onto the edge of the bed.

Juana approached her and now, abruptly, she was shy again. She stood before Meredith, wringing her hands. In a low, faltering voice, she said, "Señorita . . . ?"

"Yes, Juana, what is it?"

Juana looked away, not speaking.

"Speak up, Juana! What is it?"

"Forgive me for speaking of it, but . . . are you sure you wish to do this thing?"

"Do what?" Meredith frowned. "What on earth are you talking about?"

"Wed the señor," Juana said, her face a dark red.

"Of course I wish it!" Meredith said, somewhat sharply. "No one is forcing me to marry him!"

"I thought . . . Señor Cooper, he is your man, I thought."

Naturally Cooper Mayo would win the heart of a girl like this, Meredith thought angrily, and had to wonder if Cooper had been sleeping with the girl. "No, Señor Cooper is not my man! Whatever gave you such an idea?"

The girl looked miserable. "He is so . . . so . . ."

"Handsome? Charming? Is that what you mean?" Meredith's laughter was false. "He's all of those things, but he's other things as well." Her voice grew cold. "But what gives you the right to question my choice of husbands? It is none of your affair! Is this the gratitude I receive for rescuing you from a living hell?" Unaccountably, tears flooded her eyes. She gestured. "Now get out!"

Juana turned away and shuffled toward the door, her shoulders slumped. Shame overcame Meredith. "Juana . . . ?"

The girl stopped, without facing around.

Gently, Meredith said, "Turn around, Juana, and look at me." The girl slowly turned about. The dark, limpid eyes mirrored her hurt and misery. Meredith motioned. "Come here."

Juana approached the bed hesitantly.

Meredith took her hand. "I'm sorry, Juana. I had no right to speak to you like that. Please

287

forgive me. I know you spoke out of concern for me, and I appreciate that." She tightened her grip. "But I do have to wonder as to why you spoke up. Do you have a reason?"

The girl looked startled, then fearful. "No, Señorita. It is nothing." She tried to pull her hand free. "I should not have spoken so."

At ten minutes after four the *padre* spoke the final words, and Meredith Longley became Meredith Villalobos.

Meredith felt chilled, and her lips were like ice as she turned to Ricardo and he lifted her veil. His mouth touching hers was warm and soft, and suddenly she was clinging fiercely to him, seeking warmth from him, and just as suddenly she *was* warm.

When she finally broke the embrace and looked into his eyes, she saw that he was puzzled. Her laughter rang out, gay and inforced, and cheers and cries of congratulations came from the wedding guests.

On cue, the music began, and Ricardo led her onto the square of waxed canvas. The music was fast and lively, not the waltz that Meredith had expected. She hesitated, at a loss. Ricardo's bootheels danced a muffled rhythm on the canvas, and he danced around her. Meredith turned slowly, trying to follow him. She noticed that the guests were gathered around in a semicircle, smiling and clapping their hands, but none joined in. Evidently the first dance belonged to the bride and groom.

Finally, the music ended with a flourish, and Meredith fell into Ricardo's arms, laughing, out of breath.

"My love," he whispered ardently into her ear. "My own true love."

Meredith pressed her fevered cheek against his without answering. They moved aside now, as Luis Mendes led Doña Consuela out into the canvas. The strings thumped again, and Meredith was astounded to see the elegant, gray-haired Luis Mendes and his somewhat plump wife begin to dance. Consuela held her shawl extended and danced a slow and stately circle around her husband. Then their dancing accelerated.

Now Consuela whirled, spun, twisted. Never touching, Mendes danced around around her, smiling broadly.

Others joined in, and the canvas square was soon filled to its capacity. Ricardo looked at her, jerking his head toward the dancing couples.

"Let's just watch, all right?" She laughed. "I've had little experience at dancing, and this was a whole new thing for me. As we say in the States, let's sit this one out."

He nodded in understanding. "I'll fetch you a glass of wine and a plate of food."

As he walked away, Meredith sat down in a convenient chair, still breathless. The good smell of the food reminded her that she had eaten nothing except a roll and coffee for breakfast, and such had been her nervous state that she had nearly lost that.

The second dance was over by the time Ricardo returned with wine and a platter of beef, rice, and beans. Meredith ate hungrily, but she had to stand now as people came up to congratulate her.

The afternoon wore on and Meredith danced a number of times, with Ricardo, with Luis Mendes, and other men. She became more adroit at the strange dances, but she was soon wearied. Flushed and breathless after another dance with Ricardo, she said, "Can't we slip away soon?"

Ricardo looked deep into her eyes, a tender smile on his lips. He had taken a hideaway cottage on the beach for two weeks. Luis Mendes had stoutly maintained that they could return to the excavation without hindrance by the end of that time, if not before.

"I am as eager as you, my love," Ricardo said, dark eyes luminous. "But we should wait until the young ones have their turn." He nodded across the courtyard.

Meredith turned, looking in that direction. Señora Mendes had all the children in a ragged line, and was blindfolding them one at a time. As Meredith watched, one girl took a broomstick, and swung wildly and blindly at the *piñatas* suspended from the eaves. After the third swing she connected, and the *piñata* shattered, showering down brightly colored gifts and sweets.

Amused, Meredith watched until the last young one had his turn. Then she faced around at a touch on her elbow. Smiling almost shyly, Ricardo whispered, "Shall we slip away now, my dear?"

She nodded.

Taking her arm, he led her over to Luis and Consuela Mendes. They said their farewells and slipped out through the side gate of the patio, to Mendes's carriage waiting for them.

The carriage moved at a fast clip through the port town, and then up the coast along a road seldom used. Meredith liked Acapulco. Despite the tropic heat, there was often a faint breeze off the sea, which was blue and green in the distance; the deserted strips of beach were white as bleached bone in the late afternoon sun.

Except for the summers, the New England ocean she was accustomed to was gray and cold. She had discovered that the ocean here had the temperature of a warm bath. Ocean bathing by females in New England was still not particularly approved of, and even when a woman did dare to go into the ocean, she was expected to wear enough clothing so that not even an ankle was exposed. Meredith had noticed that here, the native women often went into the sea and were not necessarily swathed in concealing garments from head to toe.

Since her life had taken a drastic change, she had already decided that she would seize advantage of the ocean and the lovely beaches. Ricardo had told her that the location of the cottage was isolated; the only people to be seen were the natives, and there were only a small number of them in the vicinity.

The town of Acapulco was long out of sight, when the carriage rounded a headland and came upon a small cove. Thick jungle came almost down to the beach, but tucked back out of sight, within fifty yards of the beach, was a small, thatch-roofed cottage. The road, Meredith saw, ended here.

The cottage, she also saw as the carriage drew up before it, hardly deserved the name. Built on stilts, all four sides were open with only bamboo curtains, rolled up at the moment, to keep out the elements. There was a roofed veranda on the ocean side, and worn wooden steps going up to it.

She saw that Ricardo was watching her anxiously. He said, "My dear, I hope it's not too primitive for you. But with the climate here being what it is, you don't really need enclosed rooms, except when a storm hits, and those are not likely this season of the year. There is only a bedroom and a dining area. It does have a comfortable bed, however. But the cooking is done outside . . ."

"Don't fret, Ricardo. I love it!" Strangely enough, she did. At first sight she had been disappointed, but now she was falling in love with it. There was all the privacy they could desire and only a few simple housekeeping chores to perform.

Ricardo was going on, "Now that you've seen it, you may change your mind about servants. It's not too late. I can dispatch a message with the carriage driver to have a household couple sent out to us."

"No, dear, I meant what I said," she said firmly. "I don't want people around, not even household help. What needs doing, I'll do."

"But Meredith, the cooking is done outside," he protested.

"And so? I've been camping out for weeks, under the most primitive conditions. At least here there's a roof overhead. I know . . . there's a cook with the expedition, but I've been on digs with Poppa when we couldn't afford a cook, so I did it. Don't worry so much." She leaned across to kiss him. "I want us to be alone, together."

He gave that eloquent shrug of his shoulders and got down to help her out of the carriage. Meredith was surprised to see that the sun had set while they were talking. The hills rising behind them were already darkening, and as she glanced out to the ocean, she saw that it was turning a dark purple.

"Oh, it's so beautiful here!" she exclaimed, taking a deep breath. She seized his hand in a firm grip. "Come on, I want to see our honeymoon cottage!"

She tugged at him, and they ran up the veranda steps like children. In a distant part of her mind, Meredith sensed that she was talking too much and acting like a silly schoolgirl.

She put it down to nervousness. Wasn't a new bride supposed to be nervous, and expected to act girlish?

She dismissed it from her thoughts, as they

entered the dimness of what was to be their wedding bedchamber. She saw a bed and other items of furniture, but it was too dark to individualize them.

"I will light a lamp."

Ricardo took a step away and she reached for his hand again. "No, we don't need a light." She laughed. "In the States we have a custom . . . the groom carries the bride across the threshold."

"I have heard of such, but I did not think . . ." He made an embarrassed sound. "We could go outside and come back in, my love. I want everything to be right for you."

She held on to him. "I wasn't serious. Everything *is* right." She heard the carriage leaving, and knew that their meager luggage and the supplies had been unloaded.

She turned into his arms, her mouth tilted up. His face, in the faint light, seemed uncertain, hesitant. Meredith made the decision. She kissed him, her lips parted.

With a groan he crushed her into his arms, and Meredith· let herself go, all worries receding. Even the aborted excavation went out of her mind, and she gave herself freely to her husband.

They were on the bed within seconds, and Meredith was uninhibited, almost wanton, in her love-making, and she sensed, at some time during the act of love, that she was shocking Ricardo. She had to admit that she was shocking herself. It was outrageous behavior for a proper New England lady, who had not known the delights of passion until short weeks before.

Yet, that was not the whole answer. It was as if some demon inhabited her, and only by giving herself totally could she exorcise the demon.

They did not let go of one another until both fell into a sleep of satiation, and exhaustion.

Meredith awoke at first light. For a moment she did not know where she was. She moved, and saw the man in bed beside her, a total stranger.

Then it all came flooding back and she stretched, smiling to herself. Ricardo slept on, as heavily as though drugged. She turned her head. The bamboo blinds were raised, and she could see the water of the small cove begin to take on morning color.

An impish thought invaded her mind. Without further ado she eased herself out of the bed. One bare foot on the rough floor, she froze as Ricardo stirred, turning, one arm flung out as though reaching for her. Then he was still, again deep in sleep.

Meredith padded from the room and down the veranda steps. The sun was not yet up, but it was light enough for her gaze to search the surrounding landscape. Except for birds in morning flight, not a living thing moved. She ran the last few yards to the beach and waded out into the gentle waves curling around her feet. The water was deliciously warm.

Meredith had never been at home in the water, and the North Atlantic off the shores of New England had always intimidated her. In comparison, the surf here was gentle, and she soon began to enjoy herself, swimming awkwardly out a short distance, then letting the slight waves carry her onto the beach. She let all worries go out of her mind, and romped in sheer animal pleasure.

She forgot the passage of time and scarcely noticed the sun coming up. Riding another wave onto the beach, she heard a voice calling her name.

She stood up, water streaming from her body, and waved at Ricardo emerging from the shrubbery a short distance away.

"I was worried about you when I woke up and found you gone . . ." He broke off as he saw that she was without clothing. He looked both ways along the beach. "Meredith, what if someone sees you like this? It is not proper behavior!"

She went toward him, laughing. "There is no one to see, and I'm the same as I was in bed last night." She spread her arms wide. "See?"

"But this is different!"

"I'm sorry, darling. I've shocked you, haven't I?" She took his hand and raised it to her lips. "No, I'm not really sorry, since I did enjoy it. You should try it. But I will try to be more circumspect, I promise."

He studied her gravely. "There's been a change in you, Meredith."

She shook her hair out, gazing at him with a demure look. "And do you approve?"

"I'm not sure," he said. Then he gave a shout of laughter. "It may take some getting accustomed to, but I have the feeling that I will. You must remember, my dear, that I am an academic person. We are well-known for our stodginess, for adhering to tradition."

"And one of those traditions, here in Mexico, is that a female has her place, and woe be to one who dares to flaunt that tradition," she said mischievously. "Is that a fair way to put it?"

"Eminently fair, I would say."

Serious now, she said, "But at least for the time we are here, will you permit me to shatter a few traditions, without getting too angry?"

"I will try. I promise."

"Good enough." She took his hand, swinging it between them. "Now let's go have breakfast. I'm famished." She gave him a sidelong glance. "I'll clothe myself properly before cooking our breakfast."

It was an idyllic time, an interlude of love and happiness, marred only by two factors—Meredith's occasional worries about the excavation, and Ricardo's recurring, puzzling moods.

Ricardo's moods were puzzling to Meredith not only because she could not understand the cause behind them, but also because she was unsure exactly what they signified—depression, anger, unhappiness, regret over a hasty marriage? The only thing she was certain of was that they came to him, and when they did, he would retire into dark, brooding silences, during which he would prowl the beach or disappear into the jungle for hours on end. However, he did not abuse her, either by word or deed, and when the mood had passed, he was apologetic, almost humble, and so went out of his way to be kind that it set her teeth on edge.

It was infuriating! Here was a man on his honeymoon, supposedly deeply in love, yet he went into periods when she was completely walled off.

On their thirteenth day in the cottage, when Meredith awoke long after midnight, she found Ricardo gone from their bed. Going to look out, she saw his solitary figure walking under the moon, on the beach. Quickly, she threw on her clothes and started out of the cottage. On the veranda she saw him returning, head bent in thought. She sat down on the veranda steps and waited.

He came on, walking slowly. At the bottom of the steps, he stopped and seemed to brace himself before going into the house. At the sight of Meredith he appeared startled.

"Meredith! What are you doing out here?" She could see, in the moonlight, that his smile was made with an effort. "Couldn't you sleep, my dear?"

"I was sleeping just fine, until I woke up and found you gone," she said. "The question is, why couldn't *you* sleep?"

He shrugged, and came on up the steps to sit beside her. "I was restless, and thought that a walk along the beach would clear my head."

"Clear it of what, Ricardo? Are you unhappy? Is that it? This is the third or fourth time you've done this, closing me off!"

"Ah, no, my love. It has nothing to do with you." He caught her hand and brought it to his lips. "I could not be happier with you as my wife. I love you with all my heart and soul, you must believe that."

"Then, what is it?"

He sighed, looking out to sea. "Our future. I know I have talked of grandiose plans, but I live in what, in your country, would be called 'genteel poverty.' I know, I have a fine hacienda, and even a house staff. Most people," his voice became wry, faintly bitter, "would consider my position enviable. But much of it is surface. The family fortune is gone. About all I have is the hacienda and my university salary. It is very little to offer a wife, Meredith."

"Is that all you've been worrying about? Money?" She was almost giddy with relief. "Dear Ricardo, I have never been one to worry about money matters. Poppa taught me that. We never had much money. The work you do is more important that money." She laughed fully. "You're being silly, worrying about that!"

"But I envisioned us working together," he said worriedly. "On other excavations."

"And we will! Look, if we can get back to *Tonatiuhican*, and prove it to be the great find that I'm sure it is, then the world will know of us, you and I. We will have a great reputation, and will never again have trouble getting financing for other expeditions. I'll wager that even your own country will show more interest. Besides, it's more than possible that this one excavation will take years and years to complete."

"Still, having money of our own would mean that we wouldn't have to depend on others, on grants and university funding. And we could live a better life, not one restricted by little income."

"Ricardo, I can't think of a better life than happily scratching away at a dig, uncovering lost civilizations. *That* is riches enough for me!"

He said unhappily, "I agree with you, of course, yet having money would make our life much easier. Understand, my dear, it is your welfare that concerns me. I have grown accustomed to being without money."

"You are a goose, Ricardo, but I love you." She cupped her hands around his face and kissed him. "Now, let's go in to bed, and see what we can do to ease your worries."

Hand in hand, they went inside.

Both were still in bed and asleep the next morning, when a knock on the post aroused them. Ricardo went to the door and called through it, "Who is it?"

"Luis Mendes, my friend. I have news for both of you!"

"Give us a moment, Luis."

They quickly got dressed and went out onto the veranda. Mendes was sitting on the steps. He bounced up, beaming, as they emerged.

"I have great tidings, my friends!" He came toward them, his arms spread wide. "The policemen are being recalled from the expedition, and you have permission to resume your work, without interference."

Meredith exclaimed with delight, "That is good news, Señor Mendes!"

Ricardo said soberly, "How did this come about, Luis?"

"The American, Harris Browder, was found on the road a short distance out of Acapulco, bound and gagged. There was a note addressed to the chief of police, pinned to his shirt. The note stated that he had killed your brother, Meredith, claiming they had a fight, and this man Browder killed him in vengeance."

"Harris Browder? But how . . . ?" Meredith drew in her breath. "How did he come to be there like that?"

"Who knows?" Mendes spread his hands. "Does it really matter? As I mentioned in an earlier conversation, Browder was incensed at your brother. As you would say, perhaps a falling out of thieves? Forgive my placing your brother in that context . . ."

"It's all right." She gestured impatiently. "What does Browder say?"

"He denies it, of course. But since he has a strong motive, the only one so far, the chief of police disregards his denial of guilt. One would expect such a denial from a killer, is that not so?"

"I suppose so, yes," Meredith said slowly, but her thoughts were on Rena Voltan, knowing now that she had suspected the woman of killing Evan all along. But, as Mendes said, what

301

did it matter, so long as the restrictions were being lifted from the dig?

"Then we can return to work?" Ricardo asked.

"An official with such instructions will accompany you back to the excavation." Mendes smiled broadly. "Did I not promise?"

"You did, Señor Mendes!" In her delight, Meredith threw her arms around him, kissing him on the cheek. She whirled on Ricardo, her eyes shining. "We can go back to work! Isn't that great news, darling?"

Ricardo seemed deep in thought, his face grave. He blinked, focusing on her. A slow smile broke. "Yes, of course, Meredith. It is grand news." He reached for her hand.

Chapter Eighteen

Cooper, bored by the extended inactivity, was lying fully clothed on his blankets, almost asleep, when he was awakened by the sound of shouting. Immediately alert, he came to his feet, the Colt in his hand. The cooking fire had died down, but a full moon cast an eerie light over the clearing.

He saw a man hurrying toward him from the direction of the pyramid, and he went to meet him. The man came to a stop before him, panting for breath. It was the young man named Raul. He looked thoroughly frightened. He gasped out, "Señor Mayo!"

"Yes, Raul? Spit it out, man!"

"There is something you must see. The men, even the police guards, are frightened!" Raul grasped Cooper's arm and tugged. "You must come!"

"All right, all right, I'm coming!"

Raul ran toward the pyramid, and Cooper loped along beside him. What could have gone wrong now? It didn't seem possible that anything else could happen. At least, Cooper thought, whatever it is, it should help break the boredom.

Before they reached the base of the pyramid, they met others running toward them, glancing back over their shoulders in terror. They rounded the pyramid base, and Raul skidded to a stop, pointing a trembling finger. "Look!"

Cooper looked in the direction of the pointing finger, and saw a figure shimmering at the edge of the trees. It had a ghostly luminescence, but it was too distant to make out any features or even ascertain if it was male or female. Now a strange moaning noise issued from the figure and words came from it, sounding like so much pure gibberish to Cooper.

At his side Raul made a choking sound of fear. He uttered one word, *"Brujo,"* and turned on his heel, leaving Cooper all alone.

Cooper fired a cigar, remaining where he was for a few minutes, waiting to see if the figure would come on toward him, or disappear. When it did neither, he started toward it with a firm stride.

The shimmering figure remained in place until he was almost to the edge of the trees. Then it abruptly vanished. Cooper stopped, blinking, trying to make out any sign of it in the trees. Finally, Colt cocked in his hand, he stepped into the trees, warily moving a short distance.

Sensing a movement on his right, he whirled,

bringing the Colt to bear on the direction of the sound.

"You wouldn't shoot an old acquaintance, would you, Coop?" said an amused voice.

He straightened up, but didn't holster the gun. He said tightly, "You sure as hell run the risk of getting shot, Rena, if you insist on cavorting around out here like that, scaring the men half to death."

As Rena moved into view, she said artlessly, "Why, I don't know what you mean. I've done nothing to frighten anyone . . ."

"Oh, come off it, Rena! I know that was you here a few minutes ago, gotten up like a ghost, witch, or whatever."

She shrugged, taking a small cigar from her pocket. She dipped her head toward him while he struck a match for the cigar. She blew smoke and said, "You don't seem awfully surprised to see me, Coop."

"Why should I be surprised? I know you've been lurking around out here, camped somewhere off in the jungle. Who else would be behind all these things that have happened? You've frightened half our crew away."

"That was my purpose. Why should you object? The less men around, the fewer we'll have to contend with when the time comes to take over the treasure." She assumed a glum expression. "But I'm not sure that time will ever come, now with the excavation closed down."

"And whose fault is that?"

"What does that mean?"

"You killed Evan Longley," he looked directly into her eyes, "and that's why the dig is closed down, so the police can look into his death."

"Who says I killed Evan?"

"I do. You want to know how I figure it?"

She was smiling. "It might be amusing, yes."

"You found Evan Longley already here when you arrived, and you killed him. It's that simple."

"That's the way you figure it?"

"Yeah, that's it."

"But you don't have any proof, do you, Coop? If you tried that story on the police, you'd be laughed at."

"Oh, that's true enough, I'm sure," he drawled. "By the way, where's your smarmy friend, Browder? Hiding out behind you somewhere?"

She gestured with the cigar. "I have no idea. Browder just up and left three days ago. I think he was getting frightened."

"I can understand the reason. He probably thought he was next on your list to die."

"Coop . . ." She looked at him intently. "You say you knew I was around. Why didn't you try to get in touch with me, let me know why the excavation was closed down?"

"I had other things to do. What good would it have done you to know? You know now, so what can you do?"

"There has been no indications of the location of the treasure?" She touched his hand.

"Not the slightest, Rena. Not even a smell. So, if you're thinking of nosing around for it on your own while Meredith is away, you can forget it." He grinned. "I've already done that and found nothing."

Rena sighed and threw her cigar away in frustration. "I was a fool to get sucked into this thing. It's beginning to look more and more like I've spent time and money for nothing. But I'm into it now, so I'll have to stick it out to the end. Oh, well," she brightened, "at least with Longley out of the picture, there'll be nothing in the way of our enjoying each other. That will certainly make the time go easier." She gave him a sleepy look. "I've been lonely for you, Coop."

"I'm afraid not, Rena," he said gravely.

She went tense. "Now just what do you mean by that?"

"It simply means that I've gone as far as I'm going with you. I don't have many scruples, but I do draw the line at murder, and you murdered Evan Longley."

"You're a fool, Cooper Mayo." Her voice was a deadly hiss. "Nobody spurns me."

Grinning, he said, "There is a first time for everything, I guess."

"You'll regret this, that I promise . . ." She broke off to peer closely at him. "Does that also mean that you're backing out of our agreement?"

"If you mean in respect to any loot discovered at this dig, yes, it does. Call it a belated attack of conscience, call it anything you like, but don't depend on my cooperation from now on."

Without the slightest warning, she flew at him, long nails clawing for his eyes. Cooper ducked his head just in time, then seized her wrists in his hands. In the moonlight her eyes were wild, and trying to hold her was like trying to contain a sackful of scratching, clawing cats.

Then she dipped her head and fastened her teeth on his wrist. She bit down hard and Cooper let go with a bellow of pain, giving her a hard shove at the same time.

He risked a glance at his wrist to see blood bright and red, and that look came near to costing him his life. An instinct for survival sent warning signals to his brain, and he looked up to see Rena coming at him with a knife, held in both hands and raised high. The knife came down in a glittering, slashing arc, aimed for his neck. At the last moment, he twisted aside and down, coming up under her down-swinging arms. He caught her by the upper arms and clamped his hands cruelly, wrenching her to one side.

The knife flew out of her grip. Still holding her, Cooper took two steps and kicked the knife with the toe of his boot, sending it skittering deep into the rank underbrush.

Then he threw Rena from him. She hit the ground hard on her back. She was up on her elbows immediately, poised to spring at him again.

Standing over her, Cooper drew back his boot. As angry as he had ever been in his life, he snapped, "Rena, if you move so much as an inch, I'll break your jaw with my boot. It's a shame to have to threaten a lady like this, but then you're no lady."

He stood with his boot poised for a count of ten. He had never seen such a look of pure venom as was on her face. Then, slowly, she relaxed. Warily, Cooper stepped back a few feet. He nodded and she got to her feet.

With a last, lingering look, as though to imprint his features forever in her mind, she turned away, walked into the trees, and vanished like a wraith.

Cooper exhaled, a pent-up sigh of relief. He shivered, as if from a sudden chill, and strode out of the trees, his step unconsciously quickening. There was a crawly feeling between his shoulder blades until he was well free of the woods.

Cooper was the first to spot the four riders coming into the clearing from the southeast the next afternoon. Since the police had left behind several men to see that the excavation remained closed down, he had not bothered to post guards of his own.

When he saw the riders coming, he had been sitting partway up the pyramid. By the time he had climbed down to the ground, the approaching riders were close enough for him to recognize Meredith, Ricardo, and Juana. The fourth rider was a stranger, a Mexican in uniform.

Seeing him, Meredith waved. She was smiling happily. She pulled her horse in and slid down. "We can go back to work, Cooper!"

"Well now, how did that come about?"

"The murder of Evan has been solved, and through the offices of Luis Mendes, the authorities have been persuaded to allow us to continue." She nodded to the man in uniform. "He has a document making it official, to show to the man in charge here."

"That is good news," Cooper said slowly, his thoughts going back to the previous night and Rena Voltan. He had been sure in his mind that Rena had murdered Evan Longley. "Who is the culprit?"

Ricardo had also dismounted and now stood alongside Meredith. "The American, Harris Browder."

"Browder?" Cooper made no effort to hide his disbelief. "I wouldn't have figured him for it. I didn't think he had the guts."

"I suppose one never knows what is in a man's mind until it is revealed by his deeds," Ricardo said gravely. "In any event, the man Browder was found bound and gagged on the outskirts of Acapulco, with a note pinned to his shirt saying he was the murderer."

Cooper was still not convinced. "Did he admit it under questioning?"

"No, he denies it, naturally, but no one is inclined to believe his denials. He did have a strong motive, as we all know." Ricardo smiled. "Of course, Browder does not communicate well in our tongue, but since the police are content and it opens the way for us to resume digging, I see no reason for us to complain."

"I reckon you're right," Cooper said. His

310

thoughts were still on Rena. It seemed that she was going to get away with murder. Or could he be wrong? Maybe Harris Browder did kill Evan, after all . . .

His attention snapped back. Ricardo was speaking again, and there was a note of gladness in his voice that caused Cooper to tighten up inside.

". . . is now my wife!"

"I'm sorry. What were you saying?"

"While we were gone, Meredith agreed to become my wife." Ricardo, beaming fondly, took Meredith's hand. "We were married in Luis's home in Acapulco."

Cooper's glance skipped to Meredith. She was gazing at him steadily, an unreadable expression on her face. Rage boiled up in him, threatening to explode.

Ricardo said, "We would be pleased to have your best wishes, my friend . . ."

Cooper was given a moment's reprieve, as the police official came up, saying, "Could I be directed to Hernando Aragones, *por favor?*" He bounced the edge of a document against his palm. "I have official orders for him."

"I will take you to him, Señor," Cooper said, grateful for any excuse to escape for a moment, so he could get his temper under control and his thoughts in order. He motioned and started off.

"Cooper?" Ricardo called after him.

He halted and turned back, baring his teeth in a savage grin. "Sorry. Yeah, I wish you both a long and happy life together." He was looking

311

straight into Meredith's eyes, and was pleased to see her wince and look away. "I can just see both of you, getting old together and tottering around places like this one, digging into the earth like a pair of moles!"

Ricardo wore a puzzled frown. "Cooper, I do not understand . . ."

Meredith broke in, "Cooper, there is no call for your heavy-handed sarcasm!"

"Isn't there? Yeah, I guess you're right." He gestured. "If you really need my congratulations, Ricardo, you have them."

He strode on, motioning to the official to follow.

He was still seething inside, feeling that Meredith had somehow made a fool out of him. He had long since decided that Ricardo and Meredith were lovers, but had always assumed that she would eventually come to her senses and tire of the man.

But to marry him! What kind of a husband would a dull, academic type make for her? Ricardo Villalobos was a likable sort and Cooper had learned to tolerate him, but it had never occurred to him that she would up and marry him!

An inner voice mocked him. Jealous, Cooper? Well, yes, he had to admit that he was.

Damn the woman anyway! His life had been fouled up since the first moment he set eyes on her. Only the night before he had told Rena he was finished with both her and her schemes. And all out of misguided loyalty to Meredith

Longley, who had just shown what she really thought of him!

Rena Voltan was still furious with Cooper. She had brooded about his treachery all of the previous night and today, and was seized by a fit of trembling each time she thought of the scene in the trees. Several times she had been tempted to dispatch a couple of her men with rifles to hide near the pyramid, waiting for a chance to kill him. It would be easy enough to accomplish, since he strutted around the pyramid like a rooster, confident in his conceit that no one would *dare* harm him.

She had decided against having him killed for two reasons. Firstly there was a possibility that he might still be of some use to her; with Harris Browder disposed of, she was alone now, and she might need some help. She could not trust any of the thugs in her hire to aid her. If they learned that she had in her hands riches they had never dreamed of, they would fall on her like a pack of ravening wolves. But secondly, and more importantly, when it came time to kill Cooper Mayo, she wished to reserve that pleasure for herself.

She was still awake close to midnight, smoking another one of the innumerable cigars she had savaged that day, when one of the camp guards hurried up. "There is a man insisting on seeing you, Señorita Voltan," he said. "A *gringo*." He turned his head and spat.

"Cooper Mayo?"

"That is his name, yes."

Her first inclination was to order Cooper turned away. Then she changed her mind, chiefly out of curiosity, and told the guard to let Cooper through the picket line.

She was composed and cool when Cooper strolled up.

"What do you want, Mr. Mayo?"

"A word with you, Rena."

"I thought you had quite enough to say last night."

"A man should have the privilege of changing his mind, shouldn't he?" The dying fire cast enough light to show that the grin he wore was bitter and cynical, and Rena knew that he was hurting. This gave her a feeling of gleeful satisfaction and she wanted to probe at him until she found out the reason, but decided it would be best to bide her time.

"Mind telling me what changed your mind?"

"I'd mind, yeah. It won't help either of us to go into it. Just take my word that I have changed it, and I'll help you all I can from now on." He took a step closer, and she could smell the whiskey on his breath.

"Did you have to get drunk to come to me?" she asked with a sneer of contempt.

"I am not drunk, damnit!" he snapped. "I've had a couple of drinks. Well-deserved, I might add."

"Why deserved?"

He batted a hand at her. "That doesn't concern you, Rena. And let's get one thing clear . . . I have come back into the fold, in a manner

314

of speaking, but I am still my own man and not accountable to you. Is that understood?"

"Oh, I wouldn't have it any other way, Coop." She was amused now. "I would never want you to turn into a house cat." She stepped closer to him, fingering his shirt, making a purring sound. "And in that regard, why don't we go inside my tent for awhile? Unless you have to be back at a certain time and report to Longley? I understand she has returned, so that must be the reason you're here."

He went tense and took a step back. Then he relaxed, muttering, "Yeah, she's back. But I don't have to report to anybody."

"In that case, what are we waiting for?"

There was still some resistance as she tugged at his hand, but again he muttered, inaudibly this time, and came along.

Rena was still incensed at him, and more determined than ever that he would die when his usefulness was at an end, but at the same time she was exultant that her charms still drew him. It gave her a sense of power, and her pleasure was already beginning before they sprawled together on the blankets. She could sense that Cooper, in his present mood, was going to be rough and demanding, without it being necessary to prod him. She shivered.

As he reached for her, she stayed him with a hand flat against his chest. "One more thing, lover . . . if Longley has done something to hurt you, I'd be more than happy to take care of her."

"If I have any personal problems with Meredith Longley, which I don't admit to, I'll take care of them in my own way," he said harshly. "Now, why don't you just be quiet for a little?"

Work on the excavation resumed early the next morning. The crew was sadly reduced in number, but Ricardo had found a half-dozen men in Acapulco who had promised to report to the excavation as soon as possible. Meanwhile, Meredith decided to go ahead with the few men they had left. At least, with Ricardo and Cooper pitching in, they could still work at clearing the passageway, if at a slower pace.

Meredith had spent a restless night, despite the weariness brought on by her trip from Acapulco; the memory of Cooper's hurt look at the news of her marriage had been in her mind all night.

Cooper was already up when she and Ricardo emerged from her tent, and was squatting by the morning fire, sipping coffee from a tin cup. He glanced up at their approach, and his face assumed an expressionless glare. He merely grunted at Ricardo's cheerful greeting, then got up and wandered away with the cup of coffee. Ricardo stared after him with a worried frown.

Juana, who had been moved into Ricardo's old tent, was busy preparing their breakfast. She refused to look at Ricardo. She no longer made any pretense of her disapproval of the marriage, and Meredith was at a loss to understand why. At first she had thought perhaps the girl might be afraid that Meredith no longer wanted her around.

During their stay at the cottage, Juana had remained at the Mendes hacienda, and just before Meredith left for the excavation, she had tentatively asked Juana if she would prefer to stay permanently in the Mendes household. Juana had vehemently denied having any such desire, and began weeping, insisting that she wanted to remain with the Señorita Meredith. Meredith had hastily assured her that there was no need to worry, yet she was still deeply puzzled over Juana's attitude toward Ricardo.

Ricardo broke into her thoughts. "What is wrong with Cooper? He has been very strange since we came back. And that remark he made yesterday . . . I did not understand it."

"Don't ask me to explain Cooper Mayo. I have no way of knowing what is in that mind of his." Her voice had been sharper than she intended, and she had not once glanced at him.

"Meredith . . ." He took her hand. "Does Cooper care for you?"

"Don't be ridiculous! Cooper Mayo doesn't care for anybody but Cooper Mayo. And maybe his witch-woman!"

His expression told her that he was still unconvinced. He worried his lower lip. "Perhaps I should talk to him. Perhaps it is just a misunderstanding."

"No! You will do no such thing!" she said heatedly. "So what if it is a misunderstanding? We owe Cooper Mayo no explanations. I've been thinking . . . since our troubles seem to

317

be over, and we're in no more danger, maybe I should discharge him. We don't need him now."

Ricardo was shaking his head. "In that you are wrong, my dear. Gabriel Morales always poses a threat. And what about Rena Voltan? I doubt very much that she has given up. No, we need Cooper and his talents as much as ever."

"You could be right," she admitted reluctantly. "But just promise me you won't go talking to him." She shrugged. "He's probably just in one of his moods, anyway. Upset because we haven't found the so-called treasure."

Ricardo said softly, "I am sorry, my love. I did not mean to upset you unduly."

She said crossly, "Will you stop apologizing, for Heaven's sake! I am *not* upset!"

"Señorita?" said Juana's soft voice.

"What *is* it, Juana!"

Juana, holding a plate of food, backed up a step. "Your food, Señorita Meredith."

"I'm sorry. I apologize to both of you for being snappish." She shook her head dolefully and tried for a smile. "I don't know what's wrong with me."

"You're forgiven, my dear, not that there is really anything to forgive," Ricardo said, accepting a plate from Juana.

Meredith began to eat, her appetite gone. She really didn't understand why she was so touchy. Everything was finally going well—the excavation was open again, Evan's killer was in custody, and she was married to a fine, dear man who loved her. What more could she ask for?

But even as she tried to reassure herself, she was plagued by a feeling of discontent.

An hour later, back at work again, she soon forgot any dissatisfactions and became happily absorbed in her work.

Cooper and Ricardo had the crew busy working in the passageway again, and she was sketching some of the finds. But shortly after the noon meal, she finished sketching the last object and was at a loss for what to do next.

She considered going down to the passageway, but it was cramped down there, and she knew that she would only be in the way. Then she remembered the room they had discovered when the earth crumbled away beneath the two workers. Since the black rooster had been found slaughtered there, none of the men would go near it, and Meredith had remained away also.

What harm could it do to just look?

With a shake of her head she strode over to the hole made when the ground had fallen in. Standing on the edge, she peered down. On three sides was nothing but earth, but on the fourth side was a black hole. The ground had not caved in on that side, leaving a room opening.

Her curiosity was irresistible. Looking around, she saw a crude ladder made from poles lashed together. She hauled it over and dropped it into the pit. The ladder was just long enough to reach the bottom. She dallied for a moment, wondering if she should tell

319

someone what she was doing. She heard a muffled sound, like a footstep, behind her, and spun around. There was nothing there.

Without further delay, she put her foot on the first rung of the ladder and descended, testing each rung before she placed her foot on it. Finally, she reached the bottom and stood looking at the dark hole on the far side. She realized it was going to be dark inside and that she should have brought along a lantern.

But before she climbed back out, she decided it would do no harm to venture in as far as she could without a light. There was every chance that some important artifact could be found right away.

She went toward the opening with a firm step. Despite being open to the outside for some time, musty air came out, like a stale breath. Meredith had to stoop to step inside.

She advanced cautiously, carefully watching where she stepped and looking to each side. She was disappointed at what she saw. There were no artifacts visible; however, the walls of the chamber had caved in, leaving a narrow lane down the center, so there could be any number of priceless objects buried in the debris.

The light began to fail about ten yards in. Meredith halted, trying to squint into the dimness ahead of her. She could just make out what seemed to be a wall of stone ahead, and she judged she was about halfway into the room . . .

Stones rattled behind her and she whirled with a startled cry. Earth was raining down across the opening. This side of the hole was caving in!

She broke for the entrance at a dead run, but she was too late. Just before she reached it, the whole wall seemed to collapse, closing the opening like a door slamming.

Stygian darkness clamped down. She fell to her knees at the spot where the opening had been and began clawing at the wall of earth with her fingers, but even as she did so, she knew that it was hopeless. She would never be able to dig her way out this way.

How long would it be before she was missed? And even when she was found missing, they would not know where she was.

Enclosed as it was, the room had no opening for outside air to seep in. She was sealed off as effectively as if locked into a tomb. Already, it seemed to her, the room had become suffocating. How long would the supply of air last?

She tilted her head back and gulped a lungful of the stale air, her hands involuntarily clawing at her throat.

Panic washed over her in waves, and she opened her mouth and screamed, until her throat burned.

Chapter Nineteen

Meredith never knew how long she crouched there in darkness, but it seemed an eternity.

Trembling, she fought back the panic that threatened to overwhelm her reason and finally managed to regain control of her mind and body. She knew that blind fear was her enemy, and that she must try to think logically.

First, she must take stock of her resources. Rummaging in her pockets, her fingers touched a small tin of matches. This discovery cheered her immensely—just the possibility of light made the darkness less threatening. Opening the tin, she found six large wooden matches. She took one, struck it carefully on the ribbed bottom of the tin, and held it up. The small leaf of light seemed unbearably bright after the darkness.

In front of Meredith, the fall of earth loomed as thick and solid-looking as a stone wall. Quickly, she looked around her small prison, and saw nothing that might help her. And then she saw the shard, a large one of heavy earthenware, protruding from the dirt. She retrieved it just as the match burned down to her fingers. Feeling her way along the fall of earth, she began to scoop aside the dirt with the piece of pottery. It was probably comparable to trying to bail out the ocean with a spoon, she thought, but at least she was doing *something*!

Time passed as she continued to scratch at the fallen earth. Her arms grew numb, losing all feeling, but she kept doggedly on. Then she noticed that breathing was becoming difficult, and she knew that the air was running out. It wasn't her imagination this time!

Disheartened, she stopped digging and leaned forward, head falling onto her knees. Slowly, she became aware of an alien sound. It was a scraping noise, coming from the other side. Now she heard the pinging of metal on metal. They were digging through to her!

Drawing a deep breath, she shouted as loudly as she could, then listened intently. Then, at last, she heard a muffled shout in answer. She waited tensely, breathing shallowly to conserve the precious air, as the sounds of digging grew louder.

She heard a voice calling her name and she yelled in response.

"Stay back out of the way, Meredith. I think we are about to break through to you." It was Ricardo's voice, and startlingly close.

She moved back a few feet. A hole abruptly appeared in the wall of earth and light glinted off a shovel. A stream of fresh air poured in and Meredith gulped at it gratefully.

The hole enlarged rapidly. Cooper's face appeared in the opening. "Meredith, are you all right?"

"Yes, I think so."

"Sit tight, we're about to break through."

Moments later the hole was large enough for Ricardo to squeeze through. The room darkened briefly as his body closed off the light; then he was through and scrambling down the incline to her.

"Dear God, Meredith, I have been frantic!" He kneeled down and held her in a tight embrace. She shuddered, fighting back the tears of relief.

He held her away from him. "What happened? How did you get trapped in here?"

As she started to answer, Meredith saw the hole enlarged even further, and Cooper came through on all fours. She fell silent.

Ricardo gave her a slight shake. "Meredith, you have not answered me!"

"Later," she whispered, "I'll tell you later."

Then Cooper, face and clothes smeared with dirt, was upon them. Scowling down at her, he growled. "Goddamned stupid female! Didn't you have sense enough to know better than to come prowling about in here on your own? This room is a death trap, and it almost got you!"

"He's right, my love," Ricardo said. "It was foolish of you." He stood, reaching a hand down to her. "Let me help you up."

Angrily, she fended him off. "I don't need

any help." Standing, she was attacked by a wave of dizziness and swayed.

Both men caught her, one on each side, and Cooper said in a scolding voice, "Oh, no, you don't need any help. Not much you don't!"

They supported her to the opening, which was only large enough to accommodate one person at a time. Ricardo went through first, then waited while Cooper helped Meredith out.

Outside, with the full sunlight pouring down, Meredith experienced an overwhelming sense of relief, realizing just how frightened she had been in that dark chamber. It was a feeling akin to that of being rescued from the grave, after being buried alive.

The remaining crew members were already out of the pit and gathered on the edge, nervously peering down. A faint cheer went up as she emerged, but then they fell to whispering among themselves, and Meredith could catch enough to know that they were talking of the black rooster, and that they thought this area was cursed.

Restraining an urge to lash out at them in anger, she went up the pole ladder, Ricardo right behind her. Raul gave her a hand up to firm ground at last.

"We will give thanks to our God tonight for your safekeeping, Señora Meredith!" he said fervently. "You must never go near this accursed place again!"

Ricardo joined them, and taking Meredith's arm, he helped her toward her tent. Just as they were about to go inside, Juana rushed up, concern on her face, anxious to tend to her mistress.

"Wait, Juana." Meredith smiled wanly. "I'm grateful for your concern, but I'd like a few words with Ricardo first. Wait outside until I call you."

Juana remained outside, and they went on into the tent. Meredith sank down onto the cot.

Ricardo said, "I think you could use a drink of brandy, my love."

He poured brandy into a tin cup and handed it to her. Meredith drank, closing her eyes for a moment while the brandy warmed her. She began to relax a trifle, now that the ordeal was behind her, yet her thoughts were still troubled.

"Meredith, what is bothering you? I know you just went through a terrible experience, but you *were* careless, you must admit that."

Meredith opened her eyes. "I don't think it was an accident. I think someone did it deliberately."

He was shaking his head. "You are just upset."

"That's not it. I'm sure that I heard footsteps behind me just before I climbed down into that hole. I'm convinced someone caused that wall to cave in on me. Why would it suddenly give way like that?"

"My love, the earth layered over these ancient buildings is very untrustworthy. That's how the room was found in the first place, if you will recall." His eyes narrowed as he studied her. "However, I see that you are convinced otherwise. But who could it have been if you are right in your surmise?"

"Just how did you find me?"

"Well, let's see . . . I sent Raul to fetch you. He came back before very long and told me that he could not find you anywhere. We all went in search of you. Something drew me to that cave-in. When I saw the pole ladder and the wall fallen in, I knew that's where you were, behind it. We started digging frantically, and . . ." He gave that eloquent shrug. "You know the rest."

"Where was . . ." She took a deep breath. "Where was Cooper? Was he with you all the time?"

"No, I do not . . ." He paused in thought, then shook his head decisively. "We have been taking turns down in the passageway, as you know. Shortly before you were missed, it was my turn, and he went up on top. To smoke a cigar, he said." Ricardo smiled. "It's a little close down there for his cigars." His face went still. "Surely you don't think Cooper is responsible for the cave-in?"

"Somebody is, that I'm positive of."

"I do not believe Cooper is capable of that. You might as well suspect me," he said lightly. "I was also out of the passageway for a time."

"You have no reason, and he does."

"But you have absolutely no proof of this," he said slowly. "Do you?"

"No. But I could face him with it."

"That would not be wise, my darling. It

328

would only cause more discord, and we have enough of that."

"I suppose you're right." She sighed, pushing her fingers into her hair. "I'll just have to be more careful from now on."

Instantly solicitous, he touched her bowed head. "I had better leave, and send Juana in to care for you."

She nodded without raising her head, but just before he ducked under the tent flap, she glanced up. "You said you had sent Raul to look for me. For what reason?"

He frowned. "Oh . . ." His face lighted up. "I think we have reached the last obstruction in the passageway. We've broken through one corner, and can see a door just beyond. I thought perhaps you would want to be there when we remove the last stones."

"Oh, I do!" She jumped up, excitement coursing through her. Her recent ordeal was all but forgotten.

"Do you think you should?" he said dubiously. "After what you have just been through?"

"I wouldn't miss it for the world. This could be our most important find yet!"

While the last stone was being removed from the wall across the passageway, Meredith waited impatiently in the outer room.

When at last the crew dragged the great block past her, she was into the passageway before the dust had a chance to settle. Crowding between Cooper and Ricardo, she looked into the dark space only partially illuminated by the light of the lanterns.

Ricardo, holding a lantern out before him, pushed past her, and the light shone on the walls and ceiling, exposing a sight that caused Meredith to gasp in surprise and awe.

Behind her, Cooper whispered, "My God!"

The walls, ceiling and floor were coated with gleaming, white plaster, and upon this surface, vivid figures, breathtaking in their artistry, glowed with jewel-like colors.

At this point, Cooper faced the digging crew in the passageway, and ordered them outside, explaining that the room was protected by *Mictecacihuatl* and that he, Ricardo, and Meredith would enter the newly found section alone. Only if they called out, or did not return, was the crew to come into the passageway. The men left, talking nervously among themselves, and Meredith and the two men were left alone to examine their find.

Ricardo and Cooper moved cautiously forward, holding their lanterns high. Before them was a doorway, with one huge, flat stone covering the entrance. The surfaces of the door and the lintel were elaborately carved, the doorway bearing in bas-relief the form of a large solar disc, richly colored and confusing in the complexity of its detail. For a long moment they stood in silence, awed by this testament to a great civilization.

"Look!"

Ricardo held his lantern close to the door, and Meredith caught the rich gleam of gold. As if drawn by an invisible thread, she stepped toward the door, Cooper beside her. At the edge of the door, on the left side, a large seal of pure gold bonded the door to the wall.

Rectangular in shape and bearing the imprint of a jaguar's head, the seal was about eight by four inches in size.

"Here, Meredith." Ricardo's voice trembled as he spoke. Without looking at her, he handed the lantern to Meredith and reached into his pocket. Taking out a heavy pocket knife, he unsheathed a blade and reached for the golden seal.

Meredith's heart was beating furiously and she felt as if she could not breathe.

Carefully, Ricardo edged the tip of the knife blade under the seal and gently pried it free. The soft gold came away easily, and in a moment the precious rectangle was cupped in Ricardo's hand, gleaming richly.

Reverently, he handed the seal to Meredith and turned his attention to the door, pushing first one side, then the other.

As he pushed at the left side, the door moved slightly.

"Cooper!" Ricardo said excitedly.

Cooper, reluctantly moving away from Meredith and their study of the seal, set his own lantern on the floor, and stepped over to join Ricardo. Together, they shoved against the left side of the door and slowly, with the sound of stone grating on stone, the door inched inward.

Meredith feared she might faint, so great was her anticipation. Her hands were heavy with the weight of the ancient artifact, as the door swung in, and the doorway was open on two sides of the stone, which now stood parallel to the walls.

Both Cooper and Ricardo snatched up their lanterns and rushed through the openings, one on each side of the center stone.

Meredith was just behind them, and as the rays of their lanterns illuminated the area on the other side of the door, she cried out. The whole chamber shone with the warm yellow of gold. It seemed to her, in that first excited glance, that the entire floor of the room was paved with precious metal. Only after a moment had passed, was she able to distinguish individual objects—a huge solar disc against the far wall; plates; cups; small figures; jewelry, all spread out neatly upon the floor and resting against the walls; and scattered among these golden treasures, she caught an occasional flash of green jade and the sparkle of crystal.

Transfixed, all three of them stood as still as the great stone statues in each of the four corners of the chamber.

Slowly, Meredith raised her eyes to Ricardo's face. His expression was fixed—eyes wide and staring—but she could not tell whether in joy or fear.

Turning her head, she gazed at Cooper. He did not notice her and she sensed that, at this moment, nothing existed for him except the room and its treasure.

Her own elation slowly dissolved. She felt apprehension, like a breath of icy air, and that touch brought a premonition that this golden hoard would bring them nothing but unhappiness and trouble.

Then Ricardo, shaking himself like a man awakening from a dream, stepped further into the room, looking around.

"It's not here," he said loudly.

Meredith, confused, frowned at him. "What, Ricardo? What's not here?"

"Why, the Man of Gold, *El Hombre de Oro*! He is not here!"

Chapter Twenty

Cooper moved to the center of the chamber, turning with his lantern so that the light reached all the corners.

Meredith's gaze followed the sweep of light. It was true; although a wondrous collection of golden objects filled the room, nowhere among them was the fabled figure, the Man of Gold.

She placed her hand on Ricardo's arm, smiling. "But what does that matter? There are so many other things, so many wonderful things!"

Cooper grunted. "That's for sure. I don't think I ever really believed the treasure was here. My God! It's worth a fortune! What's one more statue, more or less?"

Ricardo shook his head stubbornly. "You do not understand. The find is fabulous, true, more so than I had dreamed, but *El Hombre de Oro* . . . well, he represents something more. He is legend. But," he shrugged, "you are both right. In the face of this tremendous discovery,

335

it would be insane to mourn for one piece which is not here."

Cooper had been roaming around the perimeter of the room and now he exclaimed, "Hey, Ricardo, come over here! There's another door, damned if there isn't, here next to the corner. And it doesn't seem to be sealed."

Meredith held one of the lanterns high, while the men pushed at this second, ornately carved door. Low and narrow, as if constructed with a child in mind, it yielded easily to the men's strength; it turned on a central pivot, as had the outer door.

As the door swung slowly open, Cooper fell back from it. "Whew! The air's foul in there. Let it stay open for a moment before we go in."

But Ricardo was already pushing through the narrow aperture, bending down to do so. As he entered the room, he shouted exultantly, and Meredith and Cooper immediately rushed in after him.

The first thing Meredith noticed was the stale, faintly rank odor of the new chamber, and then, there against the far wall, she saw it—the figure of a man, life-sized and shining. The room was not large, and she was not more than eighteen feet from him, as he stood erect and regal among the possessions that had been arranged all around him for his trip into the other world.

El Hombre de Oro was short by modern standards, shorter than Meredith herself, perhaps five feet one. Around his waist was an elaborately embroidered loincloth, and a per-

336

fectly preserved feathered headdress crowned him. Jade earplugs hung from his earlobes, and gold and jade bracelets ornamented his arms. Around his neck a magnificent pectoral, set with precious stones, fell to cover his breast. On his feet were sandals of pure gold.

As far as Meredith could see, he was in every feature the copy of a real man, but his body glowed with the luster of gold.

Meredith and Cooper stood frozen in place, but Ricardo inched slowly forward until he was near enough to touch the figure. Carefully, he stretched out his hand, and touched the arm of the Man of Gold, then just as carefully withdrew it.

Meredith felt overwhelmed and weak. This figure alone was a discovery without equal. Her father's vision had been proven. His name, as well as their own, would go down in the annals of archaeology along with Schliemann's.

Then Ricardo made a strange sound, almost like the sound of laughter, turned toward them, his face bearing an odd expression.

Meredith said, "What is it? What's wrong?"

He smiled wryly. "Well, we have found *El Hombre de Oro*, my dear, but like many men, he is not quite as advertised."

"I don't understand . . ."

Cooper stepped toward the figure, raising his lantern so that it shone full upon it. "What do you mean? Hell, he looks great to me!"

Ricardo faced around. "So he does, my friend. There is only one thing wrong. He is not made of gold."

337

Cooper stared at him, his expression puzzled and faintly hostile. "Just what are you getting at, Villalobos?"

"Just this."

Ricardo took Meredith's hand, and led her to the figure. "Here, my love. Touch him. Rap your knuckles against his arm, there at the shoulder."

Reluctantly, Meredith did as she was told, with the feeling that what she was doing approached sacrilege. She fingered the smooth touch of metal, but the feeling was vaguely wrong. With some hesitation, she finally rapped her knuckles briskly against the shoulder of the figure, and at once drew back. There was no ring of metal, no feel of solid mass; instead it was as if she had knocked against a figure of leather or papier-maché.

Cooper stepped in front of her, also rapping the figure. He turned a puzzled frown on Ricardo. "It's not solid gold. There's just a thin coating on the outside!"

Ricardo nodded. "Exactly, my friend. The gold is gold leaf, thicker than what we usually see, but gold leaf, nonetheless."

Meredith sucked in her breath. "Then, what's . . . ?" She tried again, "What's underneath?"

Ricardo smiled grimly. "The body of a man, my love. The mummified remains of an ancient king, or a priest."

For a moment Meredith was stunned, then the import of his words sank in. "But that's

338

even better!" she cried. "In an archaeological sense, this is much more important than finding a golden statue!"

Ricardo was staring at the golden mummy. "Yes, that is true. It is a remarkable find."

Cooper, still gazing at the figure, shook his head. "Well, I, for one, would have preferred the gold statue, but I will have to admit that it is something to see, anyway." His glance switched to Ricardo. "Why did they do that, cover him with gold?"

"It had to do with their religion, I should think. Gold was the metal of the sun, and they worshipped the sun. The ancient peoples are said to have had a ceremony where a king or a priest covered his body with gold dust, and then immersed himself in a sacred lake while the sun rose in the sky, as an offering to their god. It is the legend of *El Dorado*, my friend. Perhaps this is related in some way. At any rate, our prince, or priest, was not going poor or unprotected into the land beyond death."

Cooper gently touched the golden pectoral. "How long do you think he's been here?"

"A thousand years, I would say. Although I would have to also say that he is far more recent than the pyramid above us."

Cooper shook his head in wonder. "My God, that's incredible!"

Ricardo nodded. "Yes, it gives one a sense of humility, does it not?"

Meredith, who had been looking around the chamber as they talked, clutched at his arm. "Oh, Ricardo! There are so many wonderful

339

things here: baskets, bowls, pottery figures, and all unbroken. I can't believe it!"

He patted her hand. "Well, it is for real, my love. And it is ours."

Meredith smiled up at him. "No, it belongs to the world," she said happily. "And, oh, how surprised the world is going to be! We will be famous!"

Cooper held up his lantern and shook it. "We'd better get out of here. The lanterns are burning low. Impressed as I am with all this, I'd hate to be caught down here in the dark. Let's go above ground."

He started from the room, and reluctantly Meredith and Ricardo followed. As they left the room, pushing the door shut behind them, Ricardo said, "You know, as soon as the outside world learns of this, there will be hundreds of gold-hungry adventurers swarming over the site. I think it would be best to keep quiet about this for the moment."

Meredith brightened, then sighed. "But we promised Señor Mendes that we would notify him, and the government, the minute we found anything of value."

Ricardo raised his free hand. "I do not mean that we should keep it a secret forever, only for a short time. Until we can catalogue the items and make sure that we have a list of everything we have found. We will need some time to do this. Also, we must get everything ready for transport."

They were leaving the outer room now, and

there was a silence while the two men pushed the heavier outer door shut.

When it was closed, Cooper said, "I think he's right, boss lady. Also, there are the men to consider. I've known men to eliminate a whole village for one hundredth of the gold in that room. I don't think it would be wise for them to know about it. In fact, I think we should do our damndest to keep them in the dark."

Meredith, literally dizzy with what she had just seen, found it hard to concentrate on mundane matters, but she forced herself to think logically. "You're both right, of course. We can wrap all the items. I brought along burlap and other wrapping material. That way, the men need never know what we've found. However, it *will* take some time to accomplish."

They had reached the doorway to the outer room, where they paused before going up the steps. Cooper took out a cigar and examined it carefully. "Well, I'll go along with whatever you two decide. I don't owe the Mexican government a damned thing, so a delay is not going to bother me a whit. The only thing is, all that gold and stuff makes me very nervous just lying about down here. We'd better set up a guard, and we better make damned sure that the guard doesn't get nosy."

At that moment Meredith heard a call from above. She stepped out of the room and peered up. Raul was on the top step, fearfully looking down at her. "Yes, Raul? What is it?"

"We have heard nothing for a long time,

Señora," he said nervously. "I was afraid . . ."

"Nothing is wrong, Raul. Go back and join the others. We will be up shortly."

Meredith stepped back into the room. They were quiet again, and Meredith had the feeling that the three of them were reluctant to leave that magnificent treasure behind them.

"You know, I *am* afraid to leave it," she burst out. "I'm afraid that it might vanish during the night, as silly as that probably sounds. We've got to protect it, but how? If we set up a guard, what's to prevent him from getting curious and investigating the passageway, then finding those two rooms? Oh, Lord, this all so complicated!"

Cooper's lantern finally guttered out and he set it down. "Well, I've got an idea about that, one that might work, but it'll take a little play-acting on your part, boss lady."

She squinted at him suspiciously. "Play-acting? What do you mean?"

"The men are already frightened and nervous as hell. If you scream, then we all come piling out of here, acting as if we'd seen something terrible . . . I think that would tend to put a damper on their curiosity. What do you think?"

Ricardo chuckled. "I think it sounds like a possible solution to a difficult problem. My dear, can you manage a good scream?"

She said dubiously, "I suppose so, at least I can try. Do you want a really terrified scream, or only a slightly frightened one?"

Cooper drew on his cigar and, in the faint

342

glow, she saw the amusement on his face, but his voice was sober enough when he drawled, "Somewhere in between the two, I'd reckon. We don't want to overdo it. Then we'll all dash up the steps, and Meredith, it might help some if you pretended to faint. I'll catch you, don't worry."

She said curtly, "I think Ricardo had better handle that part. Shall I scream now?"

"Yeah. Why not?"

Meredith took a deep breath and screamed as loudly as she could. The sound, in the stone-walled chamber, was shockingly loud. Then Ricardo grabbed her hand and they ran for the steps, bounding up them as if something or someone was pursuing them.

When they reached the top, Meredith passed a hand over her eyes and moaned softly. With a watchful eye on Ricardo's position, she grace-fully folded in what she hoped was a good ap-proximation of a swoon. Ricardo caught her in his arms, and both he and Cooper hovered over her.

From beneath her partially closed lids, Mere-dith could see Raul and the rest of the crew in the background. Their faces were set in expres-sions of fear, and she felt guilty for fooling them, even if it was for a good cause.

As she permitted Ricardo to support her to-ward their tent, Meredith could hear Cooper talking to the men, telling them that the spirits of the pyramid were angry, and that for the moment, no one must go into the rooms below.

In the tent, Ricardo pulled Meredith close

and kissed her lips. Then, looking down at her, he smiled broadly. "Ah, my love. Now I will be able to give you the sort of life that you deserve. We shall be so happy . . ."

He broke off, as Cooper without warning, pushed his way into the tent.

Meredith did not bother to keep the annoyance out of her voice. "Cooper, don't you ever knock?"

"Hardly ever, boss lady." Cooper grinned, and took off his hat, bowing with mock humility. "I thought you'd want to hear how I set up protection for the rooms. I didn't know that I would catch you in a, uh, tender moment." His voice was mocking, and so was his grin, yet there was something in his eyes that troubled Meredith and made her uneasy.

Ricardo, releasing her, handled the situation with his usual gracious manner. "You are quite right, my friend. We do want to hear your report, and I think we are all due for a celebration. I happen to have a bottle of very fine brandy put away for just such an occasion. We shall drink a toast to our discovery, and you shall tell us what you have arranged."

Glasses were brought out and the brandy was poured. Meredith let the liquor trickle down her throat and felt it warm her throat and stomach. She had the oddest feeling, and it worried her that she could not get a fix on what was wrong. Nerves, she decided. After all, it had been a rather strenuous afternoon, emotionally speaking.

"We've put a large slab of stone over the

344

outer doorway," Cooper was saying, "and I drew some symbols on it, and told the crew that the markings would keep the spirits inside. I had a little trouble in getting them to stand guard, but I think I convinced them that as long as they stayed on the outside of the door, we are all safe. I told them that a guard was necessary, not just to keep the spirits in, but to keep anyone from moving the stone, and letting the spirits out." He grinned lazily, taking a sip of brandy. "Raul is standing first guard. I gave him an amulet to protect him and told him to pass it on to the next man on guard. Raul's out there now, patrolling back and forth as if the safety of the whole damned camp depends on him."

Meredith shivered. "Maybe it does."

Ricardo glanced at her with a quick frown. "What do you mean?"

She shrugged. "Oh, I don't know. I don't even know why I said that. I guess I'm just tired and a little overemotional."

Ricardo smiled. "I believe I can safely say that we are all in an emotional state. After all, it is not every day that one discovers the dream of a lifetime. Here, have another sip of brandy. It will relax you."

He turned his attention to Cooper. "Now, when we wish to enter the underground chambers to start our work, what do we tell the men then? I should like to get started early in the morning."

Cooper smiled in a self-satisfied manner and poured himself a half a glass of brandy. "Oh,

I've taken care of that, don't worry. We'll simply tell them that we're bringing gifts for the spirits; that we are placating the spirits with ceremonies and offerings; and that we are well-protected by our own magic, which we have been making here tonight. I think they'll buy that."

Ricardo nodded thoughtfully. "I believe it is an excellent plan. My friend, you have done well. Meredith and I will never forget what you have done for us. We will see that you share in the glory of the discovery."

Cooper's smile twisted briefly sideways, and his eyes darkened, before his face assumed its usual expression. "Now I really appreciate that, *amigo*. Usually I'm more interested in the money. But glory?" He shrugged wryly. "What the hell!"

By the time the evening meal was served around the campfire, Ricardo was more than a little tipsy. Face flushed, he became extremely jovial, and could not seem to stop talking about their great discovery.

Meredith had never seen him quite like this, but she thought she could understand his jubilation. All his life Ricardo's interest in archaeology had come to nothing, and now he was faced with sudden and overwhelming success. She smiled at him indulgently and became a little tipsy herself.

Cooper said very little, just drank steadily, smoked his cigars, and watched them from a face as inscrutable as an Indian's.

Ricardo finally broke off his near-monologue when Juana came bearing plates with their dinner. All ate hungrily and the food seemed to sober Ricardo a trifle. After the meal he became loving, embarrassingly so. When Juana had taken away the plates, he moved close to Meredith, put his arms around her shoulders, and pulled her against him.

"This is our day of triumph, my love, and it is one we will remember for the rest of our lives." He kissed her cheek.

Meredith darted a look at Cooper, who was watching them broodingly. Catching her gaze on him, he exhaled smoke, hiding his face.

"We are not alone, Ricardo!" she said sharply.

"What?" He reared back. "Oh . . . you mean Cooper? He is my friend, my *compadre*. He knows the love we have for each other."

"Just the same, I don't think . . ."

"I believe I'll turn in. It's been a long, rough day," Cooper said, getting to his feet. "And leave you two lovebirds alone."

With a nod, he moved off into the dark. Meredith's gaze followed him. She saw him throw his cigar away, the burning end tumbling over and over in the night. Then he stretched out on his blankets.

"Dear heart," Ricardo whispered into her ear, "shall we retire as well?"

"Let's!" she cried gaily, in a carrying voice. She stood up, pulling him up with her.

On the way to their tent, they passed within a few feet of Cooper's blankets. Meredith

347

laughed loudly and was immediately ashamed of herself.

Ricardo was more forceful in his love-making that night, taking her with an ardor that took her breath away. She soon caught fire from his caresses and responded in kind.

She went to sleep in his arms.

The sun was shining through the canvas when she awoke. Ricardo sat upright when she stirred. For a brief moment he looked disoriented, glancing around wildly. His glance lit on her and he smiled.

"Good morning, my love. Did you sleep well?"

"Like a rock." She stretched. "And I'm starved."

"So am I. But first . . ." He jumped up from the cot and began dressing. "I must sneak a look at *El Hombre de Oro*. Do you know, I dreamed about him in the night?"

"Honestly, darling." She laughed. "Can't it wait until after we have breakfast?"

"Just a quick look." His smile was teasing. "Now don't tell me you would not like another look?"

"Oh, very well," she said with feigned ill-humor. She began dressing.

Outside the tent, she saw Juana looking over inquiringly from the cooking fire. Meredith called over, "You can start breakfast, Juana. We will be back shortly, and hungry."

As they hurried toward the pyramid, Meredith noticed that Cooper's blankets were empty.

She raked the campground with a glance, but did not see him anywhere. At the pyramid, the area around the steps was deserted. Raul was not in sight from the top of the steps, and the slab was pulled aside, leaving the entryway half open. Meredith's heart felt like it was beating in her throat, and she began to feel sick to her stomach.

She looked at Ricardo, and saw that his face had gone white. They exchanged fearful glances, then Ricardo raced down the steps and into the room. Meredith followed close on his heels.

As she came into the outer room, she called Raul's name, but there was no answer, save the echoes of her own voice.

Ricardo, not waiting for her, had lighted a lantern and was already plunging down the passageway. Meredith lit another lantern, and followed him as quickly as she could.

Then, partway down the passageway, she saw Raul on the ground; he was bound hand and foot, and gagged.

Ahead of her, Ricardo cried out, "The door! It's open!"

Meredith fell to her knees beside Raul. She felt for a pulse, and after a moment she was rewarded with a thready beat. She fumbled the gag loose and propped his head up.

"Raul? Are you all right? What has happened here?"

He made an effort to talk, but the words he spoke were unintelligible.

Again, she heard Ricardo cry out. She got to

349

her feet, as he came stumbling down the passageway toward her. In the light of the lantern, his face was livid, his eyes wild and staring.

"What's wrong, Ricardo?"

"The treasure!" he gasped out. "It is gone! Everything has been taken!"

Chapter Twenty-One

With a gasp Meredith ran toward Ricardo. He slumped against the wall, as if all energy had been drained from his body. Pushing past him, she ran to the open door of the treasure chamber.

Holding her lantern above her head, she hurried into the room. The treasure was gone, as if it had never existed! In disbelief, she swept all corners of the room with lantern light, but there was no doubt—the chamber was empty, save for a few simple pieces that had no monetary value.

Meredith realized that she was moaning under her breath. My God! How could this have happened? Who could be responsible? Rena Voltan? Gabriel Morales? Cooper? Her mind shied away from this last thought.

Finally, she forced herself to duck down through the low doorway to the inner room. Had they taken *El Hombre de Oro* as well?

Standing up inside the chamber, she raised

the lantern and breathed a sigh of relief. The Man of Gold was undisturbed. Also, the pottery vessels and other artifacts had not been touched. At least they were left with something. They could still go on with the dig. *El Hombre de Oro* alone was a marvelous discovery . . .

She gave a harsh bark of laughter. She was deluding herself. Any hope of pursuing their normal work here had vanished with the treasure. Luis Mendes and the Mexican government would have to be informed now, and she, as well as Ricardo, would be fortunate if they were not immediately imprisoned. It had been a mistake not to have notified Mendes the minute they had found the treasure, and Meredith knew that she was going to regret it. At least if a message had been sent, no one could really fault them now, but how could they explain, after the fact, that their discovery had not been reported at once?

Meredith sighed again, and returned to the passageway with a dragging step. Ricardo was standing where she had left him, that stunned look still on his face. She started to speak to him, when a weak voice said, "Señora Meredith?"

"Ah, Raul, I'm sorry!" She had entirely forgotten his presence. She kneeled beside him and began working on his bonds. "Are you hurt?"

"I was not harmed badly, just tied up and then left here."

"What happened?"

She had his hands untied now, and Raul

winced with pain at the restored circulation. "It was Señor Mayo," he said sadly. "He announced his presence, then came on to tell me that he was checking to see if everything was in order. Before I realized his intention, he struck me on the jaw. Here . . ." He fingered his jaw, grimacing. "I was knocked unconscious. When I came to, I was tied and gagged, like you found me."

Meredith was surprised at the depth of her disappointment and sorrow. She had known all along that Cooper was untrustworthy, hadn't she?

She was working on the ropes around Raul's ankles now. She said dully, "Was anyone with him?".

"I think so, Señora." He frowned. "But I do not know who, or how many there were. When I came to, my face was turned to the wall and I could not see who came and went, but I heard footsteps of more than one person."

"A woman?" she asked. "Did you hear a woman?"

He shook his head. "I am sorry, Señora Meredith. I do not know."

"There, your feet are free." Meredith stood up. "I'd advise waiting until your circulation returns before getting to your feet."

Beside her Ricardo said in a thick voice, "Did I hear correctly? The thief was Cooper Mayo?"

"You heard correctly, Ricardo." She looked around at him.

His face was set in anger, his mouth working. His hands opened and closed at his sides. "I will see that he dies for this villainy!"

"It's a little late for that," she said dryly. "And since he has a good start, catching him won't be easy. How do we even know which direction he took?"

She heard her voice as if from a great distance; she felt removed from the scene, and finally perceived that she was suffering from shock.

She tried to concentrate on Ricardo's words: ". . . find him! We must leave here at once, so I can telegraph Luis what has happened . . ."

"He isn't going to be happy with us."

He rode over her words. "And he will notify the proper authorities, so a search can be instituted at once. All of Mexico will be alerted, the borders closed to Señor Mayo. He will not escape!" Ricardo gritted his teeth. "He cannot be allowed to escape! If he does, all that we have worked for so long and hard will come to nothing!"

Raul was on his feet now, and he limped ahead of them as they left the passageway and went above ground.

Ricardo had regained some measure of calm now, and he took charge. "Raul, we have to leave the excavation again. We will leave you in command in our absence. Hopefully, it will not be for long. Work will have to halt while we are gone, but it shall be your task to keep the crew together. When the men I employed in Acapulco arrive, you can devote your time to instructing them in how to conduct a dig, so they

354

will be of some use to us when we resume work."

"Yes, Señor," Raul said doubtfully. His glance went to Meredith. "Señora Meredith?"

She gestured lifelessly. "Do whatever Ricardo says, Raul. But I don't see why . . ." She turned to Ricardo. "What's the point of keeping them here? You must know that your government will never allow us to continue the dig. Not even Luis coming to our aid will help this time, and I doubt very much that he will want to now."

"We shall see," Ricardo said cryptically. "Why don't you go to your tent and rest, my love? You have had a great shock."

"I thought we were leaving right away?"

"I have changed my mind about that. I spoke without thinking. First, I must see that everything is under control here, and it is better that we get an early start in the morning. You rest, then pack your traveling things. Mine as well, as I probably won't return to our tent until much later." He smiled fleetingly and kissed her on the forehead. "Trust me, Meredith."

Meredith merely nodded and trudged off toward their tent. Juana was still occupied at the campfire. Seeing Meredith approach, she started toward her with a frown.

Meredith motioned wearily. "Continue with what you're doing, Juana. I don't need you. I don't feel well, I'm going to lie down for a while."

Inside the tent, Meredith finally broke, her state of apathy shattering like a glass shell. Despite telling herself that Cooper's awful perfidy did not matter, it did matter. It mattered more than she would have thought possible.

Tears came, a flood of tears, accompanied by great, wracking sobs, ripping at her until her muscles were sore. Once, Juana ventured timidly into the tent, and Meredith angrily motioned her out. She wept for a long time.

Cooper was not as jubilant about getting away with the treasure as he had anticipated he would be. But then, he thought wryly, Rena was happy enough for both of them. He glanced over at her. She rode along on her horse, humming under her breath, from time to time looking fondly at the four chests bobbing up and down on the backs of the mules, which plodded along between them. He could not remember a time when he had heard her sing.

She had been happy from the moment when he had led her into that underground chamber and ceremoniously waved his hand around. Her eyes had reflected the gleam from the precious metal on the floor of the room, and she had closed them, shuddering as though in the climactic moment of passion.

Then she had become businesslike, as they quickly scooped the riches into the four chests they had brought along with them. Rena's crew had been told to wait above ground until she summoned them.

Once, on her knees, Rena stopped and looked over at him with eyes almost mad in their greed. "This is the world, Coop, I've got the world here in my hands," she whispered. She held out her cupped hands, as if in offering. "You know what I'd like at this moment?" She licked her lips. "I would like you to take me right here, on the ground! Wouldn't that be a great way to celebrate?"

"This is hardly the time or the place," he said in a dry voice. "We don't have all the time in the world. Ricardo Villalobos is itchy. He might wake up at any time, and come prowling around to check on all this."

"You're right." She bobbed her head and feverishly continued picking up the gold.

She wouldn't allow him to lock and chain the chests until she had combed every inch of the floor on her knees, the lantern held high. Finally, she scuttled back to him, holding out a hand with several pieces cupped in her palm.

"You see what you would have left behind?"

Cooper thought briefly of the Man of Gold in the inner chamber. Should he show it to Rena? Somehow he didn't like to think of her greedy fingers on that ancient body. Besides, he might as well leave Meredith a token as a gesture of his contempt. Let them have their Man of Gold and his few trinkets. He and Rena had the rest of it!

When the chests were securely fastened and the large sun disc wrapped in blankets, they pulled the treasure out of the room and to the other side of the door.

Grunting with effort, Cooper said, "My God, they must weigh a ton!"

"The better for us, lover! The better for us!"

Rena chuckled and ran her hands lasciviously over the chests.

Cooper waited in the dark while she hurried above ground, summoning her men to take the chests out and load them aboard the waiting mules. She returned with the men and an extra lantern.

They lingered behind until the men had lugged the chests out of the passageway. Then, from her person, Rena produced a knife and started for the bound figure of Raul.

Cooper caught her by the arm. "What the hell do you think you're doing?" he said in a tense whisper.

She motioned to Raul and made a slicing motion across her throat with the knife blade.

Seizing her arm, he pulled her down the passageway, out of Raul's hearing, before he released her. "You're a bloodthirsty bitch, Rena! There is no need for unnecessary killings!

"And you're a fool, Coop! That kid could identify you, as well as me!"

He shook his head. "Not you, he didn't get a look at you. As for me, what difference does it make? When they find me gone in the morning and the treasure gone with me, it won't take the smartest person in the world to figure out that I had a hand in it."

"And you don't care?"

"If everything goes like we planned, and I can get out of the country with the gold and my hide intact, it won't matter."

Rena shrugged, rubbing her arm where he'd grabbed her, and then put the knife away. They began walking on down the stone-walled corridor.

She said, "It doesn't bother you that Longley will know you for a thief?"

"Not all that much. What the hell, I *am* a thief."

She cocked her head, a sly smile tugging at the corners of her mouth. "Do you suppose she will miss you, Coop?"

He plunged along without looking at her. "I can't think of any reason why she should. She's got her archaeologist."

"And you've got me, huh, lover?" She hooked an arm in his, pulling it down until Cooper could feel the firmness of her breast.

"We've got each other, would be more like it."

When they arrived on top, Rena's thugs were waiting for orders. Cooper supervised loading the chests and the disc onto the mules. They were as quiet as possible, speaking in whispers, but Cooper was tense as a strung wire every second, fearful that they would be heard and an alarm given. He did not wish to have to shoot anyone, yet he knew he would have no choice if the camp was aroused. Certainly, Rena would have no qualms; she would cheerfully massacre the entire Longley crew, if it came to that.

But finally they were away, with no hue and cry raised behind them. By moonlight, they found the faint trail leading in the direction of Acapulco and Cooper could breathe easier. Despite their getting away free and clear, and with enough booty in the chests to set him up for life, he jogged along on his horse in a state of depression. He had no explanation for it, and not by nature given to self-analysis, he tried not to dwell on it too much.

Now, here they were well on their way to Acapulco, and he was jumpy as a plucked chicken. Part of the reason for that had to do with the action Rena had taken shortly after daylight this morning. She had dismissed all of her crew, paying them off and sending them on their way, and now the pair of them rode alone, guarding a king's ransom.

Cooper kept alert as possible after the long night with no sleep, constantly scanning the trail ahead and behind, his ears straining for the slightest foreign sound.

He heard a hoot of laughter from Rena, and glanced over at her inquiringly. "Something funny?"

"You are, Coop. I've never seen you so spooked."

"I've got reason to be. I wouldn't put it past those hardcases you let go to double back and sneak up on us. They sure as hell will if they have any inkling of what we have in those chests."

"But they don't have, Coop. They're as stupid as a flock of geese."

"You have a tendency to underestimate other people's intelligence."

"And usually with good cause."

"It wouldn't have hurt anything to have kept them around, at least until we get near the coast."

"The longer they were around, the more chance they would have had of finding out." She shrugged. "They don't suspect a thing."

"You hope," he said grimly. "Don't you suppose they ever wondered why you've hung around that excavation for so long?"

"I told them that I had some old scores to settle, with Evan Longley and his sister, that the pair of them had double-crossed me. They understand things like that." She smiled and winked. "I'm not worried, lover. I have no doubt that you could handle them, if they were so stupid as to try anything."

"Your confidence is touching," he said sourly. "But it's done now, nothing to do but ride it out. This gent with the boat in Acapulco, you sure he'll be waiting? A smuggler, you say?"

"Yes, he owns a good-sized boat and makes his living, such as it is, smuggling people, among other things, out of the country. He was quite busy during the Revolution." She was smiling. "Earl Harkness is a rogue, Coop, just like you."

Cooper grunted. "Of course you know that the word is going to be out long before we get to the coast, and it's more than likely that the Mexican authorities will round up all such rogues, fearing that they might be used for what we have in mind."

"Don't worry, Coop. Harkness is a slick one. The authorities can't guard every mile of Mexico's coastline, and they have no navy, at least not to speak of. Harkness steers clear of the

361

port towns like Acapulco. He uses a small fishing village some distance from Acapulco for his headquarters. All we have to do is make our way close, get in touch with him, load these chests on board his boat, and sail away. There'll be no problems."

"You seem to have it all worked out pretty well," he said dourly. So well, in fact, that he had to wonder why she had recruited him in the first place. Certainly it would seem that now, with the loot found and spirited away, she had little use for him.

As if reading his thoughts, Rena said cheerfully, "I need you, Coop. Harkness is a worse rogue than you, and I don't trust him. He might take it in his head to pull a double-cross on me, and how could I defend myself? Me, just a woman?"

He snorted. "You can defend yourself a hell of a lot better than most men I know!"

"Besides . . ." She smiled seductively. "I need you in my bed. Nobody can come near to . . ."

Without any warning whatsoever, Cooper dove across the backs of the mules, hitting her shoulder and knocking her from her horse. They landed together, with Cooper half on top of her. The echoes of a rifle shot were dying away as they hit the ground.

Under him Rena said dazedly, "Have you gone crazy, Cooper?"

"Ssh," he said, clamping a hand over her mouth. "Didn't you hear the shot?"

She went quiet and Cooper listened, straining

his ears. The horses had bolted, but the mules continued on at a plodding pace.

He heard a rustling noise in the underbrush. "Lie there, don't move," he whispered.

Colt cocked and ready in his hand, he squirmed across the ground, until he was into the thick vines and bushes beside the trail. Slowly, he stood up and listened intently.

He heard the crackle of a breaking twig, and then a few angry words spoken in an unintelligible whisper. The jungle became quiet again, except for the angry cries of birds disturbed by the rifle shot.

Cooper quietly shucked his boots, hoping fervently that there were no poisonous reptiles in the vicinity. Then he moved on his bare feet in the direction of the sound, moving very slowly and making a sort of half-circle. Finally, he was in a position where he figured the gent with the rifle was between him and the trail. He inched gingerly forward, the Colt held out before him, his finger on the trigger.

Placing one foot carefully in front of the other, he moved forward until he saw a flash of white in front of him. He pushed aside the undergrowth with the Colt, and saw a short man in cotton trousers and shirt kneeling on the ground. A large sombrero dangled down his back, and he held a rifle pointed toward the trail, which he was watching intently.

Cooper looked carefully both ways, saw no one else, and so concluded that the voice he had heard was this gent talking to himself.

He drew a bead on the man's back, right between the shoulder blades, and spoke harshly in Spanish. "Drop the rifle, *amigo*! Now!"

The man stiffened and his head started to swivel around.

Cooper barked, "You're not listening to me! I have a bead on your back, and I'll put a bullet in you before you can turn. Now, drop the rifle!"

With a muttered curse, the man dropped the rifle.

"Now, stand up and turn around! Slow and easy-like."

The man stood up and faced around. Cooper swore. He had been right; it was one of the discharged crew.

Cautiously, he stepped out of the brush toward the man. He saw that the gent had a pistol stuck in his belt, and his right hand was literally twitching toward it. Cooper motioned with the Colt. "Up with your hands, *amigo*. You try for that pistol in your belt, and you're minus a hand!"

The fellow's hands shot up. Cooper warily stepped close, leaning across to pluck the pistol out of the belt, and toss it to one side. He moved back. "Now, what the hell are you . . . ?"

A branch snapped behind him, and Cooper cursed himself for being careless and a complete idiot. The man had not been alone, after all!

Even as these thoughts sped through his mind, he was already in motion, throwing his body down and to one side. A shot boomed out, and a bullet whistled over his falling body. He was rolling as he struck the ground, retaining his grip on the Colt. He rolled over twice and came up on his left elbow, the Colt blasting without being aimed. He missed the shadowy figure in the undergrowth, but the shot was enough to cause the shooter to flinch and miss with his second shot.

Cooper thumbed the Cold back and fired again. This time, he didn't miss. The bullet took the other man full in the chest, right over the heart, and hurled him back into the jungle. Then Cooper was on his knees, swinging around to cover the first man. At the click of the hammer drawing back, the man in the sombrero, bent over and in the act of picking up the discarded rifle, froze, staring back at Cooper, his eyes rolling in fear, the whites showing.

Cooper jerked the Colt. "Up, stand up and step back."

Slowly, the man in the sombrero obeyed. Cooper said, "Now, are there any more of you galoots following us?"

The other man tightened his lips obstinately.

Cooper fired, the bullet plowing a furrow between the man's booted feet. "Come up with an answer, *amigo*, or the next one takes off a couple of toes!"

"No, no, no one else, Señor Cooper!" he babbled in fright. "Not that I know about. Only my *compadre* and myself. That is all, I swear!"

"You swear," Cooper grumbled. He motioned with his head. "I hope it's the truth. If I see you, or any of the others around, you'll all end up dead like your *compadre* back there. Now, I suppose you both came on mules. So, collect them, sling your dead *compadre* across one, and make your ass scarce!"

The man slowly lowered his hands. His gaze jumped to the rifle on the ground.

"Uh-unh, you leave here unarmed. The rifle and pistol stay here. Be grateful I'm letting you leave alive. I should shoot you down like a dog! Now, scat!"

The man scooted, detouring around Cooper, back into the jungle where his dead companion lay. Cooper waited until he heard the sounds of a body being dragged through the underbrush. Then he holstered the Colt, gathered up the dead man's pistol, the second pistol and the rifle, then stepped to the edge of the trail.

He poked his head out, calling, "Rena? Are you all right?"

"Coop? Is it over?"

"Yeah." At first he didn't see her. Looking at the spot where he had left her lying, he could see that she was no longer there. Then, belatedly, he realized that her voice had come from the other direction, south down the trail. Glancing that way, he saw that she had chased after the mules. She was leading them back toward him.

He stepped out onto the trail, laughing softly to himself. Trust her to be more concerned with the loot than her personal safety! He retrieved his boots, put them on, then leaned against a palm and waited for her, lighting a cigar.

She came up, trying to hurry the stubborn

mules along. Dropping the lead lines, she cursed them soundly, before swinging on him.

"Who was shooting at us? Did you take care of them?"

"I took care of them. Why didn't you stay put? Did it ever occur to you that they could have nailed you, running down the trail like that?"

"I had to catch the mules," she said in surprise. "I couldn't let them get away!"

"Of course not," he said gravely.

"You didn't answer me. Who was it?"

"It was a couple of your fine roughnecks, the ones you said were too stupid to follow us."

"I didn't think they had the sense to suspect we had anything of value, much less the guts to try something like that."

"It seems you were wrong."

She wet her lips. "Did you kill them?"

"I killed one," he said laconically. "The other galoot is toting his *compadre*'s body away."

"Why didn't you kill both? He may decide to come back!"

"I doubt that very much. I put the fear of God into him."

"Sometimes you can be awfully stupid, Coop!"

"I'm not in the habit of gunning down unarmed men. Anyway, I'll bet my boots *he* won't be back for a second try. But it's entirely possible that some of the others, independent of this pair, might have the same idea." He straightened up. "So, I'd better catch the horses, and let's put as much distance behind us as possible before nightfall."

367

Chapter Twenty-Two

Once again, Meredith, Ricardo, and Juana rode into the courtyard before the Mendes hacienda in Acapulco. Meredith was not looking forward with any great pleasure to this meeting.

Luis Mendes did not come bustling out this time as they reined their horses in. The front door remained closed, and this great house that had once seemed friendly and welcoming now struck her as forbidding and hostile.

"Ricardo . . ." She sighed, weary and dirty from their long, hard ride. "Señor Mendes did receive your telegram?"

"I sent it, Meredith, that is all I can tell you." Ricardo was less immaculate than at any time since she had known him. His clothes were dusty and travel-stained, and his handsome face was shadowed by a beard. He shifted in his saddle, then reached over to touch her hand. His voice was contrite as he said, "I am sorry, my dear. I must admit that I am irritable. Too many things have happened these past few days . . . but to answer your question in a more civil manner, we must assume that he received my message."

_ "He has not come out to greet us," she pointed out.

"There could be many reasons for that. For one, Luis might not be at home . . . Meredith, Luis is an old friend, he will understand."

"Understanding is one thing," she said glumly. "But I can't see him dancing with delight over the fact that a national treasure has been stolen, and he is sure to be unhappy about our not notifying him of our discovery at once."

"Meredith, you are being foolish!" he said sharply. "What delay was there? We discovered the treasure late in the afternoon, and it was stolen during the night. We would not be expected to send a messenger until the next morning."

"But we had no intention of sending a messenger the next morning!"

"Luis does not know that, and there is no reason he should be informed."

"I feel guilty for what we had planned."

"But would you have felt guilty," he said gently, "if things had gone as we planned? If we had managed to do our cataloguing and then, when that was done, notify Luis? *If* the treasure had not been stolen?"

"No, I suppose not," she said uncertainly. "But it *was* stolen, so this conversation is pointless, Ricardo!"

"Trust me, my love. Everything will be all right, I am confident." He put on a smile. "It could even be that Luis has good news for us, that Cooper has been caught and the treasure is now in the proper hands."

She made a face. "If you believe that, you are living in a fool's paradise . . ."

She broke off, going tense, as the front door swung open and Luis Mendes stood framed in the doorway.

"Luis!" Ricardo exclaimed. He slid down from his horse and strode toward the steps.

"My friend." Mendes nodded to Meredith. "And Señora Meredith."

He made no move to embrace Ricardo and his voice was cool. It was just the sort of reception that Meredith had been fearing. Yet, when she had dismounted and moved to the two men on the steps, Mendes seemed more sorrowful than angry. He nodded to her again. "It would seem that misfortune plagues you, Meredith. I had difficulty believing Ricardo's telegram when I received it." He looked hopeful for a moment. "I suppose it is too much to hope for that it might be a bad dream, or that you have since rediscovered this treasure?"

Meredith said, "If it is a dream, Luis, it is a nightmare. Everything in that telegram, unfortunately, is true, and nothing has changed."

Mendes heaved a sigh. "Welcome to my house, my friends. Come in and tell me the details."

He ushered them in and started down the hall toward his study. Then he slapped his hand to his forehead and looked stricken. "A thousand pardons! You have had a long and weary

371

ride, and must wish to freshen yourselves before we continue."

Meredith was immensely relieved and touched. If he was going to castigate them, at least he was going to let them tell their story first.

She smiled gratefully. "Thank you for your kindness and consideration, Luis, but that can wait. I know you would like to know everything, and there *is* a certain urgency, after all."

He inclined his head. "Very well." He started on down the hall. When they were seated in the study, and he had poured wine for them, he said, "The matter is urgent, Meredith. In that you are correct. But I have already alerted everyone I can think of as to what has happened, insofar as I know it, and the borders are being closed to Señor Mayo, as much as is possible. However, I do need to know all of it."

He went around behind his desk to take his seat and make the familiar steeple with his fingers. "I am ready."

They had already agreed that Ricardo would carry the burden of the tale. Meredith listened, sunk in a fog of weariness. Except for glossing over the exact time of their find, his version was accurate down to the last detail.

When at last Ricardo was finished, Luis Mendes leaned back, sighing. "There is no doubt that Cooper Mayo is the culprit?"

"Not the slightest that I can see," Meredith responded. "Aside from the fact that he disappeared the same night as the treasure, the young man, Raul, identified him as the thief, as Ricardo told you. As to whether or not he had anyone helping him, we don't know . . ." She raised and lowered her shoulders.

His gaze was shrewd. "You have in mind Rena Voltan?"

She nodded meagerly. "I do."

"And in that you could be right, since I have learned that they were quite close in Mexico City. However, the thing that troubles me greatly is that Mayo *was* involved, and it is I who recommended him to you, Meredith."

"You can't hold yourself responsible for what he did!"

"But I do, at least to the extent that I am partially responsible for the expedition itself. I confess that I am sadly disappointed in Señor Mayo. He is an adventurer, undeniably, but charming . . ."

"That he most certainly is," Meredith said with a twist of bitterness.

"A charming rascal, agreed, but I did not think him a thief. When caught he will be severely punished. The people in high places are incensed at this outrage. Over the past few years they have been slowly growing aware of the burgeoning traffic in antiquities. At first no one cared about a few pots, pottery figures, and stone statues. But the number of poachers and vandals has grown rapidly, and it finally became apparent that national treasures, and artworks of great value, were leaving our country, and appearing in the museums of other countries and in private collections.

"Now, to have a treasure such as this, a treasure of inestimable value, stolen will have grave repercussions, perhaps even lead to bad relations between your country and mine, Meredith. However, if it is recovered," he spread his hands, "and is as valuable as you claim, all will be forgotten, I believe."

Ricardo leaned forward. "In respect to recovery, what *is* being done?"

"Everything possible, my friend, you may be assured of that. But it is a momentous task. Our country is large, much of it is relatively uncharted, and what border guards we have are spread pitifully thin. On land, it would be difficult for Señor Mayo to cross our borders, but there are many miles of seacoast and a great number of vessels out there for hire. Most of their owners have few scruples. So, you see, it will not be easy."

"There must be something *I* can do!" Ricardo was up and prowling back and forth.

Mendes steepled his hands. "I am open to suggestions, my friend."

"If I only had some talent as a tracker, I might have found the trail Cooper left. But I have never been good at things like that." Ricardo smacked a fist into his palm.

"Oh, there is one thing I have not gotten around to mentioning," Mendes said, leaning forward. "The minute I received your telegram, I contacted the police here, and a squad of men were dispatched to the excavation. Did you meet them on the trail?"

It was Meredith who answered. "No, Luis, but they may have taken a less-traveled trail. We came down the main road."

Mendes nodded. "That likely explains it. In any event, I was informed by our chief last night that he received a telegram from his men. They have found the tracks of mules leaving the excavation, which is quite likely those of our thief, or thieves."

"And?" Ricardo prompted.

"And the tracks led in this direction. However, the traffic will increase the closer they get to Acapulco, and the likelihood of the trackers losing their quarry is great."

"But that is great news!" Ricardo exclaimed. "Do you not see, that means Cooper is headed in this direction!"

Mendes was shaking his head. "Not necessarily. He could branch off on many different trails before reaching Acapulco. It does not seem logical to me that he would have such a large city as this for his destination. The scoundrel is not stupid, no matter what else he is."

"But he is, or was, headed in this direction."

"That is a possibility, and for that reason the search is being concentrated in this general area. However, it is still a large and difficult territory to cover, as you well know, my friend."

"I do know," Ricardo said grimly. "And for that reason I may be able to help. When my family was still wealthy, I spent many winters here, and learned the coastline well. I will conduct my own search. At least I will be doing something."

"It could be dangerous, Ricardo," Mendes said gently. "You will have to do it alone. Our police have spared all the men they can, and can detach no one to your command."

"I will take my chances alone. It could be better that way, since a band of men marching around could give Cooper advance warning."

"Ricardo, aren't you being a little rash?" Meredith asked.

"Perhaps I am, my love." He stood over her, his face softening. "But at least I will not feel so useless. I carry a burden of guilt over this affair, also. You recall all those times you warned me against trusting Cooper, and I scoffed at you? Once, you thought of discharging him, and I discouraged you. If I had not, this would not be happening. Meredith," he was close to pleading now, "it is something that I must do."

"All right, darling, I understand," she said softly. Disregarding Mendes's presence, she reached for Ricardo's face and pulled it down to her. She kissed him on the lips.

After a moment Ricardo straightened and said briskly, "I must get started at once. Extra delay could mean disaster." He looked again at Meredith. "Where will you stay, my darling?"

Mendes said, "Why, here, naturally. She will be most welcome in my home."

"I'd rather not, Luis." She hastened to add, "Not that I don't appreciate your offer of hospitality, but I would like to be alone for awhile. This thing has been a great shock, and I'm irritable when I'm in a mood. The cottage where we stayed before . . . is it available?"

"I believe it is, my dear," Mendes said. "In any event, I will make sure that it is."

"But you will be alone there, Meredith," Ricardo said.

"Not exactly. Juana will be with me. And I want to be alone, in the place where we were happy together." She smiled fleetingly. "Besides, what can happen to me? All those terrible things that happened before were because of the treasure. Since I can no longer be of any use to anyone in respect to the treasure, who would wish to do me harm here?"

Ricardo nodded reluctantly, still looking worried. "If you are sure that you will be all right. Hopefully, I will not be away too long."

"I'll be fine, darling." She took his hand, smiling. "Juana will be there, and she's worth any two men, fierce and protective as she is."

"All right," he said brusquely, his dark eyes swinging to Mendes. "I will leave at once. I can not afford to waste any more time. You will hear from me in several days, but do not worry, either of you." He bent to kiss Meredith again. "Farewell, my love, and take care."

He was gone, striding out of the room. Meredith stared after him, feeling an emptiness at his departure, yet there was also a certain relief. Without disloyalty to him, it would be nice to have a few days to herself, giving her an opportunity to get her thoughts in order.

Mendes stirred, getting to his feet. "I will send a man to check on the cottage for you, Meredith. Meanwhile, you should refresh yourself, and have a siesta. And at least you will honor me, and the Señora, at dinner tonight?"

"Of course, Luis." She got up. "I wish to express my gratitude to you for not being angry with Ricardo and myself for what has happened."

"Why should I be angry with you?" he said with an arched eyebrow. "The only way in which you could be faulted is for trusting Cooper Mayo, and I share that responsibility with you."

"The dig, Luis . . ." she said hesitantly. "Is there any chance at all that I will ever be able to resume my work there? There are still many beautiful things there, things of great historic value. And there is one item alone that makes the excavation worthwhile. We've barely scratched the surface, and . . ."

Mendes's eyes brightened. "What item? What are you talking of?"

Meredith took a deep breath. "Luis, what if I told you we had found *El Hombre de Oro*?"

"The Man of Gold! You mean he exists?" An expression of horror changed his features. "And they have him? The thieves have him?"

"No, no!" Meredith raised her hands. "They did not take him. Why, I'm not sure."

Mendes's expression lightened. "Thank God! But where is he? Did you bring him with you?"

"No, Luis. Let me explain."

"Yes, of course, but why did you not tell me sooner?"

Meredith shrugged. "We were so concerned with the theft of the other things that we thought of nothing else. Now . . ." As briefly as possible, Meredith told him about *El Hombre de Oro*. "And so we sealed off the chamber and the passageway before we left. And we have a trustworthy guard, the young man, Raul. As you must realize, it would have been foolhardy to have moved the mummy without the proper equipment."

"Yes, yes, I understand." Mendes wiped his forehead with a linen handkerchief. "This is excellent news, my dear. I am sure it will be taken into consideration when the question of your continuing the excavation is considered. But as to whether the authorities will let you return, who knows?" He raised and lowered his shoulders. "It is in the hands of God. All I can tell you now, Meredith, is that your question is premature."

The fishing village Rena was heading for was more than a day's ride out of Acapulco, near a small harbor. She directed Cooper to stop about a mile from the village, in a shallow glade, with a high ridge between the camp and the village.

When the mules were unloaded, her tent erected, and the chests stacked inside, she said, "Come along, Coop. Let's have a look."

He tested one of the tent ropes, then stood back, surveying the campsite. It was tucked away in a grove of palm trees, a distance from the road, and they had done a good job of covering their tracks after leaving the dim trail.

He nodded, clearing his throat. "I guess it'll

have to do. I must admit that I thought we'd never make it." His glance shifted to her. "I've had an itch between my shoulder blades ever since we were jumped right at the start, and I am goddamned surprised we made it this far."

She laughed, linking her arm in his. "I told you we'd make it, didn't I, lover?"

"You also told me that the men you let go would never attack us. You were wrong there."

"But we're safe now. Soon as I make the arrangements with Harkness, we're off to the coast of South America, Coop."

He elevated an eyebrow. "You sound awfully sure of that."

"I *am* sure. Come on, let's go have a look."

She led him up the small rise, motioning him down just before they reached the crest. On their bellies, they stretched out and parted the bushes growing along the spine of the ridge.

In the clear light of late afternoon, the small village was easily visible, as well as the horse-shoe shape of the harbor. The village itself was little more than a collection of shacks, with a single waterfront street crowded with more substantial buildings. From her earlier visit here, Rena knew there were a half-dozen stores, taverns, and one small hotel along that street. A rickety wharf jutted out into the narrow bay, and a number of boats were tied up, with several others anchored out aways.

She saw the boat she was looking for at once, and stifled a sigh of relief. It would have presented problems if Earl Harkness had not been in port on her arrival. It would have meant more delay, and despite her assurances to Cooper, Rena knew that their time was growing dangerously short. All of Mexico must be out looking for them by this time, and the most logical place would be a port town like this one. She had little doubt that Harkness had been questioned, and was still under surveillance, but Harkness *was* a slick character, and she was confident that he had had a good story to hand the police.

Rena recognized his boat without difficulty. It was old, rusty, and looked just like all the other fishing boats in the harbor, but underneath that dilapidated exterior, it was capable of outrunning most coastal vessels, and Harkness was one of the best seaman she had ever known. He would have to be exceptional to have survived at his risky calling for so long.

Rena knew his boat because of the lady's drawers he flew on the main mast. She should know it, she thought with a secret smile—the drawers were hers, white in color and trimmed with pink lace. Earl Harkness had taken them off her the one time she had been there, when she had broached her plan to him. She shivered with pleasure at the memory of that time. Harkness was a rogue, as she had told Cooper, but he was also quite a man. Built like a stump, with arms as long as a gorilla's, and about as hairy, he took a woman with an impersonal brutality that had thrilled her.

It was true that she didn't trust him; he was as unscrupulous as a Barbary pirate of the olden days, and would gladly kill her for the contents of those chests. The fact that she did not trust him was the reason she had recruited Cooper, calculating that Cooper was the only man she knew who might, possibly, be able to cope with Earl Harkness. Evan Longley certainly would not have been able to. But now her plans had changed; she could no longer trust Cooper, either.

He broke into her thoughts. "See the boat belonging to this Harkness gent?"

"No, Coop, I don't," she lied blandly. "But I'm sure I can find someone down there who will be able to get word to him."

She slid down the slope, pulling him along with her, until they could stand upright without being seen from the village.

Back at the tent, she said, "Why don't you wait here for me, have a drink, maybe make your supper? It may be after dark before I get back."

"You mean you're going off and leave me with all that loot?" He slanted a grin at her. "I don't think you've been two feet away from those chests since we took off with them."

"I haven't much choice, now do I?" She shrugged. "Not if I'm to make arrangements. Besides, I trust you, Coop."

"And of course if I took off with them, you'd have someone right on my tail, right? And me with no place to go."

"You're right." She lit a cigar and blew smoke in his face. "The only chance you have of getting out of this without your tail in a crack, and with your share of the loot, is through me."

"Now that sounds more like the Rena I know so well."

Cooper selected a convenient palm, sat down, and leaned back against the trunk. He drawled, "Run along now and have fun, Rena. But don't be gone too long." He tilted his hat down over his eyes, head cradled on his drawn-up knees.

"You're not fooling me for a minute, Coop. You won't close an eye until I get back." She laughed, and batted the hat from his head. "But Rena will be back, never fear."

"Oh, I don't doubt that for a minute. Those chests are my guarantee of that."

She struck off for the trail, feeling his eyes on her until she was out of sight.

It was long past the dinner hour when she returned to the camp. She wore the smile of a contented cat, as she paused on the edge of the palm grove. She could see the fire and Cooper sitting by it, comfortably slumped back against the same tree trunk, looking as if he hadn't moved since she left.

Harkness had been happy to see her, and their negotiations had gone well. All the arrangements had been made, and Rena was sure that they would be well out to sea with the treasure on the morrow. She still had not confided to Harkness just how much the treasure was worth, passing it off as a few stolen artifacts that could be stripped of their precious metals, resulting in a tidy profit for both of them.

She doubted that he believed her, but the evening spent in his company had convinced her that he would be easier to handle than Cooper. He was a man with lusty appetites, and Rena knew that most of the women he had known were waterfront sluts, slatternly and placid as milk cows; he had never before had a woman who could release as much passion as she was capable of. Also, he was not as intelligent as Cooper, and Rena knew from experience that it was easier to control a stupid man than a clever one.

Tonight, during their meeting, the memory of their one time together had so glazed Harkness's eyes with lust that she was certain he would have taken her across the table in the cheap tavern where they met if she had given him the word. Alternately teasing and keeping him at a distance, she had beguiled him with promises, both sexual and monetary, until he was eager and willing to agree to anything.

Now, she had one last task to perform.

She moved toward the dying fire, coming up quietly behind Cooper.

"I thought you were going to stay out there all night, Rena," he drawled, without moving the hat from over his eyes.

She tensed, then relaxed, laughing. "Sometimes, I think you have eyes in the back of your head, Coop." She moved around across the fire from him.

He sat up, pushing his hat back. "I have suspicious ears." His eyes were intent on her. "Get everything accomplished?"

"Not yet," she lied. "Harkness was out on his

384

boat. He's due back tomorrow, however, and I left word for him to meet me. Everything's smooth as silk."

"Sure. Another day to spend here," he said disgustedly. "And with a fortune in that tent. It's making me nervous as a skittish horse."

"*You* nervous, Coop?" she said mockingly. "I always thought you had nerves of steel."

He grunted. "I've never been holding this much in the pot before, and I feel like I'm bare-assed in a tornado."

"You worry too much, lover," she said lightly. "I'm going into the tent. Give me a few minutes, then come in. We'll see what we can do to make you forget your worries."

His eyes were flat and hard. "That's your answer for everything, isn't it?"

"It'll do until I can think of a better one."

She went on into the tent, checked the chests to see if they were still securely fastened, then got undressed and arranged herself on the blankets on the ground.

She called out, "I'm ready, lover!"

There was no answer, and for a few moments she thought that he was going to be stubborn. Then she heard his footsteps, and his shadow fell across the canvas before he ducked under the tent flap.

He unbuckled his gunbelt and placed it within easy reach. Rena threw the light coverlet aside and let him see her naked body. He stood for a little, staring down at her without moving.

"Well?" she demanded.

Still not speaking, he came down on his knees beside her, one hand on her breast.

"Wait!" She fended him off. "Aren't you going to get undressed?"

"Why bother? I'd just have to get dressed again. I'm not spending the night in here. I'll have to keep a watch outside."

She started to voice an angry retort, then subsided, remembering what she had to do, and his big hands were already on her. He caressed her breasts, and her nipples tingled in response. He rolled his thumbs across them, and she moaned, writhing.

His hands moved down, his knuckles like heated pebbles rolling against her inner thighs. He did not try to kiss her, but Rena was too fevered by desire to take notice.

She fumbled with his trousers until she had them open. Her hands found his hardness. She let her thighs fall apart and guided him into her. His thrusts were rough, grinding her against the blankets. Rena gloried in it. It seemed to her that her pleasure had intensified since they had left the excavation with the treasure. The knowledge that the chests spilling with riches were close enough to touch as they made love affected her like an aphrodisiac.

As she felt the final explosion of pleasure approaching, she reached under the blankets for the knife, then rose, clinging to him. As her climax neared, she pulled him down to her, raised the knife high, then started it down toward that most vulnerable spot between his shoulder blades.

He moved faster than she would have thought possible, one hand striking her right arm a stunning blow. The knife flew out of her hand, and then he had rolled to one side and off the blankets.

Dazed by the suddenness of it, her sexual pleasure still thrumming along her nerve-ends, Rena watched dreamily as Cooper scooped up the knife from where it had fallen, then stretched over to cuff her ringingly across the side of the head.

"You finally got around to it, didn't you?" he said savagely. "I was beginning to think maybe I was wrong."

The slap had broken the spell, and Rena moved back a few inches, eyeing him warily.

Cooper bounced the knife in his hand. "Well? Aren't you going to deny it?"

"Would it be of any use to deny it?" she said calmly.

"Hardly, since I caught you in the act, in more ways than one. Is this the way you killed Evan Longley?"

"Yes."

"And I wonder how many others." He sighed, slumping a little. His anger seemed to have receded. "At least now maybe I can sleep. I've been afraid to close my eyes for days, watching that you didn't slip up behind me."

"I decided to kill you when you fell for Longley," she said in a sneering voice.

"But I was still of some use, right? Trust you, Rena, never to rid yourself of someone so long as they can be of use to you." He stood up, strapping on his gunbelt. "Well, so long, sweetheart. I won't lie and say that it's been nice knowing you."

With a cry she moved around to where she was between Cooper and the chests. "You're not going to take any of this!"

"I really don't know how you'd stop me, naked as a jaybird and without your trusty knife." His laughter was grating. "But don't worry, I wash my hands of both you and the treasure. And you know something funny? I feel better than I have in weeks. I think the workers at the excavation had it right. Everything found at that dig is cursed, so you'd better be careful that it doesn't get you, Rena."

She gaped at him. "You mean you're just going to walk away like this, without anything at all?"

"Hell, I'm lucky to have my life. And at least I may get my self-respect back. And then again, I may not."

"I always knew you were a fool, Cooper Mayo."

"I should think you'd be jumping for joy. Now you don't have to share it, it's all yours. I hope you enjoy it."

He left the tent, carrying the knife with him. She sat huddled against the chests, still not able to believe that he would just walk away. It was only when she heard hoofbeats fading that she finally began to believe it.

She relaxed then, finding a cigar and lighting it, not bothering to get dressed. That would be a waste of time, since Earl Harkness would be along shortly.

She smoked, and thought about what had happened. She was frustrated that Cooper had escaped with his life, but on balance she was the winner. The loot was all hers!

Then a new thought brought a frown to her face. What if he went to the authorities? If he had gotten an attack of conscience strong enough to cause him to walk away from the loot, he might also report her to the police.

She smiled to herself. It didn't matter all that much. She would be long gone, out to sea, before the authorities could locate her.

Her head came up at the sound of footsteps. She shivered in expectation. Harkness, of course. It was time for him to show up. She fumbled for a lantern, struck a match to it, set it between the tent flap and the blankets, then arranged herself in her most seductive pose. Her smile broadened, as she imagined his face when he stepped into the tent and saw her like this.

The footsteps stopped outside the tent. Rena said, "Come on in, Harkness. It's all right."

The tent flap folded back and a man stepped inside. Rena gasped, recoiling. It wasn't Earl Harkness. He was a stranger to her, a Mexican in rough clothing, and he wore a pistol at his waist. A cruel scar zigzagged across his cheek.

His gaze moved over her, a smile parting his full lips. "Señorita Rena Voltan, I believe?" He swept off his sombrero and bowed. "I have been looking forward to our meeting, delayed as it has been."

"Who the hell are you? And what are you doing here?"

"My name is Gabriel Morales, and I am sure it does not require much imagination on your part to know why I am here."

"No!" She flung herself protectively in front of the chests.

"Ignacio!" Morales drew his pistol and pointed it nonchalantly at her. He said casually, "If you so much as move, Señorita Voltan, you are dead."

A squat, ugly man ducked into the tent. He carried a machete. He stood grinning at the taller man. "Yes, my *jefe?*"

"This is the witch-woman we have heard so much about, Ignacio." Morales gestured with the pistol. "What do you think of her?"

"*Bruja!*" Ignacio whispered, and crossed himself.

"What is the best way to kill a witch, so she will not return from the dead?"

Grinning again, Ignacio said, "One of the old ways, I have been told, is to drive a stake through her evil heart."

"But we have no stake. What other ways?"

"Burned alive, my *jefe.*"

Rena could not credit what she was hearing; she was convinced that these men were simply trying to frighten her.

Morales said, "That would take too much time. Is there not still another way?"

390

"Chop off her head." Ignacio hefted the machete.

"Ah, quick, if perhaps a little messy. But that is what we shall do."

Fear began to invade Rena's mind. He seemed so matter-of-fact, and she finally started to believe that they really intended to kill her. To have gone through so much, to have finally realized all her dreams, and now this!

"Wait!" she cried frantically. "Do you know what is in these chests? Riches beyond anything you can imagine! Let me go, and I will share it with you!"

Morales's grin was unpleasant. "Now why should I do that, Señorita, when I can have it all for the taking?" He motioned with the pistol. "Ignacio?"

The squat man stepped forward quickly to seize Rena by the arm. She screamed and began to struggle.

Out of the corner of one eye, she saw the tall man loom over her, and glimpsed his pistol swinging down. It struck her on the temple, knocking her to the ground.

Dimly, she heard that cold, relentless voice, "Quickly, Ignacio. Our time is limited."

Horror turned her blood to ice as she saw the machete raised high. Then it descended, moving faster and faster. She managed to turn her head aside, toward the chests.

The chests will be splattered with blood, she thought, my blood.

Rena Voltan died with that last thought still in her mind.

Chapter Twenty-Three

In the quiet and relaxation of the cottage, Meredith was able to forget her troubles—much of the time.

It was a peaceful period, a time of sun and water. There was no one to disapprove of her bathing naked, and during the first few days at the beach, Meredith grew brown and quite proficient in the ocean.

Juana was as happy as Meredith had ever seen her, and went about her duties cheerfully. It was astonishing, Meredith thought, how different the girl was without Ricardo around.

With a feeling of guilt, Meredith had to admit that she too was more relaxed. Since the day he had rescued her from Gabriel Morales, she had been with Ricardo constantly; it was pleasant to have some time to herself.

Meredith became so content and indolent that she was not even sure she wished to return to the hard work and discomfort of the dig. This feeling, she was certain, would eventually pass.

All her life she had kept herself busy and knew that idleness would stifle her.

But for the time it lasted, she could enjoy it, restore her jaded energies, and clear her mind.

On her fourth day in the cottage, Luis Mendes made a brief call. He had heard nothing from Ricardo, and informed her that there was no news of Cooper or the missing treasure.

"I am becoming discouraged, Meredith," he said. "If Señor Mayo has the treasure, by this time he should have tried to make good his escape."

"Perhaps he already has. Made his escape, I mean. In that case, we probably wouldn't know about it."

He nodded disconsolately. "And quite likely never will." He rose to leave. "If I receive word from Ricardo, I will send a message at once."

"I hope he is all right," she said worriedly. "I still think it was a foolish thing for him to undertake. He is not . . ."

"Not fitted for such an undertaking." He nodded again. "I know, my dear. Derring-do is not the life for an academic person. I will say a prayer for his safety."

Mendes's visit left Meredith disturbed and she found herself resenting this intrusion into her idyll. That night was a restless one, as she lay awake for a long time, worrying about Ricardo's welfare.

She fell asleep sometime before dawn, but was up at the rising of the sun. She hurried down to the beach, carrying a towel and wearing a wrapper, which she discarded before she waded out into the ocean. After a short time in the water, her troubled mind was soothed and she began to relax.

She was not aware of how much time had passed until she heard a voice calling her name. She stood up in shallow water, noticing that the sun was well up, and saw Juana waving to her from the shore.

"What is it, Juana? I'll be up for breakfast shortly. I didn't know I'd been in so long . . ."

"Not that, Señorita Meredith." Juana was smiling. "You have a visitor."

"A visitor?" Meredith frowned, then raised her voice in a shout. "Ricardo is back!"

"Not the señor." Juana hugged herself in secretive amusement.

"But who then?"

"You come now. He is waiting."

He? Still puzzling over who it could possibly be, Meredith walked out of the water, dried herself, and shrugged into the wrapper. She walked rapidly toward the cottage. Juana was not in sight, but then neither was anyone else.

She hesitated at the bottom step, as she saw movement behind the bamboo, and a figure stepped out onto the veranda. It was Cooper Mayo!

Smoke trailing from his cigar, he advanced to the top of the steps. Pushing his hat back, he leaned against the veranda post and grinned down at her.

Meredith seemed frozen in place. She had never expected to see him again and here he was, grinning lazily at her, as if nothing at all had happened. She noticed that he was freshly shaven, his cheeks glowing, and he had on the white suit, which had clearly been cleaned since she had last seen him. His boots had a high gloss.

The gall, the supreme gall of the man! She noted that her heart was beating rapidly, and that was enough to send hot rage coursing through her.

He drawled, "Hello, boss lady . . . oops! I guess that no longer applies, does it?"

"You . . . you . . ." She felt like she was choking, and had to stop and clear her throat. "You have the *nerve* to show your face to me, after what you've done!"

He shrugged. "I never told you I was perfect."

"Now I suppose you're going to tell me that you didn't steal the treasure?"

"Oh, I stole it, I reckon there's no point in my denying that. All I can say is . . ." He finally had the grace to look discomfited. "I'm sorry, Meredith, sorrier than I can ever say. But understand one thing . . . I'm sorry only because of any hurt I may have caused you. The way I figure it, it wasn't really stealing."

"It wasn't? Then what was it?"

"Let me tell you the way I figure it . . . according to your husband, that stuff has been lying down there untouched for something like a thousand years. Right?"

"Something like that." She stared at him, intrigued, her anger temporarily abating. "But what does that have to do with it?"

"And the people those things belonged to are dead about the same length of time. Right?"

"Of course, but . . ."

"So the people it belonged to are dead, dead so long they sure as hell have no legal heirs around. So who does it belong to now? You? Me? Who? I figure I had as much right to it as anyone."

"That's the strangest rationalization I've ever heard! Those stolen items are artifacts, they belong to the world, to the government of Mexico!"

"Naturally you'd say that, seeing you're what you are, but I happen to see it differently."

"Cooper, this is the weirdest conversation I've ever . . . no matter who you may think it belongs to, you committed a crime, and you'll go to jail when they catch you."

"Jail is always a risk in my way of life," he said dryly.

"But if you return the treasure now, before they catch up to you, I think I could get Luis Mendes to intercede for you."

He rubbed his nails against his shirt and studied them intently. "Afraid I can't do that, Meredith, not even to please you."

"Why not?"

He looked over her head, toward the ocean. "I don't have the treasure."

"Where is it?"

"The last I saw of it, the loot was in four chests in Rena's tent."

"Then she *was* involved in it!"

His gaze came back to her. "You figured that out, did you?"

"You mean you stole the treasure together, and then you walked away and left her with it?"

"That's about it."

"Cooper . . ." She shook her head hard. "You're not making much sense. Why, why did you do that?"

His mouth twisted. "Let's just say that Rena is not a nice person."

She gave a strangled laugh. "It took you all this time to figure that out?"

"I'm a slow thinker, I reckon."

"Where is she?" Meredith came up the steps toward him. "We can let the police know, so they can catch her."

"Nope, afraid I can't do that." He was looking away again.

"Again, why not?"

"Haven't you ever heard about honor among thieves?"

"Oh, for God's sake!" she exploded. "You are the most exasperating man!"

"Besides, it wouldn't do much good. Dear Rena is probably long gone by this time. Meredith . . ." He took her hand. "Let's sit down and talk about us." He drew her down onto the steps beside him.

"What do you mean, talk about us?" She tried to pull free, but his fingers locked around her wrist. "You steal something I've dreamed all my life of finding, you go off with that evil woman, then you show up here, talking crazy."

"Meredith, I love you," he said with a crooked grin. "It took me a long time to realize that, but it's the damned truth! And I'll have you know I've never said those words to a woman."

"Cooper, you must be insane!" Her laugh was shaky, and her pulse was racing so fast that it made her dizzy. "I'm a married woman!"

His eyes bored into hers. "Are you happy with him?"

"Of course I'm happy! What a question!"

He turned her toward him, his arm going around her shoulders. His mouth came down hard on hers. At the touch of his lips, something seemed to break loose inside her, and Meredith found herself responding to his kiss.

Then his hands folded the wrapper back, and his fingers stroked her breasts.

She pulled her mouth away. "No, no! This isn't right! We can't do this!"

"Why isn't it right, Meredith? You feel it, too, whatever it is between us. Admit it!" He shook her slightly.

"No, no. It's all wrong . . ."

His mouth stopped her, and again the touch of his lips sent little shivers of delight racing over her.

Without volition her arms went around him, her hands clawing at his back. Cooper stood up, and in one motion scooped her up into his arms and started into the cottage.

"No," she murmured. "Juana, she will see."

Cooper chuckled. "Juana approves. She went off into the jungle on a hunt for fresh fruit."

As he stepped inside, Meredith remembered her remark to Ricardo c̣ ʼheir wedding night, about being carried across the threshold, and again resistance rose in her.

She strained back, hands flat against his shoulders. "Put me down! Damn you, Cooper Mayo, you raped me once! I swore I'd never let it happen again!"

"My dear Meredith, don't be ridiculous. This isn't rape. You want this as much as I do. That other time was an unfortunate incident. I was mad at you that night, and drinking too much. Today, I'm stone cold sober, and not mad at you at all."

They were at the bed. In their journey from the veranda, Meredith's wrapper had become twisted until it barely covered her body. As Cooper put her down onto the bed, he removed it entirely.

He stood back, looking down at her. He said unevenly, "My God, you're lovely! I had forgotten. Of course, I never got a really good look at you, that one night."

He was removing his clothes now, without taking his eyes off her. Meredith knew that she could get off the bed and past him and she sensed, somehow, that he would not attempt to stop her. Yet she lay where she was, knowing that what she was doing was wrong, a betrayal of a dear, sweet man who loved her deeply. It was almost as if those glowing eyes of Cooper's

400

had her mesmerized, like a snake mesmerizing a helpless bird.

She stirred, laughing at herself scornfully. He is not a mesmerizer, she thought, and I am not a bird.

She had not moved when he joined her on the bed a few moments later. She turned into his arms willingly, and he began kissing her breasts, her throat, her mouth, her eyelids—it seemed his mouth was everywhere on her body.

Heat leaped along her flesh, in every place that his lips touched.

His hands, amazingly gentle for such large hands, caressed her expertly, searching for and finding the secret buds of her passion. Meredith felt herself stretching, blooming, expanding, shedding all reservations, under his touch.

She returned his caresses hesitantly at first, but soon all thought of the world outside this tiny cottage was swept away, and she became ardent and eager.

Her need grew great and she said urgently, "Cooper?"

"Ssh, sweet," he whispered. "There is no hurry. Time has stopped. Didn't you know that? It stopped for us."

For the first time in her young life, Meredith perceived the difference in men. Love-making was an art form to Cooper Mayo, and he led her down paths of arousal that she would never have dreamed possible. He caressed and stroked and kissed her until it was all that she could do to keep from screaming at him to take her.

Every nerve in her body clamored for release, and finally she took the initiative, urging him to her with her hands and body.

His low laughter was triumphant as he complied with her urgings and entered her, and she knew that had been his intent all along, to make *her* ask him to complete the act, but she was past caring.

Now that it began his own desire became demanding. She met his violence with a wildness that filled her with a fine madness.

Twice, her ecstasy broke, as her cries echoed in the cottage. Cooper groaned deep in his throat. "Ahh, my sweet! My love!"

Then all was still, and it seemed to Meredith that she floated in a haze of bliss, but she was not alone, Cooper was there with her. She was one with him; she would never be alone again.

He gently withdrew from her and Meredith cried out, swept by a feeling of loss. She clutched at him, trying to hold him to her.

He kissed her with a sweet tenderness, and disengaged himself from her, then stretched out beside her.

Meredith's heartbeat slowly returned to normal, but her body was still caught up in the sensations she had just experienced and her mind was a riot of conflicting emotions.

She was almost ill over the betrayal of Ricardo, yet how could she truly regret what had just happened? She couldn't even be angry at Cooper; certainly this time she could not cry rape. Except for the token resistance in the beginning, she had given him full and complete cooperation.

The paramount question in her mind was concerned with the future. No matter how she might disapprove of Cooper's ethics, his often amoral behavior, she knew now that he was *the* man. There was an intoxication of the senses, a dizzying sweep of pleasure, that she knew intuitively would never happen with another man.

Certainly it had not happened with Ricardo, and her feelings toward him would never be the same again because of that. Guilt flooded her. How could she ever face him again? A cry of anguish escaped her.

"Sweet?" Cooper turned to her, a hand flat on her abdomen. "What's wrong?"

"You know what's wrong!" She knocked his hand away. "I'm married. I belong to another man!"

"Belong? What are you, some kind of horse that you belong to someone? You're a person, Meredith, not a thing. I would never expect you to feel that you belong to me, and that should hold true with your husband."

"Of course I'm not a thing!" she said angrily.

"That's what you made it sound like." Cooper sat up in bed, found a cigar, and struck a match to it.

"Ricardo *is* my husband. I have a certain responsibility."

"In my opinion, your first responsibility is to yourself." With that infuriatingly superior grin, he put a hand on her. "Has he ever made you feel like this?"

Meredith gasped, then firmly removed his hand. "Don't do that! How can we have a logical conversation with you doing that?"

"Logic has nothing to do with it, sweet. And you didn't answer my question."

She flushed. "That has nothing to do with it, either."

"It has everything to do with it."

"What would you have me do then? Just go off with you, and leave him? Disregarding all the things you've done?"

"If you feel for me the way I feel for you, that's exactly what I'd have you do, yeah."

"And do what? Traipse around the world with you, helping you rob and steal, or waiting for someone to bring you back to me dead when you've hired out your guns?"

"I figure on living for a long time, sweet. And who knows, you might like that sort of life."

"It strikes me that you want everything your own way." She looked at him shrewdly. "How about the other way around? Would you go with me to excavations?"

"Dig in the earth like a mole?" He reared back. "Hell, no! I can't think of anything more boring."

"You see?" she said triumphantly. "You want it all your way. But it's not all that boring, Cooper. It's a fascinating way of life. There's nothing more exciting than making discoveries, unearthing artifacts left by ancient civilizations. It's really not so different from the feeling you described when you told me

404

about your love of treasure hunting. If you really gave yourself a chance, I think you would enjoy it. It could be a great life. You don't really need a background in archaeology. I could teach you all you need to know . . ." She broke off, flushing under his amused gaze. "What am I doing? I'm pleading with you to adopt my way of life, and I already have the life I want."

"Have you?" He reached for her again.

Meredith was out of the bed in a flash. She picked up the wrapper from the floor, and put it on, then started out of the cottage.

"Where are you going?"

Near tears, she wouldn't look at him. "I don't know, just out of this room."

"I have an idea. You were swimming earlier, weren't you?"

She bobbed her head.

"That sounds great. Let's go back in, together." He was getting out of bed. "Let's drop this discussion, let it simmer for a little."

She faced him defiantly. "Nothing you can say is going to change my mind."

"I don't know. People do change their minds. Even I did."

He came toward her, passing right by his pile of clothes.

"Aren't you going to put something on?"

"Why should I? Going into the water dressed is like making love with all your clothes on." He grinned down at her. "You were naked, weren't you?"

405

"Yes, but that was different . . ." She glanced away in confusion.

"You mean it's different going in with a man?" He took her arm and escorted her outside. At the bottom of the steps, he spoke again. "You stayed here on your honeymoon, I understand. Didn't your husband ever go in with you?" He chuckled. "Without clothes on, I mean?"

"No," she said stiffly. "He kept intending to, but he never did."

She pulled her arm away and walked apart from him all the way to the beach. He went into the water with a whoop, splashed out a short distance, then stood up and looked back at her. She was still wearing the wrapper.

"Aren't you coming in, sweet? It's great!"

She waited until he turned and swam away, then shucked the wrapper and went in. It was maddening to learn that he was a fine swimmer. Wasn't there *anything* he couldn't do well? Meredith had become more at home in the water these past few days, but she could not begin to keep up with him. However, it was fun in the water with someone else, and she soon relaxed and enjoyed herself, almost forgetting that she was angry at him, and determined to keep him at a distance.

Her guard down, she was caught unawares when they came out of the water, dripping like seals, and he pulled her into his arms. The passion she thought had been sated flared again at the touch of his lips. It was pleasant to be in his arms. Her defenses weakened even further as she grew giddy and weak from the assault on her senses, but when she felt him hardening against her, she pulled back, trying to tear free from his arms.

"No!" she gasped out. "I told you . . . not here, Cooper!"

"Why not here?" he said in a reasonable tone. "What better place than under the sky, and with the earth under us? What's more natural?"

"Someone might be watching."

"Who? There's nobody around but the birds and the fishes, and they won't mind."

"There's Juana," she said weakly.

"Nope, wrong again, sweet. She told me she was going to make herself scarce all day."

He bore her down to the sand, and Meredith was lost again, soaring wild and free in a maelstrom of passion and need.

Again, it was a sweet and tumultuous time of torment and rapture, and when it was over, she lay spent and gasping, yet the first sane emotion she felt was sadness.

She sat up, reached for the wrapper and pulled it around her, then sat with her knees drawn up, staring out to sea.

Cooper sensed her change of mood at once. "What is it, sweet? What's wrong?"

His hand fell on her knee. "No, don't touch me!" She turned a stony face to him. "I want you to leave now, Cooper. Walk up to the cottage and put your clothes on. When I come up, I want you to be gone."

"I don't understand any of this." He looked

honestly puzzled. "You can send me away after what just happened?"

"Yes! Because of what just happened. Don't you see? It doesn't matter what I feel for you. If I went away with you, I'd feel guilty for the rest of my life. It would destroy us." Her face twisted. "Perhaps it's that Puritan conscience we New Englanders are supposed to have."

His face grew still, and she almost relented when she saw the hurt in his eyes. She had to look away.

"Would it help any if I told you that I . . ." He broke off.

"Told me what?"

"Nothing. It doesn't matter."

"That's true, it doesn't," she said in a dead voice. "Nothing you can say will change my mind."

"Meredith, if I walk away now, you'll never see me again."

"I know. Goodbye, Cooper."

"Yeah. So long, boss lady."

She heard him move off, but resolutely refused to look around. She sat on, huddled to herself, staring out to sea, but she saw nothing. She was dead inside, and she knew that she would never be quite the same again.

A long time later, she heard Juana's voice calling from afar, and coming back to herself, Meredith saw that it was late, the sun setting in a blaze of color.

She trudged up to the cottage. Juana awaited her on the steps. She said, "Señor Cooper . . . where is he?"

"I sent him away, Juana."

The girl gave her a look of disgust, muttered angrily under her breath, and went through the cottage to the cooking fire in back. Meredith got dressed, ate the meal Juana prepared without appetite, and then sat on in the house in the dark.

Her head came up at the sound of footsteps on the veranda. Her heart gave a leap of gladness. He had come back, Cooper had come back!

A shadow loomed in the doorway and a voice said, "My dear, what are you doing sitting here in the dark?"

It was Ricardo.

Chapter Twenty-Four

So sudden and unexpected was Ricardo's appearance that it was on the tip of Meredith's tongue to ask if he had met Cooper on the way.

Then he spoke again. "Meredith? Is anything wrong?"

"Oh, no." She jumped up, reaching for the lantern on the table. "I was just sitting here, daydreaming, I guess, and didn't really notice that it was dark."

The lantern flared up and she turned as he came toward her. There was a strange, almost hesitant look on his face as he kissed her.

She embraced him fiercely, face against his chest.

His hand on her head, he said, "Are you sure there's nothing wrong?"

She stood back, giving her hair a toss. She smiled brightly. "Not a thing, now that you're here. I've been concerned about you." She hesitated a moment before asking eagerly, "The treasure . . . did you find it?"

"Not yet, my dear." Now it was his turn to hesitate. "It may be lost for good."

She was thinking furiously. Should she tell him that Cooper had left the treasure in Rena Voltan's hands? But if she did that, it would open a Pandora's box of questions. Where and how had she seen Cooper? He had been *here*? Then why had she not notified the police?

These were questions she didn't want to answer, not just yet. She was afraid that she would give herself away.

Past him, she saw that Juana had come into the room and was standing quietly to one side, her enormous eyes on Ricardo.

Meredith realized that Ricardo had been speaking, and she had not been listening. "What did you say, darling? I'm sorry, I guess I'm just not fully alert yet."

"I was saying . . ." He took a deep breath. "I have to go away for a time. I talked with Luis on my way through town, and he said that you could have the use of the cottage for as long as you wish. It should not be too long."

"But I don't understand," she said. "Go away where? And what about the treasure? Are you going to just forget about that?"

"I am convinced that the search is probably hopeless now. So much time has passed . . ." He looked away, saw Juana, and frowned at her. "I have a chance to earn some money for us, Meredith, quite a large sum of money. When I return with it, we will no longer have to exist in near-poverty."

He was behaving very strangely. She said,

"Ricardo, there is something you're not telling me!"

He moved his shoulders eloquently, his dark eyes pleading. "My love, trust me. What I am doing is for us."

"All right, all right. I trust you, you should know that, but . . ." She stopped for a moment, trying to think of the best way to pass on the information Cooper had given about Rena. "The treasure, we can't just let it slip away like this . . ."

Ricardo's lips tightened. "I do not wish to discuss the treasure just now!"

"Why not, *compadre*?" said a voice in English. "Why not tell her about the treasure?"

Meredith squinted at the shadowy figure that had materialized at the edge of the room. Then the figure stepped into the light and her heart leaped in fright as she recognized Gabriel Morales, the bone-handled pistol riding high on his waist. The scar glinted wickedly in the light.

Ricardo wheeled about. "I told you to . . . !" He broke off, darting a look at Meredith.

A gasp came from Juana. Meredith glanced at her. The girl, eyes round with apprehension, was pointing a trembling finger.

Meredith said irritably, "What is it, Juana?"

"The men . . ." She pointed first at Gabriel, then at Ricardo. "They are friends. The señor, he has been at the hacienda of Gabriel Morales many times!"

Meredith looked at Gabriel, cold knowledge spreading through her.

413

Gabriel dipped his head in an ironic bow. "What the girl says is true, Señora. Ricardo and I are old *compadres.*"

Ricardo glared at the bandit leader. "You were told to wait outside for me!"

"That is so, but I became worried." He fingered the scar. "Why do you not tell the señora about the treasure, my friend?"

Ricardo's face tightened with anger.

"What is this about the treasure?" Meredith demanded.

Gabriel smiled. "Why, we have it in our possession."

"Ricardo, is this true?"

Ricardo refused to look at her. "Yes, Meredith. I would have told you in the end . . ."

"What are you going to do with it?"

It was Gabriel who answered. "We have made arrangements to sell it, in another country. We would have been well on our way by now, but my lovelorn friend insisted on a last word with his beloved."

"Meredith, it is for us, do you not see?" Ricardo said, his voice pleading. "With the money we can realize from the gold, I can give you the sort of life you are entitled to."

"And I," said Gabriel, "can supply my army with much-needed guns and supplies."

Meredith said contemptuously, "You have had this in your mind from the beginning, haven't you, Ricardo?"

He nodded miserably. "I did not want you to know until it was accomplished, then you would have come to accept it, I am certain."

414

"In that you are wrong, as wrong as it appears I was about you," she said coldly. "I will never accept money from stolen property. You have not only betrayed me, you have betrayed your country. And your friend, Luis? What will he think of you?"

"Luis need never know."

"Oh, yes, he will. I intend to tell him!"

"You will tell no one anything," Gabriel cut in coldly. "You are going with us."

"Why?" she said scathingly. "So you can attack me again?"

"I did not 'attack' you, Señora." His smile was cruel. "You were available and I . . ."

Ricardo's head came up, and he glared at Gabriel out of glittering eyes. "What does she mean, Gabriel? Did you force yourself on her? I warned you that she was not to be harmed."

Meredith gasped at this additional shock. "*You* warned him? You gave the order to abduct me?"

Gabriel laughed with a flash of white teeth. "He wished you delayed, so he could arrive at the excavation with you."

Ricardo was moving toward the bandit. "You dared to abuse Meredith? The woman that I love more than my life? You are a despoiler, Morales!"

"Do not be more of a fool than you already are, my friend." Gabriel turned his head and spat. "What is one woman, more or less? With the riches you will have, you can purchase a thousand virgins, if that is your desire. The señora was there to be used, I used her. That is the whole of it."

Ricardo continued his slow advance. "I am going to kill you, Morales . . ."

Belatedly recognizing his danger, Gabriel backed up a step. "Do not be foolish, Ricardo! She is not worth this!"

Ricardo came on.

In one smooth motion Gabriel pulled his gun. "Do not make me hurt you!"

Hands flexing at his sides, Ricardo advanced. When he was a step away, Gabriel fired. The bullet took Ricardo in the chest, slamming him back and halfway across the room. He fell heavily to the floor and was still.

Meredith cried out and took a half-step toward him, then looked at Gabriel. His face was pale, the scar livid. In a mournful voice he said, "I am sorry, my old friend. You left me little choice." Then his voice hardened. "The girl? Where is she?"

Meredith looked quickly around. Juana was gone from the cottage. Gabriel cursed vilely in Spanish, then shrugged. "She is a stupid Indian girl. But you, Señora . . . you are coming with me."

Meredith could only stand frozen with shock. Half of her wanted to rush to Ricardo, and half of her, stunned by the revelation of his perfidy, saw him as a stranger, a man who had betrayed her.

Before she could move, Gabriel was coming toward her, and in an instant he had gripped her cruelly by the arm. She pulled back, but the

416

effort was useless against his superior strength. She attempted to cry out, and a strangled sound escaped her throat.

Gabriel shook her roughly. "Quiet, *gringa*, or I will lay my pistol alongside your head!"

A harsh voice barked in Spanish, "Drop your weapon, Morales! You are under arrest!"

Gabriel froze, his pistol half-raised. Looking around, Meredith saw that the cottage suddenly seemed filled to overflowing with men in uniform. The entryway was packed with them, and others were coming over the sides, through the openings made by the raised bamboo blinds.

Gabriel exhaled slowly and dropped his pistol, stepping away from Meredith. Instantly he was surrounded, and was led away without a struggle.

Meredith turned her eyes to Ricardo's body. Slowly, she crossed the room to kneel by his side. His face was relaxed and peaceful in death.

She said softly, "Ricardo, *why*?"

A hand descended gently on her shoulder. "I am sorry, Meredith."

She looked up into Mendes's kind face. Her tears came then, and he helped her up, holding her while she sobbed against his chest.

Finally, she stood back, looking down at Ricardo. "He did love me."

"I know that he did, my dear. My poor friend." He sighed gustily. "He was a good man, but he was weak. He could never forget the days of wealth and power of his family. The past few years have been a kind of hell for him. The temptation was too much, I suppose."

Meredith shook her head, trying to make sense out of the events of the last hour. "Luis, how did you come to be here? Did you know . . . ?" She gestured to the body on the floor.

"I did not know, but I suspected. It all goes back to yesterday. Cooper Mayo came to me."

"Cooper came to you?"

He nodded. "Yes, he came to tell me that the treasure was in the hands of Rena Voltan, near a small fishing village . . ."

So that was what Cooper started to tell me, Meredith thought.

Mendes was going on, "I immediately informed the police. Unfortunately, when they arrived at her camp, they found the Voltan woman dead, her head completely severed from her body." He smiled without humor. "The classic manner to dispose of a witch, I understand. The treasure chests were gone, naturally. But the police did find a man at the camp, half-mad with terror.

"This man, Earl Harkness by name, claimed that he had been about to enter the woman's camp, when he saw men surrounding her tent. He hid, heard the woman scream, and then saw the men leave with several chests. The leader, Harkness said, had a scar. It had to be Gabriel Morales, who else? Then, this evening, poor Ricardo visited me, and said his search for the treasure had been fruitless, so he was abandoning it. This was unlike him. Also, I knew of his friendship, or acquaintanceship, with Morales.

418

And when Ricardo told me that he was going away for a time, and inquired if you might remain here at the cottage during his absence . . ."

Mendes shrugged. "I could not help but be suspicious. I alerted the police, and we followed him here. The rest, you know."

They were silent for a bit, while Meredith digested this news. Finally, she said, "The treasure?"

"Oh, yes. That is safe. We found it loaded on mules down the road, two of Morales's men guarding it. We subdued them quietly, and now *El Tesoro del Sol* is in the proper hands."

"And Cooper Mayo?" She paused. "Where is he?"

"Who knows?" Mendes spread his hands. "With a man like Señor Mayo, who travels fast and far, there is no way of knowing. Since he was of valuable assistance and the treasure has been recovered, I will see that no charges are brought against him."

Meredith turned away, her shoulders drooping.

Mendes took her arm. "I am sorry, Meredith. But perhaps, a man like Señor Mayo, it is better this way."

"Perhaps you are right," she said dully.

"Come, I will take you to my home, where you may rest." He started to lead her out. Meredith went, looking back over her shoulder at Ricardo.

"Oh, there is one thing, my dear . . ." His voice was more lively. "I think I can safely promise you, with matters resolved as they are, that you may return to your beloved . . . what do you call it? Dig?"

Meredith was hard at work on the excavation again, but she had lost much of her zest for it and had to drive herself to keep up her flagging enthusiasm.

The additional workers had been well-trained by Raul, who was turning out to be a valuable overseer. *El Hombre de Oro* had been crated and moved to Mexico City, where he was to be stored until Meredith had time to more properly examine him. They had discovered no more treasure, but they had uncovered a great many other artifacts, and the excavation had proven to be a most valuable find indeed. Her father's name would now live on.

She should have been content. It had been two weeks since Ricardo's death, and she was beginning to make peace with his memory. She was busy at the work she loved and everything was going well. So, why this feeling of gnawing dissatisfaction?

She was unhappy, that much she knew. Often, while busy at work, she would stop everything and stare off into the distance, staring at nothing for long periods of time.

It was during one such period that she realized that she was looking at the figure of a man walking toward the pyramid. He had been in her line of vision for some time, but she was only now aware of him. The man had a shovel over his shoulder, yet he was not a member of her crew.

She started hesitantly toward him. He was tall and he wore a flat planter's hat . . .

Her heart gave a great leap of gladness and she cried softly, "Cooper!"

Before she realized it, she was running. Then she forced herself to stop, and continue on at a more sedate pace.

Neither spoke as they approached one another, and finally came to a complete stop a few feet apart.

His face unsmiling, Cooper spoke first. "I wonder if you could use a good hand with a shovel, ma'am?"

"Oh, Cooper, Cooper! I thought I would never see you again!"

She flew at him and he folded her into his arms, the shovel clattering to the ground. He said gruffly, "Like I said, a person can change his mind."

After a moment she drew back, dashing tears from her eyes. "I am glad to see you, Cooper Mayo!"

He grinned, that familiar lazy grin. "I reckon that means that I'm hired?"

"Yes, oh yes!" Her eyes widened and she craned to look past him. "But where's your horse? Cooper Mayo, walking through the jungle?"

His grin turned sheepish. "He's hitched back over in the trees. I was afraid you might not hire a man on a horse."

"Oh, Coop! I love you, love you! There, I've said it!"

She stretched up to kiss him. He held her for

a moment, then moved her back. His gaze went to the excavation, where several of the men were busy with shovels. He sighed lugubriously. "Cooper Mayo, wielding a shovel. No one will ever believe it. I don't suppose," he said hopefully, "that any country ever offers a reward, sort of a finder's fee, when something really valuable is found?"

"Coop, you're an impossible man!" she said, her breath catching between a sob and a laugh. She looked deep into his eyes. "Coop, it *is* all right, isn't it?"

"Yes, sweet." He winked. "If it's all right with you, it's sure as hell all right with me."

Love's Golden Destiny

Patricia Matthews

This is the seventh novel in the phenomenal, best-selling series of historical romances by Patricia Matthews. Once again, she weaves a compelling, magical tale of love, intrigue, and suspense. Millions of readers have acclaimed her as a favorite storyteller—the very first woman writer in history to publish three national bestsellers in one year!

Patricia Matthews' first novel, *Love's Avenging Heart*, was published in early 1977, followed by *Love's Wildest Dream*, *Love, Forever More*, *Love's Daring Dream*, *Love's Pagan Heart*, and *Love's Magic Moment*. Watch for this new book in September, 1979.*

The year was 1898, but as Belinda Lee looked landward from the deck of the *Chilkat*, it might have been a hundred years earlier. The shallow, mountain-bound harbor of Dyea was crowded

* Copyright © 1979 by Pyewacket Corporation.

with all manner of vessels, some so old and decrepit that she had to wonder how they had ever made the passage; and in front of them stretched an interminable mud flat, across which laboring men, looking like great bears in their heavy clothing, were attempting to push, pull, and carry huge piles of gear and supplies.

Gold had been discovered in the Klondike, and the rush was on, bringing thousands of gold seekers into this small harbor, the beginning point of the arduous trek over the Chilkoot Pass into Canada and the Klondike gold fields.

Belinda shivered, and tucked her mittened hands into her armpits. It was iron cold, the distant mountain range covered with snow and ice, although it was the month of April. For the first time since their embarkation in Seattle, she doubted the wisdom of her decision to make this trip.

On board there had been much talk of the difficulties of the landing at Dyea, but somehow she had not imagined that it would be as bad as this. It was said that the tide at Dyea had a spread of twenty to twenty-five feet, and that the tidal bore came in at frightening speed, often sweeping precious cargoes out to sea.

Belinda had drawn a good lot, number ten, but she still had to make arrangements to get her gear from the water's edge up past the high-tide mark.

The ship carried several landing scows, crude objects hastily knocked together for the trip, and Belinda had made sure to reserve a place for Annabelle, herself, and their gear; but since passage did not include landing costs, the passengers had to arrange those details themselves.

She turned to Annabelle, her sister, who stood beside her, her cheeks and nose pink beneath the dark fur of her hooded parka. Annabelle's full mouth was turned down, and her chin was set.

Belinda sighed, and for the hundredth time wondered what had possessed her to agree to let her older sister accompany her upon this most important venture of her life.

This was no place for Annabelle, with her dark, artfully arranged curls, pansy eyes, and pouting lips. She belonged at home, back in New York, where she could go dancing with her beaus, visit the theatres and fine restaurants, and be adored by her circle of admiring friends, mostly male. Why had she insisted on coming; and more importantly, why had she, Belinda, allowed her to come?

Around them the bustle of the landing activity grew insistent. Men were rushing to and fro, shouting, cursing, and hauling out their gear. Great excitement was in the air, but somehow she was not caught up in it.

There were few women present. Belinda had been warned that the life here would be difficult for a woman. But up until now, she had not faltered; not even when the passage was rough, the food indifferent at best, and privacy nonexistent. Even the sight of the few primitive towns along their sea route had not dampened her enthusiasm, yet the view of this dreary mudflat, and the urgency of getting their mountain of belongings ashore, especially the expensive photographic equipment, had temporarily unnerved her.

Then she smiled to herself. Temporarily, my dear, is the operative word, she thought; you aren't beaten yet.

She started to speak to Annabelle, then hesitated, as she stared into her sister's lovely but petulant face. For an instant she wondered how *she* looked to Annabelle.

Did Annabelle find *her* attractive? Belinda pictured her own face in her mind. Her chin was more pointed than Annabelle's, her nose less retroussée, and her eyes, while shaped much the same, were gray instead of blue; also, she did not have the full lower lip that gave her sister that popular pouting expression. For this Belinda was just as glad, for she did not care for the current look, although it was much admired by some. Her hair, while almost as dark a brown as Annabelle's, did not curl at all, but hung shining and straight almost to her waist, although she had trimmed it considerably shorter in preparation for this trip.

Looking at it as objectively as possible, Annabelle might be more beautiful, yet Belinda knew that she was the stronger; and that was why she should have stood firm. She should not have allowed Annabelle to accompany her. As they stood side by side looking toward the shore, Belinda had the feeling that in the future she would regret her decision even more.

Using her binoculars, she scanned the tidal flat. Among the landing passengers from other ships, she saw the hurrying forms of small, squat men, bearing huge burdens on their backs. They must be the local Indians, the Chilkats, who hired out to transport cargoes over the ever-dangerous Chilkoot Pass. She had heard that they were capable of carrying incredible loads.

The first mate was calling out the lot numbers now, and as each number was announced, the goods of each number holder were put over the side, into the scows.

Belinda touched her sister's arm. "We'd better see to our gear, and pray that we get some help. I understand that no one is supposed to claim their possessions on the beach until it is all unloaded, but I've heard that most of the passengers don't abide by this rule, because they're anxious to get their belongings safe above the water mark before the tide comes in."

Annabelle smiled brightly. "Oh, we'll have help. I've already asked several of the young men."

She looked so pleased with herself that Belinda, about to scold her sister for her flirtatious ways, held her tongue. She said merely, and with as little sarcasm as possible, "How very kind of them! However will we thank them?"

Annabelle looked at her a trifle sharply, but did not comment, as Belinda led the way aft to the large pile of canvas-covered trunks and crates neatly stacked, and lashed to the rail.

Two young men, in the motley attire that marked many of the passengers who had not had time to purchase proper clothing for this country, were already untying the canvas. They both tipped their hats as the two women approached.

"Oh, Ned," Annabelle called out gaily. "And Freddy. How nice of you both to help us! I'm sure we'd never be able to manage alone."

Belinda clenched her teeth. It was true, of course. They could not manage alone, yet it went against her grain to trade on feminine wiles to get the help they needed, and it always upset her to see Annabelle blithely making implied promises with her eyes and manner that she knew would never be kept. Men were such fools, Belinda thought angrily; all it took was a pretty face, and they fell all over one another to fetch and carry.

As the shorter young man, the one called Freddy, started to lift one of the crates, it slipped slightly, and Belinda cried out, "Careful, please! That's irreplacable!" Her whole reason for being here was in those crates and trunks, and they were precious to her.

Freddy blushed, and adjusted the crate. "Sorry, ma'am. It's all right now. I've got it firm."

Belinda sighed in relief, and her breath made a frosty circle in the air. The Graflex, which was in the valise at her side, and the new dry plates, had cost a small fortune, but the convenience they offered should be well worth the price. The preparation of wet plates, in this climate, would be an unpleasant and difficult process. Also, the new camera was smaller and easier to handle than the old view camera. The experimenting she had done in New York, before their departure, had convinced Belinda that this new system would soon replace the more cumbersome, wet-plate method.

Ned and Freddy were now joined by two other young men, who in turn touched their hat brims, nodded self-consciously to Belinda and Annabelle, and then proceeded to help load the women's belongings onto the scow, after which they hurried away to get their own goods unloaded.

Belinda had marked each of their trunks and crates with their last name, Lee, in bold letters. Despite Belinda's disapproval, Annabelle had brought along two large trunks of clothing; in fact, her personal belongings occupied almost as much space as the photographic equipment.

As soon as the last item was on the scow, they took their places aboard the heavily laden craft. Now that their gear was safely off the ship, Belinda felt her spirits rise. This was part of the landing process accomplished; surely the next part would be managed as well.

She smiled over at Annabelle, who was sitting crowded next to her, but her sister was looking the other way, boldly eyeing the young man on her left, while poor Freddy, sitting opposite, vainly tried to catch her eye. Belinda sighed in exasperation. She was going to have to give

Annabelle a severe scolding—not that it would likely do much good.

The moment the scow reached shore, Belinda jumped out, and was immediately up to her ankles in muddy sand. Undaunted, she pulled her trim boots from the mud, and began searching for a teamster as yet unbooked.

The beach was a scene of utter confusion. Many of the men were porting their own supplies, carrying them load by load to a point above the high-water mark. Others were dickering with the teamsters, whose sledlike vehicles dotted the beach between piles of gear.

Belinda's heart sank, as she remembered the horror stories she'd heard on board the ship, and she had a vision of her precious supplies being carried by the waves, out into the bay.

As she turned back toward the scow, she saw a large dray pulled by two ill-matched horses. The apparent owner was talking to a broad-shouldered man in a heavy fur parka. Both men were gesticulating; it seemed to Belinda that they might be arguing about the fee.

Making a sudden decision, she hurried over to the men. "Pardon me," she said, looking the owner of the dray full in the face, "but whatever this man is offering you, I'll pay more!"

So far she had avoided meeting the eyes of the man in the parka, but as his breath exploded in a mild oath, she turned to face him. He was older than she, but still a young man. He was only a little over average height, yet his heavy shoulders and long legs made him appear taller. His face was clean-shaven and strong-featured, with a bold nose, and strange, ice blue eyes that were arresting in the intensity of their gaze.

Momentarily nonplussed, Belinda looked away. "I'm sorry," she said stiffly. "But it's important that I get my things safely away."

He gave a harsh bark of laughter. "And you're alone in that condition, are you? What in the holy hell do you think I'm trying to do here? Is my gear less valuable than yours? Is that it?"

He was right, of course. Belinda was prepared to be ruthless, but it was more difficult than she had thought. Nevertheless, it must be done. There was too much at stake for her to quibble over a matter of business ethics. "I am sorry," she said again, more stiffly than before, and turned to the teamster. "Sir?"

The man scratched his head. "Well, the price for hauling is twenty dollars an hour, seeing as how the tide's still out, but if this feller argues with me much longer, the tide will begin coming in, and it'll go up to fifty an hour."

"I'll pay you thirty dollars an hour," Belinda said recklessly, "if you start right now!"

"You've got yourself a deal, little lady! Where's your stuff?"

Belinda turned and pointed to Annabelle, who was standing by their gear. Evidently, her feminine charms had worked again. Freddy was just unloading a last trunk, and placing it beside the others.

As Belinda mounted the seat next to the driver, she turned to look at her victim—she couldn't help but think of him in those terms.

His full mouth was set in anger, but she thought she saw a trace of something else in his face. Could it be amusement?

Well, it didn't really matter. The only thing that mattered was that she get their gear safely out of harm's way, and she had the dray!

* * *

The next morning, April 3, shortly before noon, Belinda stood next to their pile of remaining gear, and looked about her in awe. She was in a shallow valley called The Scales, situated at the foot of Chilkoot Pass. She was alone. Annabelle had gone on ahead with John, and the other bearers. On the other side of the summit, John would leave Annabelle to watch the goods ported over on this first trip, then return for Belinda and the rest of their possessions.

The squat Chilkat had insisted that they start out early this morning. It had been snowing heavily for days, and several feet of snow had been deposited atop the already heavy pack. John had explained that he wanted to be well over the pass before the midday temperature softened the snow pack, increasing the danger of an avalanche.

Belinda gazed at the mountainside—dark lines of men labored up the slope, a lock-step procession moving up a flight of twelve hundred steps worn into the frozen snow. The pace of the line was determined by the slowest man. To step out of line for any reason often meant a wait of several hours before being permitted back in. The ascent was 1,950 feet in the first three miles, and 1,250 feet the final mile.

Looking back the other way, toward Sheep Camp, where they had spent the night, Belinda saw that the line of men stretched out of sight in that direction as well.

Suddenly, she was seized with a feeling of great excitement. What a marvelous picture this scene would make!

Hastily, she took the Graflex from the valise, and the tripod from a trunk. The snow here, about twenty yards from the trail, was packed down hard, so she had no trouble setting up the tripod.

Ready to take the picture, she took a few moments to decide which view would make the best composition. She was momentarily distracted by a familiar-looking figure in the line of men. Then the figure turned slightly, and she saw that it was the broad-shouldered man she had outbid for the dray. He was carrying a bulky pack that must have weighed close to two hundred pounds, yet he walked easily, without the pronounced stoop of his fellows. Now, as though feeling Belinda's gaze, he looked directly at her, his ice blue eyes as cold as the snow underfoot.

She glanced hastily away, feeling color rise to her cheeks, and concentrated her attention on the job at hand, focusing the camera on the upper half of the Chilkoot Pass, as she took the picture.

Straightening up, she heard a sharp report, like the crack of a whip, followed by a booming sound, above her. Looking quickly up the trail, she saw a wall of snow at least thirty feet high, which had broken loose from a cliff overhanging the trail about halfway up, moving at terrifying speed, covering the trail as it went. Belinda saw a whole section of the line of men simply disappear, as though a giant eraser had eliminated them, and then she realized that the avalanche was coming directly at her, like a monster tidal wave.